Praise for
STARWALLOW, *Book II*
in The Riven Country Series

"Carrier has outdone herself as she returns with this heartwarming second installment in The Riven Country Series that plunges readers back into the world of her extraordinary characters' lives. . . This sweeping tale is as much a life story as it is a meditation on love, grief, and inspiration. Readers who love the first installment will find this one to be an absolute knockout. A quiet and hopeful literary tale that marvelously explores the meaning of life, friendship, and family. A treat for lovers of literary fiction."
~The Prairies Book Review

"Carrier has created a character who can stand her ground amongst some of literature's iconic women characters, such as Antonia Shimerda, from Willa Cather's My Antonia. *Carrier's writing carries a thread of magic throughout this book, magic contained within the character of Senga and magic without, woven through landscape, culture, mythology, and the history of her settings."*
~Morgan Callan Rogers, *Red Ruby Heart in a Cold Blue Sea*

"A unique author! Renée Carrier has a style of writing you have not encountered before. Set in Wyoming's Part of the Black Hills, the characters have the down to earth grit of the western lifestyle, and the common sense understanding and closeness to the land. You will come to a deep relationship with the main characters, and a feeling that you are there in the beautiful hills and are a part of the small Wyoming town Senga (the main character) lives near. Then, the spiritual magic sets in and seems to blend in with the western, earth centered way of life. I found the book to be filled with phrases that are memorable and philosophical insights I loved. . . Please immerse yourself in Carrier's whole Riven Country Series. You will be grateful.
~Candacelee, Fine Art and Photography

THE
SIMPLER

RENÉE CARRIER

Braeburn Croft
Hulett, Wyoming

Supported in part by an award from the Wyoming Arts Council through funding from the National Endowment for the Arts.

For All Who Suffer
May You be Comforted

THE
SIMPLER

PART ONE

Conservation of angular momentum describes the principle of force on spin. A loose interpretation: those who live near the massive igneous intrusion known as Devils Tower, in the northeast Wyoming Black Hills, are unwitting parties to this business of physics. To wit—given the rotation of the earth and the Tower's hub-like form (consider a navel, a drain or a spinning ice skater)—a spiraling gravity is thereby exerted upon those in the environs. In other words; the nearer, the faster one spins. Metaphorically or not. A more facile account might read: the closer to the Tower, the crazier. Eggs, hard-boiled and raw, are often employed to demonstrate the principle. We'd be the raw egg white, sloshing around the yoke of the Tower. See? Crazy. Present company considered, naturally.

My name is Senga Munro. I'm a migrant, like early Southerners who turned westward in droves after the Civil War. The story spirals back on itself in every generation, dragging along with it hope (it is to be desired) of greater perspective and wisdom. Not quite working up the gumption to move on, some of us stuck fast, like tumbleweed snagged on barbed wire. Whipped up by the fierce Wyoming wind, I blew onto the high plains gyre. This is why I am here, north of Sara's Spring in northeast Wyoming, making do in a small hunting cabin and earning a living as an assistant librarian and medicinal herbalist. I have savings and a few certificates of deposit as the result of a recent inheritance. My father died in Viet Nam while helping others during the evacuation. He was a hero. Mama died about two years later. She was sore tetched; I would learn the reason why.

Back on a mountain in western North Carolina, my Grannie and Papa Cowry fetched me up (as we also say). I learned herb

1

craft from Grannie and went on healing calls with her. I helped Papa farm his tobacco and he taught me to hunt. He warned me against needing to know every blessèd last thing.

After they died, I came west with a musician, Rob McGhee. We had a baby who was born on the side of the highway near the Wyoming border. After, I wouldn't leave, but Rob did; I asked him to. Our daughter died nine years later. Emily fell off the world. We'd climbed a cliff and she lost her balance. I blamed myself for years and years; the pack I had her wear pulled her backward. A man was holding her body when I reached the bottom of the cliff trail.

I've wondered what brought the man back into my life after nineteen years, after I'd gone so good and crazy with grief I thought I'd die from it (apart from the proximity of the Tower). A friend, Gabe Belizaire, who works for my neighbors, thinks nothing at all caused the man's return, but I think I may have finally sorted it; Emily is the cause, my daughter herself, and the cause of my living.

Madness, the Tower and what lies beneath may well be the cause of my dying. . .

CHAPTER 1
THE DANISH WOMAN
Le Marais, Paris

The smell of coffee and burnt toast lingered, as the grandmother clock chimed the half-hour. The sharp sound could be heard throughout the close apartment, even from the bathroom and behind closed doors. It made an excellent timekeeper. Passed down for three generations, the clock signified a certain structure in the psychiatrist's life. Something she could count on. The task of winding it weekly— *as compelling as sin,* she'd once joked. Stepping to the closed window, she pulled open its twin panes to allow fresh, springtime air. A neighbor stared at her for a too-long moment from his balcony across the way, then disappeared indoors.

April in Paris. The phrase conjures well-worn, but comfortable visions of accordions playing in Metro stations and lovers strolling along the Seine, rain or shine (mostly rain). Umbrellas moving en masse, earthbound murmurations, bobbing up and down in time to pace, rushed, or at leisure. Chestnut trees point their pink or white blooms skyward, and the first tulip leaves crack the earth in city planters. A unique smell defines Paris in April, though it could not be isolated from the myriad odors that surround it.

This is what attracted the Danish woman. It was oddly analogous to her chosen profession, psychiatry—where the object lay in rooting out *distinct* smells of pathology, syndrome or neurosis—amid the miasma of personality quirks and disorders.

The Marais District, spread over the third and fourth *arrondissements,* had immediately felt like home when she arrived years ago. Her vintage apartment stood three blocks from *La*

Place des Vosges, where Victor Hugo once lived in one of the square's mansard-roofed town homes. She enjoyed the relative anonymity of her neighborhood, though by her stunning appearance, even for Paris, she was recognized by her grocer and pharmacist and the manager of a particular bistro, where she often dined or passed Sunday mornings, reading *Le Monde* or *Le Figaro* (depending on her mood) to improve her French. Politics seemed pointless to her, but she required a basic knowledge of world affairs.

Her apartment was a find. An *extraordinary* find. With so few available, at less than exorbitant cost, she counted herself fortunate, even if the bribe entered into it. . .

Her patient was not to arrive for another thirty minutes, sufficient time to dash off an email. Leaning back into her Louis XVI desk chair, she reached for the Coke, took a sip and set it down. Her laptop waited, an address typed in, the body of the message blank. Last night's subject line read, *"What do you want? I can give it to you."*

Rivaling her attraction to Paris, or perhaps animating it, was Sebastian Hansen, her countryman. He appeared in her mind's eye, dressed simply in sweaters and jeans, sleeves pushed up to reveal sinewy forearms, lightly covered with soft hair, distinctly inviting her into his presence, He'd had a day's growth of reddish beard that day, when she and her mother happened on to him at the café in Copenhagen. She'd liked his slightly longer hair, of a color between blonde and russet. It was turning white at the temples, and his tanned forehead was more prominent; she'd carefully noted all this when she saw him—how his face was now deeply creased on both sides of the mouth. He'd stood tall, practiced good posture and had stayed fit, she also noticed, with an inward stirring she recognized all too well, then, as now. And his eyes—their blue had beckoned, like the sea in Denmark under a late summer sun.

Yet the man had not replied to any of her notes and she suspected the messages fell to a spam folder, or perhaps he simply deleted them when they appeared in his inbox. Worse, he may have chosen an altogether different address by now. Yes, more likely. *But, how to obtain it?* she wondered.

Danica Olsen was seldom denied. Colleagues might have employed a more adamant adverb. She knew this about herself, as did her mother and father, and the professional association that had recently demanded her resignation as its liaison, on account of her temper and willfulness, though these were never mentioned.

She stared at the screen for a long moment, then gently lowered the lid, exercising control and patience, not having typed a single word. She rose, lifted the can of soda to her lips and finished it, then turned toward the bathroom to prepare for her 11:00 o'clock. As she passed the full-length mirror in the hall, she smiled at her reflection. She liked to write to Sebastian in the nude. Seeing patients required clothing, however, and her costume for the day waited for her on the bed.

Danica recognized her *idée fixe,* or obsession. It did not matter. It fueled her days; as necessary as the liters of diesel for her Citroën, or the liters of Coca Cola she drank. In her mind, she had flipped the obvious with the merely suggestive, and while her own analysis (a requirement to receiving one's license) had too-gently uncovered her blindside (never truly blind to her), she had ignored her own analyst's observations; moreover, she found the game of obfuscation during their sessions entertaining, if somewhat tedious. She knew enough to tailor her responses, thus stymieing her therapist's findings and recommendations.

In the bathroom mirror, with practiced hand, she carefully outlined her lips with a rose pencil, filled in the color with light strokes and returned it to her make-up bag, which she then replaced in the cabinet. A small key locked it, and this she slipped between her breasts in her bra. As patients also utilized the room, Danica left no personal items in view. After a cursory glance and refolding a hand towel, she heard the grandmother clock begin its eleven chimes, accompanied by a quick rap on her door. She checked her teeth for accidental color, took a breath and turned.

Her high heels clacked across the parquet of her foyer to the door. Through the peep hole, her young patient's dreamy expression looked distorted in the convex lens. Danica opened to him.

"*Bonjour,* Jean-Pierre, come in, come in," she crooned, and he did.

CHAPTER 2
PAST PERFECT

April in Wyoming

It's not so much the weather, as we in the Black Hills roll over, yawn deeply, groan and stretch out of human hibernation to welcome the new season's dubious arrival. Two false springs preceded the official equinox date. One day in late January, the temperature reached a balmy sixty-two in a too-hasty desire. On the ides of March, Chinook winds brought rains, forcing the sap of wild plums to rise, only to have those same buds turn sickly brown after a hard freeze. Only a tiny portion will bloom and ripen. Premature birth, and no incubator; no smudge pots either, as employed in Florida citrus groves. Every year, I cross fingers for the orchard's fragile ovaries. Planting and hope as acts of faith. Inspired by my optimistic predecessor on the land, who decided to plant three cold-hardy Mackintoshes beside his hunting cabin, I've added to their number.

At winter's onset, another demand, or the opposite—an *allowing*—presents itself; simply to rest. While I could figuratively curl up into a ball, my ranching neighbors may not. This means I may not, in solidarity, if not for the more practical reason. Exigency describes our lives in winter as defined: demands and requirements of a situation. Winter as "situation." Claustrophobic at worse; too quiet, at best, I may never get used to it—how long winters last. When I was young in North Carolina, we gathered happy, yellow bouquets of daffodils in February—early March, at the latest.

One icy day two months ago, I struck a match to my imagination, to speculate how Sara's Spring may have appeared—the land—before the tiny community grew up. Ahead of rousing myself from fetal position, to face a bitterly cold cabin during the attendant cold snap, I pondered the notion beneath a second-hand goose-down comforter and three old quilts. My daily efforts (once upright) ran between getting to work in town on Tuesdays and Thursdays and returning home before my water pipes froze. On those frigid mornings, late afternoons and nights, the fire in the glass-windowed stove burned ferociously.

One day, I brought home from the library, where I work, an area history, replete with photographs, and I noted a resemblance between me and one of those fair settlers; read *white*. I favored the grown son in a photo. Even our builds and my usual choice of clothing were similar.

I set about making sketches of the valley sans buildings, roads or other human artifacts. Apart from rare circles of stones (not the giants) to identify past placement of a tipi (called tipi rings), American Indians practiced the original environmentalist axiom: *leave no trace*. Something else I pondered.

My "before picture" notion first occurred on a similarly freezing morning, as I passed the saw mill, whose kiln was chugging forth a puffy white cloud of steam, our very own dragon breath. The size of a large house, the wind lifted the vapor over the town, shrouding all in a misty atmosphere. Oblique rays of morning sun dazzled, I remember, and I felt pride for the small town's diligence. It punctuated a seldom-defined or considered attitude, and judgment arrived as surprise: to have lived on the limen of a great forest and seldom, if ever, to have wondered how the myriad trees figured into my personal philosophy?

I smiled. *But I had.*

My favorites represented an extended family of sorts: the juniper tree near the cabin, an ever-decorated, living memorial to my daughter Emily, by her ashes in the ground below the bottom branches. There was the venerable Grannie Tree, an old-growth ponderosa; her high crown reigned over surrounding trees. And finally, the eldest apple tree in the orchard, her companions each named and tended by me. An elder represents the most resilient specimen of her species. From whom I draw strength. . .

But, on that morning, from the mill, I perceived all forests.

In the orderly stacks of limbed logs, waiting to be turned into boards (and houses), pallets and eventual bags of shavings, the physics dropped in yet another *clunk!* of a seating gear, that matter indeed cannot be created or destroyed, but merely altered: refined-degraded; maintained-ignored; strengthened-weakened, in the tidy, tidal dance of duality. "Loved" lacked a suitable match. I held it singular. There is love, and what eventually blooms in the fullness of time: loving.

Loggers love in their exacting way (I grant) and choose wisely their quarry, like surgeons knowing where to incise. Here I have never been subjected to a denuded hillside or mountaintop removal. With Papa in North Carolina, I saw it, mercifully, but once.

Trees support the community with jobs and work, in tandem with their beauty and bi-products. Did I mention *breath?* As lungs of the earth? *Natural resource* sounds mercenary. Planetary treasure, more in keeping, and, in keeping with the respect and honor given the bison or stags or mammoths of early cultures, I bow to these forests of trees and thank them for warming me every winter, as I faux-hibernate and slow my heartbeat.

Exigencies; I could list more, but why? I await the orchard bloom, the visual harbinger of spring. Green grass shines fluorescent after recent moisture. Three days ago, six inches of snow fell, to melt within two days, making for springy soil. On a walk, I discovered buttercups (poisonous) and gathered edible wild celery, lamb's-quarter and a favorite, dandelions, whose young leaves and blossoms add a healthy, if bitter tonic to my diet.

I returned the spinning wheel to the bedroom, its place between April and December. I'd spun enough wool to roll several balls of water-resistant, lanolin-rich yarn. Apart from my work at the library, reading, correspondence, the occasional herbal client and a cabin reorganizing project brought me through the winter. All highlighted by the rare social call and supper date, and finally—Sebastian.

Sebastian Hansen is my lover. He lives between countries; *Fred* (his Black Hills home in Danish means "peace") once belonged to his Danish aunt and American uncle. Sebastian's apartment in Copenhagen is located very near to that of his daughter Erika and her family.

At present he's in Paris to attend an opening reception of his (our) photography exhibit. He received glowing reviews at the Copenhagen show, he told me. An overused expression, but he translated one of the articles and I concur: *glowing* review. Moreover, Sebastian sounded as if he glowed; I heard his lilting pleasure as he translated from his Danish to my English.

. . . I am the middle-aged subject of his photographs, depicted in various permutations of undress. Mostly undress, but artfully so; the proviso to my soul.

Yet, even *I* regard the images with a certain wonder, as to the *combination of factors* (my oft-repeated phrase for any number of plausible outcomes). Apart from one identifying characteristic (my hair, for those who know me, and those are few), the woman in the photos could be anyone. *"Everywoman,"* claimed the captivated reviewer, and Sebastian's primary objective, I believe, although we never discussed it.

I play at being critic. I could also write a glowing review, from the perspective of subject. I could describe how glowingly *erotic* was the doing of it. O to be utterly seen and lovingly manipulated. We played with my body as though it were a china doll, for placement, attitude and bearing, to produce his *tableaux,* French for paintings. Also, scenes. Of a woman's psychology and topography.

We sought to penetrate the mystery; there was no *solving* it. He titled the exhibit *The Country of Senga,* after something he once thought (he confessed) as he watched me sleep; my naked back to him, the knobs of my spine composed a veritable, miniature range of mountains—among his other examples. . .

Love ruled this country.

We made the images on a wintry day, the snowy truth; in this case, again preceding the official calendar date. The photos reflect a stark reality, and I felt (and told my lover) the physical and psychological were more available to us because of it. Nakedness of emotion mirrored that of bare skin and trees and, by the seasonal lack of color, invited the black-and-white format.

His Christmas gift to me, one of the large-format photos, stands against a wall in my tiny cabin to remind me each day of this *change* I am living. A sea-change. One might well ask how I receive guests into my home. I ignore it, meaning the photograph, and, strangely enough, my infrequent guests merely glance at it and make no comment.

But not Gabe. . .

I shifted in my blue wing chair. Seated across from me, he might have mistaken the movement for one of boredom, so I reached for the bottle of beer he'd thought to bring. One of six of his favorite Stella Artois. I drank and lowered the bottle. Upon our return from Italy in mid-December, he'd grown taciturn, as if to conserve his energy for Some Great Thing. We'd traveled there for me to reconnect with my Italian grandmother, and for him to meet his Italian fiancée's family.

As we crossed the Atlantic, flying east, he told me the story of his brother's drowning, big water having triggered memory and emotion. Then, near Florence, he discovered an American soldier's grave, etched with his own last name, *Belizaire*. The *mementos mori* took up residence, like a too-long bull ride. *Would he ever buck off?*

At my table, near a roaring fire in the woodstove, we'd been discussing words (a favorite topic). As erstwhile English professor and bull rider, he's also a Black man. Black as obsidian. An unnecessary descriptor, the last, but in light of his living in a largely lily-white state (Hispanics and Indians notwithstanding, nor ignored) the observation is not gratuitous; I include his race "just to get it out of the way," as Caroline likes to say.

"*Chatoyant.*" He pronounced it shah-twah-yon. Silent n. "Means, 'to have a changing luster,' like a cat's eye."

"Hunh. Good one. I like it. All right—'alacrity.' It's been popping up everywhere."

"Cheerfulness. Close?"

"Yes . . ." I took a swig of beer. "Why do I even try? Your turn."

"*Lagniappe.*"

"Come on! That's French too. Not fair."

"It's a Cajun word—sorry—for 'a little something extra'."

I liked that one.

Rufus and Caroline Strickland are Gabe's employers, sheep ranchers and also my friends. They took Gabe in to heal up from a rodeo injury in 2006. He later returned to the Hills from Louisiana because he missed the area. Strickland's ranch is located several miles from me, as crows fly, and we all live in the back of beyond; *upper-lower Slovobia*—as Gabe calls it.

The Lakota call it *Paha Sapa*, the Black Hills and, "The Heart of Everything That Is." This corner of Wyoming (the least-populated state in America) enjoys a portion of the forested Northern Hills—no respecter of an artificial border with South Dakota. Among the oldest mountain ranges in the United States, this is young country, historically speaking, though it's been inhabited for thousands of years by those who mostly wrote nothing down.

The people had long memories.

However, in 1868 at Fort Laramie due south of here, a second treaty was written and signed between the United States government and the Sioux and Arapaho nations, and closing the Powder River country to settlers. The treaty was broken in 1877. Three years before, George Custer had marched a column of soldiers, miners, scientists, camp followers and other self-styled adventurers onto the treaty lands, until someone announced the discovery of gold. The resulting greed knew no bounds or boundaries, artificial or otherwise.

One exigency of winter to note: I ponder.

I live within treaty borders, on unceded Indian territory, meaning they haven't relinquished title to a government, by treaty or otherwise. If "title" came into it. And therein lies the rub. On occasion I am haunted by a broken promise. I live each day in this knowledge. Is it mere tacit intelligence? As *tacit* as knowing I will someday die? The subject has landed me in hot water more than once, as unnecessary bother, so I don't often broach it.

I could move away. I discussed it with Joe Rafaela, my Franciscan friend who works tirelessly on the Cheyenne Reservation in Montana. He snorted and entreated me to "continue to live as a responsible steward of the land," (contested or not—implied) and to "just be a good person." I fail him continuously. Written parenthetically, this absolves, but is not meant to. It sets it aside to examine later.

He and his adopted Cheyenne family, Milo and Moona'e Two Bears, help me interpret my *visits*. They call them visions. None of late, I say the sightings pay visits, a derivation of the word. I haven't hosted my Montana friends since the photograph's arrival. I suppose it would be "good" of me to remove it to my bedroom for that day. Who knows? *He's a priest,* my rational mind supplies. *But it's art,* the still, small voice squeaks in my heart, *and made with love.*

Gabe, *dear* Gabe, recognized this when he first saw the photo, bless him.

"Oh, my. . ." said he, backing up for full effect; difficult, given my cabin's dimensions. I stood by a trifle discomfited, but shook it off in favor of the delight I took in the picture.

"Isn't it great?" I asked.

"In Italy, when you told me Sebastian was taking pictures, well, I hardly *realized.* . ." and he finally reached for his seat, sat down without turning and continued to take in the information. "It's magnificent, *chère*. Just beautiful," he said quietly. "I didn't know you could do that with the—" He professorially twirled his finger and pointed, ". . . *motion*—the blurring and all . . . I mean, not on purpose; *was* it on purpose?"

I nodded.

He referred to the blurring of my bare *derrière*. I'd wagged it for the photographer, Sebastian, as I peeked over my shoulder with something approaching coquetry. Having assigned the picture far less "beauty" than amusement, I'd left it where Sebastian had propped it as gift on Christmas Eve. It also reminds me of *Time*—as I am shown winding a clock. That I would trade beauty for humor suits my philosophy and I told Gabe this after his response to the image. "It, ah, doesn't *bother* you, otherwise?" I asked.

"*Bother?* Nah. Not at all. You're a fine-looking woman, *chère*; what's to bother? You white folk are too hung up on your Puritan ancestry." And with that, he inspected the image once more, made a sound of distinct approval and turned back to our conversation.

That had been in January.

Sebastian had returned to Denmark before the cold snap began, and we speak almost daily. The mermaid riddles we task one another have grown a life of their own; they are charms, spells and keys to what abides between us.

In the meantime, I abide his absence, and my Emily's. My daughter's been gone twenty years this June. I go about spring chores with the concentration and equanimity of a monk, in order to endure her loss. The yearly pruning completed, I set about gathering the twigs. Hermione is once more freed from her winter quarters in the garage. The witchy scarecrow needed some attention: a mouse or packrat had shredded a patch on her skirts. The featureless face regarded me with blank suspicion and I murmured apologies when I planted her in the garden to keep the crows company. The black birds called—cawed—for the peanuts I regularly place high on a platform. They leave the occasional found or stolen object and largely ignore my gardening efforts. A two-for-one arrangement.

As I puttered, I pondered the mermaid's latest provocative riddle. Hazarding a guess to her (Sebastian's) Christmas question, "*What did the mermaid desire more than anything in the world?*" I had finally replied, with more than speculation—

Desire.

CHAPTER 3
HALLELUJAHS

Caroline's "stray" was busy trying to rope a fence post near the Strickland barn. All elbows and twist, Joey's throw lacked a certain finesse and the lariat fell short yet again.

"You're trying too hard," Gabe called out as he made his way across the yard toward his tack-room quarters in the barn. Rufus had been working with the boy; "practicing," he'd called it, for when his grandson Jake would come at the end of the month, but he'd taken a shine to this boy, Joey, who seemed chock-full of appreciation for any little thing. Gabe knew Rufus looked forward to having their grandson for the summer, but apprehension (he suspected) tempered anticipation, not having seen the boy for the last six-and-a-half years. A sad tale and Gabe stowed it for now.

Rufus didn't know what to expect and Gabe couldn't blame him. *But you didn't know what you were getting into with Joey, either, did you?* he'd asked his boss, who'd agreed. They'd taken the boy in after his older brother Dale was arrested last fall—if not charged with manufacturing crystal meth, then for being a courier. He and another man awaited trial. It was coming up soon, reported Rufus, who kept up with county doings.

Gabe heard the kitchen door slam and watched Caroline sally forth, a pissed-off badger. "Give me that!" she said, grabbing the rope from Joey's hands. She rolled it back up and executed a perfect throw, yanking tight the noose with a flourish. "You're trying too damn hard," she told him, and Gabe saw Joey jerk his head in his direction, eyes wide. Gabe chuckled as he slid open the barn door to pass through. On second thought, he pushed it wide open, thinking the airing would do the barn good.

The young cats came running, used to his leaving out milk, never mind they'd already received their ration that morning. Over winter they'd grown, especially the ginger, and Gabe wondered if Caroline meant to have them fixed. She'd told him to sneak a couple to Senga and leave some milk to encourage them to stay. He'd considered it. Senga had adamantly declined her neighbor's *kind* offer. He snorted as he stepped into his room off the barn aisle with a "Sorry, y'all," to the bunch.

It was warm, so he walked to the space heater and turned it off. The season was such that it often felt warmer outdoors than in but, being the back end of April, anything—weather-wise— could happen. He wouldn't store his coveralls quite yet, in other words.

His eyes sought the framed photo of his sweet Francesca, where it sat on the small refrigerator serving as his bedside table. While not exactly white noise, he'd grown used to the intermittent hum, and weary of his fiancée's absence over the winter. The woman was arriving in two days. *Hallelujah!* he heard in silent echo his mother's too-seldom rejoicings. *That's the thing; when they come, they really come, and you can't begrudge the lack o' them,* he imagined her saying, or was she reminding him now?

His mother was gone and he missed her and his father and sister, who lived in Louisiana. He'd let too long pass between visits. His sister worked as cook for the rodeo stock ranch— their mother's old position. His father managed to stay busy with the stock, doing what he'd always done. "I can still *do* it 'cause I *do* it, son," he'd reminded Gabe, as though this was self-evident, when asked how he kept on doing the work and *what'sa matter wit-choo anyhow?* Gabe wanted to see them this summer. He hoped to go between sheep docking and Rufus' taking Caroline to see the Pacific Ocean, a first time for both.

It was gearing up to be a *very* busy summer.

His first collection of short stories was with the publisher and hours of work remained before that singular—? He couldn't think of the word. Too much vied for his attentions, but he wouldn't let—couldn't *allow* the collection to be buried under minutia. No, that wasn't what he meant, either. None of it was minutia; the opposite—it was all of equal value, hence the confusion.

Pleasure—a singular pleasure, he decided.

Den I guess you bess be 'bout de bidness, smart-like, eh, mon beau?

His mother's soft voice. He drew breath and exhaled, then walked to the sink to splash cold water on his face. His reflection told him it was time to shave the winter beard. *But not the mustache.* His sweet Francesca liked it. *Two more days,* and the hallelujah kissed his cheek like the warm April breeze.

CHAPTER 4
BY ALL APPEARANCES
Paris

Sebastian sat on a bench at river's edge, below the constant thrum of traffic. It was his favorite view of the Seine. Opposite stood Notre Dame Cathedral, her buttresses like a hen's wings over her brood. . . He ached for Senga. *She should be here with me, seeing this.* It had rained all morning, but he had been indoors, mounting his exhibit. The size of the photographs made it a tricky task, and he was glad to have good staff at his side. They had also complimented his endeavors, and model, unceasingly.

Work had stopped at noon. The Parisians, and most of France, ate their meals at approximately the same hours, and some might enjoy a period after to digest, depending on individual circumstances. *Horribly* civilized, he had once joked to his wife. The Normans, not those from Normandy, but Scandinavia, *his* people, were considered less than strictly cultured by the Parisians.

A young girl, with her nanny (by all appearances), passed in front of him. It was Saturday afternoon and school out for the day. Perhaps she was too young for Saturday classes, he thought. The girl regarded him and he was put in mind of Jytte. He smiled; the girl did not. *Pity.* It prompted a recent interlude with his granddaughter and his smile remained. A strong whiff of dead fish wafted by, but only for a moment. He saw the culprit; a carp, snagged in what looked to be a floating nest of twigs and debris. The girl glanced over her shoulder at him and made a face in distaste, then grinned and walked on.

Two days before, he had walked the long distance from his Copenhagen apartment to Jytte's school, to wait for her and Erika, his daughter. They had planned to visit the Tivoli amusement gardens, an unusual mid-week treat, to serve as his send-off party. Peter was away on Interpol business. Sebastian had arrived early, expressly to sit near the school yard and bask in the happy noise, a *hyggelig* activity he and his late wife had often enjoyed . . . *over twenty-one years ago, now*. The sound of children's laughter was the best medicine. His head no longer ached from the injury, owing in part to his granddaughter's humor.

Several groups of students lingered, to socialize, before biking, walking or catching a bus home. Jytte hadn't yet spotted him and he delighted in observing her and a friend play. Taking turns, they pitched and bounced a small rubber ball against the smooth wall of the building, all the while reciting some ancient (he thought) verse that accompanied the game. Simplicity itself.

Jytte stood out from her friend in height and coloring. Sebastian and his granddaughter shared both features, and her father, Peter, was similarly made. *Norman* traits. The students were not required to wear uniforms, which Sebastian found irrational. He preferred the custom; it was a great equalizer. None of that miserable vying for the latest this or that, and concentration could be preserved for learning. Shaking off the unpleasant thought, he wished he'd brought his camera, but only for an instant, realizing he would have missed the singular joy of watching his granddaughter.

He could barely make out the words of the singsong-y verses. Turning his head to better hear, he saw his daughter, Erika, beep-lock her car and turn in his direction, a dazzling smile on her face. . .

The short blast of a horn from a passing *bateau-mouche* startled him, as several pelicans flapped their prodigious wings to slowly lift into the air. The craft's prow skimmed by. Erika's lovely features dissipated with the birds' disappearance above the river. The phone in his pocket buzzed. He reached for it, smiled and pressed the button. "*Bonjour, ma chérie.*"

"We're really going to speak French, Sebastian? All right, if you insist, though I've forgotten more than I learned," said Senga. She attempted to translate her latest riddle, repeating it to him: was she asking him what danger did the mermaid have for lunch?

"No—I do not think that is what you mean at all. In English, then. Please," he begged her. "Wait, my dear; two old gentlemen are giving me the wicked eye—"

"Evil eye—*What?* What are you doing, Sebastian? Where *are* you?"

"I am sitting on a bench across from Notre Dame and watching the Seine. . . Ah! I believe they would like to sit down. Of course. I must defer to my elders." Rising, he nodded to them, one of whom carried a long box under an arm. A game, he guessed.

The man without a game grinned, bowed his head and said, "*Merci, monsieur; c'est très gentil.*"

"*Aww,* I heard him! And you *are* kind. So, are you ready for this evening, kind pooh?" She had taken to calling him pooh and he chose *robin* for her, for Christopher Robin.

"I believe so. Julien is a marvel at organizing these affairs." He wondered immediately if another word might be preferable. He spoke English as the Brits did, so bits of the language could be misconstrued by an American. He waited for her response.

"Ah. Well, I won't ask you to take pictures at your own show, but 'break a leg,' and all that. I look forward to hearing about it. Where are you staying?"

"A small boutique hotel in the Quarter—one I've booked before. I wish you were here, Senga. Paris is a terribly lonely city when separated from one's lover. Her beauty makes it all the more lonely, you see. It must be shared. . . I just realized—it's only 6:10 there! Why did you wake so early?"

"To call you, silly bear . . . and to wish you luck this evening; I wanted to be sure to reach you before you became busy with *schmoozing.* You know this word?"

"Yes, Senga. I worked in marketing, remember? It is an international insult, the word you say—but I thank you. What are you doing today?"

"Wait a second. . . I'm pouring boiling water into my press for coffee. . . All right—"

He heard her set the small timer for four minutes.

"I'm back. Um, Joe and the Two Bears are coming down—we're going to the Tower after lunch. They haven't visited since last fall when, well, when—"

"Yes, when I left so abruptly. And Senga, you will tell me when you have another, ah, *experience,* yes?" He wanted to sit down, but the benches were all occupied. He headed for the high retaining wall, to lean against it.

"Of course. Not to change the subject, but how many pictures are you showing?"

"The entire collection, my dear. Thirty-four. And do you know I have never understood the use of that particular phrase; one *is* changing the subject! I expect it is a polite means of doing just that, to soften it, yes?"

"Bingo. Um, to be less *abrupt* about it."

He felt her smile through the radio waves. "Senga, I am thinking of returning to the States sooner and we could travel to Ireland together this way. Have you decided to go? What do you say?"

As he spoke the words, eyes on his feet, someone stepped before him, blocking the sun. Senga said something, but he did not hear, for the sound of his name.

"*Sebastian.*"

"Who's there, pooh?" he heard Senga say.

"I will call you soon," he told her and pressed "off." The noise of the traffic above and behind merged with the dark river's flow. Like cold blood in his veins, a confluence of sense stimuli burst upon him; the smell of rotting fish foremost (or perhaps another passed, he reasoned, in a quick, visceral reckoning). Above the cathedral, a cloud eclipsed the sun and the edifice was thrown into shadow, its silhouette made more gothic in appearance, and he found himself slowly nodding to the left, as he had watched Senga do many times to ward away a thought. This was more than a thought, though thoughts have a way of materializing.

"Danica."

"To paraphrase *Casablanca,* we'll always have Paris," she said.

"You do not paraphrase. That is the line, I believe."

"Then I paraphrase the *context* of time. It is in the future for us, Sebastian; the very near future."

CHAPTER 5
SADIE'S BACK

Rufus Strickland stood at the paddock, arms resting on the top rail. He still felt a slight twinge in his hip if he moved in a certain way. "So don't *do* that!" his wife had directed, as if her words could magically prevent the unconscious motion. Late last summer, their ram knocked him down and he'd suffered a cracked pelvis. Not having been laid up in decades, he considered it a great slight by the universe, but felt as healed up as one could hope at his age. Senga's arnica salve helped and he took an extra aspirin now and then. The heating pad on his chair was now a permanent fixture, never mind the injury. It just felt good.

He was observing how Sadie was moving. They'd both suffered calamity. Caroline's chestnut mare had badly strained a leg in a car-gate mishap last year. The horse had only pulled a tendon, when it could have ended much worse. Gabe was mounted now and taking her through her paces: walk, half-halt, walk, turn. Joey, the "stray kid," leaned on the railing beside Rufus in much the same fashion. The old rancher got a kick out of the teenager's obvious obsession with all-things-mountain-man-and-ranch-y, but he *worked smart* too and didn't give any lip.

As he studied the horse's movement, Rufus caught his mind wandering, unusual for him, when the original subject was equine-related. He was glad Gabe knew horses, so he could check out once in a while. *Nah, not really checking out, more like checkin' in with other stuff.* Jake, his grandson, was due to arrive in three-and-a-half weeks. How would it be to have both boys here? He needed to visit with Caro and Gabe about this. Jake

21

was graduating from high school at eighteen, while Joey was a drop-out and seventeen.

"That's my girl . . . you're doing just fine," said Gabe. He'd pressed Sadie into a jog and she was moving well. No hint of favoring the leg.

"She's looking good. Try a lope," said Rufus.

Gabe leaned in and Sadie gracefully went into the gait. They circled the paddock with ease, her long flaxen mane lightly rising and falling with the three-quarter beat. It was the prettiest sight, thought Rufus, who'd ridden since he could walk. "You think Joey here is ready?" he asked his hired man and friend.

"Yep," said Gabe, leaning back in the saddle, gently asking the mare to stop. "She feels good, *patron*." He swung off and stroked Sadie's neck. "Been awhile, hasn't it, *chère?* You up for a greenhorn?"

"Hey! I've been on a horse! Once or twice. . ." Joey said, then laughed, accepting the jibe. It's what Rufus liked about him. No artifice.

"Okay, kid. Now, Sadie's Caroline's horse, as you know, so don't be doing anything cute, you hear?"

"And Senga rides her too, and you do not want Senga on your, um, bad side, or . . . is that 'back-side'," and here Gabe grinned, the reference not lost on the boy, of Senga's ministrations last fall when he was severely dehydrated and required a certain procedure involving a turkey baster.

"Okay, okay, I get the point," and he laughed at his own impromptu joke, as he squeezed through the bars and entered the paddock.

"Well, come here," Gabe gestured, "Ah, this is the horse," he said and Rufus coughed. It was an old gag between them, recalling an Army Air Corps cadet's first introduction to the aircraft he would be learning to fly, substituting the operative word.

Rufus glanced over to the house and yard to see if Caroline was around. She'd enjoy this, he thought, and he nodded to Gabe that he'd be right back. Unconsciously, he looked for his cane and remembered he wasn't using it anymore. *But I miss it—* and the thought frightened him. He turned toward the house and ambled off, looking over his shoulder once to catch Gabe watching him. *Like I'm an old, beat-up horse, too.* He wanted to kick up his heels in pat defiance, but decided he'd probably fall on his ass and that wouldn't do.

Caroline stepped around the house from the side yard as he approached. "How're you doin'?" she asked. "Looks like rain," she added, looking south.

"I'm fine. Why? Don't I look it?"

"I just mean, without the cane, old man," she said, with an exasperated look.

"Come see—Joey's going to ride Sadie. Thought you'd want to be there."

"Hell, yeah. She doing okay?" Caroline set down two empty flower pots on the bottom porch step.

"Yep." They strolled to the paddock, Rufus not wishing to push it.

"Well, lookie there," Caroline said as they came near, "He's a natural, ain't he?"

Joey sat well and appeared to be comfortable in the saddle—unusual for a second or third-timer. Gabe had him walking the mare, and a steady stream of words issued from the former professor. "That's it, you got it; just move with her—can you feel her rhythm? That's what you want to match; makes it easier for her to carry you. Good! Watch those heels now. Lots of stuff to remember at one time, I know. And lighten your hands on those reins. How'd you like to have something in your mouth pullin' this way and that? We're tender with the mouth."

Sadie moved out at an accelerated walk and seemed to be enjoying herself, thought Rufus. Her neck and head hung in a relaxed manner, and she appeared to know she had an inexperienced rider on her back. Caroline glanced up at Rufus and smiled, then did something she rarely, if ever, did in public; *though this isn't exactly public,* he reasoned. She reached for his arm and laced hers through it, then leaned on him. He looked at her, "You all right?"

"I'm just leaning on you for a change, old man," and she stuck out her tongue at him, then grinned.

"Careful, woman. I'll bite it off." He pretended to try.

"Whoa, y'all," said Gabe, quietly amused, as Sadie passed by, carrying her rider.

Joey looked down at them, grinning from ear to ear. "I could do this all day!" he said to the universe.

"Nah. You couldn't," countered Gabe. "Wait till tomorrow morning, when you first stand up, or try to. . ."

And Rufus' heart swelled with a remembered joy—when he'd felt the same way about riding. Only Caroline could fill that space now.

CHAPTER 6
A CHOICE DILEMMA

I looked at my cell phone, the one Sebastian had given me before I left for Italy last December, and I recalled Joe Rafaela's warning. My Franciscan friend had dubbed it, and other twenty-first century technologies, *tech-meth,* brooking no misunderstanding as to his appraisal.

Sebastian's goodbye had been too sudden. *Who was the woman?* The accent was not French. . .

All right, I thought; *shake it off, Munro,* and I pocketed the phone. It was still early, so I decided to hike to dispel some energy—some *dark* energy. Whatever the physics, it began to roil in my gut. I knew who the woman was. . . *Danica.* She felt something for Sebastian. I say "something," for if his comments about her were true (and I had no reason to doubt it), she was compromised in the area of feelings, I felt sure. *Felt?* No. I was certain.

What to do, if anything?

My ruminations were happily interrupted by the loud honk of a goose. I looked toward the rimrock in time to see a V winging low and flying northward. Four pairs. A restorative on this troubling morning.

Calm descended in their wake. *Thank you,* I sent the birds and stepped up my pace.

So, another trip? So soon? To Ireland. It would be wonderful to travel with Sebastian, and attend an opening reception with him. We'd discussed it. He'd asked if the photos might be a source of embarrassment and I'd told him no; that I was comfortable in my skin and felt little shame around nudity. The purpose, or premise, of his collection intrigued me and I wished to further

25

his artistic intent however I could. If my appearance at the showing could help him in any way, then I was willing. In other words, I thought I had nothing to lose.

I was wrong.

With retrospect comes wisdom (we hope), or at the very least, insight. I have too often been glib and have failed to notice when thoughtless assertions might harm others, but learning "the hard way" might, sadly, in the end, be the way some of us finally do learn; it sinks only thus into our marrow. Bone marrow transplant, I hear, is a most painful experience.

He'd mentioned a manor and a private showing, so I decided to go. I would travel to proverbial Timbuktu for him, for that matter. (Not to be glib.)

My soul sought the path of least resistance, to coax me away from thoughts of the woman, and I was distracted by a brighter, shinier object: Sebastian's presence in the near future. Not much time to prepare and he hadn't said how long we'd be away. I could always return alone, if necessary.

What did the mermaid say to another who wanted to lure the salty sailor? Thought, word and deed wrapped in slippery sea weed. I pondered what presented itself more as an answer, as questions may. It's only mystery if I choose to think it so, purely a matter of choice, as Grannie used to say. *Dearie, there are no answers; only choices. . .*

Sebastian and I *chose* one another. *My* answer.

Later in the cabin, I fixed an egg on toast, seasoned with a few drops of Worcestershire sauce, a tip from Gabe. *Perks it right up!* he'd said, and he was right. I finished the coffee in the French press, adding the rest of the scalded milk, now tepid. I liked to eat breakfast outdoors in the morning sun, weather permitting, but the air felt too brisk yet; instead, I lit a small fire in the woodstove.

Out the window, sunlight played on the trees and budding leaves, the rays shooting through the woods behind the cabin in low sweeping arcs; light and shadow . . . light and shadow. Robins, chickadees, jays, wrens, squirrels and one piercing bird call I couldn't identify, all declared that spring may come late in Wyoming, but no one may fault tardy enthusiasm.

The taste of the *café au lait* swept me back to Sebastian in Paris, with Danica, and my gut wrenched for a moment. He hadn't called back. The reception was set to begin at 8:00 this evening, Paris time. I glanced at the clock on the stove. Almost 11:00. Should I call him? I wondered. *No,* came the answer. *Let it be for now. He has an hour before the reception and will be caught up in details.* But I needed to further antidote my fear.

I stood, gathered my dishes and took them to the sink to wash, then crossed into my bedroom to my dresser. I opened the top drawer and chose two ribbons from my collection; a red one and a purple one. *Strong colors.* I shut the drawer and went to the door, opened it and walked around the porch to the juniper tree, where Emily's ashes rest beneath in a Walker's Shortbread box. The tree is decorated year-round in her memory. It's also a prayer tree and I meant to pray.

The custom of imbuing strips of colored cloth or ribbons with intentions and then hanging them in trees dates from pre-history. It is practiced in Tibet, Mongolia and other far-east countries. I've wondered if the custom reaches so far back in time to have arrived on this continent with the Bering Strait migrations, thousands of years ago, or is it a racial memory, tied to genetic markers. Both seem plausible. In any case, Emily and I had each tied a prayer ribbon to an old juniper, laced with similar cloths, moments before she fell from the waterfall cliff to her death. I hold the ribbon practice sacred now, as a link to her memory in my life; my heart-line to her, some might call it. Some might also question my wishing to continue such a reminder, since her last prayer seemed to go "unheard."

As temptation, I'd heard this cynical rationale from an ever-agonized place within me and roughly banished the thought and premise, nearly popping my neck in the doing of it. (I ward off unhelpful notions with a shake of my head.) Prayer is not a one-time phenomenon; prayers resonate through the universe like the energies they are, never to be destroyed, only transmuted. Humans are impatient, being tied fast to provincial concepts of time. We must expand our consciousness to embrace farther reaches of the universe. It's a simple matter of perspective and survival. A *whole*-ing.

I made my prayer and loosely tied the purple ribbon to a sprig for Emily, with love; then, I made my second prayer for

Sebastian and tied it beside Emily's. Fittingly. He was the last person to hold her as she lay dying. He and his father, then strangers to me, happened to be sitting at the pool below the falls that day, and we happened to find one another nineteen years later. What precipitated his reappearance in my life at this time, I do not know. *It's a mystery,* as Joe likes to say, but I'm the curious sort. I don't *need* to know; I'd just like to. Questions can be prayers, but I've made choices too and we answer our own prayers on occasion.

I answer mine with the help of herbs. These, my allies, present themselves in myriad colors, tastes and properties at this budding time of year. Marie, at the health food store, will host another workshop for me in mid-summer with a foraging component. Muriel, my sanguine supervisor at the Sara's Spring library (where I work) is an herbal client. She'd like to go foraging soon, to identify more edible plants.

Francesca will return soon and tell me news of my Nonna in Italy. I send my grandmother cards, to stay in touch. We lost one another for too many years after Emily died, but Nonna had "little" Francesca, for which I am grateful. The *little* is tongue-in-cheek, nowadays; she is gloriously Rubenesque. Gabe is as excited as Christmas for her return. They haven't set a wedding date, but my! life has certainly taken on a blush these days. *Did Papa or Grannie used to say that? Both, I think; their spirits have melded with mine in many ways. . .*

The name slipped in like a slippery fish, when I permitted my mind to wander for a moment. Danica. *What did the mermaid say to another who wanted to lure the salty sailor?* I reached for my phone to send the text to Sebastian, but set it down. There had been thought; now, words, if not communicated. Would it come to a deed?

CHAPTER 7
OF SINGING STONE

His mother had always addressed him by his first and last name—the one from her, the other from his father. *Tom Robinson, better take out that trash! Tom Robinson, how was school?* Tom Robinson had worked at the monument for twenty-seven years as chief of maintenance, and had recently found himself daydreaming about extended fishing trips. He knew he needed to work another three years to ensure a decent retirement, so why now? *Too early to be going off the rails. . .*

The season was gearing up and, already, park visitor numbers were growing. Tour buses pulled in daily with Chinese, Japanese, French, German and American-Association-of-Retired persons. School was still in session, and tour companies took advantage of the shoulder season, when students were still in *lock-up*, TR's acerbic conclusion. TR was what his minions called him, after Teddy Roosevelt, the president who had designated the monument in 1906.

Growing up in the area, Tom learned he was handy. He welcomed the fix-or-repair dailiness of his job, when dealing with people didn't interfere. His most difficult challenge at first lay in summoning the patience to explain a chore to a crew; to not say "screw it," and do the thing himself. He liked the winter season best, when he and the animals had the park mostly to themselves. The rangers were dutifully occupied and he had a good working relationship with most of them. The Visitor Center bookstore employed several people, but he rarely saw them, even when repairing a leaky faucet or installing a new counter. He ignored staff in favor of less tame inhabitants.

Devils Tower exuded its force of presence best when frosty air wrapped it in cold; when it punctuated the stillness; when a

29

slight tap to one of its hard surfaces *pinged,* like a becalmed ship's bell in the fog. The composition of the "igneous intrusion" (one of several geological theories) was porphyry phonolite—the latter term, for sound made by the rock when struck. *Singing stone* figured in Tom's way of thinking. He didn't remember why this feature impressed him, but it had since he was young. His mother had blithely told him that the rock spoke to him. So, he'd organized his life to seek work in the park, failing to understand that *leisure* time, in which to listen to what the rock might impart, would be necessarily circumscribed by long hours in service to America's first national monument.

Her gender was calculated. He'd figured that out long ago; not that the rock was female. He'd ascribed the sex to the park, herself. It may have had to do with Mother Nature. If anything, the Tower had a decidedly *male* bent. Even one of its indigenous names was Elk Penis. How he'd laughed when a ranger told him that one. No; he was married to the park and he *cared* for her— what his mother had once told him a man did for a wife. What his father had not done.

His mother had lived with him at the Tower until her death last year. He missed her. As head of maintenance, he'd been assigned one of the housing units on the grounds and felt lucky to be able to walk out his door and cross the road to the "shed" every day, where his office was located. It was a large, efficient government building that housed equipment and tools. Tom took pride in keeping it orderly and clean. It was how he liked his personal life as well.

Then came the day in Sara's Spring last fall, when he'd had to step in to keep a woman from foolishly stabbing a man with what looked to be a very large knife. She'd come unstrung at a customer who'd called her "*a lover of n—.*" His mother had taught him never to use the slur for Blacks. As he yanked the woman back, he recalled telling her trash wasn't worth jail time.

The grocery clerk had called her "a root digger," and he remembered Rufus Strickland mentioning their neighbor. Tom had noticed her from time to time in town over the years. After the incident, he'd called the ranch to see if the woman was all right. Caroline Strickland hadn't seemed too surprised by the behavior.

Senga Munro. . .

That was back in October. He'd seen her about three weeks later in the café. She was eating alone, but had acknowledged him.

Senga . . .

Lee and Mary Rogers had settled back into their Wyoming, guest-ranching life. After passing the winter in Florida, Lee was more than ready to return: "Like a green horse with the bit in its teeth, it sounds," Jim, the wrangler, had said to Mary. Besides the adult guests, they needed to prepare for the *Kids Camp* offering. Lee wanted a different name, but hadn't yet arrived at one. He hoped to entice teenagers, who wouldn't appreciate being called *kids*. Little time remained before the advertisements went out—about two weeks. They were aiming for three weeks in August. A long-enough period, Lee hoped, to test the idea.

Mary had promised to help with the more personal aspects of the endeavor; hosting someone's children involved a slew of considerations Lee hadn't fully appreciated. But, if anyone could manage it, it was his wife, with help from Francesca, who was returning on Monday.

"I think I've got an LPN lined up," Lee said to Mary, as they walked to the Lodge from their home, a separate residence tucked out of the way for privacy.

"We need a nurse, but I hope she can fill in elsewhere, Lee— you did mention that, didn't you?" said Mary.

She hadn't switched to her Lady of the Lodge wardrobe yet, he noticed. She looked comfortable in a faded pair of jeans and a sweater, with her short red hair simply brushed back, and minimal make-up—his preference. But he knew her working *cowboy-chic* style paid off in their clients' expectations and subsequent referrals. It was all part of the projected experience, and Lee loved that Mary so beautifully achieved the illusion and, if not strictly an *illusion,* then perhaps the right impression.

Mary shivered slightly and hugged herself. The Blue Wood Guest Ranch was located high in the Bear Lodge Mountains of the Black Hills National Forest, the elevation making for chilly mornings, even in April.

"Of course," Lee answered her, distractedly, and leaned in to pull Mary into his shoulder as they traversed the last few steps.

"She agreed absolutely and will come up tomorrow, around 10:00." The LPN.

"I can't wait for Francesca to get back," Mary said, as he held open the hand-carved door to the Lodge. "Gabe's picking her up. Isn't it fun to have love-birds around, Lee?"

His grin lay buried behind the white beard he'd decided to keep, but his eyes smiled in answer as they headed for the kitchen, where Lupita was already at work for the day. Lee imagined that the cook missed his son, Pete, who was enrolled at Florida State. He was due to arrive in mid-June. They were *friendly*. His term. "Good morning, Lupita, and how are you?"

"I'm good, Lee. And you? Coffee's made." His son often declared the place would squeak to a halt if coffee wasn't available 24/7. Seemed everyone drank copious amounts of the stuff. Including Lee and his wife. But Mary added all varieties of creamers, sweeteners and flavors. *Agnes Gussy,* he'd choke, *hardly any coffee left by the time—*

"Mornin'," said a voice behind him and he swung around. It was Jim, the wrangler. He would have been up for hours by now. This was his mid-morning coffee break. When he took one. He liked to see what snack Lupita came up with for the day, be it a pan of scones, a sheet cake or brownies. Didn't matter; they were all delicious. He nodded at Lee and Mary and lifted the carafe to fill their cups.

"And how's every little thing, Jim?" asked Lee.

Jim stood at a loss for a moment as he poured the coffee, then he said, "Fine, Lee," as his eyes scanned the as-yet bare-of-treats counter.

"Go on and I'll bring you some as soon as they're out of the oven," Lupita said, the "some," to remain a mystery.

Jim's expression remained the same. Far away. *In Russia,* Lee guessed, with Larissa and Tanya, the woman and child whom Jim had saved from a freezing death last fall. Lee put a hand to the man's shoulder and gave it a quick squeeze. Jim jerked aware and gave his boss a half-smile.

Mary crossed to the refrigerator for her creamer, placed it on a tray with sweeteners and sugar, plucked a spoon from a drawer and asked, "Will we require forks?"

CHAPTER 8
AN
AVUNCULAR ENCOUNTER

Gus, the Great Pyrenees, had paid an impromptu visit, figuring his domain extended beyond sheep and lambs. As the flock was newly moved to the nearest pasture, the dog took advantage of proximity to beg a treat. Which he'd received. Given a dog's olfactory talent, the smell of grilled beef likely still hung in the air from last night's supper at the house. Caroline had handed Gabe a plastic bag that held a steak bone. Gus the Great, as Senga called him, jauntily returned to his charges, large bone squarely clenched between massive jaws, on which to gnaw the next hour or two. Gabe silently willed any predators to give the huge white dog a break for the time being.

Gabe and Joey were occupied with rebuilding Julia the Cow's milking stall. She'd kicked out two rails the week before, on account of "her disposition glitch," as Rufus had explained. "She *is* Caroline's cow, after all." (The salient background information: Julia was named for a woman who'd once dared interfere with Caroline's marriage.)

Rufus had indicated the lumber he wanted them to use and headed for the house, to return moments later for the pail of milk Julia had given earlier. Joey had gotten the hang of milking, and Caroline rewarded him almost daily with creamed this or creamed that. Strawberries and cream were his and Gabe's favorite, right after peaches and cream. It was good on brownies, too.

Gabe had just returned the tape measure to his carpenter's belt and was scribbling the figure on the board, when Joey broke the silence, off-handedly.

"So, you get laid?"

Having passed the previous evening with Francesca, Gabe had returned around ten o'clock. The lights were still on in Strickland's living room, so he'd gently tapped on their door, opened it and watched the end of the news with Rufus, Caroline and Joey, before heading for his lonesome bed.

He looked up sharply and squinted down on the kid. Drawing a deep breath into flared nostrils, he stood and looked around for his tri-square. "It's in your belt," said Joey, pointing to it, a grin plastered on his face.

Irritated, Gabe pulled it out and crossed to the saw horses set up in the barn aisle.

A teachable moment like this might quickly evaporate, he thought, so he slowly replaced the tool in its tin holster, unhooked the belt and laid it down beside a saw horse. He turned to Joey, who was regarding him with question marks for eyebrows, and the silly grin began to fade. He started to say something, when Gabe interrupted him. "Come on outside, son," spoken in his best avuncular tone. But first, he stepped into his tack room/bunkhouse for two pops from his bedside fridge. These he carried into the bright sunshine. It cast dark shadows behind the hawthorn bushes in the draw. They set their chairs against the barn; the still leaf-less grove acting as wind-break against the breeze.

"That—was disrespectful, Joey. Or, don't you know any better?" He tried to sound somewhere between pissed-off and conciliatory, given the boy's earlier circumstances. Joey had told him a little about his upbringing, that rudimentary manners had prevented total chaos in his household; however, the fine tuning of recognizing the difference between decency and self-indulgence seemed to have been omitted. And so, there comes a time, Gabe decided, to shuck away excuses with the husks, in order to get to the heart of the matter. His father didn't cotton to excuses either, he remembered.

He'd taken a swig of his drink and was blankly contemplating the can in his lap, when Joey spoke. "I—I didn't mean anything by it, Gabe. It was just talk, is all. Sorry."

"I'll accept your apology, but let's talk about it; we've got a minute." He shifted on the hard, ladder-back chair and swung his ankle up across his knee. Joey did the same. Gabe waved at

Caroline, who'd just stepped into the side yard with wash to hang out. This reminded him to do his own laundry.

They sat quietly for a moment, then Gabe began.

"Joey, what you said—I want you to understand why I took offense. One, so you won't do it again, but more, to show you how it's words like those that turn people, in this case, women, into things—you know, objects; it dehumanizes them." Gabe glanced at the boy to see if he was listening. By the studied look on his face, he thought so. "Now, I'm a black man," and here, he turned up a corner of his mouth, covered by his prodigious mustache, in a smile and looked at Joey, whose eyes widened as if to say, *really?*

"Good. Means you're listening," he said and continued. "There are a lot of ways to feel superior to other people, Joey, if a body needs to, and treating others like things is one of them. And here's the tricky part: Sometimes, when we've been made to feel like we don't matter, like we're worthless ourselves, we do this weird thing; we'll sort of flip, you know? We'll turn into what we hate. It's strange, but too true, I'm afraid. . . You still with me?" he asked the boy, who nodded, as he watched Caroline pin clothing to the line across the way. Gabe searched his mental archives for an example, a proof.

He didn't want the lecture to sound like one, or a sermon, so he grounded his discourse with—"Francesca and I are lovers." *There, that should do it,* he decided, but nearly choked at the same time Joey coughed. *Okay, too much,* and he sighed. Then, he smiled to himself and waited.

"Uh, Gabe, you don't have to say anything more. I *get* that," said Joey, who looked at him with a side-long glance, the devil in his eye.

"That's the point, *mon beau,* I am underscoring it by telling it to you *plain,* as they say. Francesca and I are in *relationship.* . . We're not rutting deer," he said, gesturing toward the draw and hearing a snort from his mentee. He continued, "She's a person in her own right and deserves to be treated with dignity and proper decorum. *Especially* by you, when you start working up there. And, that's your word to look up today. Decorum. D-e-c-o-r-u-m," he spelled; then, lifting his notebook from his shirt pocket, he wrote it on a page, tore it off and handed it to Joey.

"You think your learning is over, after the G.E.D.? Think again." Sticking the can of pop between his thighs, he removed his straw hat to scratch his head and rub his forehead, then replaced the hat and picked up his drink to finish it. He lightly burped. "I know what you're thinking. Can't guys talk like that together? When alone and all? Well, Joey," he smiled now, turning to the boy, "There's a deep-ass canyon between burpin' and fartin' in the presence of other guys, and talking smack about women and your sex life . . . or, dissin' people of another color or those who call God something else because they don't happen to speak English."

He was finished and nodded once to Joey's chafed sensibilities, then he set the empty can on the ground in order to twist his torso, by reaching around for the chair back. His lower back was sore. They both heard the vertebra pop. He needed a run. Badly. After picking up the can, he got to his feet.

"*Jesus,*" whispered Joey. He sat a moment longer, finished his drink, burped—self-consciously—then stood. Gabe leaned in to pat him on the shoulder and they returned to their chore, having been greeted by Julia the Cow in a rear stall, with a loud fart.

The chore was accomplished amiably, for Joey was an amiable kid and Gabe found him disposed to it. He was one of the lucky ones. Gabe recalled a line from one of the Psalms: *Harden not your hearts, as they did at Meribah and Massah*—the latter phrase begging for follow-up. He'd look it up, speaking of teachable moments. If Joey's heart had once been hardened—and how could it not have been, given his history—Gabe would continue to massage it, exercise it and engage it, to relieve the stiffness and stupidity that often accompanied the age-old malady.

"Hunh. Nice job," he told the boy, who smiled as he gathered up the leftover wood scraps without being told.

CHAPTER 9
OPENING NIGHT SALVOS

Danica Olsen left Sebastian standing against the retaining wall above the River Seine in a state of mild confusion and turmoil, judging by his expression. Exactly her intention. She glanced over her shoulder once in leaving, to throw him one more look of calculated menace. He stared after her, but she detected a small shake of his head, the slightest suggestion, and it vexed her.

Halting, she turned and stretched out both arms to him, then crossed them to her chest. Smiling, she pivoted and continued toward the Metro station, a block away. She would go home and prepare for the evening's reception. Danica had carefully considered her attire and make-up, her entrance and, most important, her lines, deeming all as high theater and the most exquisite form of play.

Two weeks before, as she enjoyed a Sunday coffee and croissant at a favorite café, she had happened to see the exhibit publicized in *Le Figaro*. His name and profession, *Sebastian Hansen, Danish Photographer,* had jumped off the page in a mental flash above the show's description: she translated, *The Country of Senga: Intuitive Portraits of a Woman*. A thumbprint of one of the photos drew Danica's scrutiny and, finally, her ire. Something snapped in her. She had felt a bleeding sensation trickle through her body, and then, furious heat rose from the soles of her feet, to seep into her veins and travel to her heart. Her head, by contrast, had felt light and airy, as though drained of all weight of conscience. Seizing large black scissors from her desk drawer, she had cut the notice from the paper and placed it, with great deliberation, into her fringed bag. She was familiar with the gallery on Rue St. Jacques and could take a taxi.

Today's encounter by the river would serve as opening salvo of their Paris idyll—hers and Sebastian's.

The shadows alerted him to the growing lateness of the day and, gazing up, Sebastian tried to focus once more on the cathedral spire. How long had he sat against the wall, watching the river flow? And what time did Julien say the reception was scheduled to begin? He reached for his mobile and was surprised by the time; 3:40. Had he truly been sitting for two-and-a-half hours? He shrugged up the wall, dusted off his pants and turned to look in both directions. If he saw the woman, he would head the opposite way. But surely, she would be long since gone. *Or, has it all been a mirage?* He had known Danica worked in Paris, but what were the chances he would meet her like this? Strange coincidence.

Of course; the publicity.

He needed to call Senga. What must she be thinking? He craned his neck to see down the path. The gentlemen who had wanted his bench were, surprisingly, still engaged at their game, their black-clad forms stark against the cool water backdrop. Sebastian peered in the other direction and decided to walk there. He could double back to the gallery, to make sure all was ready for the evening and then return to his hotel. He wanted an aperitif. Badly. He found Senga's listing and made the call, but no answer, so he left voice mail to say he would call later.

The gallery staff had all in hand and he was told to go away by everyone, so he made his way to the small hotel, where the spry concierge with Gallic nose and soft grey eyes greeted him and wished him good luck for the evening. He trudged up the four narrow flights of stairs to his room, instead of taking the miniscule elevator. Feeling weary, he unlocked his door and entered.

Decorated in periwinkle and cream silk fabrics, he loved the opulent French accents and welcoming atmosphere, so different in style from the rustic villa in Tuscany, where he and Senga had spent several memorable nights. So different from his postmodern apartment in Denmark, where the emphasis lay in function, if also attractive purpose.

He would take a shower. This he did and opened windows to permit air. His room gave onto a courtyard and, hearing the bounce of a ball below, he leaned out to spot a red-haired boy kick a soccer ball into a small netted goal. A concession, he'd learned, to the family who shared the space, in exchange for tending the hotel's flower gardens and rooms.

Sebastian smiled and finished toweling off, then dressed in taupe slacks, a grey shirt and a light-weight jacket. A beer waited in the room's small refrigerator and he was soon seated at the tiny table, reviewing the disturbing encounter with Danica. *What does she mean—we'll always have Paris?* He wanted to speak with his daughter about this, but at the same time did not, and definitely not with Senga. *A stranger then? Or Peter?* But his son-in-law was away.

Sebastian sighed, picked up the bottle and left his room to descend to the lobby, where the desk clerk, who was a *semi-stranger* (having booked him as a guest twice before), greeted him once more, in English. He replied, first, in the French, "*Bonne après-midi, Madame Colbert,*" then asked in English if she had a moment.

She nodded, adding, "What may I do for you, *monsieur?*"

"It is a delicate situation, *madame.*"

"Of course, *monsieur.*"

"It seems I have made the acquaintance of a madwoman. . ."

The lined corners of her mouth quirked and he detected a mischievous curiosity behind her eyes.

"Go on," she said, as she stepped from behind the counter, after stealing a quick glance around the corner into the backroom, where, ostensibly, he thought, she might have a companion. But all was quiet in the quaint hotel, called a *particulier,* referring to the personal, or private, nature of its accommodations; mostly, for its previous life as a family home, either grand, or sufficiently so. She ushered him to a pair of identical, cushioned chairs, arranged by a table, upon which stood a crystal vase of salmon-colored roses, their scent warm and calming. Madame lowered, not so much as folded, herself into a chair, smoothing her skirt as she did so, then, arranging her graceful hands (he noted) on her lap, she waited for him to begin. Her expression remained one of benign expectation.

With intended brevity, he related having met Danica when she was younger, and her wish to pose nude for him; his polite refusal and subsequent entreaty, that she seek help, regarding her mistreatment at the hands of boys—or men—he couldn't know which. He had guessed a secret and the young woman had confirmed his suspicion, showing first deep chagrin, then, nonchalance upon leaving. "This was ten years ago," he explained to Madame Colbert.

"Last November," he continued, "her mother either recognized me, or my name—somehow—in a Copenhagen coffee shop I frequent, and one day she brought Danica, who had, it seems, taken my advice all those years ago and told her parents what had happened to her. . . They sought help for her and she later returned to university. She is now a practicing psychiatrist, living here in Paris. I . . . I just saw her by the river. . . Extraordinary," he added, as though responding to a silent query.

Madame Colbert's expression had changed from one of polite attention, to that of acute interest. He wished he could have memorialized the alteration with his camera. Quick to agree the circumstances were bizarre, he added, shyly, his belief that this *Danica Olsen* was possibly obsessed with him. "I do not know how else to express it, and feel rather foolish in the telling," he admitted to the woman seated beside him, whose face now looked troubled. He turned away. A clock chimed the half hour. One bright note, he noted. *Or, is it a toll?*

"Well. . . I can see how that might be possible, *monsieur; oui, une obsession . . . c'est ça.*" The older woman looked on him kindly, possibly with admiration. She may have been in her seventies, and carried herself well. Moisture pooled in her grey eyes from the late afternoon sun through the window. *"Monsieur Hansen,"* she began, then raised a finger in the universal signal for "wait," and rose to go answer a ringing telephone. She quickly settled the business and returned, after again inspecting the corridor and stairwell. He drank from his beer and set it down. It tasted perfectly wonderful, he decided, welcoming the soothing calm. He made to rise when the woman returned, but she shook her head and gestured for him to remain seated.

Smiling sadly, Madame Colbert peered down her aquiline nose at him for a long moment, as though she knew something he did not, and he expected she did. She sat once again and cleared her throat as the roses released their sweet, dusky odor in response to the time of day.

"This will be a very difficult thing, *monsieur*. Are you prepared to be in some danger?"

Danica had forty-five minutes to dress and catch a cab to the gallery. A shower in a whirlwind of motion and, after, a hasty toilette while rehearsing her lines. She slipped into the clothing and was soon standing beside the curb as the taxi rolled to a stop.

"*À la Gallery Fontaine*," she said, climbing into the car.

The reception would have begun thirty minutes before. *Good,* she thought, *everyone will be slightly—or very—tipsy with the wine and atmosphere. Perfect.*

The black silk caressed her thighs. She could feel the eyes of Sebastian on her already, as the car drove past early-evening *flâneurs* strolling along the boulevard, several wondering which restaurants to try as they paused to read the evening's menus. The driver came to a stop in front of the gallery, whose wide sidewalk was crowded with reception guests; some smoking, others mingling, most appearing to be members of the art world, by dint of dress and intensity of engagement with one another.

Danica made a quick read of the scene, then adjusted her bra for maximum exposure. Looking up, she caught the driver's eyes on her in the rear-view mirror. He did not avert his gaze and she liked that he hadn't. She rewarded him with a good tip and stepped out, wishing the man had come around to open the door for her, but he hadn't.

"Can you return in . . . forty minutes, *monsieur?*" She looked at her watch.

"*Absolument, mademoiselle.*"

Sebastian was pleased with the turn-out; more, with the beauty of his portraits of Senga speaking from the off-white walls of the gallery. The staff had done well in mounting the exhibition, with Sebastian's recommendations, of course, but it was Julien, the young, thin Frenchman, who had insisted on certain *accoutrements,* as he called his props, to accompany the nearly life-size photographs. That the collection was psychological in nature was self-evident, and promoting this detail would further the photographer's intent: beside every third or fourth portrait stood a white pedestal, on which Julien had neatly arranged one to three objects, relating to an aspect of the photograph, psychological or otherwise. *No need to hit them over the head with it,* Julien had joked to Sebastian. Subtlety counted for much in art, as in life. . .

The first portrait, perhaps his favorite, happened to be the last he had made on that day, when Senga had not realized he was making the shot. In it, she is twisting around to look at him, just as she prepares to climb the spiral staircase; a breast peeks from the silk robe she wears, a bare leg poised on the step. She appears to be inviting the viewer to mount the stairs with her. (Only he knows who shall. . .) To wit, the universal invitation from all womankind. *If the man is worthy,* he added silently.

On the pedestal, an arrangement of blowsy pink peonies mirrored the pattern on the robe, but suggesting (subtly) a more esoteric significance, in living color and fragrance. Sebastian took a photo of it and the portrait, to send to Senga. *Flowers for you, my dear. At the risk of sounding trite, I wish you were here. I love you,* he wrote, then pressed *Send.* Making sure the phone was switched to silent mode, he resolved to enjoy himself. He greeted several acquaintances, one of whom congratulated him on "this rather heady and welcome evolution" of his art, as the man gestured extravagantly. Several voiced keen interest in his model and wondered who, moreover *where,* she was. He only smiled in reply, nodding toward the photographs.

In the first thirty minutes, he sold three of the portraits and Julien told him to expect more sales. Each print was one of twenty thus, fairly exclusive, in terms of copies.

Sebastian had just reached for a glass of *Veuve Clicquot* champagne from a server's tray, when he heard an intake of collective breath. He turned at the sound, bringing the glass to his lips at the same moment. The sparkling wine tickled his throat as he swallowed, and then, it burned in response to the sight before him.

Danica stood just inside the door, wearing a black Harlequin mask over her eyes. Her blood-red lipstick gave her away, as he remembered the rouged lips from their first meeting. Her breasts, all but bare, were draped in as little fabric as possible. The seductive black silk dress molded to her torso like a second skin, and the long, wide skirt allowed her legs freedom, its length ending in red stilettos.

On her short, slicked-back hair she wore a headband, accented by a long plume; *pheasant,* he dimly noted. She commanded the room and stood riveted in his direction, as whispers and, finally, light applause followed, to grow in enthusiasm.

They think she is part of the exhibition—perhaps even the model— Sebastian steamed. He saw Julien glare at him, wondering what this was. The manager's expression was incredulous for good reason; the woman was effectively upstaging the show. She smiled at Sebastian, then acknowledged the guests by taking low, deep bows; in essence, offering her breasts to all, to yet more applause. Danica strode purposefully toward the third photograph, her sharp heels clicking like a too-loud clock.

The portrait stood alone, with no pedestal for company. None was needed. Nude, but more correct, *au natural,* Senga faced the camera. Outdoors, against a snowy background, her loose, wavy hair spilled over her shoulders and across cold-nipped breasts; arms at ease at her side. She stood straight, with heels together, on a black paving stone. She could have been sculpted in white marble, owing to a soft filter effect and her own pale skin.

Her sex, as an unintended focal point in shape and shade, vied with the triangular dark form at her feet, both contrasting with the flat-white snow. The expression on her face was other-worldly: sober gravity emanated from the eyes, relating to *grave,* he'd always thought. She had told Sebastian (after returning to the welcome heat of his hearth) that during the shoot she had contemplated revenge and how the ancient concept may have possibly originated. He had laughed, if somewhat uncomfortably . . . for he had taken the photograph from indoors, where he had hung a white gauze fabric over the window, through which to shoot.

Danica inspected the uncanny image as though she were sucking marrow from a bone, her ill posture evoking a spider considering her quarry. It was, in a word, *ugly*—and gripping at once. Others stood by, drawn to this strange visitor (though not so strange, by Parisian standards). After several moments, a server, who had read her not-so-masked desire for a drink, stepped tentatively toward her. She leaned in to kiss his cheek, leaving a bright red smudge.

Before lifting the flute of champagne from the tray, she placed both hands under her prominent décolletage and lifted her breasts to him in homage and further gratitude, with a slight purring, then, as though flipping a page, she took the glass and returned to the photograph. Nonplussed, the server drew a deep breath and spun round, laughter from a nearby couple following on his heels.

Sebastian watched with mounting concern, then felt his phone vibrate and he cursed as he switched it off. This— *lunacy*—needed to be dealt with first. He remembered what Madame Colbert had told him, and ran a hand through his hair to prompt a helpful thought. An older couple approached Danica to engage her in conversation. Sebastian could not hear what was said, but expected they inquired whether she was the model. She said nothing, but glared at him with eyebrows raised above the mask.

My cue, he thought. *I must do something before things unravel.* But unravel, they did.

The couple moved away, the man pushing air from his lips in typical French fashion.

"*Sebastian*—" Danica whispered as she moved toward him, her eyes locked on Senga's image. "*She resembles . . . a wild thing.*" When she reached him, she took a long moment to search his face, to peer into it as though it were some exotic flower. Satisfied, she then drew his face to hers and planted a deep kiss on his mouth, but he pulled away, wiping his lips with the back of his hand, now streaked with red.

"Danica, don't. . ." he said, and someone behind them made a comment, to which no one replied. She made an amused sound and he heard tittering from the crowd; this exhibition was proving more entertaining than anyone had anticipated.

She resembles a wild thing.

Danica, as a young barista, *yes,* had used the same phrase to describe a model he had once hired, *yes,* and he had shown the woman's photographs to illustrate the model's self-possession in service to Art. *The chess game,* he thought, *yes* . . . and he swore again, recalling their conversation in Denmark only a few months before. *So be it,* he submitted, as unease crept up his back. Like another wild thing. . .

Madame Colbert had warned him.

Julien approached and gestured toward the gallery office. Sebastian left Danica where she stood, after excusing himself. The buzz of conversation and music from surrounding speakers rose to fill the space with a jazzy vibe. Not his favorite. The gallery was now crowded with guests—*or, are they an audience?* he wondered.

In the alcove office, Julien indicated a small mirror, as he pulled a handful of tissues from a box to offer Sebastian.

"*Mon Dieu,*" said Julien, ". . . what is this spectacle?"

"I am sorry, Julien. She is someone I met long ago and, well. . ."

"Would you like me to call someone?"

"*Les gendarmes?* Really, Julien?"

"She is clearly disturbed, I think. *Or* . . . what does she want that you won't give her?" he asked with a wry grin.

"Truer words and all that, *mon ami.* I will, ah, think of a way to—"

"Julien!" one of the staff called. "Come quick!" she said in rapid French. He looked at Sebastian and both whirled around to return to the room.

Danica was conversing with one of the portraits of Senga, represented in profile and seated comfortably, her head resting against the low back of a chair, eyes closed, a suggestion of a smile on her lips. The masked woman, animated, was pacing back and forth, as though her subject were summarily ignoring her. Or, mocking her. Sebastian heard Danica's voice rise and fall as she recited the familiar soliloquy in Shakespeare's English.

"There's rosemary, that's for remembrance; pray, love, remember. . ."

Ophelia? he thought, then—

"Oh, look at me. . . *Look* at me!" she hissed now in Danish, striding to within a foot of the photograph. "*You* are *nothing!*"

she addressed the image. "He does not *want* you. He *despises* you! You have wasted *all* your efforts in this project, and with *him!* Look at me when I speak to you!"

She lunged at the picture. Her fists met with the acrylic glass (which fortunately would not break) and this stopped her, much as might the discovery that one had awakened too abruptly from a dream.

"*Danica* . . ." Irritated he hadn't intervened earlier, Sebastian rushed to her side, with some understanding that the woman had experienced a break. Alarmed now, he called to Julien. "Do you have some sort of coat—*anything?*"

The man nodded and sent one of the staff for something suitable. The public milled about, taking cursory interest in the exhibition, by moving too quickly from one image to another and by-passing Danica's present *object d'intérêt,* wherein Senga, undisturbed, continued to sit, the air empty above her.

"*Julien,*" a server said, "*Il y a quelqu'un içi pour la folle.*" Someone to collect her.

"I'll go," Sebastian offered. The server had called her a madwoman. He was at a loss. "Perhaps the gallery should close for the night."

Julien insisted he could handle the rest of the evening, but he required Sebastian's presence to answer questions from the patrons, should they have any.

Should they have any? What had Madame Colbert asked? *Are you prepared to be in some danger?*

He swore yet again.

The taxi driver waited by the door and scanned the room, to settle finally on his client who was being draped with a shawl. Sebastian watched the man take a deep breath and release it, the corners of his mouth curling into a closed-mouth smile. *He's not taking her anywhere,* Sebastian determined. From his wallet, he removed a ten-euro note, stepped over to the driver and handed it to him. "Thank you," he said, "but she has a ride this evening."

The man smirked and shrugged as he held out his palm for the money, then he turned and left the gallery.

As Sebastian watched him leave, an elderly woman approached him. "What are you going to do, Monsieur Hansen?" said Madame Colbert. *Has she been here long?* he wondered.

46

"Madame." He reached for her hand and lightly kissed the frail knuckles. "Most kind of you to come," he said, hoping he sounded sincere.

She gently withdrew her hand and clasped hers at her waist. Bemused grey eyes speaking first, she continued. "My nephew, Jean-Pierre, as I told you, *monsieur,* is nearly as mad as she is—" She nodded with her chin toward Danica, ". . . and if he finds you together . . ."

She paused to peruse the room, her eyes settling on a nearby portrait of Senga. After a moment, the concierge—*in every way,* he would later muse—studied him and declared, "You are obviously in love with your model, Monsieur Hansen, and she with you. Do not jeopardize this gift." And with no other word, she turned and walked through the door a guest held open for her.

He watched her cross the boulevard, pull a scarf from a pocket to cover her head and disappear around a corner. Meanwhile, Julien was trying to gain his attention from the far end of the room. Sebastian held up a hand, requesting patience. He overheard Danica's quiet sobs beneath the murmurs and music.

From Madame Colbert's direction, a man appeared and paused for traffic. It had begun to rain in earnest (as happens in April in Paris). The man wore no hat, nor had he an umbrella. His longish hair lay plastered on his head and he had a sad, bohemian look to him, as though he were homeless. Shuffling quickly across the boulevard among headlights, he dodged them and the puddles, as water turned the street into a greasy, rainbow-colored surface, and Sebastian realized in an instant the man's identity. They were linked by knowledge of the woman.

The man arrived at the gallery door, wearing an old jacket and worn jeans. A gray messenger bag hung across his body. Sebastian watched the man pull out a long coat; *a woman's,* he thought, then remembered; *Jean-Pierre. That's his name.* He called to him and the man jerked around to face him.

"*Oui?*"

"You are here for Danica?"

"Yes, *Monsieur.*"

"Come." And the guests moved aside to permit a path to the strange woman. *Soon,* Sebastian thought, *they will leave as well—the spectacle being over.* But his interest sparked anew as he observed the young man—Madame Colbert's *grand*-nephew, he decided, by his youth. Wearing the face of devotion, Jean-Pierre strode past the crowd with eyes only for Danica. She smiled in recognition, saying, *"Mon petit Jean-Pierre. . ."* and removed the shawl. His eyes did not leave hers. He then held up the coat for her and she slipped her arms into it; he buttoned it at the neck and, pulling a scarf from the pocket, he arranged it on her head, tying it under her chin against the rain, after absently handing the pheasant feather to someone.

Then, with a curt nod to Sebastian, he turned Danica toward the door, holding her up against him with an arm. They moved through the guests, most of whom had the decency to look aside. The man's face fairly glowed with dignity, Sebastian marveled, in the commission of his duty and responsibility toward this woman.

Nearly as mad as she is . . . The words of Madame Colbert echoed, and the evening would continue to haunt him.

CHAPTER 10
IN KNOWLEDGE AND
SUBSTANCE

Joe Rafaela had invited me to a late picnic lunch on Sunday at the Tower with Milo and Moona'e. Nothing like a social "gather" to clear cobwebs or presentiments, I thought, readily agreeing. Months had passed since I'd last seen the big Franciscan and his adopted Cheyenne family, the Two Bears. Sister Joan, Joe's assistant, usually made the trip with them, but had stayed behind to assist the visiting priest.

The Cheyenne Reservation lies approximately three hours north, in Montana. I consider Joe and his family kin, ever since the friar saved me from myself after Emily died. *Salvaged for what?* I've wondered, as I've lived out my days north of Sara's Spring, Wyoming; until last fall, when *some*thing shifted, or caused a shift. I'm still mulling that mystery.

Milo and Moona'e Two Bears find this white girl (me) an amusing anomaly among the usual fare. Moona'e calls me *heyoka*, meaning, "sacred clown," but she emphasizes "empath." Holy Idiot is another connotation. In Milo's discovery of the arrowhead, his wife's appraisal of me shifted to a different place, but one reserved for what?

They enjoy me; I can tell. I surely enjoy them. We trade medicinal remedies, Moona'e and I, in knowledge and substance, making us sisters in spirit, I like to think. . .

I showed the gatekeeper my pass and drove toward the picnic grounds at the nation's first national monument as I reviewed my friends' last visit, wondering what their prayer intentions had garnered; this, a shiny object meant to distract me from the reason Sebastian had so abruptly ended his call. *Danica.*

I twisted my head to the left and back, then, on my right, I was rewarded with a wholly different perspective. A tower of strength. Its appearance served to wipe away anything that was not here, now, and I rolled down the car windows to allow fresh spring air to blow through; I smelled sage, pine; a hint of ozone, I think. Clouds had also gathered.

I was craning to peer out the passenger window, when I heard a squeak and felt the slight bump beneath the tires. *Oh shit.* I braked.

"Mommy! That lady just ran over a *perry* dog!" cried a child, pointing accusingly at me.

In the rear-view mirror, I noticed the park ranger vehicle's light flash once, so I pulled over, remorse filling me like stinking gasoline into my car's tank. "*Fuck,*" I muttered.

Tom Robinson was seated beside the park's law enforcement ranger. Tom shook his head at the sight of the unfortunate prairie dog lying very dead in the road. Tourists usually respected the speed limit. This was a local, according to the license plate. *Figures,* he thought. He stepped from the SUV and, taking out his handkerchief, scooped up the hapless rodent to take it into the pines. He carefully laid it down at the base of a tree to be scavenged. When he returned, the ranger was speaking with the driver, who looked guilty as sin, her gaze fixed to her lap.

It's her, Tom Robinson realized. *Senga.*

"It happens, ma'am," he heard the ranger say, ". . . just keep to the speed limit; there's a reason it's set so low," he said, adding that he was issuing her a warning this time.

Tom Robinson studied her reaction. He stood off to the side and could just read her expression. She turned and looked at him. He held her gaze until it was she who finally glanced away, dismissing him, he thought; *or,* maybe she didn't recognize him in the context of the park. She put the car in gear and drove away. He watched her signal a left turn and proceed to the picnic grounds.

"Hunh."

"What's that?" said the ranger.

"Oh, I just thought of something. You ready?"

"Yeah."

He asked to be let off at the maintenance shed, having caught the ride from the park entrance. He'd needed a few items from the trading post outside the monument grounds. "Thanks," he called and walked to his office, Senga's name rolling over and over in his mind. The thought changed to an image of them locked in an embrace and rolling over and over, down a long grassy hill somewhere; one of those impossibly long swards he'd seen in photographs, where the grass is perfectly cut, with no weeds, stones or thistle; just a wide, long swath of cool, green grass. When he landed at the bottom, he was once more alone.

He checked his desk phone for messages and, there being none, crossed the road to his house to store the items he'd bought: milk, eggs and a box of corn flakes. The earlier niggling thought returned, nascent and barely audible. He decided to inspect the picnic shelter for the upcoming cultural program. Stepping outside, he looked to the south and frowned. There rose in the sky an enormous anvil-shaped cloud. The forecast, he remembered, had called for a thunderstorm, one of the first of the season. *Who'd plan a picnic for today?* he wondered as he walked to his pick-up, climbed in and made for the shelter.

Half-way there, he noticed Senga on foot, crossing the road to reach a trail head. A purposeful gait. She wore a jacket and a felt hat. He slowed, pulled over to permit someone to pass him, then entered a pull-out. After turning off his engine, he watched her negotiate the first few switchbacks, then stepped out of the truck, locked it and followed, unseen, at a distance.

All reason had flown. He only wanted to be near her. Hadn't she come to him?

The temperature dropped by several degrees and the sky darkened as though an eclipse were underway. He made the analogy easily, as a *kind* of truth. *She is the moon and I am the sun,* his deft conclusion. A driving force pushed him from behind, as he easily caught up to within seventy-five feet of her. She never turned.

Joe, Milo and Moona'e had arrived later than planned, and when they pulled into the parking lot at the picnic shelter, they found a note from Senga on a table, held in place by a rock, saying she was hiking the trail just across the way and would soon return, adding the time, 11:35. Joe raised his head but saw no one. His watch read 12:05. The sky threatened rain and he heard rumbling. While the shelter could offer some protection, this would likely be a *sideways* rain, as they were called. Their car would suffice; meanwhile, Moona'e and Milo took the basket and cooler to a table, away from the shelter, to be among the trees and a view of the river.

"Don't you *see* that?" Joe nodded in the direction of the massive cumulus cloud.

"I do, and my stomach says we have enough time to eat. . . Where's Missy?" said Milo.

"Senga will smell the chicken from wherever she is," said Moona'e, with a snort.

"I'll walk over there," said Joe, hitching up his robe with his belt, to allow for easier movement, his pale, hairy calves drawing whoops from Moona'e.

"Don't let her start without me," Joe called over his shoulder with the grin nestled in his thick, graying beard and mustache.

Milo chuckled and popped a can of orange Fanta as Moona'e wandered toward some plants.

"They need them some *goaties* here to eat this yellow spurge," she declared to no one. Maybe the spurge, Joe thought, as he headed toward the trail head.

He wasn't in shape to be climbing anything, he knew, but he'd felt a twinge of fear, and thought best to respect it. The first heavy drops of rain fell after only five minutes, followed by a lightning strike, and the resounding crack of thunder nearly threw him down. "*Oh, my Lord!*" he cried in surprise. "*Senga!*" he called. Surely, he must be catching up with her by now. The cloudburst occurred much earlier than Milo had predicted. *So much for old Indian tricks,* he reflected.

The red dirt path soon felt slick beneath his Birkenstock sandals, their having so little sole left. He'd meant to have them retreaded, but life got in the way. "*Senga!*" he called again, to no avail. A queer turn churned in his gut and, taking a deep breath, he marshaled his strength and continued up the side of the hill. The trail evened out and he was able to catch his breath. Joe pulled up his hood against the pelting drops, glad for its protection. A thick, steel-gray curtain of cold water prevented good vision, but the path was well established, so he lowered his head, like the bull he was, and plowed on. "Lord have mercy," he prayed aloud.

CHAPTER 11
LITERARY LESSONS

A single, clear *ting!* broke the silence. His anniversary gift to Caro had been inspired, thought Rufus; never mind it was Gabe who'd spotted the antique brass carriage clock in a Rapid City shop. He'd agreed, hadn't he? He thought he'd get a leg up on their sixtieth next year, and it surprised the hell out of the woman, proving it could be done.

He liked the clock's tone; it hung, brightly, in the air, like a crystal morning, to be interrupted—

"You're missin' that damned cane, ain'tcha?" his wife said, fixing him with a steely eye. It wouldn't do to answer and he winced; she'd just come back with some smart-ass remark. So, he did the next best thing. He ignored her and sat back down to roll another after-dinner smoke. *Where's the damn thing, anyhow?* He eyed the ladder-back chair, below the wall phone, where he sometimes hung it.

Caro harrumphed and returned to washing the dishes. With her back turned, he cranked around to check the door knob. *Nope, not there.* Setting the hand-rolled cigarette between his teeth, he lit it, inhaled and felt the smoke ease his mind. After Joey's early riding lesson, they'd passed the rest of the morning cleaning out the lambing shed—Gabe, Joey, Caro and him. The hip wasn't quite healed. A couple times he caught Gus scrutinizing him; the dog's expression asked what the hell did he think he was doing out there anyway? *When the damn dog makes you feel old, you're in trouble.* He made a sound.

"What's that?"

"Nothin' . . . nothing at all, Caro. So, what day's Jake coming; did you say?"

"I said, oh, *twenty times now*—"

He saw in her face immediate regret for the remark.

"Sometime after May 24. You know, we could go to his graduation, hon."

"Nah. I'd rather get reacquainted here." He left it at that and she left it alone. *Good girl,* he thought, as he gave her a half-smile and lifted his coffee mug for a refill.

"Joey's leaving for The Blue Wood in a couple weeks," she said, wiping her hands and reaching for the thermos.

"Came fast, didn't it? When's he taking that test? Christ, I'll miss the kid. . ."

"He's only going to the Bear Lodge, hon."

"Might as well be the damn moon." He was testy. "Aw, hell, don't mind me. I'm feeling ornery, is all."

Lee and Mary Rogers had offered Joey a job at the guest ranch, in the area known as the Bear Lodge Mountains in the Black Hills National Forest. Provided he pass his G.E.D. Gabe had discussed the first possibility with Francesca before her return from Italy. She'd relayed it to Mary. It was Lee who'd made the stipulation—"For the kid's sake," he'd proposed—and, between Gabe and Senga, Joey might earn his high school equivalency diploma. Senga concentrated on math and science, while Gabe tutored him in language arts and history. The test was scheduled for the following Friday in Sundance.

Rufus heard someone mounting the kitchen steps. Whereas before it could only have been Gabe, the presence of Joey added another ingredient to their stew of the day. After a knock, the door opened to the kid. His hair had grown to a less obnoxious length, both he and Caro thought, and a working tan lent him a healthy glow. "He's *bloomed,*" Senga observed one evening; their neighbor often talked like she'd just fallen, overripe, from a fruit tree.

"Hey," said Joey, "Gabe wants to know if we're still planning to dock before I leave or, if you're waiting—"

For Jake, Rufus filled in silently. "Well . . . oh hell, I don't know—*Caro?*" He didn't like to show indecision, but lately it'd been one damn thing after another. He thought it might have to do with the upcoming trip to California. It was using up his reserves.

Docking (and castrating—understood) entailed the removal of the male lambs' testes and shortening all tails. It could be a bloody business and made for a long, sweaty day. Necessary, however. Senga always suggested they wait until a waning moon; "Less bleeding," she'd insist.

He was glad for their smaller farm flock numbers.

"Tell Gabe we'll do it before, just to get it out of the way," said Caro, as she stepped to the calendar to check the moon phase. ". . . Up 'til the 28th, when it's new, and we'll need to sterilize everything; remind him, will ya?" She reached into the cookie jar, pulled out two oatmeal- raisin cookies and handed them to him. He snatched them up and thanked her, then said, "For Gabe?" She snorted and pulled out two more.

"Hey, what about me?" said Rufus, a look of abject disappointment in his eyes.

Joey grinned, stepped to the jar himself for a couple more. "Later," the lanky boy called; "Better make more!" he cried as he passed outside, the door standing wide open to the day. He turned to pull it closed.

"Just leave it open, will ya, hon? We got us some bad air in here that needs to leave," and, bending to her husband's forehead, she planted a loud kiss. Rufus heard Joey's laughter as he clomped down the steps.

"She'll fry you those testicles for breakfast! You got a real treat coming, boy!" he shouted, earning the last laugh.

Gabe chewed a cookie as he consulted his calendar. Spring was always busy for him, and finding time for every little thing proved tricky. But he genuinely enjoyed coaching Joey for the upcoming test. With only the one student, he could concentrate the lessons. *Might be too much, though,* he'd wondered at first, but Joey seemed to enjoy the rigor, so Gabe continued the pace.

"Gabe?"

He was lost in thought, the cookie nearly finished, when he heard his name again.

"Gabe? Hey man, you in there?"

"Yep. Sorry—what's up?"

"The stuff that needs to be sterilized?"

"Oh, yeah. Okay, come on—I'll show you. So, Rufus promised you some lamb fries, huh?"

"Um, yeah. . . About that . . ."

"No worries, man—they're *good!* Besides, any self-respecting mountain man would gobble up a bucket if he had the chance. Just don't get sick on them. You've been warned," and he winked at the boy, who, he could swear, had grown two inches since moving in.

"Well, let's go." Gabe pulled on his vest, grabbed his hat and the two headed to the shed for the tools. "How's the reading going?" he asked, having assigned *A River Runs Through It,* by Norman Maclean.

"Good—I mean, 'well.' He writes g—*well.* I'm where Jessie's brother's visiting . . . got that hellacious sunburn. Pretty funny. I know it's supposed to be true, but he writes it like a novel, doesn't he?"

"Yes. Yes, he does. He based it on his life though . . . was able to arrange events in a literary fashion, to make it more of an art form; do you see?"

The boy nodded.

"Can't remember if you've said you saw the film."

"Nah. I never went to a lot of movies. I like 'em, but we just never did. If it weren't, uh, *wasn't* on T.V., we didn't see it."

They reached the shed, stopped and admired the morning's work; then Gabe stepped to a shelf, where he found the tools he needed. These he showed to Joey, with raised eyebrows.

"Remember—do not piss off Caroline—and that's an example of not using a contraction, for emphasis," he said and chuckled, holding up the castrator.

Joey made a sound and said, "I thought y'all just bit 'em off . . . I heard Rufus talking."

"What's this 'y'all'? Yep, but we keep these on hand, in case. Always good to have a back-up plan, don't you know?"

He slipped the tools into his back pocket, including one for the tails, and they inspected the area once more, turned and left. Later, they would spread the sheep manure onto Caroline's garden, along with rakings from the chicken coop.

Gabe stole a peek in Joey's direction as they turned back toward the barn. *One kid snatched from the jaws of evil,* was how he considered it. He was proud of his and Senga's intervention.

And of course, the Stricklands'. The brother, Dale, had been convicted, along with the other man, Jacob. Both had been sentenced and were to begin serving their sentences; Dale in Rawlings, in the state penitentiary, and the other in federal prison down in Colorado.

Gabe encouraged Joey to write to his brother and to his mother in Idaho, going so far as to offer to edit the letters, thus turning them into a lesson. It gave him a window into the kid's thinking and progress. He found the letters oddly inspiring, for their innocence and adolescent naïveté, despite Joey's involvement with the Wild Bunch—Gabe's name for the gang. How Joey had remained disaffected, at least outwardly, remained a mystery (*well, there* was *that god-awful haircut*), but Senga's friend, the Franciscan friar, had declared Joey to be "one of the lucky ones," who'd had sense enough to use his discernment skills to weigh the behaviors of his companions against some ideal he held sacred, even if he didn't conspicuously use the word or consider the notion.

The Law had been written on his inward parts, Joe had suggested to Senga, and Gabe had recognized the scripture from Jeremiah 31.

Another Jeremiah earned Joey's respect, Jeremiah Johnson, whose story was based on John "Liver-eating" Johnston. Gabe also had him read Raymond W. Thorp's biography of the man, to shine a light on liberties novelists take.

He reached over and casually mussed the boy's hair.

"Hey! Quit!" Joey said and laughed.

"Say," said Gabe, "I've got an *envie* to go see Earl and Mae. Want to go?"

"*Ohnvee?* What's that?"

"In Louisiana, where I'm from, it's Acadian—or Cajun—for *I want to,* or, 'I've got a hankering'."

"Well, why didn't you just say that?"

Got me there, he thought. *No. It's who I am, in that word; it's why I write,* and he said so.

"Well now, that's just how I talk, Joey. Do you notice how Norman Maclean makes his characters talk?"

Joey nodded.

"We've got us a lot of interesting, ah, *customs* down there, and our language is one of my favorites. It's French, in case you didn't recognize it." He gave Joey a quick précis on the Acadians; their persecution in Europe, the exile in Nova Scotia, including the Great Upheaval and eventual resettlement in Louisiana. He had Cajun blood on his mother's side, he added.

"Anyway, want to?" he asked, after noting Joey's flagging interest.

They could drive up to Alzada for a burger and sweet potato fries; just the two of them. Mae would be thrilled. Joey had grown on the old biker's wife when she nursed him during an illness. Besides, he wanted to use the road time to ask the boy about his desires and needs, or sense of them; too, what Joey might expect a town, small or otherwise, to provide for its kids. He'd say "younger citizens."

He thought he heard Hamelin's Pied Piper in the ghost of a flute riff, and it sent a shiver down his spine. Many of the grown children were leaving the small communities. *They might as well have walked into the story's mountain*—his conclusion. It was true that retirees were relocating to the area, but it wasn't the same thing, was it?

He'd been mulling a story about an incident in a small western town, where the population was falling critically low. The school was in danger of closing. He figured if that happened, the town would dry up and go the way of several in the state, no longer "going concerns," like Jeffrey City, or Atlantic City, or Seeley, nearby. Signs of attrition within the civic setting of Sara's Spring had prompted his study. He'd asked himself: *is it ethical to describe a dire situation and not propose a solution? On the other hand,* he'd reasoned, *it could just be the way of it here, a natural ebb and flow, like the tides. . .*

"Nah, it ain't," the colloquial answer slipped out. It was a question of the will. Like everything else.

"Phone call, Gabe!" yelled Caroline from the porch steps, and he picked up his pace to a slow jog.

Joey called after him, "Yeah! Let's go to Earl's!" adding, "I've got me an *ohnvee* too!"

59

CHAPTER 12
PIN BALL WIZARD

The wind had kicked-up and Gabe caught the lightning to the south on the far horizon. It was something he appreciated about the West—the long vistas. *Ahh, the long view.* You could see things coming. *Well, sometimes.*

"How do they stay in business?" Joey asked, as they pulled into Earl's parking lot, beside a lone pick-up.

He grunted, switched off the ignition, put the truck in park and turned to his passenger.

"Oh, you're not the first to ask. . . They count on the bike rally in Sturgis every year and don't have much overhead—what with their daughter working with them during the summer. . . You'd be surprised how much traffic comes through this corner of Montana," he explained.

"Where's the daughter now?"

"She's a student at Black Hills State University, over in Spearfish." Gabe gave him a knowing look, then grabbed the wallet from his jacket to place in his back pocket, where it caused his sciatic nerve trouble if carried there too long.

"Hunh," said Joey.

When Gabe wasn't mulling the phone call he'd received, he and Joey had conversed for most of the hour's travel from the ranch; Gabe would save his kids-from-small-communities conversation for the ride back. In its place, he'd decided to quiz the boy, changing the insufficient noun to "young man," and ageing himself twenty years in the process. Joey showed off his recent acquisition of grammatical nomenclature with ease, and Gabe thought they just might be getting closer to the mark. An essay assignment waited on his desk, to correct and review with the "stray kid"—what Caroline called Joey. With affection.

In appearance, he had grown. Gabe looked forward to Earl and Mae's reaction. This was only the second time they'd seen him since Joey left the couple's care in November. Caroline had invited Earl and Mae to dinner once, to discuss the upcoming trip to California, where a friend of Earl's had offered Stricklands a room and sightseeing. Gabe had enjoyed seeing the two of them thunderstruck, with nothing to say, except to decline, to Earl's grin and subsequent intake of breath, followed by a long swig of his beer.

"See, I knew you were going to do that," he'd said, still grinning, "But look, this room is in their *guest* house; you wouldn't be under anybody's feet, and you'd have tons of privacy. Besides, they're dying to show you stuff—especially the ocean! Come on—they're great folks. You'll like them, and you'll have nothing to worry about . . . like *traffic*." Earl added this last point with more force. Gabe had watched Rufus turn to Caroline and she'd looked at her husband; both their expressions asking the same thing, "*What do you think?*"

Leaning forward, Gabe had quietly addressed both; "I think these folks are looking forward to your company. Earl tells me they're retired . . . not much family around, and that they're real easy-goin'. *I'd* sure feel a lot better knowing you weren't driving yourselves around. I've been there; it ain't no picnic. Please, y'all—let 'em do this."

They'd agreed, at last, if reluctantly.

Should have been a politician, he joked to himself, *or a lawyer*—at which he made a sound, waving it off to the kid as they passed into the diner.

He and Joey made their way to the counter, at which the lone customer sat, busy with his salad, it appeared. A miasma of smells greeted them: grilled hamburger, grease, beer, pizza and one he couldn't identify; sweet but cloying, he thought. They sat down and Gabe grinned into the bar mirror opposite, to Joey, who was seated beside him—same look on his face.

"Well, hey—Mae! We've got company!" said Earl, back into the kitchen, as he was exiting with a bus tub. Gabe noticed his friend's smart new goatee and shorter hair. He rubbed his chin in acknowledgment.

"*Who?*" Mae shouted through the door.

"You'll have to come see. . ." Earl put down the tub to wipe his hands on the red tea towel draped over his left shoulder, giving him a decidedly foreign flair, thought Gabe. The man hitched over to them, his prosthetic calf and foot making for a slightly uneven step. He stretched out his hand to shake Gabe's, then Joey's.

"Sorry I haven't brought him up sooner, Earl." He and Rufus had stopped in, but never with Joey, to Mae's disappointment.

The man dismissed the apology, grinning ear to ear—upon one of which hung a dainty gold loop. *Has he always worn one?* Gabe wondered. Mae bounced through the door and squealed at the sight of Joey. "Well, look at you!" she cried and stepped around the counter to where they sat. On her head, a flour handprint dusted her black bandana.

She always wore the same black apron, similarly accented with ingredients. Joey stood and offered a hand to be shaken, but Mae would have none of it and grabbed him in a bear hug. Gabe saw Joey's eyes widen as she jerked him up and down, nearly off the floor.

"'Bout time!" she said, then stood back to appraise him. She raised a hand to brush something off his shirt. "You've *grown!* Caroline's a good cook, but not *that* good; what else you been doin', besides eatin'? Hey, Gabe; how's it going?" she asked, to be polite, her gaze quickly returning to the main attraction.

Joey looked to Gabe for help, but his tutor let him twist in the wind for a moment longer.

"It's going well, Mae, and maybe it's his hair growing out," said Gabe, "Gives him at least another two inches." He didn't mention the kid's dental work.

"Okay . . . but nah; you just look healthy, kid; that's it. Damn, it's good to see you—both of you. Well, sit. What are you having? I assume you're here to eat? Hope so. We need the business—"

"Mae, be nice," said Earl, "And I need to give you a couple of phone numbers for Rufus; my buddy says he'll pick them up at the airport and take them back."

"That's generous of them, Earl," said Gabe, "But I'll tell you right now, Rufus doesn't particularly like being obliged to anyone. How can we make this work?"

The room grew still, save the solitary diner's smacking at the end of the counter; rhythmic—like dripping water.

"I've got an idea." Joey broke the silence. He'd climbed back onto the stool, while Mae continued to smile and touch his hair, at which he finally scrunched up his shoulders to discourage her.

"Mae, quit—you're bugging him now," Earl said gently. "What is it?—your idea," he asked Joey.

After scanning the room, as if viewing it for the first time (and it may well have been, as ill as he'd been, thought Gabe), Joey nonchalantly slid back off the stool and sauntered over to a pin-ball machine. "It's gotta be a gift, I think," he tossed over his shoulder, ". . . you know, like—from *all* of us. Then, he can't feel funny about charity." Joey shrugged his hand into his pocket and brought out a couple of coins. These he placed in the slot and the machine whirred to life. He pushed the ball launch and set about wildly pressing the flipper buttons, as Gabe and the others stared blankly at him, then at one another.

Out of the mouths of babes, thought Gabe. *I'll forgive him the use of* like, *this time.*

"Damn. He's right," said Earl. Mae kept grinning. Even the man at the end of the counter sat nodding his head, having undoubtedly overheard the exchange. "Okay, kid," the old biker said, "What do you propose?" Earl began replacing clean glasses from his tub on the shelf behind him.

"Their anniversary's coming up, right?" Joey said over the electronic din. "We could all chip in and give Earl's friends something for doing all this. I know they just want to for nothin', but this way, the piper would get paid, right?"

With brows furrowed, Gabe considered his student, wondering when he'd ever mentioned the Pied Piper. He hadn't, as far as he knew. "Joey, I think you have a good plan." The pin-ball wizard threw him a flash of a smile between plays. Gabe looked at Earl and Mae. "What do you think? Would your friends go along?" he asked.

"Well, I suppose. . . They don't need the money, Gabe, but I guess they could always find something to do with it. Okay; I'll get on it."

They heard the game ringing through a series of loud bells and whistles, to finally settle back down. A low chuckle could be heard from Joey, who'd evidently passed some time, ill-spent or not, on such entertainment.

"*Oh shit!*" cried Mae, as she whirled around the corner of the bar, and burst through the kitchen door.

From the other end came a gruff voice, rising in volume, "I was afraid you was gonna burn my dinner, woman, and it happened! Just get me a bag o' them chips, Earl; will ya?"

"Sorry, Jerry . . . um, wait a sec," said Earl and he stepped into the kitchen to see if the man's order was salvageable. Happily, it was and arrived with a complimentary cinnamon roll—what Gabe had detected earlier among the usual fare.

"I'll have one of those," he said, pointing, as Earl passed with the freshly frosted example, "And a cup of coffee; oh, and scrambled eggs. Joey? What do you want, now that you've solved our dilemma?"

"Dilemma: a predicament or quandary."

"Smart-ass," said Earl. "He always like this?"

"Nah, but isn't it sweet to hear the gears churning?" said Gabe the Professor.

Just then, a loud crack of thunder shook the walls of the pre-fab building, and he was glad to be indoors among friends. He'd sort that telephone call later. . .

CHAPTER 13
QUEEN TO KNIGHT, CHECK
Paris

Sebastian sat among the few hotel guests in a dining room that once served a family, judging by the intimate size and furnishings. There remained several possible "residents" from the 17th century: a tidy Henri IV hutch, a sideboard (for the buffet-style continental breakfast) and two Louis XIII chairs, propped against the wall, never to be used, evoking a pair of elegant old men, living out their days, tucked away and all-too silent.

The observation did not aid Sebastian's disposition. His gaze fell to a small, cast-iron fireplace that had once burned coal, just to his left. Three fat, white candles flickered there now, their flames lightly succeeding in improving his mood. From hidden speakers, strains of a symphony played at a proper volume, to both enliven the room and to offer a screen for conversation. He sat alone at a table for two, sipping his café au lait. His thoughts drifted as he looked through the open window into the orderly courtyard garden, teeming with bright tulips, herbs and sunlight. No sign of the young soccer player this morning.

Drawing a deep breath, he released it slowly and picked up a croissant, its buttery flakes like gold leaf, and he smeared it with butter and strawberry jam. After dunking it into the bowl of coffee, he let the excess drip and carefully lifted it to his mouth. The combination of sweetened coffee and hot milk, cold butter, strawberry jam and crisp pastry conjured Senga. While it was true that at home, he could duplicate the taste, smell and textures, the accompanying setting and view through the window marked it quintessentially French—never mind the soft murmurs. But Senga remained the feast for which this tiny, if exquisite, example prepared him.

As though she read his mind, Madame Colbert brought him two additional pastries and, using tongs, she placed them, *spooning*, he noticed, on the white porcelain plate, with a slight bow of her perfectly coifed head. The expression in her eyes was pained, he noted, and he asked her to join him.

"*S'il vous plait, madame*," he added, ". . . and thank you," he said in English, smiling at the newly charged plate.

"*De rien.* Good morning, *Monsieur Hansen.* How are you this morning?" she asked as she gently sat down, as a ballerina might.

"I'm not sure, *madame.* And you?"

Madame Colbert scanned the room discretely to ensure their privacy. "Jean-Pierre telephoned late last night. He told me the woman—this Dr. Olsen—left a message at the gallery. An apology. *En principe.* He said he was able to entreat her to eat something. It seems she had eaten little all day and blamed the champagne for her behavior. He only alluded to the woman's mode of dress. What do you think, *monsieur?*"

"Ah, no, *madame;* I believe the woman is unwell and should be under the care of professionals. But I am not a physician. She . . . has been sending me emails for some time—you know *emails?*" he asked. She glared at him. "Sorry." he added. "I did not open them after the first. It was disturbing enough. What else . . . did your nephew tell you, if I may ask?"

Madame Colbert stood, finger raised in the familiar gesture and walked to the sideboard, where she took the carafe of coffee to other tables, making short remarks with the guests. She left the room for a few moments, to return with slices of cut baguette, arranged in a basket. This she placed on the sideboard as an older gentleman made his way to replenish his plate, for which he thanked her. She glided back to her chair beside Sebastian. He enjoyed watching the woman's movements. *Yes, I suspect she danced in her youth.*

"Did you dance, *madame?*"

She smiled and raised a well-groomed eyebrow. "One must never cease to dance, *Monsieur Hansen,* else, without it, the body may reject this paltry life."

Touché. So she still danced. He smiled at the thought; *but, of course,* and reviewed the instances she had been in his company;

how she moved, her poise and composure, bearing and presence. Each step, calculated and executed with grace, and accompanied by an inward music. What was playing in the background? *Ah, yes.* He recognized a Saint-Saëns cello concerto. *Jacqueline Du Pre,* he thought.

"Do you have photographs from a favorite performance? I would love to see them."

"*Bien sûr,*" she said, cocking the other eyebrow. "Now you are flirting with me, *monsieur.* But I am flattered." She smiled and lowered her eyes; *not her head,* he noted. She cut them to the window. Still focusing outdoors, she said, "Do let us return to our present trouble, and it *is* trouble, is it not?" She met his eyes. "For my nephew, for you, and—I do not guess—for your lover, wherever she is . . . the woman in the photographs?"

My lover. He listened for Senga's breath in his heart. He needed her. "I am going to pay her a visit—Danica—I must make her see reality."

The dancer chuckled. "I wish you luck, *monsieur.* I think this task is probably impossible. But, if I were you, I would certainly ask a doctor to accompany me for such an errand. An *advocat*— do you know? I do not trust this woman. I have seen what misery she has caused in my nephew. I never said, did I?"

He shook his head and a shiver followed.

Several guests were preparing to leave and Madame Colbert indicated she needed to return to her station in the foyer.

"What are your plans for the day, *monsieur,* if I may ask?"

"Please call me Sebastian."

She nodded graciously. "Then you must call me Simone," she said as she rose. He stood abruptly, as though an old school master had tapped his shoulder with his *baton.* In the doing, Sebastian bumped the table and his bowl of coffee tipped over, spilling the remaining light-brown liquid. He was mortified. "Oh, I am *so* sorry," he said, as he reached for the napkin to dab it.

"*Non, Sebastien!*" She pronounced it in the French. "Please— else I'll have *two* stains. . . Let it be . . . The housekeeper will take care of it, and do not worry—it is nothing." All this, as she deftly plucked away his napkin, removed the breakfast service to the side and lifted the white tablecloth to reveal intricate marquetry beneath, the inlaid wood pattern made of several species. A treasure.

Her words rang—*else I'll have two stains.* . . He tried to recall a quote by Shakespeare, about the ill done by mistaken efforts to improve a situation. *To mar what's well.* Yes. *Was this such a case? What he proposed to try with Danica?*

After dropping by the gallery, and learning the astonishing news of eleven sales between last night's reception and noon today, Sebastian wanted to call Senga, but it was too early in Wyoming. His agent emailed him a link to a review, wherein Danica's "contribution" was noted and carefully described as "genius"— including her dramatic departure with "a street urchin character from *La Belle Époque.*" It had been perfectly choreographed, cited the critic.

So, she succeeded, Sebastian thought wryly. *Proving the critics' dearth of sense.* His deserved delight in the sales, however, was spoiled by the circumstances and he sat down before one of Senga's portraits to be with her.

A small yellow sticker near the price read "SOLD," in French.

Julien walked up behind him and stepped over the bench to sit astride. "You look miserable, *mon vieux,* when you could be celebrating. I will call for a *coûp* of champagne, yes?"

"No, Julien, but thank you. How long will these sales remain exhibited? I did bring other prints, you know."

"Yes, yes. They are in the back. We exhibit the sold photos here for several days, unless the buyer wishes them right away, in which case. . . You were in marketing, Sebastian. It is merely a ploy—to bait the public with a *sold* sign."

"And you are sadly correct. Now, something else. . . I want to find help for this woman. Do you know of a good psychiatrist?"

Here Julien's face underwent several permutations. Sebastian was sorry, yet again, for being without his camera. "Well?"

"Ah, *non, mon ami.* You are a friend, Sebastian; not only a client. Please, divorce yourself from her acquaintance. She will bring you only sorrow. I . . . have heard things."

"Julien—what *things?*" He was rapt and had to know, as the anxious, unholy desire and curiosity of a knowledge, *particulier* or not, squeezed his testicles and he felt pain.

The thin Frenchman sighed, swung his leg around and rose, and gave Sebastian a long, level look. "Come into my *cabinet* of an office and I will tell you, but I do so under duress. No one likes to pass on such disagreeable gossip. At least, I do not."

Forty minutes later, Sebastian emerged, ashen and shaken. He turned right on Rue St. Jacques and began to walk, simply *to* walk, paying scant attention to his direction. A conflagration of emotions gripped him and he considered stepping into a bar for a stiff drink, but reason told him this would be unwise, so he continued to walk—the sight, sound and smell of Paris becoming a milieu unto itself into which he disappeared. With a burden of knowledge.

At five o'clock, he found himself at the *Place des Vosges,* the oldest square in Paris, where a true conflagration was in progress. He moved to a corner of the tree-lined park, where others gathered to watch firemen extinguishing a blaze at one of the mansard-roofed residences, dating from the 17th century. It concentrated his mind to such a degree that he was momentarily freed from the effect of Julien's discussion. He watched, engrossed, as tall ladders were swung into position, and yellow-clad men climbed to reach the flames. Great flumes of water spewed into a gaping hole at the top of the house as all Sebastian's fears and misgivings returned, magnified in that one blackened void; an ugly, smoking destruction.

"Destruction."

"*Pardon, monsieur?*" Someone spoke at his elbow. Sebastian had responded aloud, unconsciously. With a small shake of the head, he addressed an old man who looked up into his eyes with some concern. Sebastian was taken aback. The man was dressed in what appeared to be vintage garb, including a top hat. As well, he sported a well-groomed white beard and round spectacles. Sebastian could have sworn. . .

The man moved his umbrella handle to his left arm, in order to proffer his hand. "You are curious about my costume, *monsieur.* Be not alarmed," he said, with a twinkle in his eye, as Sebastian took the hand—solid as could be.

"*Monsieur Hugo?*" he would hazard a guess, knowing the author had once lived in a house, now a museum, very near that which was burning. He could not remember which, however.

"*Ah, non, monsieur;* but we resemble one another—a *very* little, I think," and here Sebastian recognized the Austrian accent and hesitated to entertain the obvious. But he needn't accept it to simply ask a question. "May I ask you something, *Herr Doctor?*"

"I have time. Yes, certainly. I want to see this nasty business through," he said, pointing to the fire with the end of his umbrella. Sebastian glanced at those standing before him. Their attention had not strayed from the spectacle.

He spoke quietly. "I am in the throes of a drama with a woman whom I believe to be insane."

"Well, *monsieur,* to admit such is the beginning, but it depends on your definition of—insane. . . Your conversing with *me,* for instance, is suspect," and here, the old man tipped his shoulders back and forth in a kind of dance, his feet remaining still. Sebastian noticed the *spats.* Perhaps he was an actor and was merely taking a break during rehearsal. . .

"I assure you, I am not," the man spoke to the air, and Sebastian jerked back to the man's face. "So, what is your question, old son?" What his father had called him on occasion.

All right, then, thought Sebastian, *may as well profit from this. . . What would Senga say?—this "helpful coincidence?"* No. *She would not.*

"How can I help the woman and not become further entangled?"

The man turned and gazed upward, to regard him full in the face, his expression supplying the reply, adding, "You cannot, my friend, sadly. Are you a trained psychoanalyst? No? I thought as much. Insane is a powerful word, *monsieur,* for a yet *more* powerful condition. I notice—and dread—how lightly this generation treats it. They believe, 'Everyone is insane, so, no one is.' A dangerous and shocking hypothesis."

"May I at least go tell her goodbye?"

"*Monsieur,* look!—the fire is contained. How marvelous it didn't spread to the adjacent home. Victor's is too close, however. I must pay him a visit. . . Fires, *monsieur,* seemingly go out, but beware the smoke! This can kill as dead. Good bye and good luck to you!"

Sebastian watched, in a mild state of bewilderment, as the gentleman shuffled toward the corner of the square, to disappear amid the dispersing crowd. A light breeze carried an over-sweet perfume from behind and, when he turned, he was staring into the haunted eyes of Danica.

"You wished to speak with me, Sebastian?"

He watched her unlock the door of her apartment. They had ridden the tiny lift to her floor. She had insisted. The tight space had required their bodies to touch and he'd felt his fingers throb. He was disgusted. The loud perfume intoxicated him.

"Welcome to my parlor, said the spider to the fly," she recited, as she tossed her bag onto her sofa and passed into the small kitchen area. A string bag contained several items from the market and these she removed to the refrigerator, leaving two tomatoes on the counter. "I noticed you in the crowd, Sebastian. You stick out, do you know? I had just stepped into the park to see what the commotion was and there you were. You seemed to be speaking with someone. I came up behind you, but you were so mesmerized that you didn't notice me."

Had he spoken aloud? he wondered. About her insanity? It did not matter. Things were as they were and he tried to remember what the good doctor had said to him. The gist, he recalled, that he was not trained—

"You want to say something to me, Sebastian?" he heard her say.

"Danica. I wish you would consider getting help."

"Help? Why do you believe I need help, Sebastian?" and she crossed in front of him, moving toward another room. "Sit down, please," she said. "We can talk, but I want to change."

His inner alarm sounded, but he sat, marshaling his senses for what may come, as he watched her enter a bedroom. Quickly, in his mind, he sorted through possible openings and decided on one. The only one. "Danica, I am in love with someone. I cannot be with you."

She reappeared at the doorway, smiled and reached into her bra for something before turning away. *She's ignoring me,* he thought, not knowing how to proceed. He watched her pass into a bathroom that opened from her room, as well as from the *salon,* whose door now stood ajar, so he could just see her step to a cabinet and unlock it.

"*Oh Gud—*" he groaned, when he saw what she'd pulled from the shelf. The phone in his pocket vibrated and he recognized Senga's number.

It was the proverbial sign and he treated it as such.

With no other remark, he stepped to the door and left Danica's apartment. He flew down the stairs, hearing Danica's shriek, and only when he'd crossed the courtyard, leading to the great wooden door at the outside entrance, did he dare answer the phone. "*Senga?*"

CHAPTER 14
EXPLICIT OR NO

Sebastian? What's wrong? You sound—"

"Oh, Senga, I am sorry. Please, allow me to call you in five or ten minutes. I must find a place to sit," he said, his breath labored as he walked briskly, often looking over his shoulder. Would she follow him? *Yes,* came the answer.

"All right. You sound upset . . . I'll be here," she said, and he pressed off. He was still shaking with nerves from the revelation and the hasty run down the several flights of stairs. The time difference between him and Senga felt like the barrier it was, strictly speaking, distance-wise and he cursed, drawing disapproval from an elderly woman who stood beside him. It seemed his tone, never mind the Danish language, was sufficiently offensive. They waited for the sign to cross the busy boulevard. When it came, he mumbled an apology and scurried across, to head in the direction of a café.

Glancing behind once more to no sign of Danica, he darted into the somber place. A table was free in the back, where he sat facing the entrance to gather his shattered wits. The café felt reassuring, in the manner of his favorite in Vesterbro, and, as refuge and means of sustenance, he welcomed the hectic nature of the place to that end. A waiter nodded to indicate his intentions.

Sebastian wished his son-in-law were available. Peter was away on a case. But Sebastian thought he'd try his number anyway, just in case.

"*Hej!*" answered Peter. "You caught me. I was just leaving, but I have a moment. How are you? How did your show go?"

"Several sales, but it is a long story and will keep. Be safe, and call when you can." They hung up and he sighed. He wouldn't involve him at this time. The waiter approached and he ordered a hard cider. He had told Senga he would return her call within ten minutes, but he was still at a loss for words. He surveyed the clientele. None were smoking, banned now in public places. Sebastian longed for the strong smell of *Gauloise* cigarettes. The Turkish tobacco would have extinguished any molecules of whatever scent Danica had been wearing. Hannah Arendt's phrase, paraphrased, came to him, slowly twisting in his gut. *The utter banality of evil.* He would *not* grow accustomed to the woman's shocking predilections.

Cider delivered, he took a large swallow, then thanked the server—who looked at him with some concern, but turned away. Reaching for his phone, Sebastian dialed Senga's number, hoping he would know what to say.

"Hello? Are you sitting down?" she asked first, as though she had news requiring the position.

"It is good to hear your voice, my dear, and yes; I'm in a café. Ah, Senga . . . I wish—" and he stopped. He did not particularly wish her there at the moment; this he knew. He would mention the sales. Something positive. "We sold ten photographs, and the gallery believes more will sell." He waited for her response, but heard nothing at the end of the line. "Senga?"

"I'm here, Sebastian. Are you planning to tell me about the woman? The one who was saying your name before you hung up yesterday?"

Was it only yesterday? he wondered. "Ah. Of course. It is . . . a long story, Senga, and still in play, I'm afraid."

"What do you mean? 'Still in play'. . ."

"I wanted to ask Peter for his help with this, but he is leaving, so I didn't bother him with it. Senga, the woman is troubled."

"As you have pointed out. What has she *done,* Sebastian?"

He could see Senga as clearly as if she were sitting across from him. Her tone stung, but he felt a sudden lightness with it, as with the release of pain from a cut after salve is applied.

"It has just come to me to contact her mother in Denmark. I knew if I waited for it, a possible solution might appear, and hearing your voice—well. . . You have a talent for throwing light on darkness, my dear. Thank you. I *miss* you, my Senga," he said, then groaned. *Darkness* is *upon me,* he thought, and then, he shuddered.

"Are you . . . *safe*, Sebastian? Can she harm you in any way? You're frightening me."

"I will relate all when I have this in hand. But you—how are *you?* I regret this drama. Has Francesca returned? And how go your lessons with the boy?" He sorely needed the small talk.

"I'm . . . fine, Sebastian, and Francesca arrives tomorrow . . . I'm working with Joey today, in fact. The test is in a week—then he'll go to the Blue Wood. Rufus and Caroline will miss him, but their grandson arrives soon, so there's that."

He half-listened after she said she was fine. He knew she didn't like to describe her state by the word, so it could mean she was not. He thought it had to do with Danica. *Yes, most likely,* and he sighed, too late realizing he was groaning and sighing too much. *Come now, old son!* he could hear his late father say.

"What's that? You all right?" she asked. "You don't sound all right. That woman is starting to piss me off, Sebastian."

He chuckled. "No-no, my dear . . . I am picturing you as my avenger—my own *wonder woman.* Let me attend to this, and then I'll look at flights to Rapid City."

"Deal. I love you, Sebastian. Oh! And *how* did the mermaid cross the ocean to be with her lover? Goodbye for now. I love you."

He repeated the phrase to her and she hung up, as distance and time whooshed into the here and now for him. For the next several moments, he sat amid the rippling-water language that is French, while mulling the riddle, welcoming the distraction. He thought of adverbs, points of marine navigation and modes of dress—or undress. When he finally settled on the image of a whale—harkening back to Senga's dream—he smiled and felt warmed. A respite, but short-lived. The memory of what Danica had pulled from her bathroom cabinet and her appearance flooded back like a nightmare. . .

He again felt the hot prickling on the back of his neck, to Danica raising an element of one of Senga's portraits, cut with some precision, even artfully, from the full image. He had recognized it immediately, and the tortured expression on Danica's face had curdled his blood when she saw his own mirrored reaction.

Aside from the piece cut from the photo, Danica's newly-naked, pale breasts were scored horizontally with several shallow cuts, the blood dripping eerily like stalled rivulets of deep red stuck to the inside of the pot after his mother had poured out scalding raspberry jam. The analogy disturbed him. He could not remember crying out before leaving, but he had.

How had she acquired it? (The print from last night's show.) Simplicity itself, he knew: money transferred; artwork delivered by courier, sans framing.

Sebastian finished the glass of cold Breton cider in one long swallow, set the glass down and stood to leave, dropping the necessary change on the table and, stepping into the early evening, he chided himself for his cowardice and turned back toward Danica's street, but only after placing a call to his daughter, Erika.

He had been able to reach her, but only just. She was preparing to turn off her phone, as Jytte's piano recital was set to begin. She took down the name and told her father she would do what she could and entreated him to be careful. He had omitted Danica's self-harming for fear of alarming her.

His stomach growled and he realized he hadn't eaten since breakfast. Not that he had much appetite. The smells from restaurants assailed his senses, however, but more, gave him upset. He stepped up his pace and was soon outside the large step-through, wooden entrance that opened to an inner courtyard and Danica's apartment above. He took the stairs by two and was soon at her door. This stood open. Her neighbor across the landing peered from a chained crack in her door.

"Bonjour, madame. La docteur est là?" he quietly asked. Was the doctor in?

The woman's eyes grew large as she slowly nodded, then closed the door. Reopening it, she whispered, *"Elle est complètement folle, monsieur. Soyez prudent."* She is completely mad, sir. Be careful. He knew enough French to translate the worried tone. She closed the door again and he stood for a moment to gather his wits. What would he do? More importantly, what would he find?

The telephone rang inside the apartment. He heard Danica answer, *"Allô?"* Then, she began to cry. He heard her speak in Danish—to her mother, he guessed. Had Erika been able to reach her so soon? But that was thirty minutes ago, he realized. He heard Danica tell the caller she was simply emotional and there was nothing to worry about. By the end of the call, Danica had regained her composure. He heard her say goodbye in a frightening change of tone. He stood riveted to the spot, wondering what to do next.

"Sebastian? Is that you? Come in. I am sorry I scared you," he heard in his language, and then, she was at the door, utterly nude and, with a sharp intake of breath, he tried to back away. She reached out and pulled him to her by the lapel on his jacket. He put out a hand to separate them and Danica stepped back, so he could take her in . . .

Her body was well-formed, taut and slim, but also a living roadmap of hell; crisscrossing scars and marks, most old and white with age, some newer and pink with healing. At the reception, her uncovered décolletage had shown no sign of injury. It must have been the only area on her body unharmed, save her face and hands. And now, it wasn't.

"Danica. *How* can I help you?" he asked, careful to engage her eyes and disguise the horror in his mind. Erika had once proposed that people who cut themselves needed to produce a physical reason for their incessant emotional suffering. In some cultures, it accompanied grieving.

"That was Mother on the phone. She asked the very same. Have you spoken with her, Sebastian? I think you must have, else why would she have called? She rarely calls. I am out of sight, so out of her mind."

She laughed at the accidental wordplay and turned toward the open window. He noted her total lack of self-consciousness, different from his Senga's, whose relationship with her body was healthy, while Danica's need was not. "You are being kind," she said as she surveyed the cloudy sky.

"Do not mistake my kindness for weakness."

"What a strange thing to say, Sebastian." She turned her head to regard him and smiled, if sadly.

Several long scars crossed her back and shoulders. Even her buttocks had been cut. She backed to an upholstered chair beside the window and sat, her legs spread apart onto each chair arm in invitation, her pelvis tipped up. He turned away. "No, Danica," he murmured, as he moved toward the still-open door to her apartment. The neighbor was back at her post, taking it in. He felt repugnance as he shut the door. And then, he felt his cock stir and more disgust. The mindless thing knew no shame and he surveyed the room for a throw, something with which to cover Danica, who was now regarding him while touching herself and bringing her fingers to her mouth, and returning them to her pleasure.

He wanted her—and the idea began to transmute into an acceptable solution, or answer. A rationale. He treated the contrary as a framed picture, turned to the wall, or, as though he had simply walked from one room, into another. *Is madness infectious?* The question escaped as quickly as it was posed.

He stood watching her for a long moment, lost, and vaguely registering the recent cuts on her chest. They had been cleaned; though long red lines, such as what a calligraphy pen might make, still scratched the white velum of her skin. His photographer's eye noted the lighting on her thighs, how the raised ridge of an old scar caught the light, a thin shadow just behind, as though her body had been inscribed or engraved, and then, he gasped. She had effectively lured him to study her nakedness long enough to *read* her, and he stumbled backward and onto the floor, clattering against the desk leg. With her eyes locked on him, she began to moan, then, by the bright glint in her other hand, he spotted the razor blade.

Scrambling on all fours, he lunged for her hand and she let drop the small blade to the floor.

. . . After, he offered to help her rise. They exchanged no words. There were none. She crossed to her room, where she put on a robe. A light tapping at the door startled him. Sebastian took a deep breath and walked to it, opening to Jean-Pierre and his aunt, Simone Colbert, who stood behind.

"Monsieur Hansen—*Sebastien*," said Simone, taken slightly aback. "My nephew would like to take the . . . ah . . . *doctor* to hospital. Are you in favor of this? And—" Hesitating, her attention focused behind him. He turned to see Danica leaning in her bedroom door, robe open. Reconsidering, Simone continued, "Have you seen what she has done to herself? Your *name?*" Simone looked on him no longer with compassion, but with shrewd accusation; he saw it in her sharp gray eyes, lit now by the wall sconce beside the door. The nosy neighbor was again eavesdropping.

"*Au nom de Dieu, madame!*" he shouted and the door clicked shut.

Name of God, indeed. Simone Colbert stared at him, like a man clothed in darkness. A sweet-salty smell exuded from his pores; his appearance was bleary-eyed, wrung out and spent.

"Yes, *madame*," was all he could say. Yes, he'd seen his name. The letters of which were carved into Danica's skin, here, there, in horrific mutilation serving only to bring her fixation to the evening's conclusion. She had worked a sort of sympathetic magic on him, to conjure his—his *what?* "Danica," he called out after a moment. "I . . . I am sorry," and with nothing more, he swept past them and made his erratic, uneven way down the flights of stairs in a fog, void of emotion, insensible to whom he apologized.

Jean-Pierre cried out from above, the words reverberating round the hollowed stone stairwell. "*Monsieur,* she had *me* cut your name in her! Now, *you* have been cursed! It is *I* who am sorry for you!"

CHAPTER 15
BEATITUDE

After speaking with Sebastian on my magic cell phone, jacket drawn over my head against the rain, I'd returned the device to the inside pocket. Mumbling to myself, I met Joe as I stepped back on the trail. We both looked the worse for wear. Earlier, I'd tripped over a fallen limb, to land face down into a mud-filled patch, while Joe's robe hung limp, stretched of all recognition, to resemble a second-hand store bathrobe. I told him he looked like a wet grizzly bear.

"And you picked a fine time to go on a walkabout, Senga," he said, moving to embrace me. Deciding against it, he favored a light peck to one of my cleaner cheeks. "Are you cold?" he asked. "You look cold. Milo's got blankets in his trunk. I hope," he said, as we tramped back to the picnic shelter.

I turned once to an eerie sound; imagination no longer spoke for the unreal. It sounded like the lonely breath of a wooden flute, but through the rain it could have been anything. Joe made no sign of hearing it, so I returned my attention to the trail and we were soon back at the picnic shelter. Moona'e shook her head upon seeing us, and Milo walked to his car, where indeed the trunk held several thick blankets.

"I know, I know; stupid white girl doesn't read sky and gets caught in rain. Yet again," I joked, through the shivers. "Papa Bear here looks worse."

"No, he doesn't, Missy. Are you hurt? Looks like you tumbled," said Milo.

"I'm not hurt." I raised a hand to my forehead, smeared with red mud. "Have anything hot to drink?" I asked, while wiping my hand on my jeans.

Moona'e reached for a thermos and poured a steaming cup of coffee. She kept stealing glances at me and I began to feel self-conscious. "What is it?" I finally blurted.

"You. You look like you've seen a ghost."

"No. No ghosts." I held the warm cup between my hands and let heat penetrate them. I began to feel human again. *Why would she say that?* I wondered. A gust of wind carried on it a faint high note. I turned in its direction. Nothing.

"Want to move to the car and turn on the heat?" Milo suggested. I nodded and Joe agreed. Soon, we were enjoying a car picnic, with the heater blowing hot air over us. The windows clouded with steam.

"How is Sebastian?" asked Joe.

I was silent a moment too long.

"Senga?" he said, as he took another bite of his peanut and apple butter sandwich. (Apple butter made with my apples, Moona'e informed us.) I accepted a crusty chicken leg.

"I don't know how he is. When I talked with him earlier, I heard a woman say his name and he said he needed to go. We spoke a little while ago; he seems . . . troubled." I gave them a half-smile and saw them exchange looks. "This, ah, person who called his name," I added, "she's a bit *tetched,* as we used to say in the mountains." I didn't want to say more. They grasped the simple and all-too-familiar explanation.

"How's the boy? Joey?" asked Joe, changing the subject.

"He's doing well," I said. "The tutoring and all—he'll take the G.E.D. test next week, and go to the guest ranch the week after."

Someone knocked on the driver's window. Milo rolled it down just enough to be polite. "Yes?"

I recognized Tom Robinson and scrunched down. Moona'e regarded me with a questioning look, but said nothing.

"Hello, folks. Your picnic got rained out, didn't it?" he said, unnecessarily.

"Yep," said Milo, never one to embellish.

"That's too bad. Well, just checking to make sure everything's all right. You camping?"

"No."

Like pulling teeth, I wanted to whisper to Moona'e, but held my nervous tongue.

"Okay, then. This should blow over soon."

He turned and left. I noticed he was drenched, himself, from what I could glimpse through the window.

Joe grunted. "What else is there to eat? The weather's worked up my appetite."

"Oh, it's the weather this time, eh, *Joe-He's Big,*" joked Moona'e.

"Blessèd are the hungry, for they shall be fed," he proposed and Milo chortled.

"Making up new Beatitudes?" he commented. "What next—a new Commandment?"

I laughed. "Good one, Milo. Let's see—Thou shalt not. . ."

"Thou shalt not mock thy friends!" said Joe—rather proudly, I thought.

We finished eating and caught up on our news. The clouds eventually scudded away, to allow a bright, if humid afternoon. They asked me to join them, but I had things to do and asked, tongue-in-cheek, for a rain check when they returned later in the summer. Joey needed a review, for one thing and, I wanted to work in the orchard and garden, for another. It may not have rained at the cabin. Spring squalls are often localized.

As I crossed the parking lot to my car, I again heard the low, voice-like keening of the flute and stepped up my pace.

The Black Hills, Circa 1820

High Wolf played for his wife and her mother. News of the suicides had thrown the tribe into a deep chasm of sadness, and the warrior knew the music of his flute might assist in carrying the grief along the path it needed to travel. So, he continued to play. He knew his wife, She Who Bathes Her Knees, was caught between attending to her mother's sorrow and feeling her own. Looking once again in the direction of their tipi, he suspected she busied herself with the evening meal. It was something she and her sister, Lona, had always prepared together.

Lona and her Little Eagle lover, a man from an eastern tribe, lay three days dead, left together on a scaffold at the bottom of a cliff from which they had stepped off. A half-day's journey from this place. Their bones (those that remained) would later be gathered and placed elsewhere. Possibly nearby. The clan had camped here in order to offer prayers and to take time to heal. The great stone had many names, but he'd grown up calling it *Nakovehe*. Bear Lodge. For good reason—for here slept bears. It was simply a matter of avoiding them, and sentries were posted. Even as he played, a friend insisted on accompanying him to his perch above the camp, where the song might waft down among the tipis.

High Wolf was grateful he could concentrate on the playing. He blew long and mournfully, even to the point of bringing tears to both his and his friend's eyes, for Lona, *The Beautiful One*. He hoped she would hear the music and it would comfort her and accompany her where she needed to go. *Both of you,* he amended. But he mostly played for the living.

As he did, he remembered the first time his father brought him to this place. He'd been only seven. His father was preparing him for *a 'wonderful thing,'* he'd declared.

For weeks before the journey, he was instructed in crawling, much as the hunters did when approaching a herd or a flock of ducks on a pond. "It will require strength and patience," his father had told him; but foremost, he must comprehend how fortunate he was to have been given the opportunity to see this *thing*.

His grandmother had sat on the council. The elders had deliberated long before granting permission for him to visit the hidden place the *Tsitsistas* held sacred, but he was not told why he must crawl.

When his father thought him ready, they departed. His mother had packed the rawhide *parflêche* with dried meat, berries and dried breadroot, and High Wolf—then named *Pup*—heard her tell his father, in no uncertain terms, that he'd better bring the boy back. *Alive.* She had looked on her son with pride mixed with fear. He would learn to recognize the emotion in himself.

After two days of travel, the small company reached a ridge, where they studied the great stone in the distance and then proceeded into a valley. They were twelve, counting him. He was glad he had been given one of the swift horses to ride. His had grown old and he didn't like having to continually press her to move along. But this one! Riding him was as much an event as what he was going to see, yet unknown to him. It was sacred knowledge.

He had camped at the Bear Lodge before, and was familiar with its wondrous contours and environs, never mind the truth of bears living among the huge boulders at the base of the massive rock. He understood what a bear could do to a dog, horse or person. The children were taught by being shown consequences. And, sometimes, by living with those consequences, like his cousin, Blue Heron, whose face was disfigured by the clawing of a bear cub.

High Wolf paused in his flute playing at the memory, then closed his eyes to remember the passage, and he wondered if death were somewhat like that crawl had been. . .

After posting three sentries with the horses near the river, he and the others had made their way toward the towering monolith. The day had been warm, with a light breeze, he remembered, and he'd felt good. They had all eaten and drunk their fill from the flowing stream, then rested in order to digest their meal.

He followed behind his father; his eyes peeled for bear and whatever else that could pose a threat. He particularly feared badger and the mouthful of sharp teeth. This looked more like badger country than bear, he mused. "Watch where you're stepping, Pup. Snakes—" A warrior quietly spoke to him from behind and he jerked at the word. The man chuckled lightly.

"Do not frighten him," his father chided, then said, "But yes, there are snakes," drawing mirth from the rest of the group.

High Wolf noticed everyone wore their older clothing; certainly not their best for such an auspicious journey. His mother had laid out his everyday shirt and breeches. "They will get dirty—" her only explanation.

PART TWO

CHAPTER 16
WITH RESPECT TO RESPECT

Gabe lay half-dreaming, imagining the surrounding country similarly in the half-light, holding the weathered ranch buildings and paddocks in the peaceful crook of its arm; *so to speak,* he added, to excuse the cliché. The Stricklands' forebears had chosen wisely the location of their home and outbuildings, in order to benefit from the valley's best sunlight arc during long winter months.

His wakefulness expanded, much as a camera lens may pan out to include the wider view. Gabe knew he dozed, rendering consciousness a delicious comfort. He flung it (his consciousness) higher to view the ranch as the robin did, calling now from the nearby grove, the birdsong bright and cheery on this, his birthday. *Maybe it's Mama,* he wondered sleepily.

The bird called again, a short, melodic trill, closer now. Gabe habitually left his window raised an inch to the fresh air and for precisely this reason—to hear birds. Possibly lion, if another ranged close by. He heard his father's, *"Ole Wampus?"*—the cursed cat from Southern folklore. Gabe wanted to ask Senga if her grandfather ever told her the story about the hapless Cherokee woman who, having broken a taboo, was shape-shifted to a mountain lion, to forever roam. A story to persuade children to stay close to camp, like other boogey-man—in this case, *woman*—tales. He took a long breath with eyes shut, to test if he could detect lion, the musky odor unmistakable. No, he smelled only horseflesh, sweet hay from the loft and his own sleep-soaked body, born after all in the stable/stubborn sign of Taurus, the bull. *Naturally.*

He was sensible of his birthday in May, having yearly celebrated in the rising, sticky temperatures of Louisiana's midspring, but in northern Wyoming it was a toss-up. A late blizzard could dump several feet of wet snow on greening fields and blossoming trees (as had befallen Senga's trees two years before, he dimly recalled). But so far this year, they had received only a mild snow storm before the usual last frost date of May 15. Changing weather patterns made the date no longer dependable, his friend and neighbor had lamented. But for the time being, her flowering orchard was gloriously (he hoped) safe.

His thoughts turned to his Italian fiancée, in fairness.

Francesca had returned two days before, and his toes still thrilled to the memory. They had stayed in Rapid City after her late flight's arrival, the city's venerable hotel again chosen for its old-world charm. Gabe had requested, and acquired, the same room as before her departure last November.

They hadn't yet chosen a date to be married. It was to be a small ceremony in Italy, a condition her mother found utterly irksome. Francesca wanted to wait until Gabe's collection of short stories came out.

"But *why?*" he'd asked.

"Because it is important, *caro mio,*" she'd said, "First things first, no?"

"But *you* are first, sweet Francesca, don't you know?"

"In Italy—" She cleared her throat and began again; "In Italy, a mistress can be, and is often, first—"

Gabe made to interrupt, but she raised a resolute palm and closed her eyes. He desisted.

"I tell you," she resumed, "I will *share* you with the writing and, I think, in this case, she—the book—comes before; *sì?* As gesture of my respect and . . . *come si dice* . . . ah! goodwill for this . . . this—"

"Arrangement?" he had suggested hoarsely as he raised his head, then snorted and snuggled between her breasts again, squeezing them against his cheeks as he blew, like a bull. This had produced in her a fit of hilarity. How he loved her laugh!

She had returned to work at the Blue Wood Guest Ranch, ahead of a group from Italy. Gabe had wanted more time with her before the busy period set in. "*C'est la vie,*" he said aloud to the early morning, sighed and threw off the covers. "Get on up, you silly bag of bones," repeating his late mother's soft-spoken wake-up call and, rolling over, he decided to linger a moment longer, to allow morning to sink into those bones.

It was still early, judging by the pale light at the window. He loved the way it reflected through Caroline's Tiffany-style lamp on his desk. *Like a little bit of Christmas every day,* he'd decided. He watched dawn grow brighter and the stained-glass shade's colors increase in brilliance. "Sort of like my life right now, ain't it?" he asked no one in particular, so—everyone.

The tang of dried horse sweat reached him from the saddle blankets, hung upside down over the saddles. He found the earthy, warm smell comforting. Always had. It reminded him to have Joey clean the leather tack soon. The neat's-foot oil, even in memory, engendered more, and might create some for the kid, he hoped.

The phone call on Saturday had come from his publisher, who told him the book release date had been moved up, and could he attend a "pub party" in New York next month? Gabe told him he'd get back to him and he hadn't. *Better do it this morning,* he thought, as he rose and stepped to the sink to rinse his face. Joey's test was in two days. Was he ready? Gabe thought so. He wanted to review a couple of weak areas, but couldn't remember what all Rufus had on the agenda for today. His mind was full of his sweet Francesca.

"Happy Birthday to me," he sang as he pulled on his jeans.

Francesca had hand-carried the tablecloth for Senga from Italy, embroidered by Senga's grandmother, Maria Teresa, along with several small family keepsakes: Senga's father Andrea's small, wooden horse, carved by his Italian grandfather; his first report card from elementary school, with a sample of his careful handwriting; and a trophy he'd won for high school wrestling in North Carolina.

Francesca held up the cloth to Mary Rogers.

"It's just gorgeous, Francesca," crooned Mary in her Floridian drawl. "It looks tedious as sin—all those tiny stitches—but I'm glad someone has the patience."

"She said it is something she began over twenty-five years ago for Emily, to give to her on her wedding day. She stopped working on it after . . . but started again after Senga left last

December. It is all she has been doing, she says. *Beh,* that—and spending time with my *Nonno.*" She grinned. "They are like a painting, Mary; Maria Teresa brings her work basket to our home in the early morning and, after a cup of coffee with *Nonno,* they both go to sit on the chairs beside the front door, like two, ah—"

"Old folks?"

"*Sì!* Old folks. This is correct, no? They talk a little, she sews; he points to someone walking on the road with his chin, says something silly and she laughs. It is very sweet, do you know?"

"I think it's wonderful. I'm happy for them, and for you. We take such joy in other peoples' happiness. I don't understand why it isn't in the water."

Francesca furrowed her brows at the expression, but didn't question her employer; instead, she asked, "So, Lee is ready for his great experiment with young people?"

"Mmmm, not quite. You met the LPN? We're not sure about her yet. What did you think?"

The middle-aged woman in question turned the corner from the hallway into the commons, where Francesca and Mary were talking. "*Oh, spit,*" said Mary under her breath.

"I heard you, and what are you not sure about?" the *tall drink of water* spoke as she headed toward them. Jim had taught the expression to Francesca, who collected western idioms.

"Hi, Gloria. All right—" Mary set down her cup and rose to fetch the carafe. "Would you like a cup, dear?"

"Sure." said Gloria, and eyeing Francesca with something like mistrust, she took a seat beside her.

"Good morning, Gloria." Francesca chose reserve in light of Mary's statement, but she understood what Mary meant. She had felt it as well. Something wasn't quite *suitable* about the woman. No, that was not it and she searched for the word in Italian; *inquietante.* Disturbing.

"Gloria," said Mary, as she set a mug down and poured a cup of hazelnut coffee. "You heard me. So, can you tell me why I'm having reservations about your working here?"

Francesca admired her employer's courage. No skirting the issue for her. She wondered if she shouldn't leave to give them privacy. She made to stand, but Mary placed a hand on her forearm. She settled back into her chair and reached for her cup, all the while looking at Gloria, who was glaring at her.

"I don't know what your problem is," the woman said, as she continued to stare at Francesca; then, turning to Mary, "You don't have a problem hiring Mexicans, I see."

Francesca blanched. As an olive-skinned Italian, she had rarely experienced discrimination, and had dismissed the incident with the man at the bar in Montana (who was locked in jail now, according to Gabe). She lowered her eyes in distaste and wanted badly to leave. Mary's hand returned to her forearm.

"Francesca is a valued employee *and* friend, miss, and I'll demand respect toward her—*and* Mexicans." She glanced to the kitchen where Lupita worked, whose parents, she'd learned, had emigrated in the nineties. "Further, I'm not required to justify my hiring to you or anyone else. I'm sorry, Gloria, but I don't think you'd be a good fit here, and I hope you can change your mind about some, ah, *things,* before you get much older, else . . . else you're bound to grow even *more* bitter and angry." The last phrase was spoken quietly, for emphasis.

Brava, signora, thought Francesca, as she peeked into the troubled face of Gloria. The woman prepared to make a retort, when the heavy door to the Lodge opened and in stepped Lee and Jim for their morning coffee break.

"Hey, Francesca!" said Lee, as he hung his jacket on one of the pegs near the door, while Jim headed for the facilities, calling, "So happy you're back."

She felt the love.

"So what are you and Gabe doing for his birthday? His 40th, isn't it? Thought I overheard that somewhere," continued Lee, not realizing he had stumbled onto an awkward scene. Gloria rose to leave and Francesca felt, if not pity, then a semblance of compassion, as the woman was clearly disappointed. Perhaps she could not help her disposition, Francesca wondered.

Lupita entered as if on cue, carrying a tray of assorted sweet rolls and cookies, always a welcome antidote, Francesca believed. She smiled at the pretty cook, who beamed with the satisfaction of the appreciated. To Lee's question, Francesca answered, "*Gebb* . . . he and Joey are coming here! Lupita is baking a cake for him. . . Gloria," she addressed the woman who had turned to leave, "you must try one of Lupita's sweets. They are wonderful. Please have one." The woman wanted to, Francesca could tell by her expression, but she could not release the chain tied to her resentment.

CHAPTER 17
TWO BIRDS, ONE STONE

L upita had outdone herself by Gabe's cake. Francesca had somehow wheedled out of him his favorite recipe. She liked the word, *wheedle*, and added it to her growing lexicon of expressions. It was the humble pound cake, the one his mother used to make. "A pound of flour, a pound of butter, a pound of sugar; you know—a *pound* cake!" Mary had been fairly confident their cook could bake it.

Everyone had gathered in the Blue Wood commons. Pete— Lee and Mary Rogers's son—had arranged to arrive in time for the party, to Lupita's great delight. It may have been Gabe's birthday, but the girl was celebrating something else, guessed Francesca. They had invited Rufus and Caroline, Joey and Senga, Earl, Mae and their daughter—whose name she had forgotten— so there would be fourteen. Maybe. Carey, the housekeeper, wasn't sure she could stay.

The first ranch guests would arrive in a few days, and Mary was happy to have a get-together before the "season" began. "It helps to get everyone on the same page," she explained, not entirely clearly to her Italian liaison. Francesca had looked forward to the evening and wore a new top for the occasion. She took a last look at herself in the mirror. The rosy blouse accented her best feature, and she didn't mind sharing it with appreciative friends.

She pronounced the image *bella,* but added a swipe of lip gloss and sashayed out her bedroom door toward the commons. The room buzzed with conversation and laughter. Lee, Mary, Pete and Jim were drinking beer and sampling Lupita's cheese nachos. Lee whistled at Francesca, as though he had just witnessed the perfect touchdown. She grinned in reply.

On the buffet against the wall, the perfectly plain, yet exquisite cake rested under a glass dome on a pedestal stand. Francesca had nixed black decorations, though Mary couldn't resist hanging a narrow banner that read, "Lordy, Lordy, look who's forty!"—citing they had to embarrass *the kid,* "just a little."

When Earl, Mae and their daughter arrived, the old biker guffawed at the sign and praised whoever had thought of it; that they were to be commended. "That would be me," responded Mary. "Commendable."

Conversation turned to Joey's high school equivalency test in two days. Gabe had earlier reminded Lee they were docking next week and he'd bring Joey over after. Francesca hoped he would do well on the test—for Gabe's and Senga's sake. *Beh, the boy's too,* she amended. He would bunk with Jim, the wrangler and foreman.

At precisely seven o'clock, the large carved door opened to the Stricklands, followed by Joey and Senga, then Gabe. Though it wasn't strictly a surprise party, everyone yelled "Surprise!" anyway. Gabe appeared nonplussed for a moment, then he laughed, pointing to the sign and shaking his finger and head at Mary. Francesca clasped her arms round him for a hug. Pete shouted, "Kiss! Kiss!" and they obliged him. Gabe had worn the cedar-orange fragrance she had brought him from Italy last year and he smelled like Christmas. She beamed at him and said quietly into his ear, "Happy Birthday, *caro mio;* I love you."

He grinned and repeated the words in Italian, then spotted the cake and his reaction brought tears to her already moist eyes. "Aw, y'all. What have y'all gone and done for me?" He crossed to it, lifted the glass lid and leaned in to smell the golden-brown crumb. After making a sound, he said, "Lupita? You did this?"

She nodded.

"I thank you, sugar. From the bottom of my heart. It looks perfect and I can't wait."

He gently lowered the lid, turned to his friends, smiled and said, "Thank y'all. I am a blessed man."

The room grew quiet; too quiet for Lee, evidently, and he said, "All right then! What'll everyone have? There's beer, wine and tea in the fridge—and appetizers; then, steaks on the grill. Let's move outside. Pete? Would you put some of those drinks in the cooler?"

"Okay, Dad," said Pete, unwillingly pulling his eyes from Lupita, noticed Francesca.

She also noticed that Senga did not seem herself. More withdrawn than usual. Stepping over to her, she asked, "Senga, what is wrong, *cara?* Did something happen?"

"Oh, Francesca . . . let's wait 'til later. It's complicated and I won't spoil Gabe's party. I'm sorry. Let's all just enjoy this, okay? I want to. What are you drinking? And you look beautiful! Gabe's a lucky man. Have you set a date yet?"

Francesca saw through her friend's tactic and refused the bait. She recognized the misdirection. "Senga. You will tell me now. So, beer or wine?"

"Wine. But no—I really don't want to discuss it." She snorted once. "Mainly because I don't *know* what's happened, Francesca. That's the problem. But yes, let's get some wine. And here comes Mary. *Shhh,* now."

Francesca understood and took a breath, then smiled and planted a kiss on her friend's cheek. "Wine, Mary?" she called.

The Lady of the Lodge held up a bottle of beer, so, no, she did not. Francesca turned toward the kitchen, then Senga and Mary stepped out to the patio area, where the grill smelled of sweet apple wood and burning charcoal. Rufus, Caroline and Joey sat at one of the wrought-iron tables with Earl, Mae and their daughter, Lily—as she was introduced.

"Lily has just finished her first year of nursing school," announced her proud papa.

Overhearing this, Francesca and Mary exchanged glances.

Francesca and I took our glasses of wine to a bench set a good distance from the noisy patio. Seated beside a row of mature Black Hills spruce trees, we watched the sun set behind a far ridge. Private nooks offered guests (and others) solitude, or a place for a quiet visit. Such as this one.

I turned the stem-less glass in my hand, raising it to the fading amber light. The red legs of the wine against the clear cup made a stained-glass effect; beautiful—if oddly melancholic.

"Mary serves good wine, doesn't she?" I said and felt its truth rising.

"Senga. Is it Sebastian? What's wrong, *cara?*"

"I don't know. That's what bothers me, Francesca. But something is wrong." I took a drink of the Malbec and waited for it—the truth. *In vino veritas.*

"What is the matter? When did you last speak with him?"

"Just today. . . All right—there's a woman. A Danish woman he met years ago, who—well, I don't know what all she wants, but he's part of it, I know. I *feel* it, you know? Like when you can sense a storm is brewing—in your bones. But, she's sick, mentally. He says he needs to help her, but I'm afraid for him, I guess. It's fucked up. . . Sorry." I looked up at her. Her expression had grown cloudy.

"You don't have to apologize to *me*, Senga. I hear this word as the truth sometimes," she said and smiled. "But you say you are going to Ireland for the show. This is good, no? Away from this—this woman and her *boolsheet?*"

I laughed at her pronunciation. "Yes. Yes, I am, and you're right; this—*boolsheet*—will not prevail." We sat in silence a moment. "Thank you. I feel better. It's been an undigested piece of meat in my craw all day." I chuckled, then pointed in the direction of the sun just sinking below the ridge, peeking from beneath a bank of clouds.

Francesca took a drink and said dreamily, "I like this place. I *don't* like it when I come and someone is here already. It is *boolsheet.*" We chuckled at her joke—how I took it, anyway. Sardonically.

And someone is there, with him, I pondered on our way back to the party. *Where is he now? With her?* No. I was not going to play this game. The wine may have emboldened me, but medicinally, resolve may have been prescribed by my heart. For my heart.

Back at the party, they were playing a game. Pin the tail on the bear. I suppressed an eye roll as I glanced in Caroline's direction. She grinned. Someone had drawn a fairly good rendering of a grizzly, sans tail (as nowadays), on a piece of tag board, and Rufus, blind-folded, was carefully heading for the image, tacked to a panel of sheet rock. The "Bear Lodge Game," I later learned, had apparently become a popular diversion for guests. The constellation *Ursa Major* depicted the ancient tailed bear, better known as the Big Dipper.

Laughter and cheers followed Rufus' deliberate placement of his tail. He whipped off his bandana and pumped a fist in the air. His was the closest so far. I lost myself and my concerns over the next two hours in reveling with my friends. Whatever Sebastian was about at that particular hour, I'd trust he was asleep. Alone.

Gabe wore a paper crown, courtesy of his fiancée. Watching them together stung; I missed intimacy. *Now, stop,* I told myself. I would further my acquaintance with Earl and Mae and their daughter, Lily, who seemed to be getting on with Joey. Behind me Mary whispered, "So, Francesca and I are wondering if the girl would hire on for the summer."

I turned too quickly, nearly spilling my wine on my host. "That was close—I didn't get any on you, did I?" I asked as I looked her over.

"No, Senga," she replied, checking herself all the same. "She's passed a first aid course and *seems* stable—important when working with kids."

"Work here, you mean? I didn't know—"

"Oh, we thought we had someone, but she . . . well . . . it didn't work out. Joey's *clearly* interested."

"Not appropriate criteria, Mary," I suggested, "Let me visit with her for you; do you mind? You mean to have someone with medical training, for when the kids come, right?"

"You got it, darlin'," she said, winked and walked away toward Lee, who'd been monitoring us. I expect he knew what his wife was up to, the sly dog.

I screwed up my social courage and crossed to the table, where sat Joey, Lily and Jim.

"Hey, y'all," I said, setting down my now-empty glass. Jim, ever gallant, whisked it up and headed for the bottle on another table. Joey and Lily looked somewhere between relaxed and ill-at-ease. How much was bravura and how much, genuine? I wondered. The girl—young woman—was leaning forward in her chair, toward Joey, I noted. Elbows on the table, hands clasped, she reminded me of a Vermeer painting; her expression one of benign amusement, and a natural poise I couldn't fathom. Her eyes rested on Joey, when they weren't following the speaker. After Vermeer, I conjured her as a young doe; bright, curious, quick. She was pretty—in an easy way. In other words, she didn't appear to spend too long at her toilette, as some do.

She seemed shy, and yet, did not. She would make a good nurse; her learning would override timidity.

"Good to see you, Senga, when you're not making me learn something," the boy said.

"You too, Joey. How about tomorrow? After I get off work?" I suggested. "I'll stop by." His test was soon and he needed a review.

"That'll work. I'll be glad when it's over." He looked at Lily and grinned.

"Joey says you're a good teacher—that you explain science well." The girl spoke articulately, thus earning brownie points in my book. Refreshing, given she didn't know she was being considered for a job she may or may not want. I knew she worked for her parents at the diner in Alzada during the summer. Would they agree to a new arrangement? I needed to speak with them first. *How quickly things complicate.* I sighed, while my heart and mind welcomed the diversion.

In Paris, Sebastian and Julien had drunk every night since Sunday. After gallery hours, of course. During the day, Sebastian walked. He must have explored twenty square miles of the City of Lights. Julien finally asked about the woman, the *arlequine* who had disrupted the opening reception. Sebastian had demurred and Julien had pressed. They were well into the bottle of brandy.

"All right. I will tell you, only because I need to," he slurred. "I do not want to. Do—do you understand?"

"Of course, *mon ami.*"

"And why are the French so damned cock-sure of everything! You all sound so superior with your '*bien sûrs. . .*'"

Julien made a sad, lopsided smile and took another small sip of the Calvados. Pointing his finger at the photographer, he said, "And you Danes are so certain you grasp reality, *n'est-ce pas?* Let us ignore stereotypes this evening, *Sebastien.* I can see well enough you suffer. Tell me, my friend."

He told him. The Frenchman sat back and whistled, or tried to. It sounded like a deflating tire. When Sebastian could no longer tolerate the seeming scrutiny, he abruptly stood. "I need to piss," and he made his way to the WC. The café was crowded for a Wednesday night and he was made to wait outside the toilet a few moments. The brandy had rendered him insensible, but he welcomed the respite from sensibility, even remorse. From a place of supra-consciousness, he had overheard himself tell Julien about the incident, in insipid shades of grey, like a poorly developed photograph.

Sebastian had moved from Madame Colbert's hotel to a room closer to the gallery. She had not been in when he checked out, for which he was grateful. His vague plan would have him remain in Paris until the end of the week, when he would return to Copenhagen. He needed to ground himself at home, he knew; but first, this madness must be worked out. *Exorcized* came to mind.

When he returned to their table, Julien had ordered food; for each, the traditional *croque-madame,* with egg that aided in sopping up too much drink. Sebastian offered no opinion of it and sat down. Such were his sentiments, or lack thereof.

"And, what of this other woman? Your model, *mon chèr?*"

He shot a look at Julien in warning, then slowly took a bite of the sandwich, cutting it with a fork and knife, as was the custom. It tasted of comfort, of his Senga and their shared love of quiche. His deed had left a hole—or was it emptiness?—in his gut, and now, in his heart. A paradox—to feel nothing now, where before he had felt such love—for Senga. There was no justification, no excuse. *But I do love Senga*, his intellect cried beneath his stupor.

"You will simply live with it, *Sebastien,*" said the man who read his thoughts. "And, please stop judging yourself. It never helps; it only harms. *I* certainly do not judge you, *mon ami.*" The man then tucked into his meal.

He has already passed on to the next thing, thought Sebastian, and his eyes blurred as he lowered his fork and knife and asked, "Then, why the whistle? I should like to, Julien—move on. It would help if I knew the woman was being helped."

"*Mon Dieu, Sebastien!* Let her go, man. She is not your concern. I do not understand your . . . your—*comment dit-on?* Your compulsion." He took a sip of water and dabbed his mouth at the corner, then picked up his fork and knife and continued, "I *whistled,* as you say, only for the grotesque and macabre nature of the encounter. Nothing to do with moral principle. But, *en principe,* you my friend are feeding her, ah . . .

fantaisie. Do you not see this? It is *elementary* psychology, something we *Français* comprehend better, I think, than you Danes."

At this Sebastian choked, but with quiet laughter. The first note of levity in days. He brought his napkin to his mouth, then raised his near-empty glass to Julien and said, "*Salud*," in marked agreement, thus terminating the line of conversation and Sebastian's confession. A healing sense of absolution, however, would require time. If forthcoming.

He reached Senga the next morning, her time, to say he was sorry he had neglected her, that he was leaving for Denmark the following morning, and had received word of the exhibition dates in Ireland. Could she meet him there? He would purchase the ticket.

She was quiet. It was a workday for her, he knew, so she would be preparing to leave, but her reticence disturbed him. "Senga?"

"I'm here, pooh. I—I'm sensing a distance, I think. I tried to call several times and it went to voice-mail."

"Yes, yes, I know, and I'm a fool. I was caught up with the exhibition." No. He wouldn't prevaricate. "And . . . with something involving Danica."

Silence.

What did you expect, old son? he heard. "She is being evaluated in hospital, Senga. I want to wait to tell you about it. May I? Please, my dear?"

"Of course, Sebastian."

Those words again. Words that accuse and dismiss at once, and he skipped to the details of the Ireland show and other trip notes. When he put his phone away, he realized he had forgotten to ask about her week and his error disturbed him.

When he was five years old, he had killed a baby bird. His mother had forewarned him never to lift one from the nest, as parent birds might not accept the strange smell from a human hand. The bird had actually died in his palm, frightened to death, or so his mother had told him.

His *robin*. His Senga. He became fearful for her.

CHAPTER 18
THE HEART OF EVERYTHING
THAT WAS

Grannie's *usefulness* cure ever at hand, staying busy proved the best remedy for my unyielding malaise: digging my garden, potting a geranium or two, cleaning windows, airing the mattress, blankets and pillows, and, finally, working on notes for the late summer herbal workshop. Being useful also carried an unspoken understanding with Grannie; that one strives to be useful to the benefit of humanity. I counted my tutoring. Joey passed his test with flying colors, as they say. (Imaginary medieval flags and banners fluttering gaily in the breeze as he informed me.)

Gabe and I bought the kid a new pair of boots to celebrate, and I've seldom felt such appreciation from someone. He's at the Blue Wood now, as is Lily, who accepted the challenge. I spoke with Earl and Mae the night of the party, and they believed a camp experience could only help their daughter. I admire Lee and Mary Rogers for their willingness to supervise two hormonal teenagers.

Sebastian. . .

More than a truce (on account of there not having been a war), our ship warily tacked back toward our preferred course. Where mermaid and whale occupied their proper ocean current; where Danica was nowhere to be seen and her name not uttered. Which could have raised a question, but I shook my head to the left at the thought.

He emailed my airline e-ticket for Dublin and I made necessary arrangements with Muriel. She was beginning to wonder if I wanted to stay on as an assistant. I assured her I did.

Meanwhile, I planted my garden with beans, corn, tomatoes and squash, and trusted the rains to nourish the rows. Dear Hermione stood guard and Gabe promised to come water, if need be, while I was away. His parting words left me unsettled—

"Daddy told me that's his Uncle Thomas—*my* great Uncle Thomas—who's buried in Italy; that grave we saw?" I nodded. "Well," he continued, gazing into the sky, "I asked him how come I didn't know that and he just said there'd been some big family fuss around his uncle's going to fight—that somehow, they all knew he wouldn't come back—for any number of reasons, I guess. Anyway, things catch up with you, huh?" He turned to me.

I'd agreed, citing my grandmother's reappearance in my life, even if in distant Italy. Gabe seemed less haunted, knowing who was buried beneath the Belizaire gravestone. But there was always—and may there always be—his sweet Francesca to smooth his rough patches. Before he left (after I showed him my watering routine), I kissed his rough cheek, hidden under a buffalo soldier beard.

"Now, you take care over there," he instructed me and I noted the troubled furrow between his brows.

"So long, Gabe, and hugs to Caroline and Rufus," I added, and then I packed my bag.

CHAPTER 19
THE EMERALD VASE

From the air Ireland rose into view, a patch-work crazy quilt; no rhyme or reason to shape and dimension, her fields hemmed by stone walls and shrubbery. And *green*. Emily would have loved it.

I was met at the Dublin airport by a stylish driver named Seamus, who smartly grabbed my carry-on, saying, "Follow, please," which I did—my mind proving too disorganized for much else. It was 6:30 in the morning and I hadn't slept on the long flight. I'd missed the erudite company of Gabe, whose conversation on our flight to Italy, just six months before, had helped pass the time.

Soon, Seamus and I were flowing with traffic on the left side of the four-lane highway. The Emerald Isle glowed, once we left the urban areas, and I understood, finally, viscerally, what *Kelly* green was. The air was mostly dew; soft—and the light more diffuse than Wyoming's, where atmosphere is thinner; the sun, brighter.

"It's only about seventy minutes, miss," said Seamus in his lilt. I groaned something in reply and tried, really tried, to keep my eyes open to Ireland, but couldn't. My senses shut down entirely. . .

"We're here, miss," I heard through a fog and, when I opened my eyes, an imposing gate reared before us of black wrought-iron. Seamus lowered his window and spoke into an intercom, "I have a guest with me." A voice asked my name. "'Munro,' is it?" the driver asked over his shoulder. I said yes and we waited for the gate to swing open.

Rubbing my eyes, I wondered how I must look and smell. My hair was mussed, so I quickly loosed and re-braided it, suppressing a yawn. "I'm sorry, Seamus—I wasn't much of a traveling companion."

"Not to worry, miss; glad you caught a bit o' shut-eye," he said, as we drove on through a wood, carpeted with what looked to be bluebells and populated with great, sprawling trees. I detected no sign of human interference, save the macadam road.

"Have you ever been here, miss?"

I coughed. "Um, no, Seamus; this is a first. It's nice, I hear," I suggested lamely.

"Oh, I suppose you could say *tat*." He made a sound like a small, hiccupping giggle.

Leprechaun, I thought.

We rounded a curve and there appeared something *like* interference; more adroitly—undaunted will; an edifice unlike any my imagination could conjure—save when reading Jane Austen or Dickens. Devoid of distracting signage and crass publicity, the singular, gray Palladian structure spoke entirely for its grand self. Ballyfar was a "great house," in every sense of the phrase. Four columns stretched from the wide stairway to the top of a gabled portico, between two wings, reminding me of a gray White House. A wide graveled area allowed vehicles to deposit their passengers, their bags to be whisked away to their rooms and their car parked or their limousine (such as my conveyance) driven away by the hired driver.

I was met by a dignified coterie of staff, with introductions made and hands shaken.

Guided into the rose-peach entrance hall, I marveled at an impressively sized antlered skull. "That would be our ancient elk, madam."

I startled at her voice and noted my new title.

"He's upwards to 10,000 years young, we've been told," explained the wholesome example of Irish womanhood standing behind me.

"Oh, it's huge!" Something to tell Rufus when I return home.

"May I offer you water or a glass of our own apple juice, madam? Or, champagne?"

I was tempted by the wine, but resisted. "Water would be wonderful."

Caitriona (her name tag read) offered me a bottle from a basket of several. I had just taken a long swallow, when I heard a familiar voice.

"Senga."

"*Oooo,*" I spun round. Sebastian blended with the surroundings as though born and bred in the place. Slanting morning light through tall casement windows lit his most welcome face. By comparison, I felt tired and must look it, I lamented.

With arms extended, he gathered and held me close for several moments.

"I need a nap, Sebastian."

"Try to wait until after lunch, my dear," he said, winking.

We climbed a staircase; "cantilevered," he called it, as it hugged two walls of the large room to reach the second floor. Life-size portraits of the home's early inhabitants decorated the powder-blue walls. I followed him down the hall to our room. He used a real key to open the door and stood aside to allow me entrance.

Well.

Words fail, but I must try—

The canopied bed claimed the middle of the room, its gold-festooned drapes spilling over the head and foot boards. A feminine vanity stood against a wall. A round table, laid with a white linen tablecloth, stood by a pair of matching chairs. An armoire hid a television (Sebastian informed me) and another wardrobe stood directly across for our clothing. All was placed symmetrically, with a dresser poised across from the vanity. My luggage had been brought up.

"Sebastian. . ." I tried to speak, but stood—mouth agape, I expect. Our room was, in a word, stunning.

"There are drinks in here," and he showed me. The small refrigerator was housed discreetly in a wooden cabinet. Within were Cokes, the hotel's apple juice (from the walled orchard), sparkling and still water and lemonade. I'd guzzled the water I'd been given upon arrival.

"*Mmmm,* the lemonade, please," I said, still thirsty, and he handed it to me with a flourish. "This is . . . incredible, Sebastian. How did you. . . I mean, who booked your exhibition *here?*"

He smiled, allowed me a good, long swig of the lemonade, then reached for the bottle to place it on the table. "You haven't seen the bathroom, my dear." He took my hand and led me into a room—larger than my cabin (which isn't difficult, but *still.* .); an immense bathtub dominated the area, ample for two. *Oh joy! We can repeat our Italian bathing,* I thought. Double sinks, marble everywhere and a separate shower with seating (again, for two); the toilet hidden for privacy, and a French (*Italian*) window giving over a courtyard to the lake beyond—all made me sigh.

"I want a bath, Sebastian; I require a bath," I insisted and began to remove my jacket.

"I've some things to attend to, so will leave you to your ablutions," he said, lightly kissing me. My nether regions stirred. "Enjoy," he said and was gone.

I changed my mind about the bath and took a shower instead, believing I might have drowned for falling asleep.

When he returned, he suggested a walk to show me the grounds and we made our way outdoors. *Serene* came to mind. No; *sublime.* Called a "demesne," for the area the walled estate comprised, the home had been built in the Regency style as a country dwelling, for the main purpose of entertaining.

During the Irish famine years, the construction of the perimeter wall provided work for people and, for a recent period it served as a boarding school. An artful visionary bought the property and proceeded to renovate all, including the landscape, gardens and orchard. Several apple trees were 130 years old. The grounds included several "follies," including a round tower. Sebastian had been given the grand tour upon his arrival two days before and now played guide for me.

"It says *Grotto,*" I read. Placed at knee height, a small green sign with an arrow pointed the way. I smiled. "I want to see it—that's a cave, right?"

He nodded. "Let's do," he said and we set off.

We approached quietly, almost reverently; yes. Brambles choked the sides of the path. A morning rain had sweetened the air and I felt young again. The capstone of a central, arched entrance had been perfectly placed, which precluded *too* ancient an origin, strictly speaking. We ducked and entered the cool, dark interior. The hillside cave could have been created as recently as the turn of the century, or excavated thousands of years ago. Humidity enveloped us, like misty amniotic fluid, while *fecundity* and an unspoken demand as to our purpose here both bloomed in my mind.

I was wondering about rites, either in the distant past or of late, when I recognized the certain play of molecules, *or were they photons?* I expected to "see" something momentarily. I stayed Sebastian's arm, to hinder him, as my vision adjusted to the gray light within. Tightening my grip, I lightly shook my head and raised a finger to my lips, cutting my eyes to him in warning. He remained still and quiet as I backed us nearer the wall.

In the center of the room, I perceived a shadowy couple, *coupling,* on what could only have been an altar stone (no longer present). The woman stretched across its rough, dark surface on her belly, facing me; her knees drawn up, with arms outstretched and hands gripping the edge of the stone as a man thrust from behind. In appearance, he looked wild; his features and expression, intense, dark and riveting; hair, long and black with a spotty beard. His body was sinewy and pale-white, with dark hair on his chest and arms.

The woman's face froze me. Her lips were stretched tightly over what few teeth remained, in a grimace beyond pain and pleasure. She appeared less than young. Flaxen hair, long and loose, spilled over her body, nearly touching the ground. All was silent and trance-like. I was drawn—first, to one, then the other. And just as quickly, the image blurred and the scene dissipated, as so many champagne bubbles rising in a glass.

Yes. Ritual had been performed in this place.

"Look down," said Sebastian, when I released his arm and exhaled and moved.

As with herb tea, a sighting must steep before sharing. "I'll tell you later," I murmured, wondering if he caught the husky tone in my voice, rising from my womb. Could one hear sexual stimulation?

I looked down. At our feet lay hundreds of pebbles and stones, laid in a mosaic of light and dark concentric circles. A recent fire had burned, judging by a blackened area and several coals in the center. *Where the stone had stood,* I observed. To our right, a niche in the earthen wall held a candlestick, with requisite matches. I stepped over to light it. Shadows jumped about the cave. Behind Sebastian, I spotted a bench and, stepping to it, I rapped it with my knuckles, to assure its reality.

Mmmm.

"Sebastian," I said, smiling.

"Someone might come by, my dear. . ."

I ignored this and began to undress, holding his gaze. Biological imperative had gripped my body. Folding my clothing neatly on the end of the bench, I said, "I need you." It was enough.

He wasted no time in undressing and we were soon standing skin to skin, the dripping water marking time. We kissed, deep and long, resisting an urge to be hasty. "I've missed you so," I said as I explored his mouth and face. He tasted of black-currant jam and bitter black coffee, and smelled (always) of sun-dried linen, sandalwood, lemon and musk—the scents mingling with that of damp humus around us. With a low chuckle, he moved his fingers over my breasts, lightly teasing my nipples. Bending, he took one in his mouth, sending me into paroxysms.

With his hand, he held my wrists above my head against stone, near the low ceiling, cocking his head to inspect me, my dark underarm hair holding particular fascination. "I need to behold you like this, my Senga, as though you are at my mercy," he said quietly, and his eyes traveled the length of me. "But it is the reverse, isn't it?" he whispered, expecting no reply, as his free hand explored my neck, breasts and crotch while I shuddered.

I *was* at his mercy.

My body bucked in wanting him. I heaved and begged. My nipples and womb tingled. Feeling vulnerable rendered me all the more desperate. Candle-lit, sparkling runnels of water seeped through the dirt walls, rendering the grotto a life of its own. In this place, in this ancient land, I felt the god in him rise and a wild creature stirred in me as well. He turned me round, pressing my buttocks against him, to cup my breasts and belly and further fan the fire below. We moved to the bench, where he sat and had me straddle him backwards, then, entering me easily, "My robin, but you are *wet*," he observed, rightly—we rocked to an age-old rhythm.

I could have been a ship's figurehead, plying the waves, as he held my waist. When I opened my eyes, I detected a shimmer, mirage-like, where had been the altar stone. I dismissed it.

He groaned and uttered something like an ejaculation in Danish (in the grammatical sense) and we moved and quickened and both cried out. After, I turned round to him and we clutched one another tightly, gasping—our sweating bodies cooling and slick with moisture.

"Here . . . sit—I want to taste you."

I did as I was told and, leaning against the back of the bench, I drew up my legs, which he spread wide.

"Your very own *Sheela-na-gig.*" Whispering, I explained the carved stone woman, whose exaggerated vulva is occasionally depicted over ancient church portals. His eyes grew wide with impatience, mocked or no. Kneeling on the hard mosaic, he took me with his mouth and I vibrated with hunger and love for him.

Rough magic, indeed. . . While I keened (*not* in mourning), he made noises of pleasure, "*Oh Gud,* Senga—it has been too long . . . too long—"

"*Shhh,*" I interrupted, whispering "*Someone's here. . .*"

Sebastian froze, then lifted his head to listen. We heard voices; a man, speaking French, was taking his leave, and a woman (perhaps) made a low reply. Sebastian slowly reached for the candle stick, to blow out the flame. Motionless, we barely breathed.

A hooded figure hunched below the archway, wearing a voluminous coat or cape, further darkening the grotto. I could barely see from my position, but Sebastian's back may have been visible and I sensed the person staring at us. I heard her make a sound, but she said nothing, turned and left. I say "she," only for hearing a similar low snarl from the mountain lion I'd had to kill only months before in Wyoming, that happened to be female.

We remained still; breathing shallowly, until the voices faded away, then I inhaled deeply in relief and sighed.

"Easy for you, my dear. It wasn't your backside in *flagrante delicto.* My knees are pulp," said Sebastian, and he took my face in his hands and kissed me—tenderly, gently, lovingly. His cock responded to my touch, again, and after a quick intake of breath, he repeated my own earlier admission, "I need you," and I obliged him. No one else interrupted our tryst in the grotto and we stayed longer, honoring old gods.

"Well . . . now I'm famished. What's for lunch, pooh?" I asked, rhetorically. He grinned.

"Won't the bed be a welcome comfort tonight?" he asked, glancing back at the grotto's eerie entrance on leaving.

While he scanned the lake to our right, our intruder sat against a nearby tree trunk to our left, thirty feet away. The cloaked form faced away from us. Nearby, cut into the hillside, I spotted another, smaller cave entrance. "*Ahhh,*" the mouth seemed to say, as its throat led to the grotto, I presumed, and I felt the knowledge ice the blood in my veins. We had been observed—as *I* had observed. . .

Lunch was served in the conservatory amid orchids and a view of a garden folly, a water feature and a statue of a nymph. Sebastian suggested we start with *foie gras,* move to carrot soup and finish with quiche, our personal favorite. My appetite had flown, but not for fault of the chef. The nap couldn't come soon enough, but I ordered a coffee anyway. When it arrived, I described what I had seen in the grotto and outside, feeling curiously nervous doing so, which was odd, given my disposition. His eyes grew round, but he reserved comment.

"So, who booked your exhibit here?" I asked again, gazing into the green distance.

"Ah, yes," he said and paused. "It was Danica, actually." He glanced at me to gauge my response and looked away.

My response. . . I remembered feeling this way only once in my life—when I was thrown from a horse near the post stables in North Carolina. The wind was knocked out of me, how I felt now, and I waited for deliverance.

"Da—*Danica?*" I blurted; the very name stung like a jolt of electricity. I stood, laid my napkin beside my plate and walked away. I asked a server where I might find the restroom and she escorted me. Blessedly alone in the room, I chose a stall, sat on the closed lid and practiced deep breathing for several moments. Anger and pain coalesced between my womb and the recently exercised path to it. *Fire, indeed.*

A woman is born knowing several things. These include biological imperatives, necessary for our survival—now, as in ancient days. One is knowledge of one's mate and his unconscious sensibilities toward you. I recognized this in Rob, my daughter's father—that he simply wasn't (as they say) "there" for me. In all fairness to him, neither was I present for him. In positive reciprocation, there exists a convenience, plus, it saves time; but, when one-sided, something like this gut-ache ensues.

I could be wrong.

Occasionally, I mistake matters of *grave* importance. My Grannie warned me to always pay attention. The warning had to do with the use of herbs, but translates (and should) to all of life. I hadn't paid attention and I was angry—at myself. I'd ignored the mermaid riddle that had come unbidden, a cosmic clue: "What did the mermaid say to another who wanted to lure the salty sailor?"

I shook my head in my manner to banish the thought; now, to discourage a rival, it seemed. Standing, I found I felt better and a sense of calm returned. On a shelf behind me, I noticed an emerald vase of some bygone era. (*Etruscan?*) Etched into the glazed terracotta was a bi-tailed mermaid, her breasts bare and free, her hair adrift in sea water around her. Taken by surprise, I then sighed and thought I heard whispering. "*Yes. . .*" I replied. Had I jumped—vaulted—to a conclusion earlier? *Like a mermaid breaching the waves,* I mused, *or, a giant whale?*

I discovered Sebastian in the hall.

"Forgive me. I'm an idiot," I said.

"Senga," he said, with a look that told me I wasn't. "Do you want to see the exhibit?"

I nodded.

"But first, I want to speak with you—about Paris," he said, placing his arm round my shoulder. My cheeks flushed in dread. We returned to our room, where we sat in the chintz-covered chairs and he told me about meeting Danica by the Seine, the concierge, the reception and the man who took her home. Apparently, she'd learned his agent's phone number and one day the man had called to say she'd arranged to have an exhibition here, at Ballyfar.

"An unusual venue for an art show, but given the subject matter. . ." said Sebastian now.

At this I bristled. "*Subject matter?* Sebastian! Did he say this, or is this your opinion?"

"Well, Danica had used the phrase. . . Senga, please don't become upset again. And . . . she's not well; show some compassion, my dear."

"Is this why you didn't return so we could travel together?" I squinted at him, trying to read him and found myself thwarted. The other shoe fell. "Did you . . . sleep with her?" I finally asked. Both humiliated and compelled.

He looked long at me. Saying nothing.

"*Oh God, oh God,*" I said and ran into the bathroom, where I vomited into the toilet.

"Senga, no—" he cried, following me. "You misread me. I would *nev*—"

He stopped. And I knew; either he had, or he had wanted to. The biological imperative served up with coffee, toast and black-currant jam and ambiguity. *But desire!—God, he's allowed . . . he's allowed that.* My own words to him returned to mock me: *You are now free to pursue your own passions. . .*

I might have been more explicit.

Desire is . . . everything. And, it is nothing. Where is the truth in that paradox? I wondered.

Crossing to the sink, I extended my arm, open palm against him for distance, rinsed my mouth and brushed my teeth. I inspected my reflection. Stress marked my features, so I rearranged them and rinsed my face with cold water. The white streak at my crown was growing in wider. I loosened and brushed my hair, the chestnut waves reaching mid-thigh. Separating the length into three tresses over my right shoulder, I knitted my fingers into the old pattern for the second time in a day. Sebastian watched as he leaned against the door jamb, wearing a mixed expression of awe, concern and something I couldn't identify. "I *love* you, Senga. Forgive me for hurting you. *Please.*"

I took a deep breath, blew it out and smiled—if wanly—then, I wound the elastic around the braid's end. Putting my hands to his cheeks, I pulled his face down to mine to kiss his forehead.

"Let's go see our pictures." He embraced me and I felt an oxytocin surge. Grace.

"Have you ever seen a double-tailed mermaid?" I asked.

"Is this your riddle for today?"

"No, absolutely not. Just wondering."

"Why, yes. They're ubiquitous, my dear. Starbuck's logo?"

I swallowed a curse.

CHAPTER 20
A CERTAIN SIGNIFICANCE

A couple passed us in the hall, followed by a group of six women, obviously enchanted with their surroundings, as was I. An impeccably dressed woman ushered them; their friend and host, I guessed. Sebastian led me into the Drawing Room, where the exhibit waited, asking if I would do anything differently regarding placement. The magnificent, high-ceilinged room took my breath away for the exquisite crown molding alone—frothy dips and swirls of whipped cream, frozen in place. I ignored the photographs on their easels, until at last, my gaze floated from the ceiling to eye level, to encounter my own image.

"Oh!" It startled me. A server did a double-take as he recognized me as the model. He smiled and nodded imperceptibly toward me, in admiration, I believed; not cheek. His eyes cut to a fellow staff member.

The photos were well positioned throughout the large room. I couldn't help but notice the juxtaposition of the black-and-white nudes—even those semi-clothed in the silk robe—with the rich gold and white fabrics dressing the room. It was brilliant of Danica, I thought, despite my weighty concerns. Sebastian had confessed he thought she was losing her mind. . .

I studied the flow of the pictures and suggested Sebastian exchange only two, for nothing more than a feeling. Given the exhibit was psychological, I dismissed reason for emotion. One of the enchanted ladies made a quiet, glib remark and a companion groaned in response; I watched them admire Sebastian and one sighed. Five of the group left the room after conferring with someone, regarding the time of the following evening's reception. A sixth woman, tall and distinguished, remained behind to further study one of the photographs. She looked an artist herself, of indeterminate age, judging by her manner.

I excused myself, feeling a sudden urge to lie down. Sebastian wished me a good rest and offered to wake me in two hours—unless I needed more sleep. I asked for three. He kissed my cheek, in European fashion, and I wondered if my being his lover was an advantage in this venture. *Doesn't matter; carry on,* I hastily added, as I climbed the cantilevered stairs to our room. The moment I lay down on the fairy-tale bed, I fell asleep.

The reception was well attended by exquisite guests, specifically invited to the private showing. Shimmers and soft rustling of silk, and even a white fur collar rested languidly on a woman's bare shoulders, like a familiar. Expensive perfumes competed in the most subtle way. And, while "fashionable" would never describe this model's talent for clothing, it suited someone whose very skin had already made the necessary impression.

I again wore the long olive skirt and silk blouse I'd worn to the concert in Lucca, appropriately décolleté for the venue and expressly for Sebastian. (I covered several love-bites and a bruise with make-up borrowed from one of the covey women; the artist, naturally.)

Sebastian was dressed more formally than I had ever seen him: a dark suit, a dark purple tie and a charcoal shirt that contrasted his light coloring. He looked *fetching,* as they say. I might have wished the room magically cleared of anyone but us, if only for the few moments required to mate like minks on the formal Louis XVI settee. Meanwhile, the fragrance of appetizers wafted from the kitchen and I could smell pastry and mushrooms—the scent oddly reminiscent of the grotto.

These were my thoughts (worthy or not), when I noticed the striking woman poised at the room's entrance, wearing (what I could now distinguish) a taupe silk cape, its hood lowered. The red-gold setting sun through the glass lit the garment with iridescent dark fire. I was seated on one of the Louis XVI chairs, with my back to one of the floor-to-near-ceiling windows, watching with interest, as the woman projected an air of what I could only describe as rapt sensuality. She fairly dripped with it. Heels gave her a commanding height, and her short, styled hair accentuated her stature.

I watched her lift her hands to a clasp and remove the cape with an easy grace. She held it out expectantly and a server took it from her. Blond, with flawless complexion and make-up, she wore a high-necked, long, caftan-like dress of several colors. A fringed, woven bag swung from her shoulder. She appeared to be alone and scanned the room carefully, a lioness considering her prey, and when her serious regard halted at Sebastian, I guessed her identity—and that of the hooded figure at the grotto. She moved in his direction. It was Danica, of course, and I rose from my chair, but waited to see what would happen.

I watched my lover make polite, if restrained conversation with the woman. He glanced at me and back to her with an imperceptible frown, but I saw it. Nearby, I heard the covey (*coven?*) of six women—a colorful flock of disparate birds— busily discussing the exhibit with varying degrees of opinion. While they deemed it worthy of praise and merit (one woman in particular, the artist, critiqued the exhibition with knowledge of photography), I wondered if any might choose to buy one. I'd also wondered earlier about the photographs' dimensions; how does anyone get them home? No worries, Sebastian had assured me, the cost of shipping was included in the price. These observations vied with a more taxing interest: my lover and the woman.

Her voice now rose above her neighbors', breaking into my reverie, and I returned my attention to the woman, even as spectators and spectacle began to merge in my mind. Incipient fear, in the form of one of Gabe's tiny Mardi Gras *bébés* materialized, as Sebastian and Danica argued in Danish. I watched with mounting concern as he escorted the woman by the elbow from the room. This raised the curiosity of the guests, naturally. The coven [sic] was interested, but overcame, in murmurations of nonchalance.

I took a deep breath as a guest approached, flourishing two glasses of champagne. "You might want this," he said, as he nodded in Danica and Sebastian's direction. I'd only assumed it was she. . . *Why didn't I introduce myself and find out?* I didn't want to appear distrustful or jealous, I told myself—when I felt both. I watched them pass into the adjoining room.

"Thanks," I said as I took the glass, craning my head to see where Sebastian would go. I felt warm, as though the temperature in the room had doubled.

"She's not an admirer, I take it," champagne man said, a twinkle in his eye. I hadn't been introduced the model in the photographs, but clothing or no, the braid was obvious.

"I've never met her, but, no; I guess not."

I hadn't understood the Danish spoken between them. Frustrated, I took a long sip of the sparkling wine, glad for its effect. The man wanted to say something, but either lacked the words or the courage. At last—

"These pictures are full of a *certain* significance, do you know?" he lilted.

I smiled, but not too broadly, in acknowledgement or, perhaps, encouragement.

He continued, "When I look at *tat*—" he said, gesturing to a photograph across from us, in which I am contemplative: elbows on a table with hands clasped, sitting on a bench, my nude back to the camera, three-quarter view, left breast visible. My head is in profile, before the large window in Sebastian's home in the Black Hills. He resumed, ". . . I perceive an idea— or, an ideal, I *tink*. Did you identify your intention as you were posing? Or, did the photographer?"

He was Irish; his t-h's spoken as t's, I noted. *Hmmm, the photographer, yes; where is he?* I wondered, and why is he leaving me alone with strangers? I sipped again and glanced past the man's shoulder to see if Sebastian was returning. I replied, distractedly, "Um, no; we just moved from one to another, but I held a purpose in my head, I guess." I was guessing a lot, I realized, but champagne man seemed to like this response and smiled.

"Excuse me, please," I said and edged toward the doorway.

In a blur of movement, I watched Danica twist away from Sebastian—who was grasping her forearm. Her hand plunged into her shoulder bag as his arm again reached for hers. He failed. I watched her quickly cross the threshold toward me and, in one fluid gesture, she seized my braid. With her other hand, she cut it off at my nape with a pair of large black scissors. These I registered peripherally, as a furious raven's beak, attacking me.

Stricken dumb, I beheld my twenty-five-inch rope of hair being raised to the air as trophy, the room's occupants gasping as one. Then, Danica collapsed to the ground; first, to her knees, then forward, onto an open scissor blade pointed to her heart and held fast, to the sickening sound of sucking.

The body as clay, once more.

Once, years ago, as I rode Sadie, she stepped into a viscous mud puddle, *gumbo*—what bentonite is called when saturated by rain. The horse recoiled with some difficulty. The sound was similar. Then I heard someone scream, as another cried.

My shock and the initial reaction from the guests were then met by silence, even in the rapid course of Danica's suicide. All had transpired in less than seven seconds, to pass into a growing *banshee* cry of my suppressed keening—part rage, part grief, equaling horror. Sebastian's expression of utter disbelief mirrored mine, even after he'd tried to intervene, but too late. The violation of Danica, the self-harming and her final tragedy had arrived, cloaked in a fatal guise. *She had suffered.* This, I knew.

The six women, having shifted from covey to coven to Greek chorus, delivered their collective asides as to *what to do? What to do?!* as the concierge made desperately reserved telephone calls. . .

Later in our room, I sat mutely considering my altered image in the gilt-framed mirror of the vanity. In retrospect, I'd witnessed the events in a series of slow-motion frames, as though time itself could make no sense of the circumstance. The horrific scene had unfolded like a time-lapse, origami fortune teller, one action leading to the next, until the woman's final deed revealed her fatal intent: my hair may have been shorn, but she lay dead, the braid beside her, soaking in a growing pool of crimson blood.

I fixated on the folds of gold brocade, draped, expertly pleated, from the vanity top down to the carpet, in an example of absurd attention, or was it self-preservation? The mental distance between my unfamiliar reflection in the glass and the dressing table's lovely purpose magnified in significance and I accepted a silent suggestion of irony with a cheerless spirit of grace. Not by any effort on my part, but as gift; and now, very slowly, I reached for the brush I'd only that afternoon used on my hair, and I began to wonder how to navigate this redrawn map of myself. There were no stars in this new, bleak heaven.

I trembled. In my core, my spirit, my body. *Who* was *this woman—Danica?* I wondered. The *why?,* I knew, would never be answered. And I saw, more than consciously watched, Sebastian's hand lift the brush from mine and, standing behind me, begin at my crown. With great care, he moved it through my now, mostly white, clipped hair, newly shaped by the hotel's hairdresser. *Not unlike Danica's,* I dimly realized. I closed my eyes in surrender to his ministrations and to my fate—bartered, it seemed, for Sebastian. A strange conclusion, I grant. And I also knew, in a blinding flash, that in the grotto, I had unlawfully observed a rite, through no fault of my own. Payment had been exacted.

What had the mermaid said to another who wanted to lure the salty sailor? Nothing.

But, the one on the emerald vase had implied that I was "fortunate," I remembered. *Yes,* and I sighed.

CHAPTER 21
THIS ROUGH, DARK BEAUTY
Ballyfar, Ireland

They lay awake. The placement of the bed allowed a view of the lake, now cloaked in darkness. Pale silver light shone around them and they were quiet. She lay in the crook of his arm, her tousled hair and head on his chest, softly rising and falling with his breaths. By her inhalations, uneven and interrupted, she was conscious. *And thinking,* he guessed.

His own thoughts, a dark-winged butterfly, alighted on what Julien had counseled. *You will simply live with it, Sebastian. . .* Atonement enough? He wondered, as that late afternoon in Danica's naked, maddening presence returned to him. Like the specter it was. . .

After the razor blade (poised to inflict more ghastly harm) had dropped to the floor, she had raised her pelvis to him and he'd forgot himself. On his knees, he put his mouth to her poisoned cup, made so by pain, and she made a sound he'd heard only once—when his late wife Elsa had given birth to Erika. After pulling Danica off the chair and onto the floor, his hands squeezed her breasts as he sucked them, mad with desire. He groaned and she cried out and he was not himself; he was possessed by *her* obsession. *Of him.* The woman reached for his belt, loosened it and pulled his swollen cock deep into her mouth and he cried out in pain and ecstasy and they persisted until the air grew chilly, the room dim, and their appetites sated. His seed had been spilled. The woman had smeared it on her body and onto recent cuts. No; he had not completed the act, feeling somehow the less *weak* for it. Danica had made a low, wry laugh.

He heard it now, in the gun-metal darkness of a corner of his and Senga's room. *Where it lives,* he thought.

Visible through the window, one of the house's great columns stood to the right of a bright star, or was it a planet—*Venus?* he wondered. He was not superstitious by nature, but the juxtaposition intrigued him. Senga moved to better position her head, then settled.

"It's beautiful," she murmured.

"My . . . robin. . ." The pet name came tentatively, then easily, as though only this appellation, as incantation, could calm the fury and upset she must have experienced beneath her spoken observation.

Indigo sky stretched upward into black. They lay still longer, simply together, watching. From below, a floodlight illuminated the column, rendering it massive and, in a way, portentous. A force able to uphold whatever meaning he wished to ascribe it. Reviewing the evening, Sebastian shuddered anew. Senga again moved beside him.

"It's going to be all right," she muttered, as she rose to an elbow. Her shock of hair caught the light. An errant lock fell into her face and he lifted his hand to tenderly curl it behind her ear.

"I love you, Senga. I feel . . . wretched about what happened. I should have—"

She laid two fingers to his lips. "*Wretched's* enough. No, Sebastian. . . Let it go. Danica was—" She let it go. *Almost.* "So, her mother will arrive in the morning, you said?"

"Yes." His daughter *had* reached the woman after all. He repeated what Erika had told him, adding that Birgitte felt responsible for not having left for Paris immediately. "She is utterly devastated. . . Oh, *Senga*—" His defenses cracked, but not to crumble, and then, they did. His usually sturdy composure broke as he turned Senga toward him and, with both hands he held her face and smoothed her hair. Stabbing guilt pierced his heart.

"*Nooo,* pooh," she murmured, kissing his tear-filled eyes; first, the right, then the left. He choked on the memory of Danica's final breath. She was not finished with him, apparently.

Senga rose from the bed and walked around to the window. "I want it opened," she said as she tried to lift the sash, ". . . to the night—" She grunted with the effort, "To the . . . *beauty*, Sebastian."

The age-old custom occurred to him; open windows and doors permit spirits of the dead egress.

When it was evident Senga could not, he slipped off the bed to help her. The window lifted easily for him and they embraced in the cool breeze. Senga had earlier questioned the lack of screens on the windows. "What, no mosquitoes in Ireland?" He noted the occasional glint on the dark water. *Starlight?* It punctuated the stillness, due, *most likely,* he thought, to the absolutely remote setting. Denmark was concentrated, even in her small, rural distances; but tonight, Ireland's heartland felt singularly *free*, as though unshackled by time or space.

"Let's go for a walk, Sebastian."

"Now?"

"Yes. I need to be out in this . . . this . . . *dark beauty*." She spoke un-self-consciously and he smiled sadly. What she had witnessed in the grotto—dark beauty, yes—but her sense of transgression—*more, perhaps, from having merely spoken of it,* flooded his intuition. After telling him, she had uttered exactly what Julien had said to him; that she would simply live with it, whatever *it* was. *And then today's—no—it was yesterday. It is in the past.*

They pulled on clothing and made their quiet way down the grand stairs, toward the massive entrance. The night manager at his lonely desk appeared startled by their 2:30 a.m. appearance.

"We, ah, wish to go out for a bit," said Sebastian.

"Of course," the man said, as though it were the most natural thing in the world. "And would you like a blanket against the chill, then?"

Senga nodded and the man stood and crossed to a cabinet, where several were neatly folded. He chose a green plaid and returned, to hand it to Senga. "And you'll be wanting a torch? Tis as dark as they come tonight." He bent to a desk drawer, opened it and produced a Maglite. "May I help you with anything else, sir? I could have a beverage brought, or—"

"No-no; not necessary. Thank you. You've been more than kind. These will do nicely. It's, ah, been a day." He did not mean to remind the man of the horrific events, but reticence seemed absurd in light of the fact.

With typical reserve, the genteel night manager simply said, "It has been that, sir, and tomorrow will bring the sun again, even if it rains. Enjoy your outing, sir." He addressed Senga as "madam," and resumed his post behind the desk. Sebastian noted the deep compassion on the man's beautiful Irish face, and would remember the expression with no aid of photography.

They stood before the great house, awake with it alone save for another single, faint light gleaming from a far window on the opposite wing. Senga had left a similar one for their return; "A candle in the window," she reminded him.

"Which way?" asked Sebastian, as he surveyed the shadowy directions.

"Toward the lake?"

"As you wish," and they set off.

He was glad for the torch—called flashlight by Senga. She carried the blanket while he lit their way. A well-marked path led to a boat house, where two flat-bottomed boats waited, moored to a dock. He grinned at the sight, remembering summers with his brother. How long had it been since he'd been on the water? *If you have to think about it, old son, it has been too long.*

"Let's take one out, shall we?" he proposed.

"In this darkness? Really?"

"My eyes are adjusting. Haven't yours? Oh, Senga, let's," and he proceeded to inspect the placement of the oars—not paddles, he noticed. Yes, it was exactly ordained, he thought, and as he shone the light into the boat, he heard Senga sigh and toss the blanket in.

"I suppose they have life jackets somewhere, um, in case the lake has its own Loch Ness monster or something," she suggested, ". . . as if jackets would save you."

He chuckled and illuminated the wall beside the door through which they had entered. Several life jackets hung from hooks and Senga stepped over to take two. "Okay. You up for this?" she asked as she held one out for him, and then shrugged into hers.

"I am. Climb in and get settled. There is nothing like being on water to put things to rights, my dear." Hoping he was correct and not simply offering empty platitudes and false courage, he fastened his jacket.

His heart ached. For Senga, for Danica and, for her mother.

When Senga was seated, he shone light on the ropes, set down the torch and quickly untied the boat. He grabbed the torch and handed it to Senga as he climbed in, then, he pushed against the dock and they drifted out of the shed.

They soon floated beneath a sky made brilliant with stars, as soft lapping of water lulled and night noises came from the nearby wood. The near-invisible silhouette of the stately house stood by, steady as a guardian presence, and Sebastian guessed the night manager had followed their objective—by jouncing light—to note they were on the water. He took comfort in this. For the moment, his over-wrought nerves welcomed the task at hand, to simply, if not easily, use all his strength to move oars through dark water, with no particular destination in mind; only the *moving through* would do for now, with Senga, facing him; a rough, dark beauty.

CHAPTER 22
GHOSTS ARE PETTY

Sebastian and I were prevented from leaving Ballyfar for another two days, while the Garda completed their inquiry. I watched with mild distaste as one of them scowled at the exhibit, as a possible trigger for the woman's suicide, "evil influence," or the like. I banished my speculations.

They interviewed us separately, and I trembled as I relived and described the *incident* (for lack of a better word). It was a woman who spoke with me, and I was grateful. She was kind, if direct. At interview's end, she asked if I were a tourist. I answered no—that I was an American woman, which drew a puzzled look. Then, I was quiet—unnerved and saddened by it all. Had she amassed enough information? I wondered. Whoever could?

Knowledge is a tricky thing. A teacher in high school once told us we are responsible for all we learn, and obligated to apply such knowledge where possible; if not, at the very least, process, hone and polish it. In many ways, this has made sense to me, and I do my level best not to amass it for its own sake. Once, Papa warned me about the *glamour* (my word) of knowledge—as a kind of useless vanity. He used the word "vain."

I waited for Sebastian in the library of the great house, its high-paneled walls lined with all manner of books and knowledge of all stripes. As I sat, idly leafing through a glossy magazine, steaming cup of *café au lait* before me on a table for the purpose, one of the covey women approached, tentatively, by the way she halted, turned and resumed her intent. *The artist,* I saw out of the corner of my eye. I set down the magazine and addressed her.

"Hello," I said. Not "good morning."

"Hi."

American or Canadian, I'd guessed earlier.

We assessed one another, reading faces and body language, then she asked, "May I sit?"

Nodding, I scooted and slid my coffee over. "Would—ah, you like some coffee, or something? I see the girl near the door." One needed only to ask and any sort of refreshment, from water (still or sparkling) to afternoon tea would be brought to you. Like magic.

"Sure. I'd like a Bloody Mary, actually. Oh, sorry—" she said, when she saw my face alter. (The image of blood.) I waved it away. She studied me a moment, then said, "It was awful for you. Your beautiful hair. . ." Someone had thought to bring my braid to me, like a severed limb, in a plastic bag. It sat beside me. Washed of Danica's blood, it was still lightly tinged, but they'd tried. . .

I swallowed and said nothing, but looked in the direction of the attendant, standing by the door. She immediately came. "May I help you, madam?"

I'd never get used to being called madam. "Um, yes—my friend would like a Bloody Mary," I looked at my new friend and asked, "What do you want in it?"

"Vodka, please, with all the garbage—or, is that what you call it over here?" she asked, referring to garnishes.

"No, madam, but we know what you mean. And would you care for anything at all?" she asked me—pronouncing it *a-tall.* When I shook my head, she turned smartly on her heel and left us alone.

I sunk back into the deep sofa and exhaled. I wasn't *a-tall* sure I wanted company, but, as Joe likes to say, *this is what God put in my path today,* so I arranged my face and braced my nerves for a visit. Extending my hand, I introduced myself. "I'm Senga Munro, and you are an artist. I overheard you talking with your friends."

"Carla. Carla Jenkins. How *are* you?" she asked in a tone that told me she meant it.

"I've been better . . . I'm . . . sorry everyone had to see that."

"Whoa, there . . . *not* your fault," she stated unequivocally. "We all saw what happened. It's always tragic when someone

gives up like that, but don't you *dare* take responsibility, Sen—
what? I've never heard that name."

I couldn't place her accent. Midwestern? She smiled, looking
cozy in her long, draping dress and shawl. I wanted to crawl into
her lap and suck my thumb.

"Senga. Uh, it's the reverse of—"

"Agnes! Yeah, I love it! Did you change it yourself?"

I nodded. "When I was fifteen. . . Um, so did the police speak
with everyone?"

"I don't think so—only a few of us. Usually, an event is seen
differently, depending on one's point of view, but not this time."
She paused. I could tell she wanted to ask a question, but resisted
the impulse out of politeness. I appreciated it and stayed mute.

She changed the subject. "They did a nice job with your
hair," at which point I felt hot tears spring to my eyes. I think I
choked.

"*Ohhh,* I'm sorry, Senga; I didn't mean—Oh!" She pounded
a fist on her knee, on the exclamation. Here I was, struggling
with my response to shorn hair, while a woman had taken her
life before everyone's eyes. Not a worthy balance. But, if I added
the weight of Sebastian's—what *was* it? then, I could
acknowledge, or justify my confusion and upset. It was merely
the artist's observation stupidly affecting me at the moment—
and, that she might think me callous and petty. *Ghosts are petty,*
whispered the library ceiling. I looked up. Carla followed my
gaze. "What?" she asked.

"Oh, nothing. I thought I heard—All right, I will tell you
something," I said to her, then paused, as the server arrived to
place a tray on the table. A big tumbler of Bloody Mary, heaped
with *garbage,* and a bowl of mixed nuts. Carla thanked the girl,
took a sip and said, "Wow. . . Okay—I'm listening."

I suppose you are, I thought, then turned my head to the left,
again, to banish peevishness. I was composing my thoughts,
when Sebastian entered the vast room and abruptly stopped. He
resembled a subject in an impressionist's painting and I squinted
down on him, as we were taught, to better ascertain shapes and
colors. I couldn't read him and it disturbed me. Excusing myself
from Carla's presence, I crossed to him. He looked worn out.
We hadn't slept much the night before, having stayed on the
water until four in the morning. Not talking. Only listening. The

chirp of robins before daybreak induced us to return to our bed, where I fell into a rough sleep, but still, *sleep*. We were awakened at 8:00 by the manager, to say we were needed by the Garda, to go over the incident. *The incident.* I hope to rename this in memory, to something more—respectful. . .

Sebastian watched me approach and held out his arms. I didn't comply. His eyes spoke and I answered I wanted to remain a while longer; I'd be up after a while. Through the Drawing Room doors, I noticed the exhibit; the room sat vacant, save my image—alone and (when not in Aunt Karen's silk robe) naked, surrounded, albeit, by priceless antiques and gilt. *Freudian slip?* My photographer looked at me, then over my shoulder to Carla, who sat serenely peering out the casement window to the grounds. "Then, I will see you when you are ready, my dear," he said.

The extraordinary thing, I thought, was my complete and utter disappointment in myself for showing spite. And if not *spite,* then what?

No. I would not speak of this to a stranger, I decided, as I walked back to her, but I needed to hear what *she* had seen; I required corroboration of my inward experience. An artist could provide this. Sebastian was too involved, said my soul. And I apprehended, at last, what the mermaid on the vase had intimated. Indeed, I was the fortunate one. I could have been killed.

He ponderously climbed the stairway to their room, each step arduous and requiring more will than he possessed. *Am I losing her? Have I?* Even now, with the ostensible cause of this imbroglio gone with the coroner yesterday, Danica's presence seemed to hang in the very air. Sebastian did not believe in ghosts, per se, but psychological ones were another thing altogether. He sighed as he reached the top tread, turned and made his preoccupied way to the jewel-like room at the end of the hall. It had been cleaned and all was in perfect order. The small refrigerator had been restocked and he chose a bottle of apple juice. "Old son, get a grip," he said aloud, then drank deep and set the bottle down beside the bed. He stretched out on its inviting spread after removing his shoes and was soon asleep, lulled by a fragrant vanilla and lavender sachet left on the pillow, the sweet taste of apple lingering on his tongue. Later, he would wonder if the juice harbored some ingredient foreign to the usual recipe. Surely, the hotel could not have all its guests subject to hallucination, whether dreaming or not.

He is in the rowboat on the water with Senga. No moon; only an expanse of stars and the glittering path of the Milky Way above them. He feels a sense of déjà vu: The oars swishing through the water, the squeaking of wood against the rowlocks, chatter from the nearby forest; muffled sounds, small noises and the annoyed squawk of an awakened bird; then, an owl— not its wings—he knows these are deadly silent; rather, a 'hoohoo hoo!' Another, and after—silence.

He stops rowing and lets the oars drag. Even the water stills its lapping against the sides. As though a pause button has been pressed, he dimly observes.

His attention is drawn to Senga, sitting across from him near the bow, saying nothing, seemingly gazing straight through him, as though he is not there. He cannot see her eyes for the darkness and this unnerves him. No glint of spirit visible in her pupils. 'At least the stars—' he considers and looks up, but—now there are no stars; there is nothing, save this luminous darkness, as in caves, where he can only see what is not there. . .

A faint smell of fish surrounds them. Unmistakable. He moans, but hears nothing. A suffocating fear presses from beneath him, from the depths of a murky unknown, and, frozen, he watches a hand and arm break the surface. Then, another arm. They gleam pale green in the night by some source of bioluminescence. He hears scratching on the side of the boat and watches in horror as the two hands, with long, pearl-like fingernails, followed by head and torso bob from the water to clasp the gunwale and begin to rock the boat back and forth, back and forth, with increasing violence. He sees Senga's eyes grow wide as she reaches for the sides to hang on. From the water, he hears a choked cry as a pale face turns to him—Danica, in the guise of mermaid. Not Senga's, he notes abstractly.

He can say and do nothing, but watches paralyzed as Senga tumbles overboard into the dark water, whereupon Danica's fishy form flips to dive for her catch. He again tries to cry out, but cannot; to move to save his Senga, but he cannot. He can barely breathe.

Choking on his breath, he was making tortured sounds, when he felt hands on his shoulders—someone, trying to shake him awake.

"Sebastian! Wake up, you're dreaming; come on—wake up!"

Heavy. So heavy. Weighted down as though in deep water, the load of remorse and fear filled his pockets. He recognized Senga's voice, but why was it *so hard* to reach the surface? he wondered. *But she is there,* he vaguely apprehended. *She is there— and alive.*

No small relief, to learn a nightmare was only that; a nightmare. He managed to roll to his side, and when he did, the tears came as her body scrambled over his, to embrace him as best she could, saying, "*Shhh* . . . it's all right, pooh; it's all right. I'm here. *Shhh.*"

CHAPTER 23
TAKE ME BACK TO
THE BLACK HILLS

When I was young and living with Grannie and Papa on the mountain in North Carolina, one rainy Saturday afternoon we settled in to watch a movie on television. *Calamity Jane,* with Doris Day. In retrospect, an utterly impossible portrayal of Deadwood in 1876, or anywhere, but I loved it. I wanted to be Calamity, as depicted in the film; not the reality. Sad to say, the woman had a *serious* drinking problem and most likely, syphilis. Loving Wild Bill chewed up her dignity as well. Still, I felt a kinship. I liked the song Day broke into as, indubitably, *anyone* would, while trying to slog through a street full of deep mud and shit. (In fairness, I believe she sang the song while riding shotgun on a buckboard and it *was* a beautiful "Black Hills" day, as we often experience.) I sang the opening stanza for weeks after seeing the movie. Not that I could sing. I caught Grannie and Papa smiling in amusement more than once. And so, here I am, living in these Hills.

The song title returned to me when we were aloft, on approach to the Rapid City airport, in the way thoughts make connections and surprise us by finding meaning where we'd least expected. I felt an unfamiliar sense of *coming home* I'd rarely experienced. (In truth, it was more the desperate need to *get* home I felt.) I'd been merely marking time, since that day at Ballyfar, cutting notches on a mute talking stick. Speaking of which, the use of one, I thought, might help Sebastian and me ease from our respective black holes and I nudged the notion into my pocket for later.

We planned to stay at *Fred* for a couple days before returning to Wyoming. His late aunt and uncle's home, bordering the National Forest near Spearfish, was waiting, its name meaning peace in Danish.

We sorely needed some.

It was the morning after we'd returned, both having fallen into bed exhausted after a long day of travel. I'd helped him sort his gear and began a load of wash, including mine. We worked quietly, with no conversation, save the necessary. He tuned the radio to a classical station (thank God for Mozart's cheer), so speech was an interruption anyway. I blurted a couple of times, but caught myself. He examined the paltry contents of the refrigerator and made a list, then left for the grocery store. The car wheels crunched the gravel, overriding Mozart, and I was jettisoned into the *Great Lonesome*, as Papa used to call it. His word for God, he once alluded. *That's why He made us,* he'd explained.

It occurred to me, like a match struck to my brain, that this impasse was plainly ridiculous and I said so, aloud. I stepped outdoors and began a search for a *suitable* talking stick. This was important, I thought, as it would be imbued with intent and needed to convey a certain gravitas. I listened, as I would to an herb, finally settling on a short piece leaning against the wood pile. Somehow Sebastian's, or his uncle's, conscientious arrangement of cut wood into the rick lent the piece power and I grabbed it up, mouthing *thank you.*

Indoors, I scoured drawers for bits of yarn or ribbon his aunt may have saved. I found four lengths that would serve and wrapped, then tied them on the thickest end, content to have a physical task supersede the mental. The principle of the talking stick ceremony held that whoever clasped the stick might speak without interruption. A person could expect respectful attention, to be listened to deeply and with (it is hoped) compassion. One might respond to what was said, when their turn came to hold the stick, or not. It was truth-telling and a cathartic exercise, useful for communicating when circumstances have eroded opportunities or inclination. The latter gripped us. We were *dis*inclined to speak of things. *Things,* with a capital T. Or, *Tings,* as the Irish say.

"And how are *tings?*" the manager had asked upon our leaving Ballyfar. Sebastian and I had looked at one another and we honestly did not know. He'd recovered from his nightmare (he said), but refused to recount it, citing some version of bad luck. We shook hands with the staff before leaving, and thanked them. I was handed into the back seat of the hired car and he'd chosen to sit in front beside the driver, who was arranging our baggage in the *boot,* as the trunk was called. I lightly chided Sebastian for superstition and he glared at me, then—

"You can say this to me? You?—who see ancient Irish *fucking in caves?*"

This stung and put a damper on our travel. To mix metaphor, I was drowning in confusion *and* walking on eggshells. (Maybe oyster shells, long pulverized; more analogous.) I'd never seen Sebastian so tightly wound and it was painful to be in his presence; similar to constantly hearing, in the back of my mind, fingernails on a chalkboard. *Yes. Like that.* And, he'd never seen me so despondent. *Ever.* So, the talking stick.

Two hours passed. What was taking him so long? Maybe he thought we needed some time apart. *For more perspective? The dark boat ride wasn't enough?* Soon, he would leave for Denmark and another reception in New York. I would stay home. His agent had waxed effusive regarding sales, after hearing the numbers from the Ballyfar exhibit. *People are strange,* I decided, after Sebastian told me how many photographs had sold: three to the covey women, six more contracted to be shipped to the continent, and one to remain at Ballyfar, which sent shivers up my spine.

Feeling at loose ends (understatement, but apt), I decided to call my cousin Colin in North Carolina. I'd asked him, a financial adviser, to invest a portion of my inheritance—the proceeds from my grandparents' home—and he'd agreed, if reluctantly, not being in favor of working for relatives. I assured him I could be dispassionate, when it came to the vagaries of money markets, etc. He'd chuckled and said he'd help me, but with a limited amount, and advised me to find a second broker. We'd keep the funds in CDs and similarly safe options.

"Hello? That you, Senga?"

"Yes. How are things, Colin?"

"We're good here. What's up?" He sounded winded, as though he'd been running.

"You jogging or something?" I asked.

"Ha! Good one. Nah. I'm helping my son move into another house. I keep telling him he's already got way too much stuff for a college kid. So! Been a while. How're you doing?"

I took comfort in the soft, tar-heel accent. Like biscuits and syrup after a long time.

"Oh, I just returned from Ireland with my, ah, boyfriend." I wondered why I balked at the word. *Because you wonder if he still is?*

"You don't sound too sure, Senga. Is he or isn't he?"

God, You're coming through Colin now? And then, it slapped me in the face, figuratively. *Of course this is how it works, you fool.* And, if not a complete fool (my compassionate side retorted), I'd foolishly allowed pride too much rein. *Stinking pride,* I could hear my Grannie say, but not to me at this moment; she'd quit coming through last winter. It was just a phrase I recalled her using. *One of the seven deadlies—pride.* The worst, I remember. Got Lucifer thrown out of Paradise and it threatened to nudge me out, right behind him. It had certainly wedged itself between me and my heart's desire. . .

"Senga? You there?" I heard.

"Oh! Sorry, cousin. Daydreaming." *Jesus.* "Okay, and yes— I've got me a boyfriend," I said with conviction, if a little forced. "I'm just calling to check in, you know, like you asked me to. But it doesn't sound like a good time to visit. Don't hurt your back," I advised, my voice tired. I'd never realized how difficult it is to help when you're low. "Bend from the knees," I added, pressing goodwill into my tone.

He chuckled again. "Yes ma'am. I'll talk to you soon. Bye, girl," he said and we ended the call. I stood holding the cell phone, staring at the end call button, then, backing up to the bench in the foyer, I sat down with a *plunk!*

The first time I'd sat there, eight months ago, Sebastian had gently nudged away my hand from my task of unlacing my boots, to do it himself, kneeling before me. *Like a knight,* I remembered thinking. *Only eight months ago?* We hadn't yet recognized our love. I say "yet," for the truth of it. It had required all those years, nearly twenty, as we lived our separate lives, mine "caught between the tides," I'd once told Caroline.

Time expands and contracts just so. But the simple gesture of moving aside my hand to unlace my boots had felt as charged as the action of unlacing a corset, had I been wearing one.

His further explorations had uncovered me.

One proof leaned against a timbered wall in the living room: a framed photograph, five-and-a-half feet long, perched horizontally along the back of the side board. Printed in sepia tones, instead of black-and-white, I am shown on my bare stomach, in long profile. Lighted from above for better contrast and Sphinx-like, weight on my forearms, I face away in a three-quarter view. Anonymous. A long braid meanders in the foreground like a frozen waterfall, a rounded breast visible behind it.

I reflexively raised my hand to where my braid should have been, a phantom limb now, and moved my head to the left. For the image, I lay on a woven rug of dark, muted shades, the very one that greets guests in the foyer. It contrasted with my pale limbs, the line of my raised shoulders and backside undulating like a wave. . .

I studied the picture for several moments and tried to be objective by taking myself out of it. What came to me was this: I don't need to know the details of Sebastian's encounter with the woman. He was compelled, I believe, by compassion, but had yielded to her madness. The artist at Ballyfar believed Danica had declared war. "She was a *seasoned* seductress, Senga," she told me, after describing the horrific scene, never mind the dead woman's tragic, earlier circumstances, as provocative as any of the photographs (and, never mind the subject, me, wherein Sebastian had sought to capture a healthy sensuality). I'd happened to provide a useful conduit is all. Danica had succeeded in freeing herself of all emotion. All, but hate.

The artist's thoughtful opinion had lain to rest any notion of "fair ingénue infatuation," either toward or from her. In the end, it was I who had allowed pride to blind me to her capacity for chaos.

Sebastian would be appalled at my facile analysis. It wouldn't be the first time. I sighed.

The satisfying sound of crunching gravel. *Such good timing, Sebastian,* I thought. My nether regions agreed. Did *I* need the talking stick exercise? I did want to hear what, if anything, he might say. *On the other hand, what if he's made peace with it? What we are striving for, after all. . .*

I heard the door open behind me and froze in indecision.

"What did the ancient mariner say to the salty mermaid after plying the seven seas?"

"Oh, it's 'ancient' now, is it? And did they ply them together?" I asked, for clarification. The door clicked shut behind him and he gathered up a sack, to pass behind me to the kitchen. I stood, unmoving, still considering the photograph. If I imagined hard enough, I could conjure scales and a tail fin on the figure's lower half. And so, I did. *Presto-change-o.* It might help me solve the riddle. Then her head dropped to her forearms in utter despair. Desire wasn't enough to recreate legs from fins.

"Is it ply or plow?" Sebastian halted mid-way to the counter.

"Ply," I said, my voice betraying weariness. "To 'ply' one's trade. Something done repeatedly, you know? Like us when we're fucking. . . Like your ship, sailing back and forth on the seven seas. . . Like—"

"I see! I see. . . Senga, you do have a way with words, my dear," he said over his shoulder, "Well? I await the riddle's answer," he said quietly, earnestly, as he set the bag on the counter and began putting the items away: cream, croissants, yogurt, butter and cheese; several fresh vegetables and a package of short ribs. It resembled the ingredients for soup, with the pastry for now, I hoped. I craved sweetness.

I thought a moment. Then, I stepped over to the talking stick, picked it up and crossed to him. He regarded it curiously as he lifted the cutting board from its slot. "What is this?" he asked, his *chatoyant* blue eyes catching the sunlight through the tall windows behind the dining table. I caught a twinkle in one of his eyes, absent so very long. "Are you going to beat me with it?"

"When you—we—hold the stick, we talk and tell truths. It's like Wonder Woman's golden lasso. You know Wonder Wo—? Of course, you do. And the other . . . listens. Here—" I handed it to him. He examined and recognized it, I saw, by the smile curving his lips.

"It's from the wood pile."

"Yes. Bravo." I silently addressed *stinking pride* by mentally pointing, tersely, arm outstretched, away from the open portal of my mind. (A long flaming sword may have been involved; I've got friends in high places. *What?? Is that you, Humor?*) "So, what *did* the, ah, *ancient* mariner say to the salty mermaid after they plied the seven seas?"

"This is not fair, Senga. That is *your* riddle."

"*This is not fair??* That's your answer?" I gave him a raised brow and picked up the kettle to fill it for coffee. He saw I was serious.

"No-no. All right, but let us sit down, shall we?" He regarded me as he moved into the dining area to his uncle's arm chair. I set the kettle down; it would keep. He sat, holding the talking stick between his hands, elbows on the table. "I have heard of this—a long time ago." He lowered his arms to his lap and leaned back in the chair. Sunshine lit his face and hair again, like a blessing, and he appeared calmer. At peace. The house had worked its magic on him. My stomach growled audibly and he smiled at me, then, he was quiet for a long while as he stared at the stick. The clock, removed from the side board to a shelf, chimed eleven times, to break the silence. A charm.

"Well?" I pressed.

Leaning forward, he brought the wood to his lips and kissed it, then lowering it, he spoke: "The ancient mariner . . . told the salty mermaid . . . he only ever wants to ply her in the time he has left, and—" He raised a forefinger and looked at me, ". . . that he is done with the sea; she is too demanding."

"The sea? Or, the mermaid is too demanding—"

"The sea, Senga."

"Good . . . answer," I replied slowly, catching my stinking pride slink away with accompanying qualms. There exists *healthy* pride; it smells better. Like sage, after rain.

Clever man, I thought, but wondered how one plies a mermaid outside the environs of the sea. I let it go. Our eyes locked in the crucial understanding and I sat down beside him, my usual place to his left, against the window. "Sebastian—" I began.

"It is over, my dear," he said simply, studying his lap.

My stomach wrenched. "*Wha—?*" I must have grimaced.

"Oh, my dear—oh, I am sorry! No. I mean the, ah, sorry business in Ireland—*it* is over," he said in a near whisper as he reached for my hand, turning it over to kiss my palm. *Sorry business* sounded better than *The Incident,* anyway. Similar to one's sad story, or, a sore subject, a sorry business is traditionally kept under wraps, as it were. I didn't know how to proceed, given my epiphany—that of permitting pride between us. I would instead allow myself some breathing room to just let it be, as the Beatles counseled.

Sebastian proposed a second solution. He held onto my hand and, standing, looked on me with such longing. I would've had to have been blind *and* insensible to ignore the stirrings in my body. With my hand clasped in his, we climbed the spiral staircase to the more-than-ample bed, and there, we fell on one another with every scrap of a too-long ignored passion.

All of nature is conscious, I heard, and, *Permit the healing.*

We would heal in one another. In time.

I would come to rue my glib prediction, time not being what we think it is. . .

"Oh, *Gud,* Senga—" His God, in Danish, became mine in English. We were tender at first, almost tentative in our touching, as the slow recollection of our senses and topographies dawned. I moved my hand along the length of his torso, using only enough pressure to assure his presence, where all senses became one—the sun-dried linen warmth of his skin, the sweet taste of his mouth, the soft hair of his belly, his groans. I wanted to devour him and almost did.

He yelped.

"I'm sorry!" I rolled onto my back and, wrapping my legs around him, I lifted my arms over my head, to cling to the headboard, to open myself to his need and, by default, mine. I wanted his very being to infuse mine; to steep in me, to effect a chemical reaction of some unknown magnitude. *Nothing short of fusion.* "Could be done," I muttered.

"What did you say?" he looked up from his work.

"I said it *could* be achieved, fusion—during lovemaking—and maybe it is . . . you know? Why not? If two people love each other enough and the sex is, ah, *volatile?*"

He grinned and made a particularly explicit movement with his tongue, causing my hips to jerk in response. I made the sounds and was very soon scaling the proverbial wall.

"Your turn," I panted dreamily, as I reached for his cock. He quivered.

We burned for one another, while cool sweat made our bodies slick. I smelled his musky odor and sniffed my own arm pit, wondering. He laughed quietly and lifted my arm to reveal my patch of moist, dark hair. He inhaled my scent and, without warning, pushed into me deeply, said my name, and I groaned with desire and certainty that he was mine and had ever been; the sorry business to be totally eclipsed by *our* transit; his ancient mariner, to ply *this* particular sea, beneath which the Black Hills once lay nascent and where he had taken me, *was* taking me.

CHAPTER 24
EVENT HORIZON

Caroline and Rufus settled in their seats for the second leg of their flight to California. Salt Lake City to San Francisco. At 79 and 80 years of age, they were taking their very first vacation. Rufus had suggested his wife take the window this time. Soon, they were cruising at altitude and could sit back and relax. For someone who had flown only once, in a neighbor's small Cessna, Caroline felt oddly at peace. As did Rufus. Maybe it was age, she thought, as she twisted to look out the window to passing clouds over the Wasatch Mountains. She noticed her husband had closed his eyes and snoozed, as best he could in the cramped space. He'd managed to get around without the cane for nearly two months and didn't complain.

Engine hum, even and loud, functioned as white noise and her thoughts hung suspended, like miniature airplanes, in the peaceful space of her mind. *Which one to choose?* She settled on Joey first, then she'd pass to Jake, their grandson. Joey had passed his GED test with a high score and she'd warmed to hear him name Senga and Gabe as the reason. It made her happy to hear his pride in accomplishing this thing, even if it meant his leaving. It was a natural progression, one she and Rufus had felt happy to have aided. Caroline smiled to herself, then sighed loudly.

"What's the matter, Caro?" asked her husband, one eye trained on her.

"Oh, nothin', hon. Just thinkin'. I miss the little cuss. Joey."

"Yeah, me too. But he's in a good place. Gabe says he's working out for them. Making a good hand." Her husband turned his face to her, the side that had escaped the fire. He knew she "chose" (if such a thing were possible) to see him as he'd appeared before the accident, when he was nineteen. Memory worked that way.

"Jake—" she began and paused. ". . . He's been working with you and Gabe for almost three weeks."

"Yep."

"Well, you ain't said much. His manners are decent and he shows some sense, as far as I can tell," she said, as an attendant reached their row and asked if they'd like a beverage and a snack.

"What do you want?" Rufus asked her.

"Oh, a Coke, I guess. And some of them nuts." She smiled up at the woman.

Caroline also wanted Rufus' estimation of their grandson. The six-year absence from their lives had been long. She'd gleaned temperament from simply observing the boy, who was affable, if shy with them, but a person's character was better revealed when working, she knew, and she hadn't had the opportunity. She'd felt estranged and it burned. That Rufus hadn't said much did not bode well. Maybe he was giving the kid room to sort things out. He'd grown up in the city, after all. She'd give him some time.

If he just didn't look exactly like Rufus at that age. . . She sighed again.

"I'll have a ginger ale, please," said Rufus, ". . . and pretzels."

They sat quietly sipping their drinks and munching the snacks, when Rufus turned to her and said, "He *ain't* Joey."

This made her sad. She didn't want a stranger to assume a grandson's place in her husband's affections. After making a sound, which he might have taken negatively, she turned her eyes to the window and mulled which tiny airplane to pluck from the store of the possible.

Senga.

She and Sebastian had returned from Ireland. Her neighbor's long hair was gone and she hardly resembled herself. Caroline had gasped when Senga walked through their door only days before. Rufus had stayed mum, concern burning on his face. All their neighbor had said, in her unnerving way, was, "It's a long story and can wait." Caroline had walked up to Senga, first, to give her a hug, then to peer into her eyes, to see if she was all right.

No, she wasn't, but Caroline didn't press. Her friend would eventually find the right time to tell her, probably alone, and then Caroline would tell Rufus. Sebastian, walking in behind her, had offered no explanation. He remained too quiet, she thought. And his eyes looked—*haunted.* That was the word.

Senga had asked about Joey—how did he like the Blue Wood?—when Jake and Gabe walked in.

"*Whoa*—" had been Gabe's initial reaction, even if inhaled softly, and Caroline watched him study their friend, who may have sent him a silent message. He'd left shortly after, saying, "I'll see you later, *chère.*"

"Christ, what *happened?*" Rufus had asked after the visitors left. Senga had brought bottles of Irish whiskey for Rufus and Gabe and, for Caroline, tea towels, whose intricate stitching she studied to set her mind on *some*thing.

"She'll say in her own good time, hon. Asked if she could take Sadie out this week—I said of course. They didn't look too good, did they?" asked Caroline.

He slowly shook his head. "I don't like it. Hell—let's try the whiskey," he'd said, meaning, *medicinally.*

Caroline turned to him. "What else did Gabe say about Senga?"

Even at 40,000 feet, his wife still gnawed that bone. Rufus shifted in his seat. "Oh, let it go, Caro. She's all right—or will be. Chrissake."

He closed his eyes. . .

. . . That night, he'd watched for Gabe's truck lights to bounce back over the car gate and, after giving the man a few minutes, he crossed the yard to the barn. Later, he reported to Caroline that they'd hemmed and hawed a few moments, then Gabe reached for two small glasses to sample Senga's welcome whiskey gift. Rufus had sat at the desk, while Gabe leaned against his pillow and metal headboard. He rose once to turn on the fan against the heat and drifting paddock smells. Two of the six cats bounded in for their evening treats, which Gabe provided in the barn aisle. He shut his door against further invasion.

"This is good," said Rufus, raising his glass, having already imbibed with Caroline. Gabe had nodded and, after relaying the sad tale as told by Sebastian and Senga in her cabin, he assured Rufus that the Dane was doing "his level best" to attend to Senga.

"It took a writer to tell it," Rufus later told Caro. "I never heard such a *god-awful* story in all my life."

"*Your own is pretty god-awful,*" she'd muttered under her breath.

"She's all right," was all Gabe had said and Rufus repeated it, though it could have been whiskey courage—or wishful thinking.

What else can be done? wondered Caroline. Not a damn thing. She sat quietly staring out the window to thin wisps of cloud. And then, they saw it—sparkling silver water to the horizon. The sun hung in the western sky and Caroline sat back, so Rufus could better see. They sat starboard and the aircraft was banking inland.

"*Ohhh,*" said Rufus. The sound groaned from deep inside, like the sound an engine makes from a far distance in a snow-covered wood.

Caroline loved to catch any bright sparkle in his eye, and now it watered. She handed him the moist napkin from under her drink. The captain spoke to say they'd be landing within twenty minutes, and that the fasten seatbelt signs were in effect.

"*Ohhh,*" Rufus repeated. "I . . . never thought it'd be so . . . *big.*"

She leaned in to kiss his scratchy cheek, the one that still grew whiskers. "That's what all the girls say," and she winked at him.

He raised his white beetled brows to her. "Ain't you the frisky one," he whispered. "Ever hear of the Mile-High Club?" he said, gazing back at the ocean.

"Yeah, and we're too damn late, old man."

He made another sound. "Let's see . . . we're around 40,000 feet. Divide that by five thousand, close enough; we get, ah— eight make-ups." He winked at her sidelong and shifted back to the water.

"Actually, we're way lower than that. Didn't the captain say we'll land soon? But, nice try, Superman. Ha! Eight. *As if. . .*"

They landed without incident. After retrieving their bags, they were met by Earl's friends, Harry and Jane Wilson, whose sign for recognition read, "Wyoming Sheep Farmers, Unite!"

"That would be us, hon," Caroline said as she jabbed Rufus in the ribs. It caught him off-guard and he stumbled, but she reached out to right him and slipped an arm through his.

"You Earl and Mae's friends?" she asked the couple.

"That'd be us," the tanned man said and they all shook hands and were soon in traffic, heading south. She figured their hosts were only a little younger than they were, maybe early seventies, but it was hard to tell these days.

Almost an hour later (because of traffic), when the sun was nearing the horizon, they pulled into a wide, red brick driveway, bordered by tall trees; eucalyptus, they later learned. "*Here?* This is your place?" Rufus asked, his facial features trying to arrange themselves appropriately, Caroline saw. Hers were doing the same.

"Yes—this is us. And Jane and I are so glad you're here. I hope you enjoy it. We do." Harry held out a hand, in case she needed it. She looked into his bronzed California face and slowly shook her head, but nodded toward Rufus, who was still sitting. Harry walked around to the other side of the SUV and waited for Rufus to unfold himself. Jane laughed at his machinations and grabbed Caroline's bag from the back. She was fit, Caroline noted. *Could probably buck bales with the best of 'em.*

"Let's go in before the sun sets. We like to watch," she said coyly, smiling broadly at them all with her perfect white teeth.

The cypress wood home appeared smaller from outside than it was—the interior dimensions belying first impression. The house was built over a sloping cliff, Harry explained, with the major portion invisible from the road. Once inside, the space multiplied, as stairs descended to a large room with a two-story stone fireplace. Through floor-to-ceiling windows, the Pacific Ocean glittered before them. The scent of something green, like Christmas trees, filled the air. She detected lemons, too. She was oddly reminded of Gabe.

A high cathedral ceiling mirrored the azure water below. Off the deck, to the right, a series of wooden walkways and steps led to the beach. Music began to play from nowhere, or everywhere—the strains surrounding them. Rufus' eyes grew wide.

Jane said, "I've been thinking about this. Earl said you two had never seen the ocean, so I wanted to make it special and play something fitting. It's called, "In the Middle of This Nowhere," by Hammock. We play it a lot; it's our soundtrack. Now it can be yours!"

The woman was downright *perky*. No, that wasn't the word and Caroline thought harder. She remembered the Lawrence Welk Show and his bubble machine, and wouldn't have been surprised if some burst from the air conditioning vents. She kept searching for the appropriate word. *Senga would know. . . Bubbly?*

Harry led them outdoors, where the soaring music suited the overwhelming vision before them. In the background the surf pounded massive rocks, sending spray in rhythmic arcs; roiling waves, by turn, crashed, then receded. They were shown a love seat and Caroline sat down beside Rufus. The astonishing view was unobstructed by railings (on account of there being none), as they watched through a clear plexiglass barrier. The great, red-orange sun melted below the horizon.

"It's just . . . so *beautiful*," sighed Caroline, as she leaned into Rufus' shoulder. When she turned to look at him, he was trying not to cry as he lifted his forearm to dab his eyes. With his other arm, he pulled Caroline to him. She heard him choke back tears.

"Oh, hon," she murmured, turning to their hosts. Harry and Jane had left them alone.

CHAPTER 25
THE FORAGER

O
n Sunday, as I sipped an early morning coffee at my table in the cabin, something silky brushed against my bare ankle. Involuntarily, my foot jerked away. Looking down, I squeaked (as women do in movies, I later realized). I'd come *this* close to stomping on the bat, in reflex, bare foot or no.

What *is* it about these things that startle us so?

Biology again, came the answer. Are we somehow wired against them? Somewhere deep in our history, was it us against the critters? *Really? A dystopian past? And are you really asking this question, Munro?* my reasonable side asked. I remembered the more sinister species and another great gear clunked into place in my personal philosophy. *Vampires.* Thousands of years ago, vampire bats ranged farther north, and recent evidence showed they might be returning from their *long* vacation in Mexico, Central and South America, due to climate change.

Well, fuck.

I pushed my chair back, in order to give the furry beast room. It was little and brown, hence, its name. Little Brown Bat. The half-folded wings dragged behind like the train of a macabre wedding dress. *Unfortunate bride,* I quipped silently. It seemed to be experiencing some torpor as it crawled—time of day and all. My heart rate had almost returned to normalcy and I practiced deep breathing as I watched the world's only flying mammal struggle across my floor, like the misshapen assistant Igor in early Frankenstein films. *Where was it going and whence had it come?* I wondered. Some narrow ingress between the cabin's outside walls and its roof, I suspected, followed by a full-body shiver.

145

Rising carefully, I stepped to a cabinet for a jar. After taking a lid from a drawer, I slowly walked back to the bat, leaned down and captured it. I made myself study the not-quite-cute face, body and wings—one of which spread to full length, about five inches. *Myotis lucifugus,* indeed, I thought, after quickly looking it up. I took it outdoors and released it onto the wall of the garage, where I permitted it to find shelter under its rafters, if it so desired. *Myotis* referred to mouse ears, the obvious connotation, but *lucifugus* means "to shun light." Fascinating.

Great; maybe it owes me one now.

Two nights ago, we'd sent Rufus and Caroline off with, if not style, then a fair amount of hoopla. The only one absent was Sebastian, for an appointment in New York he couldn't postpone, via Denmark first. He traveled a lot, I realized, if abstractly; I couldn't have kept up the pace if I tried, and was secretly pleased I didn't have to. We'd parted with heavy hearts and no new mermaid riddle, I later noted. I was also still reeling. It would be a matter of time and equanimity. Our love-making had proven a loading dose of remedy, with attendant side-effects; awkwardness, but one. Yes, we'd require time.

At the bon voyage party, Gabe had grilled burgers and I'd managed a garden salad. Caroline made brownies and everyone supplied their own libations. I limited alcohol, being too familiar with its effect on frayed nerves, choosing instead a calming oat straw infusion to sip all evening. Jake and Joey were handed beers, "Just this once!" said Rufus, knowing full well he'd foreswear himself. They were quite the trio and I smiled in spite of myself. With Jake, it was as though his six-year absence had summarily blinked out, like a star, to be replaced by a swirling galaxy.

I was reminded of the nova I'd witnessed on the dark flight home from Italy last year. A colossal wink from the Cosmos, extraordinary grace I'll never forget. Like this party. My neighbors accepted our gift—per Joey's suggestion—with some hesitation, then Rufus simply said thank you, nothing more, while Caroline beamed.

As I reviewed the evening, I straightened the kitchen, got dressed and anticipated a morning on horseback.

I knocked on the tack-room door that doubled as Gabe's bedroom and he opened with a smile, electric shaver to his cheek.

"Come in, come in, *chère,*" he said, gesturing me in. "Have a seat. Caroline said you want to go riding." She and Rufus had arrived in California, safe and sound.

Gabe was shirtless and it took my breath away. He was beautifully made. Taking another breath of appreciation, I nodded to him and started to remove my hat, but left it on. Dropping my eyes to the step, I entered his quarters, the use of the word a leftover from having lived on an army base when young. Officers lived in *quarters;* we others, in "housing." Gabe filled the former rank in my mind.

As he resumed shaving at the sink mirror, I studied him a long moment. A man's naked back tells a tale and proves a rule; in this case—strength, beauty and perseverance. Backbreaking work, shouldering responsibility and more, the idea of a shield, or shielding, belonged to a good man's back. The thoughts still playing in my head, I made my way toward his print of *The Annunciation* by Henry Ossawa Tanner. The colors and ineffable subject worked their subtle way with me and I made a sound. Turning, I caught him now studying me out of the corner of my eye. He wore a frown.

"How're you doing? I mean, really. No bullshit," he said.

My attention returned to the picture and back to him. *How am I doing? I could fall to pieces,* I thought, but I resisted, willing his gaze to impart strength.

It did.

"Thanks for asking. Grannie once said that just asking after someone was healing, too. Shows caring."

He half-smiled and consulted the mirror to make one last pass against his neck, then, after tapping the razor against the sink, he put a cap on it and tucked it away on a shelf.

I monitored his economical motions with interest, the kind that qualify as helpful distraction, and reversed the inquiry. "And how are *you* doing? A lot has happened. You and Francesca going to be able to go see your dad and sister? Not the best time of year to visit Louisiana, I hear, but you've said your dad's not well." I rambled on.

"Now don't be turning this around, woman," he said as he quickly rolled on deodorant, reached for a tee shirt and pulled it over his head. The bright turquoise color was meant for me, I'm certain, so I claimed its protection and allowed the blue shade to infuse me with courage.

He added, "I'm pretty sure what happened in Ireland involves more than I know, and I'm wondering if—well, if you've been able to sort it out."

"That's going to take a while, Gabe. I don't know. But I appreciate your—concern. It was horrendous."

"We're friends. I had a feeling there was more. . . All right then. . . Well. Sadie could use a long ride. It'll be good for you both. Ah, do you want me to come along? I can hold off on my chore."

"Nah. I'll be okay. And you're right; it'll be good for me. We'll take it easy. I've been looking forward to this since I asked Caroline. Is she—Sadie—with the others?"

"Actually, she's in the paddock waiting on you. I put her up a few days ago. Jake's learning to ride too, so. . ."

"Oh yeah? He's a sweet kid—I like him. But almost *too* sweet, you know? He needs to, oh, I don't know, do something rebellious while he's here."

Gabe quietly laughed. "Yep, I know what you mean." He lifted the water bottle from his desk and finished the contents, then pitched it into a box with other empties. "Me, I think he was starved for what his grandpa's feeding him. Attention, I think they call it. Oh, and don't worry; he's managed more than a couple, *deeply* dumb-ass moves. . ." He snorted, grabbed his hat and gestured for me to follow him to the paddock and Sadie.

"Like what?" I asked, hustling up beside him.

He sucked in his cheeks, what he did when considering something. "You can't tell Caroline."

My eyes grew wide and I gave him a meaningful look that said, "Get on with it."

It wasn't original, he said, or even remotely daring; he would have given the kid a C-, if assigning grades. "The minus for stupidity; the C for mediocrity. Aw, it really doesn't bear telling," and he left it at that.

I just said, "Hunh." The sun was blazing hot already, so I tied my chambray shirt around my waist. The tank top felt breezy and free. I unconsciously moved to toss the absent braid out of my way. Muscle memory once more. Papa's fedora kept the hair out of my eyes. The sun as well.

After currying and brushing the mare, I worked on her mane until my fingers ran through easily. She snuffled with the attention. Gabe brought out Caroline's saddle and bridle and, together, we finished tacking up. I lengthened the stirrups and Gabe held her head as I mounted. I'd thought to stretch in the morning, but expected to feel the groin pull that evening. Part and parcel.

"Do I need to come looking if you don't return in a couple hours?" he asked, pulling his brim down against the sun as he gazed up at me.

I grunted. "Oh, I don't think so. I'll make toward the river, so you'll have an idea. In case." I nodded at him and, reining away, waved without turning.

It felt good to be astride a horse again. I'd forgotten how soothing it felt; the smell of horseflesh, the squeak and ease of leather moving under me to a horse's even gait. Moving through air, above the ground; a meditation in motion. I'd learned to ride at the army post stables in North Carolina, a "stable rat" among other young girls my age.

I concentrated on Sadie's movement. It appeared she'd healed from her encounter with the car-gate. "Good girl," I whispered while stroking her neck, her ears twitching back and forth as we descended to the draw's deer trail that would lead us to an old dirt track. I'd have a few gates to open, a nuisance, but small price to pay for the privilege.

The sweet smell of a horse works like magic, a nervine as effective as any calming herb. I may associate riding with peace, a good tonic. Sitting up tall, I pulled in my stomach. Remembering my horsemanship, I squeezed with my thighs and calves, to rock with the horse. Sadie was quiet and moved out well. She was ready for some one-on-one time; I'd neglected our relationship, I thought, and then, I swore. *Enough regrets!*

The sky shone cobalt blue and no cloud interfered. Storms were forecast for the following day, so I'd chosen well and felt a smile break on my face, in unconscious surrender to the occasion. I'd play the centaur this day. No mermaid.

We passed the neighbor's pasture, where a herd of horses watched us approach. One whinnied and Sadie answered; social creatures, they. I reined her away from the fence line, to continue our descent toward the river, lulled, tempted or seduced by a returning sense of freedom; moreover, freedom from recent memory. An intermittent view of the lazy, winding water soothed my thoughts, but only for a moment. I was doused by memory's next wave: last night's discovery. Twisting a hand into Sadie's mane, for courage, I leaned back as she picked her careful way down the steep hill to the river . . .

I'd discovered the letter by accident as I dusted my books and shelves. (Not a task I perform with any regularity.) A tiny corner of the white envelope peeked from the top of a book and I slowly pulled the volume from the shelf. It was one of Grannie's old herbals I'd brought with me from North Carolina nearly thirty years before, when I'd hurriedly packed some of what I, nearly six months pregnant, thought I might need on an adventure with Emily's father, a musician. He'd questioned the heavy box of books.

I'd never consulted it, having other reference books I prefer. After using the dusting cloth to wipe the old leather binding, I held it to my breast for a moment. Grannie had used it to teach me the fundamentals of botany. As a child, I'd sat for hours copying schematic drawings, and then coloring them. (*Stigma, style, ovary.*) I took a breath and slowly extracted the paper. It was a letter, addressed to me. In my Grannie's hand. I replaced the book on the shelf absentmindedly.

She knew me better than I know myself.

One afternoon last fall, I'd tossed a packet of letters from her, most unread, into the fire, including one from my mother who'd died when I was ten. She was killed in a car accident, but only after regaining some semblance of sanity. You see, I am more than acquainted with madness. Fear had thrown away the letters and the secrets therein.

On the plain envelope (the kind she'd used for bills), my former name, *Agnes,* sweetly called in Grannie's soft mountain accent. I slowly inhaled, blew out and walked to my blue wing chair. There I sat with it for several minutes, before carefully opening it with my pocket knife. I had the sense to murmur a prayer, invocation or charm for protection.

Granny wrote that she had "seen" me pitching a packet of letters into the fire of a black wood stove. She said these "*keeks*" of scenes came to her; they hadn't begun until she was done with her courses (*like me*), and she wondered if I'd have the sight as well.

"*So,*" she'd continued, "*I'm writing this second letter, mostly about my Lucy, your mama, so's you'd know the truth of it—why she weren't quite right in the head—and that she couldn't help being the way she was. I always feared you thought it was some ways your fault. Like a child will do. It weren't.*

"*Like I wrote in the other letter—the one I seen you burn—Old Scratch, he come to see us. In the guise of a young man. Papa, he hired him to help at the still. Your mama, she weren't no weak-willed child, no sir, but there was some other trouble there. Papa, he was drinking his recipe too much and couldn't see what's what. Our Lucy, your mama, was hurt real bad by this young man. He had his way with her for weeks. One day, Lucy wrote me that he was gone—had just up and gone. I was gone to that nursing school in Kentucky, but I quit it when I got home at Christmas and learnt the truth—and here's the Truth—you've a right to hear it: Papa, I believe he did something unholy to that young man. We never spoke of it, but I'd see him staring at his shotgun on the wall with a hollowed-out look now and then.*

"*Your mama—she tried—'specially that last month we were all together. She got right with God and herself. But I want you to know, she was happiest when you and your daddy and her were all together. Both times he was gone to that war, she got scared, like half of her was gone, which it was, I suppose.*

"*So now I've told you, and I don't know if you'll read this 'un, but I ain't had any more pictures of you feeding your fire. It's all right, dearie. It'll be all right. I love you.*"

It was simply signed, "*Grannie.*"

What does a body do with something like that? Climb on a horse and keep riding?

No.

When I turned back from the river, I let fall the letter's words behind me, like Hansel and Gretel's bread crumbs. Maybe the crows would discover and take them to their fledglings. Maybe they could eat words.

By the time I returned to Stricklands', the sun was high overhead and I was hungry and thirsty and empty inside. Knowledge is a two-edged, sharp-as-a-razor sword and I was ready to beat it into the proverbial plowshare, but there's truth to the adage, that once you learn something, it cannot be unlearned (with apologies to G.K. Chesterton).

Emotional knowledge can, at last, be made useful, *like compost.* I knew my mother had suffered. It was just a part of me. It sat between me and Emily's loss in my heart. I just hadn't known the why of Mama's sorrow, and had always hoped she'd found peace during that last, joy-filled month. No—I am certain she had, for if she hadn't, I'd be a much different person than I am now. . . Did I benefit from learning what had happened? If I were to describe it, I'd say it was akin to ingesting a tablespoon of the bitterest herbs. They have their place in healing and to season a pot of soup.

I unsaddled Sadie, groomed her, cleaned her hooves and led her to the pasture to join her friends. Gabe asked me to stay for lunch, but I begged off, thanked him and drove home to spend the rest of the day in my garden, after eating a peanut butter and honey sandwich and drinking nearly a quart of cold, oat straw infusion.

After speaking with Sebastian in Denmark and describing my ride (making no mention of the letter and its contents), I wanted to assign him a mermaid riddle, but none came to mind. Instead, I wished him well and good luck for the upcoming New York show; also, to convey my regards to his daughter Erika, Peter and Jytte.

No doubt about it, my heart was leaking from a tiny puncture wound; nothing aspirin or nitroglycerine could plug.

Muriel called after my soup supper to confirm our plant walk at the Tower the following morning, and to ask how I'd been. I thanked her for her concern and went to bed early, even as the air still glowed in the *gloaming,* as Grannie called it. Having taken skullcap and valerian to help me sleep, I also took St. John's Wort against muscle pain (and perhaps to ease my melancholy for Mama). Following my nightly remembrance of Emily, I drifted off—a horse's ambling cadence as lullaby—and slept through the night. . .

————

I woke with the robin's song, before light, and after coffee and toast, I grabbed my walking stick and stepped out for a much-needed walk. First, I squatted and pressed my palm to the earth beside my cabin, in gratitude. Walking along the road is good for contemplating horizon and sky, but on cross-country hikes, I keep eyes downcast as I step, mostly on guard against the rare rattle snake. Herbs and mushrooms are also there for the sighting, as gift, if one has eyes to see. Over at the Tower, however, nothing may be legally harvested or taken, but I'm not prevented from reviewing herbal theory: I may learn *where* a plant grows; i.e., north side of a hill, or when it flowers (conditional on water and sunshine). I can transfer information of, say, when an herb is ready to be harvested to where else it grows and may be taken.

Despite a sound sleep, Grannie's letter troubled me, and my understanding at last spread to grasp her intent—that being in possession of the truth is healing in itself. But I hurt for Papa, and wondered how much more my heart could stand, in both senses, and decided to carry a few aspirins and my tiny bottle of nitroglycerine against occasional angina. I love my herbs, but they generally work more slowly than drugs in emergencies. It's what accounts for their safety, as well.

Returning to my Starwallow less sore, I filled a water bottle and left for the Tower.

At 9:30, Muriel and I met at the picnic shelter. I brought her St. John's Wort oil against her own aches. She told me I could have waited until I came in to work the next day, and this frustrated me. "Why wait for it, Muriel? I'm sore from riding yesterday. You can bet I took some last night or it might've been worse."

Her shoulders hurt, either from arthritis or bursitis, we thought, and the herbal oil helped. If applied regularly. I had her rub some on before we set off, the warming red color and sweet smell two of my favorite properties. The sky threatened, so we may have rushed a normally, pleasant opportunity.

I helped her identify *chamisa,* or rabbit brush; wild celery; and pineapple weed—whose anti-inflammatory and calmative properties mimic those of chamomile. The wind came up after an hour and she left. I continued around the great stone, veering off the trail when a familiar plant caught my eye. My old childhood herbal notebook open to a blank page, dark green color pencil in hand, I was fixin' to sketch the young shoots of the shepherd's purse (Grannie used it when catching babies, to clot blood and hasten labor) when I felt the first, heavy drop of rain on Papa's well-worn fedora. Another drop came with the certainty of a second summer drenching. Glad for my jacket, I pocketed notebook and pencil, and turned back in the direction of the shelter.

From where I stood, the structure was hidden and only part of the parking lot visible. No vehicles save mine. Turning back toward the trail, I was met with the person of Tom Robinson.

"Oh! You startled me . . . I wondered if that was you the other day . . . at the prairie dog village," I said, almost sheepishly, omitting the car picnic with my friends. Suddenly, a violent gust lifted the hat off my head and I twisted to catch it, but failed. It tumbled through the yellow brush below us, as though borne by a hopping hare. Surreal. I think I laughed.

"I'll get it," Tom offered as he jumped over sage, and another blast reanimated the hat, in Buster Keaton fashion. I wondered where it was going to wind up, as heavier raindrops stung my face. I turned toward the direction the hat was moving, when Tom's expression clouded, *colluding with the weather*, I remember thinking, and we stumbled on through the brush.

We were nearly to the hat, finally snagged high in a standing dead, whose gray and black twisted limbs rose stark and skeletal against the darkening sky, when I heard him say, "Come see." His lips quirked in a small smile and I, seldom one to miss a curiosity, obliged him, ignoring the hat for now.

Soon, we were standing beside a collection of giant scattered boulders; originally, sections of a six-sided column of the Tower. In a blinding flash, lightning struck—immediately followed by ear-splitting thunder. *Too close.* It reverberated through my body and substance. My heart skipped a beat, as if resetting itself. Then, I heard a strange thing: the pealing of a bell after being struck; a *ringing*. It resonated at a high frequency and I was mesmerized.

"You hear it," Tom stated, his eyes shining under the bill of his cap.

"Yes. It's in the stone?"

"That's right. Come see," he repeated, gesturing hurriedly for me to follow.

And I did.

CHAPTER 26
MEMORY AND OTHER MELODIES
The Coast of California

"Hey, Grandpa! How's it going? You and Grandma having fun? What's it like?" Jake peppered Rufus with questions, so much so he had to rein him in.

"Whoa, son, hold up. I can't keep up, and yeah, we're having fun. I hope you'll see this someday—if you haven't already." He caught himself wondering, *Hell, I don't even know if my grandson's seen the ocean. I should know that!*

"No. I haven't. Mom wanted to go a couple of years ago, but Dad—well, he couldn't get off work."

Rufus heard the excuse and changed the subject. "I went swimming for the first time in, oh, sixty-some years, if you can believe that—and you should see where we're staying, your grandma and me. Real nice digs. So, what have you and Gabe been doing? I'm not checking up on you, but yeah, I sorta am." He chuckled. A pause, then—

"We've been working, Grandpa. Painted the house red, like Grandma asked."

Rufus's eyes bulged and he swung around to his wife. "You did *what?*"

"Ha! Gotcha, Grandpa! It was Gabe told me to say that. No, we've just been going down the list you left, and then some. The sheep are down in the south pasture and we're working on that east line today. It's about done. Rained an inch a couple days ago . . . what else? Oh! We picked beans. Here, Gabe wants to talk to you. Hi to Grandma, and have fun!" he called as he passed the receiver to Gabe.

"Hey, boss. Sorry about the joke. You knew Caroline wanted the trim painted red; thought I'd exaggerate a bit." He laughed at hearing Rufus groan. "Y'all doing all right?"

"Yeah, we are, but I'm ready to come home. Nice place to visit and all that. A lot of people, but at least fifty percent of the view is water." He paused to gaze at it. "It's so pretty, Gabe. I wobble around for hours on the beach, just looking, then sitting, then sort-of-swimming. Floating, mostly. Drinking some beer, too. Caro does stuff with that gal, but I'm happy to just hang out—and Larry's good company when he's around."

"How's the hip?"

"I'm fine. Can't milk it any longer," Rufus said, though it still ached. The doctor had recommended a hip replacement, but he'd bucked that notion off entirely.

"It can be tricky, staying with folks," said Gabe.

"Ah, hell, son, they've got us in this fancy guest house, with all kinds of room. A full view of the ocean, too! They stocked the fridge with food and beer and other drinks; we eat dinner with them most of the time; lunch sometimes. They've hauled us to vineyards and on long car rides to see the country. It's something, all right. Just too many damn people! Gabe, I know you said y'all got together and compensated the Wilsons for this, but I can't imagine it being enough, not to sound fussy—"

"*Patron*—" Gabe interrupted, "Earl and Mae have assured us that his friends are lovin' every minute, and they're the ones who are grateful. Didn't I mention they don't have a lot of people? No kids, apparently. They've loved having you. Hey, enjoy it! And everything's fine here. The kid's doing great; takes after his grandpa, as far as I can tell. You can be proud of him, boss."

"Hope he isn't standing right there—it'll go to his head."

"He's out of earshot; no worries."

Rufus made a sound. "But I am—proud of him. And thanks, Gabe; you set my mind at ease. I've been imagining all kinds of trouble. Don't know why. Not used to being away from the place, I guess. All right. Take care, and we'll see you soon. Oh, and Caro says hi—she's got her nose in some girly book."

He replaced the phone on the cradle, on the bedside table. He and Caro were set to do something they rarely, if ever, enjoyed back home. A nap after lunch. They'd instituted the habit the day after they arrived at the Wilson's. Such a simple luxury, Rufus thought. *Why are we so all-fired up to get everything done in a day?* he wondered as he moved to wrap an arm around Caro to pull her to him. He was leaning against the upholstered headboard, arranged for a view of the ocean beyond the sliding glass doors. These gave onto a narrow balcony, furnished with a small table and two chairs—off to the side—providing an unencumbered vista.

"Everything's okay?" asked Caro, placing a bookmark in the novel she was reading, borrowed from Jane's eclectic library. After setting it on the bedside table, she snuggled her soft contours against her wiry husband of sixty years.

"Yep."

"Jake minding Gabe?"

"'Spect so; why wouldn't he?"

"Oh, I don't know. Well, good. Heard you say you're ready to go home. I am, too. Feeling a bit—oh, you know, like a dull horse that's kept in a paddock all the time for the owners to admire." She smiled up into his face. "Not that I'm sad we came, hon. I don't mean that. It's been a little bit of heaven, seeing this . . . being here," she said as she glanced around the perfectly appointed bedroom, done in light grays and blues, and a color they'd always called pink, now "blush" by Jane Wilson. *Restful colors,* the woman had explained. *Like a sunset.*

Caro turned back to Rufus and he felt her hand on his groin. She raised her eyebrows to him in question.

"Uh, it's kinda sleepy, Caro. But do your worst," and he grinned, reaching for his belt buckle.

She rose and left the room, to return in a moment. "Thought I'd better lock the door—in case they deliver pizza or sushi, or *some*thing." She cackled as she climbed back into the bed, the covers having been turned back. The heavy sound of the surf breaking on the rocks below added an exotic element to their lovemaking. "I hear you can get these sound machines with this. Might have to get us one. Ain't it grand, hon?"

He took a deep breath, thrilling in the force of the seascape. The water! *All that beautiful water!* He was brought to tears once again, in concert with it, this moment, this woman, this wonder.

"Oh, Caro. I love you, hon. You do know that, don't you?" he asked her, massaging her shoulder and arm as she lay against him, staring out the window.

"I know, old man. I've always known it. Since we were—oh, seven and nine. Seems like yesterday and a thousand years ago, don't it?" She continued to rub his pelvic area and moved to his cock. He shuddered. They had long ago given up intercourse, on account of its discomfort to her, but they'd found their way, in other ways. It required imagination, something called *lubricant* and time. He felt absolutely at ease with any suggestion his willing wife made. He loved her taste, the warmth of her body, the grin plastered over her face when he rubbed her *sweet spot,* as she called it.

Rufus groaned as his cock woke up. And then, the old lovers froze, to floating music. Hidden speakers, he suspected, and he jerked his head to ascertain direction. Caro's eyes grew large as she whispered, "*Is someone here?*" quickly drawing up the sheet to cover their nakedness.

"No—I-I don't think so, Caro. I think it's just the music. It's that same song they played when we got here; remember? Probably some remote-control thing. *Christ.*"

She cocked her head to listen a moment. "Yeah, it's the same. Guess they thought we needed us some background music—the whole damn ocean ain't enough?" She resumed her ministrations and he took in a sharp breath.

The first time she had played with him like this he was twenty. How *crazy* were those early years . . . He was recovering from yet another skin graft, at home this time. His parents were away for the day and Caro had offered to "baby-sit," she'd joked. It was mid-September, a warm, Indian summer day and she'd insisted they sit outside in the shade of an old cottonwood. He'd agreed, just to be agreeable, and they'd sat quietly watching his mother's chickens peck for grit, when Caroline abruptly stood and slowly walked around to his side, lifted the green plaid blanket off his lap, knelt and began to unbuckle his belt, ignoring the prize rodeo buckle, all the while boring a hole into his eyes with hers.

It was the most sensual moment of his young life and he'd relived it time and again in more quiet moments. He recalled a horse whinnying, followed by another, and then felt her strong hand on his groin. Her eyes never left his destroyed face; she held his will in hers.

When she put her mouth to him (and he'd immediately ejaculated), he'd understood where his life might wind up after all: forever staring into the willful countenance of Caroline and being devoured by this *something* called love.

"Whoa there, girl!" He was wrenched back to the present.

She paused, eyes on him, "I ain't no horse, Rufus, so you can quit sayin' that."

He felt a dream-like stupor and well-being wash over him, as he surrendered to their lovemaking. She kissed him and then, he watched, amused, as she considered his wrinkly, old pink cock, against the silky sheets beneath.

"Well, we're shittin' in high cotton now, ain't we?" she said, then, she kissed him all over; his belly, arms, chest, neck, and last, every square inch of his face, especially the injured left side, where his external ear should have been. She licked him, like a she-wolf cleaning her pup, and he allowed it, sensing some great need or significance for her.

They had never spoken of the accident that left his face scarred. He had never placed blame. *What good would it have done?* he'd pondered, only once, then dismissing it for good. Why he found himself thinking about it now, he didn't know.

After a horrific fire destroyed the historic family barn and a prize stud (among other horses), leaving Rufus badly burned, area gossip ran that Caro's impromptu date to the Strickland's annual barn dance had started it with a carelessly tossed cigarette. It *could* have been dry lightning—what the insurance company had covered. But Rufus had learned another possibility, most likely the truth, given the circumstances. It had been Caro's cigarette. Friends of Rufus were also smooching behind the barn, near enough to Caro and her highfalutin' acquaintance, Henry-something, whose maiden aunt lived in Sara's Spring. The friends mentioned the cigarette, as a postscript, after relating this Henry's groping of his Caro. *His Caro* was how he'd always thought of her, since they were both too short to climb onto a horse without help. This other guy, Henry, was just, well, shiny.

He's the one gave her those pretty lamps. Well, I got her in the end, didn't I?

He held his Caro now in one arm and, with the other, led her to her joy. For the first time in their lives (he thought), she dropped the reins completely and he lay in awe.

"Caro," he said after several moments, "*I know.* I just want you to know it; I always have and it's *never* made a lick of difference."

He felt her stiffen, then sink into the mattress, into stillness, and then, he heard her whimpering.

"Oh, no . . . Damn it, Caro . . . *shhh, hon* . . . I didn't mean to make you sad . . . chrissake, no. I just think you've carried it way too long and, for some reason, it occurred to me here and now, and I guess I wanted to say it. I'm *sorry*—hon; please, *please* don't cry. . ."

She buried her face in the pillow and began to sob. He gathered her up to comfort her, feeling terrible for upsetting her. He hadn't thought this through and berated himself for being an idiot. "Caro, hon, it's all right, really. . . I'm a jack-ass," he said. Finally, she lay quiet; her breath even.

"You really . . . *knew?* About the cigarette?" She turned to face him and searched his eyes, his once perfect eyes, those she always saw.

He was sorely tempted to utter some smart remark, but refrained. Humor had its place, but at the moment, she needed more. He looked at her, their faces inches apart, and he summoned all his mercy for her, every drop, and poured it into his regard, that the *certainty* of his love might at last cross the too-many years of her secret pain and guilt.

He'd waited too long—his stinging regret.

They'd lived like a couple whose only child had died; any word of the loss forbidden—to protect the other—when the very mention, spoken with affection, might have eased their suffering. *One of those i-ronic things,* he figured. *Senga would know . . . but her child* did *die,* and he squirmed in recognizing a false equivalence.

Caro squinted at him, to read him, he knew, and her lips curled into a sad, slow smile as she moved to kiss him, a deep, long and precious kiss on his crooked mouth, to the soothing music of the waves and other melodies.

PART THREE

CHAPTER 27
THE HEART OF
EVERYTHING THAT IS

In a casual manner, he gestured to the woman much the way he'd once seen his mother do, the day she pointed out a robin's nest in the old apple tree. *Tom, Son of Robin!* she'd called. He'd been five, and now remembered the aftermath with grue in his gut. He'd leaned toward the branch where sat the nest, when the smooth, blunt snout of the snake (in this case, a nonvenomous bull snake) reached around a leafy twig, opened its jaws and snatched the babies, not quite fledglings, in one fatal lunge.

Shrieking, the boy had fallen backward off the chair and lay quaking on the ground.

His mother had ignored him to run into the kitchen for a broom with which to chase away the snake. He'd lain paralyzed with fear as he watched the serpent slither down the trunk of the tree, the hapless prey bulging behind the jaws, to crawl silently beside his catatonic body and pass within five inches of his face.

The recollection had crystallized into one, dark burst of energy and Tom Robinson blew out in response. He gestured for Senga once more to follow.

The rain fell harder and he could offer her shelter. In his secret place.

He watched her consider a moment and move forward, tentatively. Like a fawn. Stepping over several, now-slippery stones, he offered his hand to her in assistance and, at last, he spied the large, rounded boulder to be rocked in and out of place by a steel tamping bar, stored nearby for the purpose. The rain pelted them, driving out all other sound, save thunder. Working quickly, he set the end of the bar into a notch on the boulder, then leaned the bar over an entrenched rock, sharply ridged— his fulcrum—placed to require the least force and, stepping back, he pressed with some effort on the far end of the tamper. The rock shifted and slipped into another position, to reveal the black maw of a hole. He replaced the bar beneath a fallen trunk and beckoned again. Seeing her surprise amused him, and was that wonder?

He drew a breath and lowered himself into the space, then called to her to follow. It widened to reveal a small entrance. He gave her room to enter, by retreating into the darkness, then motioned her behind him, in order to move a screen of sorts into place.

Each spring, he'd cleverly (he thought) woven a new "portal" of pine boughs and dried grasses for camouflage whenever he paid a visit. He mimicked a previous tack to protect the entrance to this hole in the earth. As chief of maintenance, it was his duty to guard against such hazards, never mind the discovery. In the low light, he saw her squint in deliberation.

"Where does it go?" she asked, as she tried to peer down the *throat*. His word. He saw her shiver.

"*Shhh,*" he said, finger to lips and, reaching behind her, his eyes holding hers, he produced a wool blanket hanging from a root protruding from the wall. She drew a quick breath in astonishment. He explained he kept one against cooler temperatures and rainy days like this. Facing her, he held the blanket up behind her, spread it between his arms and shook it against possible insects, then he wrapped it around her shoulders, handing her the corners to hold. A more intimate encounter, he could not recall. At close proximity, he caught her scent; *rain fresh and minty*. Through the pine screen, the gray light played with her appearance; she resembled a wild person—an early inhabitant of the region.

"Oh, one thing, *Root Digger*—promise never to speak a word of this place to anyone." He waited, watching her eyes for hollow falsity. She frowned, then nodded solemnly. "Say it," he insisted.

"I promise."

It had cost her to say the words and he wondered why. "When I first saw you, I loved your braid," he said as he studied her hair. Embarrassed to have uttered the personal statement, he looked away. He didn't want to see her reaction, for fear she might find him amusing. He feared being thought amusing most of all. Cocking his head in the direction he wanted her to follow, they advanced.

He bent low and gestured for the woman to do the same. Squatting through the narrow passage, he smelled dank earth, and then remembered he'd left them absolutely in the dark. He was familiar with the route, but the woman might be frightened, so he reached into his inside jacket pocket and withdrew his cell phone for the flashlight feature.

He heard her half-gasp behind him as the light illuminated their narrow way. They were descending at an almost thirty-degree pitch. From her perspective, they may as well have been traveling through a worm hole. A *large* worm's hole, he imagined she'd think. The narrow dimensions would bother someone with claustrophobia, and he felt remiss at not considering the possibility. He asked, "You all right?"

"Where does this go?" she repeated, but her tone implied no suffering, so he didn't answer. *Less said, best mended,* his mother always said.

"I *said,* where does this *go?*"

"*Shhh. . .* You'll like it, I promise; now, be quiet . . . please."

"Tom, come on—how long? I'm expected somewhere."

"Just a bit more. It's worth it."

He lost track of time, as happened on these *journeys*—how he thought of them. He'd read his Jules Verne. . . The center of the earth was a real place; *the heart of everything that is.* The Lakota got that right.

Behind him, Senga sighed, then swore as she bumped her head on the low ceiling. As he'd once done. Repeatedly.

"Okay—now you have to crawl on your belly for this part, but it's only about twenty feet. At the end, you can stand up. Ready?"

"*Fuck, no, I'm not ready!*" she whispered harshly. "You've got to be kidding, right?"

That she was easily provoked, he knew, having witnessed the grocery store incident, but he didn't think she was *timid.* Would she turn round and leave? She'd be in the dark; so maybe not. He spoke to her.

"You're not a coward, woman. I saw you pull a knife on a guy. This is easier. Now, buck up," and he moved to continue, with or without her. He heard her swear again, but it sounded resolute.

This was his least favorite part of the passage, but he knew what lay beyond, turning it into a quest. He relished the thought of being the one to show her. The effort required to scoot, prone, on one's stomach, never grew less tedious, even along a downward slope, and he could hear Senga's grunts behind him. The blanket could pose a hindrance and she may have cast it aside, but no matter. There were others. He was glad he'd cleared debris from the tunnel last year, making the crawl less loathsome.

At last, he reached the end.

Carefully, he set the phone out of the way ahead of him and advanced the last few feet, until he was completely through, then, he took up the phone, pressed something and an LED bulb lit the area. After a quick surveillance, he determined that nothing had changed. Nothing ever did. The scene was a particular and solitary frame, lifted from a sequence long gone. One sound could be heard here, sometimes two, as now; water dripping into water, to create a singular, wet echo, and the rolling grumble of muffled thunder.

My forehead was sore where I'd knocked it against the top of the tunnel. On stone. I'd managed to drag the blanket with me as I struggled across the ground and, at last, I felt a cool breeze— no, not so much a breeze as the clear certainty I had reached the end of a trial. I also saw a semi-luminous glow. While not the proverbial light at the end of the tunnel, it passed.

"Tom?"

"You're here."

Where's here? I wondered, sore and out-of-sorts.

Finally able to stand, my body stiff in several joints, I pulled the blanket around me, and when I'd taken a deep breath and analyzed my circumstances, vis-à-vis various bumps and scrapes, I nearly fell back to the ground. Tom caught me under my arm and raised me up, as I heard him say, "Whoa there, woman," for the second time in seven months. Same pitch and emphasis. The first time involved his pulling me off someone, my digging knife in hand, ready to do harm, I believe.

"I'm okay. *What*—" I was rendered speechless.

He laughed lightly, as he directed the light over his head into a vast cavern. When my eyes adjusted to the dim picture, I tried to adjust my brain to what I was seeing.

"I have another light. Wait here," he said, as my eyes grew wide with frustration, as in *where would I go?* He turned and stepped away, leaving me in the dark, and I watched him approach an odd collection of rubbish, as the British would say. Why this word came to me, I don't know, but it described what one might find in a boy's tree house: a small table, roughly fashioned from three boards into a U shape, to raise it off the ground; a cushion (to sit on, I presumed); a wooden box (for treasure?); and a clear bag—the kind blankets are sold and stored in, and in fact, there was the blanket. Tom unzipped the bag and pulled one out. There remained another and the flashlight. "We can have a fire, if you like," he suggested quietly, as he returned with the light. I turned it on and lit the near-apparition before me.

I felt a damp chill, whereas before, I hadn't. The cavern was dank and no wonder, for before me lay a black pool of water, nearly round, measuring possibly seventy-five feet in diameter. I wouldn't have been able to see to the other side, if not for a glittering outer ring of some bright substance that reflected the light. *Mica? Fool's gold?* After my sharp intake of air, I heard Tom whisper, "It's gold, Senga. Can you believe it?"

No. Frankly, I couldn't believe my own eyes.

"Look up," he next had the nerve to say, even if in a hoarse whisper.

What next? Tinker Belle?

My wits must be returning, I thought. To be glib, even in my thoughts, signaled my usual defense against the truly bizarre, but I had another tack; crouching, I placed a palm on the ground, to ground myself, to touch earth—an action I had not felt necessary in recent memory, now made twice in one morning. Minute dark grains, like dead fleas, clung to my hand when I held it up to the light. I swiped and clapped it clean with my other hand, flashlight resting under my arm, and then I rose. Humidity hung in the air, reminding me of a moonless, cloud-covered summer night in North Carolina before an all-night rain, and I understood why Tom whispered in this place.

It was a *dark,* dark place. Who knew what could be awakened?

Remembering my ruse, I told Tom, or *Tom Robinson*—his preference—I really needed to go, that I didn't want to cause worry.

"*Look up,*" he spoke again, ignoring my plea.

I did. Stalactites, of a size I'd never seen in any *National Geographic* magazine, pointed to the pool from the pale, lace-like ceiling of the cavern. My guess—at least forty feet above the water. "Are there bats?" I asked and immediately regretted it. Of course there were bats. Millions of them. They comprise twenty percent of all mammals.

"Come sit down, and I'll tell you an incredible story."

"No, I'm leaving, Tom—*Robinson.* I can't stay. Rain check?" I said brightly and turned, but he put out his arm to prevent me and I caught the imperative in his intent. *I would best comply,* it told me.

"I'll go and tell them you're with me. There's food in the box, and water. I'll be right back. Please, Senga? It's a great story."

He must have thought I was meeting Joe, Milo and Moona'e again. He sounded so reasonable, so . . . *sensible,* and I found myself nodding, even as I felt conflicted.

"Good. You'll love it. I know you will . . . you're . . . someone who would."

Someone who would. . . He guided me to the cushion, where I sat down, cross-legged and wrapped now in two blankets. He set the makeshift table to one side and the box on the other. I noticed the box was fitted with a small padlock. Reaching inside his shirt, I watched him pull a chain over his head. A tiny charm dangled from it. "Here's the key. For when you're hungry and thirsty. You have the flashlight with you."

"Yes," I stated abstractly, my mind still on the key; *locked against whom?* Taking a knee, he slipped the chain over my head.

"Good," he added, gently. On rising, he extended a hand toward my blanket-covered head, but held back, and then he stepped behind me.

Over my shoulder, I asked where to pee if I needed to. Silence. When I turned in the direction of the tunnel, to utter darkness, it was too late; I was alone.

CHAPTER 28
WHEN BIRDS QUIT SINGING

Tom Robinson knew he needed to restock the box in the cave, but the superintendent had emailed a long list of work requests. After a quick bite to eat, he hurried to the maintenance shed and began. When he next looked up, the sky was dusky, with filaments of light blue, layered between apricot-colored streaks, too light for a first star, but later than he thought.

He swore and quickly completed the oil change. Snatching up his wallet, he placed it in his back pocket and started for the store on foot, located just outside the park. The temperature felt mild, so, no jacket required.

He dreaded this time of day, between daylight and dark. Dusk felt otherworldly to him. Give him either absolute darkness or high noon, any day, he'd once decided and, quickening his pace, he lengthened his stride to let his mind reach for secrets he held in his heart and in his hidden place. He hadn't returned, preferring the knowledge to the evidence of his secret.

At the Trading Post the clerk greeted him, a regular customer, by name. He bought bread, peanut butter, several protein bars and two liters of water. He set out again, walking briskly beside the dark road and watching for the trail head. His back to oncoming traffic, he heard an engine rev, and caught the wavering flash of headlights gone awry. He twisted round. After a sickening crunch, he felt himself flung upward, still somehow grasping the plastic bag. The dark road rose to meet him, then came a *crack!* from the area of his head, followed by silence.

A camper reported the accident as a hit and run, a car having made a quick U-turn out of the park, and Bob Mills—the law enforcement ranger—arrived shortly. After covering the semi-conscious victim with a blanket from his trunk, he asked the camper to describe the vehicle. The man shook his head. "I can't. Not really," he admitted, but nevertheless tried. "It was older—maybe a 70's model, shaped like one of those long-ass cars, you know? Like boats? All I know is the poor dude went flying into the air."

"His name is Tom. Where were you exactly?"

The rough-looking man wheeled to get his bearings before pointing to the sign about prairie dogs. "Me and my boy, we'd just reached that, to read it. He's pretty good at it, for a seven-year-old."

The ranger noticed the flashlight in the man's hand, and winced at the thought of a kid having to witness the incident.

"My boy, he says to me to look at the car driving funny, so I did, and then's when we saw the guy gettin' hit."

"Where are you staying?"

"The campground—where else?" answered the camper. The boy stuck like a bur to his father's pant leg and said nothing.

Ranger Bob Mills thanked him and requested his phone number. He told him to stick around, adding, "Please," at which the man smiled, saying, "We ain't goin' nowhere for a couple days, at least."

Bob swore under his breath and made a note. Deadwood, South Dakota, was hosting a car show and dozens of vintage autos were swarming the area, rally-like. This would be tricky, he knew. He placed several calls.

The ambulance had arrived and EMTs were carefully lifting the injured maintenance man onto a gurney, to slide him into the vehicle. Barely groaning, he was badly injured, from what Bob could see, his head already wrapped in a bandage. *Internal injuries,* someone suggested. They were barely acquainted, he and Tom Robinson. The man wasn't a talker and kept to himself. Bob had only met the man's mother once, and now she was gone, he remembered. Who, if anyone, to contact?

Flashing lights on the ambulance marred the once-serene park atmosphere. Bob was grateful they omitted the siren, but it was strangely quiet; the birds had long quit singing; the prairie dogs had scurried into their holes. A group of silent onlookers, none of whom were witnesses, stood off the side of the road, needing to know what happened.

The next morning, Bob spoke to the emergency room staff. Tom Robinson was placed in a medically induced coma, while physicians conferred. He'd been hit squarely in the pelvis and thrown, to land on his head—what the camper had seen and heard. Why Tom hadn't suffered a broken neck was anyone's guess. The danger lay in brain injury and the hip was broken.

Bob returned to the site and recovered the grocery sack, still containing a plastic jar of peanut butter, as well as two-liter bottles of water. The empty wrapper to a protein bar and a bread bag, torn apart, lay a few feet away. *Food for wildlife*, he dimly observed. He gathered the items and, as he stood idly gazing toward the picnic shelter across the prairie dog-pocked field, he noticed the car. A gray Honda hatchback. It'd been parked in the same spot for a while. He'd been trained to notice things; *what day* was *that?* The model was ubiquitous and must have blended with other vehicles. Berating himself for negligence, he walked over to it. A local license plate number. He ran it and learned it belonged to one Senga Munro, who lived north of Sara's Spring. He called the admin building to ask if anyone by the name was registered to camp. No, came the answer.

"Well, hell," he muttered and after trying the doors and finding them locked, he checked the interior through the windows. Nothing remarkable or amiss. He called Chief Charlie Mays in Sara's Spring.

"Hey, Charlie. It's Bob at the Tower. How're things?"

"Oh, can't complain. Pretty early yet though. What are you up to this morning, Bob? Never mind. I know what you're up to; how can I help?"

Bob's prominent brows knit in puzzlement. "Uh, I've got a car here—been parked for a few days. License says it belongs to a Senga Munro. Know anything?"

"Senga's? Didn't you have a hit and run last night? Heard it on the scanner."

"Yeah. That's a stickler, too. So, who would I call to ask about this woman?"

"Want me to? Sounds like you've got enough going on."

"Yeah, would you? Let me know and, thanks, Charlie." Bob pressed the button to end the call and started back, toward the stretch of road where Tom was hit. He still wore a frown and, raising his hand to his forehead to rub it, muttered, "*Damn* it, Tom," as he began to comb the area for anything that might have broken off the car. Any clue at all.

Chief Charlie Mays had a *semi*-soft spot for Senga. He'd helped deliver her baby on the side of the interstate highway back in '84, when he served as a state trooper. And later, after joining the Sara's Spring police department, he kept tabs on her while she twisted off in the months following her daughter's death. His jurisdiction being narrow enough to allow it, he'd given her just enough rope to buck it out of her system, like a too-wound-up yearling mustang in a round pen.

He'd escorted her back to her house in Sara's Spring from the bar on more than one occasion when she could barely stand. Another time, he remembered—and wished to God he didn't—yanking her ass out of a pickup cab, stinking drunk, where she was getting ready to give a hunter (judging by his fluorescent orange vest above unzipped pants) some attention. And finally, one fine day, Charlie realized he hadn't had to jerk her line in a long while and, when he next saw her she seemed sorted out, even peaceful. They had never spoken of it.

So, now what's she gone and done? He called Muriel, who was his girlfriend and Senga's supervisor.

The phone rang, just as Gabe was fixin' to slide his and Jake's eggs out of the skillet. "Want to get that, Jake?" he called. Rufus and Caroline were in town running errands and easing back into their routine.

"I can't!" he heard from the bathroom.

"Oh, all right." He quickly set the pan on an adjacent burner, covered the eggs with a lid and reached for the wall phone. "Hello."

"Mornin', Gabe. It's Charlie. Say, Senga Munro's car's been parked out at the Tower for a few days, I guess—Bob Mills just called. Know where she is?"

"Senga? Um, no; I guess I don't. Last time I saw her was, oh, about two weeks ago, when she took Caroline's mare out. It was a Sunday. Are you concerned, Charlie?"

"Well, she isn't registered to camp and, yeah, it's bothering me some. Had a hit and run last night, too."

"*What?*" Jake entered the kitchen and Gabe gestured to the skillet on the range. "I could run over to her place, if you like. Hey—you have her number? Her cell number, I mean?"

"No. Better give it to me."

He did and they hung up. Charlie had also told him that Muriel had met Senga at the Tower the previous Monday for a walk, but she hadn't shown up for work since. Muriel hadn't worried because Senga might have just gone off on another one of her trips, but, "It's not like her not to say."

No. It isn't.

Gabe felt queasy. He told Jake he'd be right back; to go ahead and eat. The boy's features altered to those of concern. *Damned if he isn't the spittin' image of his grandpa*, thought Gabe, qualifying the notion in light of Rufus' once fiery circumstance. He told Jake to go ahead and feed the critters, if he wasn't back in thirty minutes.

Gabe backed his truck out, crossed the car gate and was soon heading north toward Senga's. Pulling up at her mailbox, he opened it and withdrew four bags—Monday's, Wednesday's, Friday's and yesterday's. *Today's Tuesday;* he had to think. A little over a week. *The days get away from you.* He shut the mailbox and turned onto her drive. When he stepped from his truck at her place, he noticed an utter presence of absence. It was deathly quiet and he shuddered. Not a cricket, cicada or frog. July was normally abuzz with honey bees pollinating plants in the area, but not today. He closed the cab door with as little noise as possible. Taking the mail bags with him, he crossed to the cabin and, stealing a glance toward the garden, frowned at the wilt. Nothing had been watered in days and the storm must have passed south. He noticed the sprinkler, dropped the mail bags and, after entering the enclosure, walked to the water pump and pulled the lever. A burst of spray shot into the air. He could almost hear a sigh from the plants.

A red geranium on the porch looked worse for wear, too. He touched a finger to the pot. Bone-dry. Beside it stood a plastic jug of water. "Here you go, *chère.*"

Her door was unlocked. Senga only locked her cabin when away for the day, or when traveling—the circumstance having increased, he'd noted. He felt uneasy, lifting the latch. . . On entering, it smelled faintly of herbs. Several bundles hung beside the door, drying, but he was overcome by the stronger reek of trash and under the sink sat the culprit. Rotting chicken skin and parts. He quickly pulled open the window above the sink.

"What the hell, girl?" he asked aloud. Glancing in her bedroom, he only saw her bed, properly made. He took out his cell phone and swore at seeing "No Service." He pulled the trash from the cabinet and tied the bag to take outside, then watered a second dry red geranium on the table. Using the landline, he dialed her cell number. It went directly to voice mail. "Senga, hon, call me when you get this. Please."

He wished she had an answering machine, but Senga, being Senga, didn't. Sebastian's photograph of her gave him a start. She stared at him. "Where are you, *chère?*" he asked the face.

Gabe was rarely one for presentiments; he considered himself pragmatic—if ever hopeful—but something tugged and didn't feel right. He pulled open the drawer in her table, where he knew she kept writing materials. Pushing aside her journal, he sat down to scrawl a quick note, asking her to call when she got back. Maybe her friend Joe had given her a ride somewhere, he speculated.

Sebastian. He knew him to be in New York City this week, where Gabe should have been, but he'd asked his publisher to reschedule the publication party for late September, when he and Francesca planned their honeymoon. It was a good solution, they'd thought. But first, he picked up the receiver to call Francesca at the Blue Wood.

"*Gehb?*" she said, "Where are you? Senga's, you say?" She sounded sleepy.

"Yes, I am, darlin'. We, uh, can't find her. Have y'all talked in the last few days?" He didn't want to alarm her, but how not to?

"No, I have not talked with her, not since she and Sebastian returned, *Gehb*. Now, I am afraid. She is not herself, do you know? What happened to them in Ireland, *caro mio,* it scared her."

Gabe didn't want to admit his fears, but he'd also noticed Senga's altered state of mind. "Don't worry," he told her, "I'm sure she's just gotten busy with something. I'll let you know when I hear something."

They hung up and he stared out the window, across the ravine, to the red cloth dangling from a twig on a tall ponderosa. She'd told him about the Indian, possibly a scout, who was there and then not. *Whoever you are,* he began, *find her? Please?*

He looked down at his phone and located Sebastian's number.

CHAPTER 29
TO PICK AT A CARCASS

The trail ride wound through the Black Hills National Forest. Yesterday's rain meant footing was slick in places for the horses. They could have waited a day, thought Jim Wilson, as he brought up the rear. Ahead of him, the paint gelding had nearly dumped his rider when the old horse's hindquarters splayed, then recovered.

"Matt, how're you doin'?" Jim asked the remarkably composed boy. The wrangler enjoyed the kids, most of whom had never ridden.

"I'm all right, Jim. You?"

"I'm good," the wrangler replied.

All boys, their ages ranged eight through thirteen, and Joey rode point to his intrepid line of campers. Jim had made sure to take the new, young hire out several times before the young campers arrived, to ensure Joey's ease when the day came. Apparently, his strategy had worked, but Joey was a quick study. Jim mentally sent Gabe thanks for starting him. He chuckled to himself. The Kid, as Joey was nicknamed, minus the *Sundance* bit (no sense in glorifying that one, he'd figured) had managed to transform himself into the fantasy of every boy's dream. *Well, at least those when I was growing up,* he amended. Jim had helped The Kid collect the proper regalia, much of it gleaned from his own, seldom-culled wardrobe. Some clothing was fifty years old, but how Joey had chirped when he saw it, as if he'd discovered gold. Jim figured the shirts and vest looked authentic enough. For good reason. They were the old-time duds the kid liked, and not a rhinestone to be seen. Ms. Mary, now *she* liked her rhinestones. Mostly on her backside pockets. But then, she rarely rode. *Seems like those would pinch like hell,* Jim mused as he ambled along, lost in his daydream.

The string of horses and riders moved in single file, through bracken growing along the narrow path. They were headed for a particular, old-growth aspen grove for a picnic, one of his favorite places in the range. Every fall, golden leaves and white-and-black bark of towering trees blazed against the deep blue autumn sky. It thrilled his soul. For some reason, the image put him in mind of Larissa Ivanovna. Last fall he'd pulled her and her child from a snow bank not far from here. . . Thoughts of the woman accompanied his horse's ambling gait with a bittersweet cadence. He didn't shrug it off.

Lee Rogers and Lily, the new student nurse, were to meet the riders around noon with the grub wagon, commonly called a pick-up. Jim's stomach was already growling and they had at least thirty more minutes to go. They would soon join the Forest Service road, and (he hoped) meet no logging trucks to spook the horses. He listened. Nothing but quiet, counterpoint plodding of hooves on the sometime-squishy earth, squeaking saddles and occasional comments from the boys.

They were good kids. Not a brat among them, he thought. *But it's early.* They'd arrived three days before and, after the first evening's Welcome (what Mary called it), he thought his boss's experiment just might work. (They strove for as much authenticity as possible, being reminded often, by Pete, of a young person's nose for hokum.) Lee's perpetual grin peeked from his snow-white beard. Lupita and Pete happily worked together, preparing meals and organizing picnics and "special events," under Mary's instruction. Francesca assisted Mary and continued to rustle up new clients from Europe by tending the website and paperwork.

Joey had been a damn good idea, Jim thought, recognizing how much *he* did on the place. Now he had a hand. That the boy had been involved with the Berry place concerned him some, so he paid extra attention to his new bunkmate's behavior. *So far, so good.* Besides, Gabe and Francesca vouched for the boy, which counted for something. And, his younger age proved helpful with the campers.

A beep interrupted his ruminations; he had a text message. Unlike driving, checking a message while riding posed little trouble for him (if annoying), as Mike, his trusty mount, could fend for himself. All day, if necessary.

Have you seen or heard from Senga lately? read the text from Francesca, back at the Lodge. He typed one word and tapped *send*.

No.

Gabe reached Sebastian, who told him he'd be on the next plane from New York City. *Who has seen her?* he'd asked, not having been able to reach her by cell for over a week. He'd believed she was simply immersed in work or other activities. Gabe could only speak for himself. Caroline and Rufus, as far as he knew, hadn't spoken with her since their return from California. But Muriel, Senga's colleague at the library, had been on a plant walk with her nearly two weeks ago and reported she hadn't spoken with her since that morning.

"Look, man, Muriel thought she was with you," Gabe said, then heard the Dane groan on the other end. "Charlie—the police chief—questioned her; she's angry at herself for jumping to a conclusion. . ." This would do little to lessen Sebastian's irritation, Gabe knew; he omitted what else Charlie had said to his girlfriend—"Not to worry," that Senga was, "one of those free-spirit types." An observation he'd foolishly repeated to Gabe; it denoted lazy thinking, for a cop.

After speaking with Sebastian, Gabe felt his guts churn. He'd called from the ranch road turn-off, where cell reception was better. He needed to make another call, but could use the landline at the house. *Where are you, girl?* Scrolling his phone numbers for Fr. Joe Rafaela on the Cheyenne Reservation, he found he didn't have one, so he put his truck in gear and drove home, all the while shoving away dire thoughts and worry. He needed a run.

"Hey—" he called to Jake and Rufus, as he jogged past them toward the ranch house. They were heading to the paddock. Rufus gave him a short wave. Gabe sprinted around to the kitchen door, let himself in and went straight for the telephone on the wall. On the red counter, sacks of groceries waited to be unpacked. He raised a finger for "wait" to Caroline, who was preparing to speak. From Information, he acquired the rectory and Fr. Joe's phone number. He dialed it and a woman's voice momentarily confused him.

"St. Kateri's," she'd answered.

"Ah, hello. This is Gabe Belizaire. Is Fr. Joe Rafaela there, by chance? It's important."

"Yes, and is this an emergency?"

"I'm not sure. I'm a friend of Senga Munro's."

"Senga? This is Sister Joan and, yes, she's spoken often of you, Gabe. I'm surprised we haven't met."

"Sister Joan, yes; me too. Ah, is she up there? No one's seen her for over a week, and her car is parked at the Tower. I thought—hoped—she'd gotten a ride with y'all or something."

A moment of silence, then, "No, Gabe. Joe hasn't seen her since May. They're planning to go soon, though. I'll get him; he's over at the church. Can you hold, or do you want him to call you back?"

"I'll hold and, thanks," he said. Caroline was standing at the counter, concern crisscrossing her features. He was sorry for the two, deep furrows between her brows. They appeared more pronounced lately, despite the much-needed vacation.

"Senga's gone?" she said quietly, as she emptied a sack.

He put a hand over the receiver and took a breath. "No one knows where she is, Caroline."

He watched her slowly shuffle to a chair and sink down.

"Hello? Fr. Joe? Yes, it's Gabe Belizaire. Have you seen her, or spoken with her in the last week or two?" No, the Franciscan hadn't seen, nor talked with her, but he'd received a letter about three weeks ago, describing what had happened in Ireland, and he'd planned to see her when next they came.

Gabe read the man's tone. *Worry.*

He hung up the phone and after a moment turned to Caroline. "He hasn't seen her, but they'll be down . . . says his adoptive father is good at, ah, tracking." He scarcely believed the word he heard himself saying.

Caroline slowly stood and crossed to the refrigerator, opened the door and pulled out the pan of last night's roast chicken. "I'm making soup with this. Better stay busy," she said, as she turned away from him, so he couldn't see her face, he thought, and the groceries forgotten on the counter. The telephone rang. "Will you get that?" she asked.

It was Sebastian. He'd rent a car from the airport. Gabe told him it wasn't necessary, that he'd pick him up. After jotting down the particulars, he hung up. "He gets in tonight at 10:30."

Caroline only nodded as she picked the chicken carcass and placed the meat in a bowl.

CHAPTER 30
RECAPITULATION
Cave Notes

Cavern sounds invade my dreams. They come moist and tinkling. Of drips, their stretched silences extend over eons. I could measure time by them, like grains in an elongated hour glass. The rock breathes. My own breath, magnified, I suppose. Candles lay unlit; I postpone their use. Velvet fluttering of wings. First, a soft shhhh; then, a squeak and whoosh! as possibly thousands fall from pitch black above, to turn as one in dark murmurations, in stereo to my charged sense of hearing. I dare not shine the feeble flashlight beam upward. The bats swing to and fro for several moments. A great pendulum. I wonder if they're cognizant, but indifferent, to my presence in their lair. In their story. I can't tell the species. Do they know mine? Do they know my story?

Little brown bats were naturally small, near-feathery things. More likely, these were the Big browns, and I recalled they roosted in caves and emitted a high-pitched sound, their echolocation, which prevented their careening into my hair, the ever-mythological fear. Still, my gut lurched as I wondered exactly how far under-ground I was.

When Tom didn't return, I steeled myself to find a way out; twenty-or-so-feet of crawling again, then through the wider passage. *Piece of cake,* as Papa used to say. I buttoned my jacket, to secure my notebook, and turned on the flashlight feature. I had less than 10% battery life available to me. The difficulty lay in grasping the phone and crawling, so I'd reach, lay the phone down, scoot to it and repeat.

Until I couldn't.

Something blocked the tunnel—a huge stone, by the look of it, and in my prone position, there was little I could do to budge it. I managed to twist around in the narrow space and press my feet against the obstacle, but gave up after several tries. My anxiety mounting, I paused to breathe slowly and deeply. When I felt sufficiently calm, I started back for the cavern, all the while practicing even breathing. I calculated the amount of time it took to crawl back into my black hole and figured the pitch, an estimate, including that of the time from the entrance to the obstruction. Granted, a guess.

This rough math occupied me for several minutes or maybe hours.

The gift of thinking is not to be understated. Neither is the gift of a temper tantrum—which I unleashed upon my innocent environs. I leaned over and pounded the earth fiercely with both fists and I screamed; I thought she could take it. *How could I have been so stupid?!* Then, with my desperation reverberating, I settled back down near the box and blankets. *Strange*—no response from the bats. I lit the stub of a candle I'd set on the table. The flame was consuming too much of the wax, so I blew it out and carefully trimmed away a quarter inch of the wick with my knife, judging this between my fingers. When I relit it, the flame burned shorter, but adequately. A tiny sense of agency returned.

My calculations put me approximately fifty feet underground and it was impossible to judge direction. The trail I'd taken lay a short distance from the Tower, and I'd begun near the south side to hike easterly. The cell phone lay useless. In any case, the bats appeared to be the only critters, but the dripping water and glitter of gold, fool or no (when I'd trained the dim light on it), took on eerie characteristics of the living. I could imagine too well a sleeping dragon, Tolkien's Smaug, guarding his hoard as he lay camouflaged by boulders and unidentifiable objects, his long tail encircling the pond; his reptilian eyes closed, *or were they?*

What could loosely be called *time* passed—days? I hadn't decided to explore as yet—not for fear of dragons; not really. My mind conjured other dire possibilities. The real variety. To counter this monkey chatter, I chose to employ a method I'd learned along my curious way. *Recapitulation*—a Toltec shamanic practice. Sebastian had once asked why I occasionally turn my head as I do, as though I have a crick in my neck. I explained it's a habit to ward off certain thoughts and it seems to work for me.

I'd alluded to the Toltec method one evening, but it was late, we were both tired and I dismissed it.

"*So, Sebastian, if you're there. . .*" I whispered.

First, what did I want to release from my mind? Fear? Betrayal? The reason for my mother's sadness?

Where I grew up in Appalachia, "ruined" is pronounced *rernt*. The people there put more store on whether an object is *rernt* or not, as there is so much less available, and means with which to buy. Things are cared for over decades and not tossed at the first sign of decay. They are repaired. When a thing is ruined, it is *truly* that and mourned as though a death has occurred. I learned what a ruined girl was, but until I read Grannie's letter, I'd never fully appreciated my mother's state; I'd only experienced her symptoms.

In a small home with thin walls, a child may overhear conversations, and as Grannie tended to the area's women, some would appear at our front porch, to sit a spell. One of these *rernt* women squeezed her heart out like a dishrag to my grandmother one day, when I was just inside, doing my homework. I don't know why this particular memory occurred to me now, but it did, so I let it unfold to cover a growling stomach. I was also reminded of acute hunger.

The gist of the woman's complaint, confession or ailment was that she'd often been used by her cousin when she was young (I'd noted the verb, *used*). She proceeded matter-of-factly, with not much feeling: when she was married a few years later, she couldn't abide her husband's touch, or the act. "I *hate* it," I heard her say in a strong whisper, this *with* feeling. She'd come to Grannie for some kind of charm to help her "like it more." I'd listened harder for my grandmother's lowered voice, and caught the woman's sniffle, then her crying.

Grannie came through the door, glanced in my direction and went through to the kitchen, where she opened the squeaky pantry door, and I could hear her shuffle something on a shelf. When I stole a peek as she passed, she was grasping a *sang* root. Ginseng is purported to improve libido, but I didn't know it then. I also heard her tell the woman to stop drinking anything stronger than coffee, tea or water immediately. That the *sang* couldn't work with it.

"What's the matter with her," I asked Grannie, after the woman left.

"Oh, dearie, she's just *rernt,* that's all," I remember her saying, ". . . but, she likes the *likker* and that'll kill any shine she has for the man. The root I give her may or may not help, but it could give her some comfort and courage—like she's doing something for herself."

Oh, Mama. . .

So much came down to agency. *And a good place to begin,* I sighed.

The last water bottle was nearly empty and I hadn't found the nerve to test the pond, for fear of too much alkalinity or base salts—what the Black Hills steep in. High pH can be lethal. Alkaloids are the poisonous or drug-like properties of a plant, i.e., caffeine, nicotine, cocaine. The smell of my urine after a meal of asparagus occurred to me in an odd sensory apparition. The odor is the alkaloid *asparagine* being sloughed off. An example of a less-poisonous effect, if, to some, unpleasant.

I resolved to investigate the water, to see if I could distinguish any white residue that might indicate alkali. It was either that or go bat-shit crazy, which was something I *could* smell, even as I thought it. *Guano-loco.* How long could one survive in a place encrusted with it? *Shit.* And could I find water where bats hadn't flown *over* it?

The former idea seemed the wiser choice over *crazy.*

To learn something had been Emily Dickinson's solution when beset with difficulty. But first, *Recapitulate!* I ordered myself and began.

Sitting cross-legged, with the blankets pulled round my shoulders, I breathed slowly to quiet my thoughts. Even the bats hushed. A loud *plop!* caused my eyes to fly open, but all was still after, and I attributed it to something falling into the water from the high ceiling. (I felt an affinity for the element of water, for speaking to me in this way. I felt less alone.) Closing my eyes again, I exhaled as I turned my head to the left.

What exactly was I recapitulating? The intent was to weaken the effects of a particular trauma and to recover my energy (or power)—twin purposes of the practice. But *never* had I wished to lessen the impact of Emily's death—however traumatic it was. No; it would always be a part of me, as much as my lungs, my liver and my heart. Our energies were one. Intertwined.

And therein lay the proverbial rub.

The gentle epiphany, like an invisible velvet wing, brushed my cheek.

We cleave to myriad associations in remembering an event: music, the weather, scent, the occasion and place; but *emotion* may adjust to reminiscence (as strong as any musician's *muscle* memory, as I once heard Rob explain it). Painful associations may be reduced, even released.

To begin, we bring to mind the sum total of our recollection, including *all* our associations with an event (consciously accepting the *unconscious* as a given) and, in particular, how we feel about ourselves around it. Of course, the emotions are paramount. In a way, we paint a canvas (or compose a symphony, or construct a building, et cetera). The exercise eventually scrapes, or peels away, the overburden of paint to reveal a blank canvas. One serenely weightless. This is to be hoped for. . .

A French philosopher—which, lost to me now—believed we [*truly*] have only two choices: to live or die. I inserted "truly" and dismissed the philosophical angle. *Was it Pascal? Sartre? Camus? Descartes?*

So, what was I recapitula—? Before completing the word, I knew. Tom Robinson's betrayal for one, but more important, I'd once told Sebastian he was "free to pursue his own passions . . ." I'd meant it as observation, with regard to his photography—his art no longer ruled by advertising overlords. Could I recapitulate my own naïveté? *Or,* Sebastian's frailty, in light of (*O God, let there be Light!*) the woman's madness? Both? *All,* I heard and understood.

I understood.

The growing possibility of my death had taken root and, the sense of probability, even in this poor soil. Aiming to prepare, I yearned to forgive and self-forgive for having held a thing poorly, unskillfully, in my heart. For lack of wisdom, love and compassion. Tom Robinson was—incidental, if also. . . The image trailed away, replaced by his pulling me away from doing harm that day last fall.

So, I began, and when finished, I inhaled long, slow breaths through my bandana and felt peace rise from the earth.

I was in the underworld. No *king* had abducted me to where I had followed my daughter after her death. I had dispatched some shade of myself as envoy to the surface to live out the years. More Demeter than Persephone. The woman reflected in my cabin window last fall is here too, in whom I sit. She managed to cross some barrier to find me, to lure me here. *To effect a reconciliation?* I've often wondered what precipitated Sebastian's reappearance, as though chance demands a reason or explanation for our meeting nineteen years after our singular encounter.

But I was posing the wrong question. . .

The more salient query demanded: was I going mad? Here, in this dark place? I avoided the obvious, germane to my survival or my death, afraid to test the water.

Literalities boggled the mind.

I shook my head to dispel dizzying notions, laid my pencil and notebook beside the candle, careful not to drip hot wax on me, and reached for the bottle of water. After a small sip, I screwed the cap back on, twisted around to replace it in the box behind me, closed my notebook and put it and the pencil in my pocket. After moving the candle to the ground and twisting it into the dirt, I steeled my nerve to stand, still gripping the blankets. My muscles felt stiff and cold from the damp and I had little energy. What food I'd discovered in the box was long gone, save part of a protein bar I was rationing.

I needed to get out. No one was coming. There was no future in this place (I wasn't being glib) and the past did not exist.

Crumpling back down into my blanketed cocoon, I moaned in discouragement. Tom Robinson's blocking the tunnel entrance demanded another solution. It was time—in this place of *no* time. Counting drips had only served to exercise my *sense* of time passing, when the truth lay closer to my inhabiting a time loop, where action, sound and circumstance were cyclic. My being in this place was the anomaly and, if another existed, I would find it.

CHAPTER 31
THE LIFE

Across the border in Montana, at Saint Kateri Tekakwitha's Church on the Cheyenne Reservation, Joe Rafaela studied his reflection as he pulled on his chasuble for Mass. He'd continued to think of himself as a friar, or *Brother* Joe, despite his ordination. He wore the brown robe and white cincture most of the time, for its familiar, comfortable significance. As uniform, surely, and imbued with meaning. His assistant Joan, also a Franciscan, wore street clothes (as she described her wardrobe), harkening back to her work in troubled neighborhoods back east. In short, she didn't resemble a religious. It's something he appreciated about her: a complete aversion to false piety. The shorter veil and "lighter" habit (since the Vatican II revolution) made little difference to her vocation. *The clothes maketh not the monk,* she once quipped. He'd disagreed with her reasoning and they'd left it at that.

That morning, he'd awakened with a long-dead Cheyenne chief on his mind. High Wolf. Senga Munro had drawn the likeness after seeing a man near her cabin last year. It reminded Joe of George Catlin's 1832 painting of the chief at a younger age. After a short search, Milo, talented at tracking, had uncovered an arrowhead in precisely the spot Senga had watched a deer bound away from her subject's loosed arrow. Joe's research determined the chief had likely died at the hands of unhappy tribesmen. He speculated it might have pertained to High Wolf's refusal to trade with the *voyageurs,* who trafficked in liquor. He'd meant to write Senga his findings, but had been more than busy lately.

After telling Milo of Senga's disappearance, the old Cheyenne confessed a dark shiver down his spine and told Joe it was time to go join the search. Not until after a parishioner's funeral Mass and burial, Joe had reminded his adopted father. Exhaling, Milo admitted he'd forgotten, and that he and Moona'e could prepare for the trip. After the ceremonies, they were expected at the meal. Milo would speak with the widow and explain the circumstances. It would go down better from him, he told Joe. They could be at the Tower by mid-afternoon.

His grandpa laid down his fork, leaving half his supper, and gestured for Jake to join him on the front porch. The boy finished his meal lightning-fast and Caroline threw him a look, then motioned for him to go, adding she'd take his dessert to him. He grinned, wiped his mouth on his napkin and pushed the chair back in order to stand. After thanking his grandmother, he told her it had all been good (bacon and eggs, hash browns and toast) and he was soon seated beside his grandpa, who was hand-rolling his after-dinner cigarette.

Evenings shook and spread out their long tablecloths in July, with nature's banquet to last hours. The sun shone late enough to light a chore, or, like this evening, for resting easy on land one had worked hard. Coos from rock doves answered cicada rhythms, and Jake felt confident that nothing could ever spoil the peacefulness. He'd lived in a city all his life and the difference yawned too wide to cross, even when state of mind entered the argument.

A quick motion in the trees interrupted his thought and he scanned the area beside the barn and paddocks, something Gabe had taught him—that ranching was mostly a matter of paying attention. *Like everything else,* the black man had added with a grin. Jake liked Gabe a lot, but he loved his grandpa, who, with his grandmother, had been able to make him feel needed, relatively important and loved in just over six weeks. Even from California, their phone conversations had been real; their rapport, genuine.

No surprise he'd taken to The Life.

Gabe had presented it capitalized, with a flourish of his ebony hand, unabashed enthusiasm and an easy sense of duty;

"It's *almost* a religious calling," Jake had heard him suggest. In any case, sheep ranching tickled Jake's fanciful imagination and, by the time Gabe made his introductory remarks, Grandpa was able to "slide into home," he later joked, by greasing up the more tedious aspects of *the life*—lowercase. Jake snorted quietly with the memory.

"Here you go, kid—" Jake heard Grandma Caroline say as she came through the door.

He made to rise from the steps, but she told him no need and set the bowl of chocolate ice cream down beside him. Heaped high.

"Thanks, Grandma!"

"Want some?" she asked his grandpa, who shook his head, lost in thought.

"They'll find her, hon," she said to him, as she lowered herself into the Adirondack chair.

He leaned back. "They're still hard, even with the damn cushions, Caro."

"But they're better, ain't they?"

"Maybe a little," he said and squirmed. "Going to be a late night for Gabe—going all the way to Rapid for Sebastian."

"You think they'll stay at his place near Spearfish, or come on? I mean, if there's a search, at least he'd already be here," Grandma Caroline said.

His grandpa shrugged.

"Has this lady ever disappeared like this before?" asked Jake.

His grandparents both looked at him; *lady?* Then, at each other, and each took a deep breath. Grandma Caroline spoke. "Only once. Long 'ole time ago. She took off and was gone for a few days. That was before we knew her—when she still lived in town. We'd only heard things—like you do."

"Oh, yeah? Like what?" the boy twisted around and asked.

"Nothing that's any of your concern," his grandpa said, with accompanying look to his grandma.

"Sorry." Jake looked back at his bowl. He wasn't entirely used to his grandfather's appearance, as it was, but seeing it employed to drive home a point soured his stomach.

"Hon, now look what you've done. The kid's upset."

"Damn it, Caro—I didn't mean. . ." He stubbed out his cigarette and hauled himself to his feet (a little wobbly, thought

Jake) and nodded tersely for him to follow. Jake gobbled up the last bite, stood and set the bowl and spoon on the small table, with a quick glance to his grandmother. She nodded and gathered up the bowl to take inside.

"I'm not upset. Thanks for the ice cream, Grandma," he remembered to say.

"You're welcome, son."

Rufus rarely entertained qualms. He believed they turned your thinking off and worse, off-course. But qualms were different than hunches. Those could actually solve a mystery. He reviewed this notion as he made his way toward the barn to make sure the cats had milk. It was on Jake's list of evening chores, but supervision is supervision.

His grandson caught up with little difficulty. Rufus remembered being spry and quick as the boy. Seeing Jake at the same age he was at the time of the fire was giving him a turn of sorts. They looked that much alike.

"Grandpa?"

"Yes, son?"

"I-I didn't mean to. . . I mean, it isn't my business, that lady's stuff."

He chuckled. *That lady's stuff.* She'd think that was funny. He grunted, to dismiss the comment and get on with it. *But damn it, where are you, girl?*

Jake stepped ahead to slide aside the heavy door and they stepped through. The cats let out various meows and two impassively gazed up from their repose. Apparently not dying of thirst, Rufus decided. He took another deep breath and released it slowly, then pointed to a couple chairs. "Let's sit a bit," he said and crossed the aisle to where dusty chairs waited beside an empty stall. He smelled fresh wood shavings and smiled. *Good boy,* he thought. Might have been Gabe, but it didn't matter. The boy was learning the ropes. One of the cats silently appeared and brushed against his booted calf, to twist and repeat the affection.

"She's saying thanks, huh?" said Jake.

"That—or, 'more, please?'" He snickered, leaned down and stroked the big ginger.

They sat and listened for several moments. To the silence, within and without. Then, a night hawk whirred outdoors as it swooped for insects.

"Jake," Rufus began, "I'm grateful you came. Caro and I can't tell you how much it means to us. And I'm sorry—"

Jake had learned when to interrupt and when not to. "Grandpa," he broke in, "I'm . . . *sad* about the last six years, but I don't—I *can't* look at it as a waste. Nothin's *lost*, Grandpa, and I hope you don't think so. I figure I'm just getting the concentrated dose to make up for it—if nothin' else. . ."

Rufus made a sound between a grunt and a choke.

Jake stared at the ground as he made his point and Rufus understood. Some matters were often impossible to utter straight into another man's face, as though the words might somehow catch fire, or, dissolve in the communicating. No, this way was better and he waited, in case his grandson wanted to add anything.

The kid went on for another quarter-hour, quietly rattling off everything that had occurred to him since he'd arrived: his joys (in finishing a fence line); his frustrations (the same fence line); his wonder at being around sheep; and (most important) his gratitude. His grandson's soft talk purred like the cat. Rufus marveled at the kid's reasoned acumen for organization and priority. Some of it was Gabe's influence, surely; but Rufus detected his own father's voice—his sensibilities and dreams—the very ones he hadn't been privy to at the time, for having had his and his parents' lives interrupted by the catastrophe. *Hadn't been for Caro,* he reflected, ignoring her possible mistake, *I'd 'a been worthless,* he concluded, then he spit, barely missing the cat.

"Grandpa?!"

"Guess it better learn to keep out of the way. . . Uh, what did you say just now?"

"Oh. . . Well . . . Just, I was hoping you and Grandma might let me stay on, and I could maybe take some classes over at Black Hills State."

"That's what I thought you said." Rufus made another sound, paused, then regarded his grandson full in the face—for this had to do with *the heart* of a matter. *Like getting married,* he supposed. "Jake, son, it would make us proud to have you stay with us. And school's a good idea, too. Your mama, well, she'd buy that, now. Ha! I expect you thought it all through, didn'tcha?"

Jake nodded, a smile crossing his lips. "Gabe—he's the one told me to take classes. Ag, you know? So—did you ever?"

"Nah. But life was different then. Come on. Let's go tell your grandma."

Jake held out a hand and Rufus took it. When he gained his feet, he reached to embrace his grandson, the boy's heft made of heartier substance and stability, and Rufus closed his eyes to draw in every sense and force of the hold. They stood a moment longer before Rufus released him.

"Love you, Grandpa."

Rufus smiled. "Love you, son; your grandma does too. Well . . . come on; she'll be wondering."

CHAPTER 32
VERISIMILITUDE

"You there, woman?" Caroline heard as she neared the top stair from the basement. Rufus only called her that when he had something to say. *Well, what is it this time?* she wondered. *Maybe news of Senga,* she hoped.

After listening to Rufus' false efforts to downplay their grandson's monumental proposal, and showing her own unrestrained delight (which her husband finally shared), Caroline asked about the cats. Rufus and Jake had forgotten to bring back the milk jar. She offered to return for it, as an excuse to get out of a house that couldn't contain her joy. Once there, she refilled the barn aisle dish, then replaced the empty jar in Gabe's bedside refrigerator. Task accomplished, she was drawn to his writing desk and the magnificent lamp.

While the sun set on the opposite side of the barn, Caroline watched the muted play of soft pink, diffuse light from the east-facing window paint the colorful lampshade and reviewed her recent trip to Rapid City. She'd found an interested party for what she'd determined decades ago to be genuine Tiffany lamps, given to her by the mostly clueless suitor.

Leaning over, she nudged the bronze base a quarter turn, to better view the rosy, stained-glass grape clusters. The lamp lent an uncommon beauty to Gabe's writing efforts in the rustic room, never mind his saying, often, that he *liked* the smell of saddles and horse sweat; she'd hoped the lamp might inspire him. The second of the pair served a similar purpose in Jake's room—if not for writing, then in theory. The lamps had guarded their secret significance for more than sixty years.

She'd decided it was time to reveal it.

One day last week, she'd leaned against the door jamb of Jake's room to admire, maybe for the last time, his lamp's shine, color and *exquisiteness*, a word reserved for only them. She had made up her mind to "make them useful for her own designs." This was not the way Caroline normally thought or spoke. She'd read the phrase in a romance novel in California. In fact, the story had prompted her to have the lamps finally appraised, to sell them, and, to make it a surprise.

She'd traded out both with less inspiring models plucked from storage, and sealed the box with tape, declaring, "There you go, my pretties; make someone happy, wherever you wind up." Having prepared the box with sufficient packing material to safeguard her treasures, she'd met the broker in Rapid City. The quicker the better, to avoid second thoughts. An antique dealer in the city might give her something close to their appraised value, to have money left over after her proposed purchase. Or so she'd figured.

Following their meeting, Caroline had driven home, not necessarily dejected and, eventually, strangely calm. . .

Like now, she thought. The feeling may have had to do with Rufus' news that Jake was staying on. She'd found the idea oddly fitting and, more, welcome. *On the other blessèd hand,* as her mother used to say, the lamp he'd inspected was "not authentic," the broker had sadly informed her. After a sharp intake of breath, she'd pointed out the *Tiffany Studio* stamp on the base.

"Yes, yes," he'd said, ". . . they provided every possibility of verisimilitude."

She'd asked him to explain and he had; then, determined to hide her disappointment, she'd maintained her dignity, thanked him for meeting her and apologized for bothering him. He'd assured her he wasn't disappointed, as the lamp was breathtaking; that he'd rarely seen such workmanship outside the genuine article. Did she wish to sell it anyway?

She'd squinted through the bright café window to the busy city street and back to him as something tugged at her. She didn't show him the second lamp; one disappointment was enough, thank you. "No. I appreciate it, but I'll take it on home with me. What do I owe you?"

The broker shook his head in answer.

He didn't *seem* like a dishonest person, if he was, but she'd had little experience with the antique trade. No big deal; she'd do more research, she reasoned, as she stood and gathered up the box to leave the restaurant. He could pay for her damned coffee and pie.

On the way home, she'd cried for every second she'd invested such misplaced pride in the gifts of one phony like Henry Hollis Hannity Peterson. Her mother had been right. "Nothing's *free*, Caroline," she'd warned her.

She smiled half-heartedly as she switched on the still-*exquisite* lamp for Gabe's late return. The room glowed. In her mind she held back fear, palm up and stiff-armed, and demanded Senga to get on home, wherever she was. Unconsciously, she surveyed the room and her eyes strayed to a picture tacked on the wall beside the window. On closer inspection, it revealed a figure Caroline guessed to be Mary, beside a bright, vertical dash of yellow-white; *the angel*, she supposed. *Gabriel.* "Hunh," she grunted.

Caroline rarely paid visits to Gabe in his room and felt slightly snoopy.

Empty quart jar secured under her arm, she stepped down into the aisle, closed the door and returned to the house to join her husband and grandson.

CHAPTER 33
SINGULARITY

I thirst. What Jesus muttered from the cross. The bottled water was gone. I experienced a sketchy sense of time—it was merely a concept *once* known to me, like recess in grade school—the period dedicated to leisure, or school-yard gossip, or activity, like tether ball. A ringing bell to signal its end. *My end?*

I thought I heard a poorwill call. *Through stone?* Not likely. I felt abandoned by whatever force of nature gathered home the tides. Yes; I was finally lost at sea, where I'd run when I was seventeen, the Powder River Basin, emptied for eons, on my threshold.

God, I'm thirsty.

If I had a segment of *Echinacea* root, I could somewhat mitigate the feeling. The root produces saliva. Indians used to chew a small piece to give them stamina when crossing dry country. They still might. . .

Several beetles kept me company. They survive on baby bats. *Was this a mother cave?* The light buzz of insects came and went in weird circadian rhythms. They eat guano, they shit, sleep, eat more guano, shit and sleep again. Forever?

Days and nights collided in darkness. Up was down, down was up. Magnetics whirred between my ears and the obscene gravity of my situation grew. The reek of ammonia infiltrated the mask I'd made with my bandana, and I remembered something called *histoplasmosis fungus,* or cave disease, affecting those with low immunity. I banked on my reserves, which I'd thought to be healthy (save heart concerns).

What's right in front of you to do? I asked, and the pool of water beckoned, black and oily, like the slick city street it resembled when I'd first waved the flashlight over it.

I decided to boil a small quantity. I had matches and, strangely, kindling. Tom Robinson had built a fire here at some time, judging by the charred evidence. Charcoal smudged my hands and probably my face. I'd grind and stir a teaspoon of the substance into the water against likely bacteria.

Oh God, how I thirst. . .

Rising wobbly from having sat too long, I grabbed the metal cup from the box, lit the last so-called "emergency" candle (the flashlight batteries having died) and made my careful, shuffling way to the water, almost distracted by the glint Tom Robinson had called gold. The cool sand, soft and gritty at once, stuck to my wool socks, as my feet lightly sank into squishy earth. The bats swarmed and I crouched low, crooking my arms above my head and shoulders, drips of hot wax stinging my hand. After several moments I rose, and finally reached the edge of the dark water that simply *was*. No lapping. How elemental, how bedrock, how . . . desperate.

Candle aloft in one hand, with the other, I dipped the cup and mostly filled it, listening for the growing echolocation noises above me and deeper in the cavern. I vaguely speculated how high the cavern's ceiling extended, as one might blithely wonder how far the vault of the sky reaches. When Tom Robinson had aimed his phone LED light, tips of pale stalactites eerily dangled, like multiple swords of Damocles, from a dangerous darkness. *Above me. Now.* I may have said or thought *Fuck,* but if I did, the curse held no force. It was uttered in acquiescence, maybe humility. Even *awe.*

Back at my so-called camp, I arranged the kindling and set the cup in its midst. I used paper torn from my notebook to light a fire. The smoke rose straight up and I sensed no threat by fumes, save those from the *pissy* guano. *How combustible is ammonia in these conditions?* did cross my mind. I continued to wear the bandana over my nose and mouth. Meanwhile, I scraped charcoal from a burnt piece of wood onto the top of the box, then mashed it into a powder with the side of my knife blade.

How long to boil the water? I wondered. One minute? Two? I waited two minutes, counting, listening to it fizz and sputter as

I added small pieces of pitchy kindling, holding some back, in case. I would imagine no further than "in case," but dehydration concerned me. I'd risk the water to which I added the black grains, making a slurry of sorts.

After it cooled a little, I lifted the mask and took small sips. My throat stung with the moisture, then relaxed. I nibbled on the last bite of a protein bar from the box, constituting my meal, warmed by the dying embers of my fire. The average temperature in caves at this latitude (I'd once read) was forty-two

degrees. Holding the warm metal cup in my cold hands to my lips, I savored the trickle of warm, if thickened water on my tongue and the grainy richness of my morsel, chewing slowly to prolong it. Afterward, I wanted to cry, not because it was gone, but for the pleasure. But I didn't cry. No tears available, it seemed.

In absurd fashion, the matter of dark matter occurred to me, while trapped in my singularity where time and space stop. *Something* was binding my molecules together... *Dark matter may be more accurately described as 'invisible matter,' as it doesn't emit, absorb or reflect light,* occurred a phrase from one of Joey's science lessons. I'd begun to *believe* (how unscientific) I could nonetheless see (*sense?*) photons of light as pinpricks and bright spots, viewed as through a colander. I inhabited the colander.

Hallucinations, reason suggested. Yet, these persisted and I allowed fancy to do her will with me; *The Lights*—my loved ones through the years, come to comfort me in my private Gethsemane; *sorry, Jesus.* Then (I thought) I saw torch light beyond the pond, retreating and disappearing into another passage on the other side of the water. Remembering what fresh horror those torchbearers had ultimately brought the god-man, I wept dry tears in fear, despair and desolation, for the terrible mistake of Emily's backpack; for the worry my disappearance might cause; for not having sufficiently loved my soul.

"*Sebastian!*" I finally cried aloud, my voice hoarse and unfamiliar. "*Gabe? Rufus? Caroline. . .*"

Shrill echoes rang round me, as though my cries had rearranged molecules along sound waves. For a long moment, I feared earthquake and I froze. Then, the poorwill called again, answered by another. *How?* I wondered, and my overworked mind prepared to shut down, even as the bats renewed their explorations. I accepted the very real chance I was surrounded by half-a-million of them. *What's a half-million?*

I sipped the remainder of the water in a daze; it tasted of wood and then, metal. For simply being heated in it, I hoped.

After stirring sparking embers with a length of kindling, I shoved the box farther away so I could lie down, curled beside the comforting glow in the darkness. The ravaged face of Rufus appeared behind my eye lids and I wished him and Emily goodnight.

CHAPTER 34
SMALL COMFORT

On the rural, mostly two-lane scenic route to the regional airport to pick up Sebastian Hansen, Gabe's thoughts bounced scattershot toward—one, his friend's disappearance; two, her boyfriend; and, three, a work-in-progress about Wyoming small towns and their predicament. If not exactly *predicament,* then a situation that might predict—*demise?*

Having merged onto the interstate, he passed the national cemetery near Sturgis. *Tidy rows of white dominos.* The phrase occurred to him naturally, if sadly, by association, recalling the memorial in Italy Francesca had shown him, Senga and Sebastian. The image of a stark gravestone marking his great uncle's remains continued to haunt him. Peripherally, more compelling than an idea one simply accepts. His little brother's death by drowning, more than a quarter century ago, fell under *Things Hard to Accept,* along with meanness, willful ignorance and arrogance.

Sebastian's plane met with delay in Minnesota, so Gabe visited the city library to research a question scratching the minds of Wyoming legislators; *some, anyway,* he amended: What makes one small town successful and, conversely, what contributes to another's demise? *That word again.* He'd explored rejuvenation and considered it (*maybe*) key. Possibilities inherent in the arts, technology, education and tourism suggested a common nexus—one that required better broadband capacity. Better communication in general. Trickier might be the willingness on the part of residents to acknowledge and address root causes of scarcity, addiction and stagnation, with solutions embedded in the very questions.

Examples and solutions jumped out at him like roadside deer at nightfall—only to be run into by a speeding pick-up on a lonely, dim stretch of road. Slowing down seemed to answer one condition, while increasing bandwidth speed addressed another. A paradox, where answers often lay. Days of relying on oil and coal to fund state government programs were past. It was time to move on; not out of the state, necessarily, but hitched to a new star, or paradigm, by pulling a sturdier wagon.

The fundamental hitch remained: *who might be left behind?*

When the library assistant whispered near his ear that they were closing, Gabe was astonished at the time. He'd found good sources and was engrossed in an article, taking notes, but would pack up and drive on to the airport. After making copies of the material, he left with a tug on his hat brim to the librarian. The airport restaurant came to mind and what he might choose for supper, when a chill passed through him. In August. Senga was somewhere, unknown to him, her lover and her friends. In his gift for concentration, he'd managed to put this aside, or *compartmentalize*, as some used the word. He picked up his cell phone and called the ranch. Caroline answered.

"Hey. Heard anything yet?" he asked.

"Nope. You?"

"Nah. I told you those friends of hers from the reservation are coming down, didn't I? The one is good at tracking—not that it's anything we'll need, right?"

She ignored the comment. "I'm gonna make up a bunch of sandwiches. 'Spect you'll need 'em when folks show up to help."

"Why do you say that, Caroline? You know something I don't?"

"Nah. That's what we do, women, when there's an emergency, Gabe; we make a shit-load of sandwiches to feed people, you know? Gotta go." She hung up abruptly, as usual. He recognized distress in her more-than-usual brusque manner.

At 11:30 p.m., he watched Sebastian stride purposefully toward him, duffel in hand and shouldered satchel. The man looked bleary-eyed, as though he hadn't slept in days.

"Gabe. Thank you for coming. I would not have had you do this, my friend. Please, any word?" They clasped hands after

Sebastian set down his bag, and Gabe slowly shook his head. He wondered if he should mention the tracker. *Not yet.*

"You hungry?" he asked the Dane.

"No, thank you; I ate something earlier. Ah, shall we go straight to Senga's cabin? I'd rather be there. Do you mind?"

"Of course not."

The traffic at night was normally light and they were soon headed northwest, toward Wyoming. Gabe stole glances at his passenger to judge his state. *Not good* was obvious. To make small talk or not, he wondered. Sebastian beat him to it.

"When did you say your collection is being published?"

Gabe might not consider it small talk, but treated it as such. "Thanks for remembering, man. . . Um, it's been pushed back till next month. Francesca and I are planning our, ah, honeymoon in the city. May as well go *big* city, *eh, mon ami?*" He took comfort in Cajun talk, its sweet cadences and terms of endearment.

"I—*we*—look forward to both occasions, Gabe; your wedding and reading your book. Was it postponed for a reason, may I ask?"

"Well, yes and no. My dad's been sick, but he's doing better. Allie—that's my sister—wanted to come to the reception Caroline is hell-bent on hosting . . . in the barn, of all places. I don't think it'll happen. Their coming, I mean. And the publisher wants me to attend a pub party and all the hoopla that goes with it, as close to the publishing date as possible, so. . ."

"Ah. I see. I'm sorry to hear about your father. Serious?" Sebastian reached into his duffel at his feet and pulled out a light sweater. He pulled it over his head. "I feel a chill," he said.

Gabe looked at the man and started to speak, but didn't; then, "Kidney trouble. Daddy's undergoing dialysis. Francesca and I may go see him, but not until—" He couldn't bring himself to mention Senga and wouldn't speculate. He glanced through the window to the passing darkness. *Where are you, girl?* The image of her face from the cabin's photograph loomed briefly in the dark sky. "How did the show go in New York?" he asked.

"Ah. We did well. Sold several, it seems. Senga's a star. Gabe—" He began, then paused and gazed into the distance. The moon was waxing full, illuminating the far hills. "I am . . . in trouble, as you say."

Gabe shot him a look, then back to the road. "What . . . do you mean?" he asked.

"I'm sorry. That was dramatic. It is a language difficulty, I think. I am *most*—" He choked up and Gabe glanced back at him, then activated the turn signal to pull over. The truck rolled to a stop, he put it in park and twisted in the bucket seat to better consider Senga's friend.

"We'll find her, man. Likely, she'll turn up on her own. She's resourceful, you know. More than most. My resilient friend—I mean her; not you," he added with a half-smile.

"You are right, Gabe. I feel an enormous burden of guilt since Ireland, and I do not know how . . . how to *reconcile* with her. What I mean is—we have lost something precious, or I should say, *I* lost it and would do anything to have it back. Do I make sense?"

Gabe took a deep breath and silently composed himself. He nodded in reply. "Let's maybe leave all that for now and find her first, how 'bout?" Gabe projected as much compassion as he could muster. How to help beyond that? Relationships were, and always would be, a complete mystery to him—his parents', his and his sister's, Rufus and Caroline's, his and Francesca's. He was mulling this when he found himself staring at the Dane, who had broken eye contact to gaze out the window.

"It is beautiful, no?" Sebastian said. "I love this country—I mean this particular countryside."

"I knew what you meant, man." Gabe pulled the gear shift into drive and they rolled back onto the road, absolutely devoid of traffic.

They had driven a couple of miles, when Sebastian leaned forward, as though searching the side of the road for something. "Please—stop here, will you?"

Gabe swerved and abruptly slowed, to stop once again. "What is it?"

"I . . . want to see if it's still in place."

"If what is?"

"Oh—come and see, if you like." Sebastian unbuckled his seat belt, opened the door, stepped out and closed it quietly. First, he surveyed a ghostly horizon, the black and gray of the hills under bright moonshine, iron-red in daylight. A breeze lifted his hair off his forehead and Gabe noted the wistful and tormented expression on the man's face. The Melancholy Dane in person, he reflected, then removed his seat belt, stepped out and followed his mysterious friend down through the borrow pit and up the opposite side. They tramped through tall summer grass to reach a thing he couldn't see. *How did*—

"*Ahhh,* it is still intact. Good."

"What's intact, man?"

"Oh, I created this little shrine for Senga's daughter. Did you know this is the very spot where she was born? Yes! You did not know?"

Gabe shook his head and pivoted to gain his bearings, then leaned over the shining bowl, its golden letters reflecting brilliantly. He squatted to better inspect it.

"Do you have any water in your truck?" he heard Sebastian ask. Spoken words interfered with written ones in the bottom of the bowl: *Here were you born . . . flaxen-haired child. . .*

He turned on his heels toward Sebastian in a slow movement; time and motion converging in a moonlight epiphany. Smiling at the man, he stood. "You thirsty?" he asked.

"For the bowl, Gabe. It . . . it is part of the magic, you see."

He did see, and he saw Senga's friend and his suffering and the solution. More love—the *only* solution. "It's beautiful. What a thing you've done. So, when did you—"

"Last fall, before I returned to Denmark—" His phone chirped and he reached for it, excusing himself. He spoke Danish to the caller, while Gabe wondered why Senga had never mentioned the shrine. He returned to the truck for the bottle of water stored behind the seat. Holding it up for Sebastian to see, he then tramped back through the deep grass, twisted off the cap and poured the contents into the waiting bowl. The letters wavered, as though dancing. He sensed the magic and the significance; water had to be represented. The elements—fire (by the bowl's manufacture), earth (in the clay) and air (by virtue of being surrounded by it and, on occasion, by the bowl containing nothing but). Gabe brought two fingers to his lips, then held them over the place for a moment, in blessing and prayer; for Senga, for her lover, and, for the child.

After Sebastian thanked him for stopping, they drove several miles in silence, then he related the call from his daughter, Erika. "She's upset. You see, she's grown not a *little* fond of Senga."

Gabe coughed. The man showed a talent for understatement and subtlety. *Sort of like small towns in Wyoming.*

It was nearly 2:00 a.m. when Sebastian bade Gabe goodnight from Senga's cabin and watched him drive away under bright moonlight. Reaching down, he plugged in Emily's tree, thus learning the reason for Senga's devotion. The light created company and he felt less alone; moreover, he felt her near, if merely invisible. *Where are you, love?*

Beyond tired, he faced the yard and groped for the seat beside the cabin door and lowered himself to it. He would sit a moment and allow a place named *Starwallow* to soothe his rankled nerves. The stars, the moonlight on the opposite ridge and a night bird's two-note call conspired to calm him. He turned to the tree to send a thought, its mirrors yet glinting and waving in the light breeze, then he bent to unplug the cord for the night.

Indoors, a rank odor hinted at the trash Gabe had removed. He opened two windows to create a draft, then brewed a cup of linden tea. As he waited for the water to boil, he regarded the large framed photograph, still propped where he had placed it on Christmas Eve. He regarded his lover's image and exhaled slowly.

As the tea steeped, he lit a scented candle, one of several adorning the cabin's three rooms (if the bathroom were included). The flame encouraged him. He was glad Senga had adopted the Danish custom. The electric water kettle clicked off and he waited for the boil to rest, then infused two teaspoons of linden leaf. Meanwhile, he took his bag to the bedroom (requiring an airing as well) turned on the lamp and raised the window. On the bedside table, he noticed a letter; its pages casually open at the crease, as though someone has just laid it down to take up again after a task. He deliberated, then lifted it, easily justifying a look, if it could shed light on her whereabouts.

The handwriting was scrawled and spidery, much as was his grandmother's, and he turned to the last page for the signature. *Grannie.* The woman was long dead, he knew. Chances were, he would learn nothing, but he would read it, nonetheless—only because his Senga had done so recently and it might bring her closer to him. He carried the pages into the main room, sweetened his tea with honey and, settling in the blue wing chair, began.

Waking with Senga's name on his lips, Sebastian groaned and, turning to her pillow, he inhaled her scent. He had slept poorly to the plaintive bird call. The letter's tragic contents wrestled with her disappearance. *Are they related?* He rose, made the bed, closed the window against the morning and walked into the kitchen area to heat water for coffee. How pronounced was her absence. Everything he touched was imbued with *her* touch, intention and life. Reaching for the coffee press high on a shelf and, bringing it down, he saw *her* actions. He and Senga were one, it seemed. The same had happened after his father died. In extending his own hand for a thing, he saw his father's.

This felt like that.

The coffee was brewed, but the milk had soured, so he poured it outdoors on a shrub, as Senga would have done. He noticed a lone crow inspecting him from a branch and so, proceeded to the garage for the peanuts he knew Senga kept for the birds. Platform refilled, the crow sailed down to it, only after Sebastian had reached the porch steps. Back indoors in a cabinet, he found a box of graham crackers and ate three. His watch read 7:50 and Gabe would come at 8:00, he'd said, to take him to the Tower, where a search party gathered, including the Blue Wood Ranch staff and guests.

Gabe would be late.

CHAPTER 35
OLD MEDICINE
Circa Early 1800s

After first crawling through the narrow tunnel on their bellies, High Wolf, or "Pup," as he was then known, was happy to be able to stand at last, and he stuck to his father's tracks as well as possible, insofar as he could. The earth seemingly fell away with each moccasin footstep, in rapid descent and, once, he tripped forward into his father, causing him to knock the man before him.

"Pup! Watch where you're stepping!" said the man behind him, who was carefully wielding a burning torch of pitch pine, its smell competing with humus and age. "You do not want to be burned," he warned. Each of them carried a bag, slung on their backs and tied securely in front.

The boy apologized quietly and wished he were back in camp with his playmates.

The underground passage appeared to have been in use for a long time, he decided, as he noted the evidence. Objects filled niches: shards of old pots; a beaded pouch; a handsomely carved antler in the shape of a spoon. He was surprised by the last. A utensil was usually offered to someone for use, surely, and not cached away like this. He wondered why as they continued, single-file, to descend where, he did not know. But he would learn presently, and this motivated him to attend more closely to his movements, the quiet swish of his leggings urging him on.

Far ahead of him and his father, he heard the insistent call of a poorwill, the night bird. His father replied in kind to the leader in front. He loved to hear his father's imitations. Some said his calls were the best in camp. He never appeared to work at them;

he would open his mouth and out they came, like startled butterflies on a fruit tree.

Pup paired images with sounds, always. And vice-versa. They awakened him on occasion.

After a long while, the line halted. Pup watched and listened with interest, as ahead more torches were lit and his eyes widened in wonder. They were standing at the mouth of a great cavern. His father pulled him close, as a noisy wave of bats appeared, swirled and rose higher. Pup wondered where. High above the small group, beyond the firelight, all was blackness, but ahead, with the aid of torches, he made out a lake or pond of sorts, round, with shining matter circling it. He had heard of a substance the white men particularly craved. They called it, *gold*. Is this why his father was being so secretive?

He wanted to ask, but dared not speak, for fear of bringing shame down upon his father. He would wait and watch. Someone passed him a skin of water and he drank, grateful for the fresh taste. He handed it to the man beside him. The black water looked more than brackish. He had been taught to avoid such.

Someone gestured for the group to squat, in order to rest, and Pup was glad. They formed a tight circle. The medicine man began to speak in low tones and, now and then, his father and the others would respond with the voice of agreement. Pup absorbed all and it was given him to understand that they were here to leave the medicine bundle of a certain old man, and more. He and his wife had died in the not-so-near past, childless, their bleached bones collected from the scaffold upon which they had been laid. The man had died of venerable old age, while his wife had chosen to end her life, in order to be with him and not burden the tribe. Pup remembered his mother speaking to his father about it one cold night after the bones were retrieved. It had moved him.

The shaman reached for his bag, as did the others, and each withdrew a sinew-tied bundle, apart from the dead man's medicine bag, which was smaller. Pup's father had carried this and now he held it out to Pup, speaking to all, "This is my son, called Pup, who will one day carry his people's troubles, cares and joys, not unlike this bundle."

Pup stared at his father in dismay. He did not know what to do and glanced at the man beside him, who gestured with his lips for him to take the bundle from his father. Pup stretched out his hands and accepted the soft leather bag, rolled and tied on both ends. He held it in his lap. In the poor light, it resembled an ordinary bundle. He'd seen dozens. But what his father had just pronounced circled his mind, like a bobcat eyeing a possible meal. He wanted to rise and run back through the passage, back to his mother's side. And then, he felt ashamed.

"Come," the medicine man said, and all stood with their share of bones and crossed to a wall, where they were instructed to leave them in specific niches, after being removed from the leather hides. Pup looked on, fascinated. He wanted to ask questions, but remained silent, hoping to speak with his father later, in private. The medicine man then instructed him where to place his bundle and this he did.

After the ceremony, in which the shaman burned sage for blessing and purification, wafting the smoke toward the recessed ossuaries with an eagle feather, the group spent time in circle to smoke the pipe. They passed it over Pup, who was too young. His father leaned toward him to wipe a smudge of dirt from his face. His garment was filthy, *like everyone's,* he'd noticed in the firelight, from crawling through the beginning of the tunnel.

His father whispered to him, out of ear-shot of the others, "This day you are witness to a *thing,* my son, and no—not only what we have just done with Old Badger's bones. . ."

"And his woman," the boy supplied.

"And his woman," his father gently agreed. "When we leave this passage and are once more above ground, we will each do our part to seal the entrance, so none may enter and uncover our sacred burials. More and more, the strangers come. Do you understand, my son?"

The boy nodded solemnly. "And the . . . *gold?*" He watched his father sigh.

Half-smiling, the man said, "That you know the white man's word for it saddens me, for you have surely also learned of its accursed importance to them. But, yes, the knowledge will be buried with our peoples' bones in our Grandmother Earth. And hear me now—" he whispered more forcefully, ". . . you are entrusted with a great secret, and one day you may tell *one* other, but not for a very long time, my son. . ."

The others had risen to their feet. "Come. Let us go from this place," he said to the boy, extending his hand. Looking about wistfully, he added, "It is a *wonder*, is it not?"

Pup recognized his father once again in the man's awe and turned to commit the place to heart as well as he could, given the poor visibility. After, he fell in place, the torch-carrying warrior once more behind him, while they made their strenuous climb toward the entrance, through a passage that would take long. Would it be dark when they emerged? he wondered. *And how will we seal off the way?*

Pup was put to work gathering boughs and small stones, all his size and strength would allow, and, after a lengthy and difficult effort, entailing the placement of large boulders and many smaller ones, the once-discoverable entrance to an ancient bear cave (it was told) would be so no more. He stood back and watched with a shudder, as hundreds—likely thousands—of bats escaped from the shrinking portal into the dusky sky, as his father and the others continued to haul stone after heavy stone, and chunks of fallen timber and earth in the now-empty skins. They would close the entrance for good, where before, a simple structure of clever camouflage had concealed it for generations. Some said, since long before the time of Sweet Medicine.

A poorwill call woke me from a dead sleep. A small mound of burning embers persisted, in contrast to outer darkness. My throat was scratchy and dry, and when I tried to swallow, my tongue felt swollen. I'd dreamt of Rufus. Strange, to see him scar-free and vibrant. He'd said nothing; only smiled at me, looking like Christmas morning. The bird called again and I rose on an elbow with difficulty, to better listen. Another answered from a distance. I'd heard them earlier, I thought, but dismissed it as impossible. And here they were back. *How?*

The second bird call left behind a deeper-than-possible silence. I'd set about rearranging the increasingly moldy-smelling quilts around me, when I was startled by the glimmer of moving torchlight out of the corner of my eye. My heart skipped a beat. I felt a squeeze and anticipated the angina. My hand flew to my pocket, where aspirin and nitroglycerin waited. *I* waited too and mercy won, but the torchlight's glimmering shadow remained. Hope welled in me. I pulled on my boots and quickly drew the laces tight through the grommets. Moved to finally stand, I secured the blanket round me, leaned down to where I'd squirreled away the candle stub—nearly tipping over from weakness—and touched the wick to a coal. A flame danced and I gained inspiration by it. Having begun to explore the now-glowing part of the route twice before, I trusted my steps to a tapping stick and, advancing slowly for my faulting balance, I made to carefully ring the edge of the water, keeping an eye on the eerie glow across the way.

When I realized it was retreating, seemingly deeper into the cave, I hesitated, then whispered, "*Fuck it,*" and continued, but afraid to call out. I discovered a new path (of sorts), devoid of hidden objects to trip me, aided, as mentioned, by one of the long twigs my captor had somehow managed to carry in, strapped to his back (I'd imagined), like an old-world peasant. The path appeared to lead in the direction I wished to take, my candle glow bobbing up and down and, after several minutes of training my eyes between it and the dark ground (the flame actually making it more difficult to distinguish depth), I risked blowing it out, to rely on my stick and instincts, and whatever they might bring. I was glad for the quilt, however, and kept moving, hearing only my labored breathing and the skittering of insects. No poorwill. An occasional sound of water turned my head, but I'd quickly return my attention to the far-leading glow.

After a long climb, the light weakened, the passage tightened and I was forced to crawl. I abandoned the quilt. This tunnel, unlike the one I'd arrived by, smelled differently; I detected the pungent scent of burned sage and welcomed it. Another old-old odor arose, like the boxwoods in my Grannie's front yard, or what escapes after opening a long-closed chest. I took comfort in all and persevered, the faint light as guide—and hope. The incline took reserves I would never have thought I possessed, and I heard myself (as though my consciousness inhabited the entire cave) sob at one point in desperation, frustration and, yes, anger. My crawling form could either die down here or keep moving, the choice. I slammed back into my body and kept moving.

"EIGHT SECONDS, GIRL!" I heard loudly in my head—*Rufus?*—as in a bad dream, and all I had to do was wake up. I snorted then coughed—the dry, wracking fit causing my limbs to convulse. And then, I saw it—*light*. Whether twilight or bright moonlight, I couldn't tell; but diffuse. Not torchlight.

I didn't wait for halleluiah choruses, but muttered thanks.

"SEVEN SECONDS!"

Like one kicking harder to reach air after being submerged for too long, I scrambled, grunting unearthly noises of desperation.

Then came the bats.

I felt them rush over and beside me by the hundreds—maybe thousands. I figured (from some dim corner of my left brain that still functioned) that I occupied an area approximately thirty inches in diameter. Lying flat, arms crossed over my head, I felt their webbed wings and bodies lightly push the air as they passed, and I pressed my forehead to the earth. Their smell recalled the furry sweetness of kittens I'd snuggled with at Caroline's last year.

"SIX SECONDS, GIRL; *MOVE YOUR ASS!*" It *was* Rufus.

The bat squeaks grew louder and louder and, once again, I was thrown into darkness as their numbers blocked the light. I wondered how many more there were, but within moments I was alone once more, and for the pearl-like presence ahead, I renewed my efforts.

"FIVE SECONDS! *HOLD ON.*"

I tried to evaluate my condition, but dismissed this as asinine and continued my jerky, painful drive toward my sole intention, anxiety crawling up my throat in absurd analogy. All else had vanished into the seemingly shrinking shape of light ahead as I struggled to remain conscious and evade panic by repeating what Rufus had earlier cried in his raspy tone: *move your ass, move your ass;* and then—

"FOUR. . . THREE. . ."

All the time I had left. *Before the bull stomps me.* That much I'd figured out. My notebook kept catching through the jacket fabric and, after struggling for it, with a mighty heave and cry, I pitched it forward, into the light.

When and if I did pass out, I would be *on* the Earth. Not *under* it.

CHAPTER 36
JUST SITTIN'

Caroline was passing a fitful night. She lay still, listening to a persistent poorwill through the open window and mulled the opinion of the antique broker. Having gotten up twice, first to use the toilet, then, to stand at the picture window, overlooking the moonlit ridge, she sensed something wasn't quite right and couldn't put a finger on it—*besides Senga gone missing,* she added. A frown twisted her face as she returned to bed. She rubbed the pinched area between her brows, then rose a third time. Reaching for her chenille robe, she thought she'd go sit on the porch. From the mantel, her anniversary gift from Rufus chimed three times.

The front door stood open to the screen, in moon shadow. She paused. Rufus had had the same idea and there he was, sitting in the Adirondack, his back to her, in his tee shirt and long john bottoms; *just sittin',* he often called it, cigarette fixings ever beside him. Visible from his position near the railing and lighting a good deal of him, the bright circle shone high in the sky, washing all nearby creation in a quicksilver bath. Gus sat beside him, staring off in the same direction as his master.

The poorwill called again. Caroline, watching and listening from inside the screen door, couldn't make out what Rufus was intent on. She decided to leave him be and quietly turned round. Funny she hadn't noticed he wasn't in the bed. He never took up much room, unlike her. She climbed back in, laid her rough hand on his pillow and finally fell asleep, listening to the night bird.

In the early morning, she was awakened by Jake's gentle call. "Grandma? Grandma, wake up, please. It's Grandpa."

She rolled over to no Rufus. "What's that?" she asked Jake to repeat himself.

He held up her robe for her. His face looked—*all cockeyed,* she thought. "What's the matter with you?" she asked.

He said nothing, but led her from the bedroom, looking backward two or three times, as though she might disappear herself, like Senga. When they reached the front door, he stopped. "He's out there, Grandma. In his chair," he said and extended his arms to embrace her.

She knew what the matter was.

"*Oh, nooo*—" she moaned, though it sounded more a loss of vital breath, an aborted attempt to cry, the last syllable lost to the breeze.

Rufus was sitting in the too-hard chair, despite a cushion; his head resting against the back; his forearms stretched on the seat's wide arms. In near perfect posture, he seemingly gazed at the grove beside the barn fifty yards away, where he'd often watched for wildlife, or to simply admire the cottonwood, chokecherry and ash trees. He was peaceful, and he was gone.

"Get a blanket, Jake, will ya?" she told her grandson, then stepped around to face her husband. "God damn it, Rufus," she muttered, as her knees buckled, then she crumpled, her head dropping to his lap. The right arm slipped stiffly and awkwardly from the arm rest to find her back, as though on purpose, and his torso shifted in response. She wasn't going to cry; no, she wasn't and then, she did. Gus, who'd been standing by, not expressionless, slowly ambled over and leaned against her. He let out one short whine.

Gabe had just stepped through the sliding barn door when he heard Caroline. He pulled it closed and hurried toward the ranch house, where he could plainly see the front porch.

"Oh, no—oh, *Lord, no*—"

At 6:10 in the morning, the air was fresh and he filled his lungs with it, then uttered a quick prayer of one word: *Jesus.* Jake was passing through the front door, holding open a blanket. The boy visibly deflated, or relaxed, when he saw him; Gabe couldn't tell which. Jake moved his head slowly from side to side, then spoke to his grandmother.

"Grandma, Gabe's here."

She sat back on her heels after clinging to her dead husband; she sniffled and wiped her eyes on her sleeve, then patted the cold hand of Rufus that hung in the air. Pushing herself off her knees to stand, she reached for his thick shock of white hair to lovingly comb her fingers through it—*to tidy it,* Gabe thought. He slowly walked up the porch steps and drew another deep breath.

The clouded eyes of Rufus rested calmly on the grove.

"Mm, Miss Caroline, may I?" asked Gabe, his palm reaching for the white forehead, as though to shield it from the morning sun. She nodded and he moved to pull down the lids, but couldn't. "Aw, *patron.* . . Here, Jake, let's move him indoors. There's a chill," he said, unnecessarily.

Caroline snorted and burst into tears again. "God damn it, hon," became her refrain between sobs. The body was stiff and carrying it through the door and into the bedroom required some effort. Caroline covered Rufus with the quilt after they turned his body on its side. It was frozen in the shape of the chair. "I don't know whether to laugh or cry," she said, choking on the words. "Now, him, he'd-a thought it's hilarious!"—which only brought on another crying jag.

Gabe agreed that Rufus would have thought it funny.

He glanced at Jake, made a tortured sound and reached for Caroline. She clung to him, mewing, as he said, "I'm so sorry, hon. *So* sorry. He surely didn't do this on purpose," he said *with* purpose, at which she grunted a mirthless laugh amid the cries. Gabe spoke soothingly into her ear, "Now Jake's here for you, you know, and so am I. We'll help in any way we can. You know that, *chère.*"

He held her until her breath returned to normal. *What's normal now?* he wondered. *Damn, Rufus.* A knife twisted in his guts.

After his friend and boss was somewhat properly laid out on the bed, covered with the quilt he'd slept beneath for most of his life, Gabe set about fixing breakfast, whether or not anyone was hungry. He brewed a strong pot of coffee and fried bacon and eggs. Jake took care of the toast. Caroline sat at the kitchen table, charged with making a list with the pad and pencil Gabe had pointedly handed her.

"We need to call the coroner, Caroline . . . and your girls. Someone will come for Rufus and take him to the funeral home. It'll take a while to get here, so y'all have some time."

He hoped he was saying the right things to his friend, more than mere employer through the years. His heart broke for them all.

"Jake—how many eggs do you want?" he asked.

"Um, I guess two or three."

"Which? Come on, man—"

"Okay. Three."

"Caroline?"

"I don't want nothin', Gabe, but thank you."

"Nope. Won't do. Just a little something to sop up that coffee. You'll, ah, need your strength, hon." He stood beside the stove, ready to crack eggs, his watering eyes fixed on her. She stared back with equally determined, if bleary, brown eyes.

"All right. One egg and a piece of bacon. Be right back," she said, pushing her chair back and disappearing down the hall.

He needed to call Sebastian. *What do I do? Go look for Senga? Or, stay and tell the man to take my truck?* He sighed as he adjusted the heat under the pan.

Caroline returned after a few moments and told him what he was going to do. "I'm gonna call Haley and Leigh, then that coroner . . . Jake's here with me . . . and you're gonna go look for Senga, you and that boyfriend of hers. We'll do here, Gabe, but before you go, we got us more sandwiches to make."

She managed to eat a few bites and down a long swig of lukewarm coffee. After wiping her mouth on the paper towel napkin, she looked, *for all the world,* he thought, like a fragile, completed puzzle, unsupported, that might break into its million pieces on the spot. But he knew she wouldn't. She'd had her cry. At least the public one.

CHAPTER 37
SILENT WITNESS

Sebastian and Gabe arrived at the monument's picnic shelter in the shadow of the colossal stone and parked beside Senga's hatch-back. The Blue Wood Ranch van was also there, as well as several pickups and cars, including a National Park Service vehicle.

"We missed them," Gabe said, when they saw no one, save a family of campers playing what appeared to be a board game.

"I could have come alone, Gabe, as I said," Sebastian repeated. He felt sick about Rufus. How he felt about Senga was unspeakable. It was all too much. He tried to call her cell yet again, but voice mail answered. He made a small sound of frustration and stepped from the pickup, quietly shut the door and, seemingly entranced by the sight of Senga's vehicle, placed his hands on its roof. The massive rock stood silent witness to *something* here, and he made a private plea for assistance.

Gabe spoke in a low voice, "They've likely split up to search, and nah, man . . . Caroline and Jake—they'll be . . . they'll be all right. And they need the time. I should have called you, but I couldn't say it on a phone. Sorry."

"No, Gabe; it is I who am sorry." Sebastian turned from the Honda, rubbed his face, rough with a three-day beard. He ran both hands through his hair and tried to stave off growing anxiety. Gabe averted his gaze.

From the nearby campground, beside the river, came soft flute music and little else. Sebastian wondered if it was often this peaceful here. Even the air was still. The day had warmed as it neared late-morning. He thought he smelled sage. *No; it's sweet grass*, he decided. Senga had once burned the aromatic for him.

219

High against the Tower flew several birds. One screeched. *Perhaps a falcon,* he thought. Hearing conversation, he turned to its source and recognized the Franciscan, Joe, and his adopted Cheyenne father. The two were walking a well-maintained path between the parking lot and the road. When they approached, Joe spoke in a hopeful, jovial tone.

"Sebastian. It's good to see you, friend. She'll show up; I have great faith in Senga. You remember Milo Two Bears?" said the hirsute Brown Robe. His garment was hiked up to reveal stout, hairy calves and feet, secured in what looked like worn-out Birkenstock sandals.

"Yes, of course," Sebastian said, extending a hand. "Joe, Milo. Anything yet? I am completely at a loss. I should have wondered when I could not reach her by phone. . . Gabe and I have just arrived and, ah, have sad news. Rufus Strickland has died. During the night. Senga's neighbor—"

"*Oh, no,* and yes—he was dear to you both, like family," said Joe to Gabe, to whom he introduced himself and Milo. "I am so very sorry for your loss, Gabe. It was sudden, then?"

"Ah, we don't know what happened. He was just sitting in his chair on the front porch. The boy found him this morning. We . . . don't know what happened," he repeated.

They discussed where the search party had already looked, and that all were to meet at the shelter soon. Joe and Milo described the location of their campsite, having arrived late-afternoon of the day before. Moona'e had chosen to stay at the campground to pray and attend to their needs. *The flute music?* Sebastian felt restless and needed to do something, anything, but the Franciscan persuaded him to wait until the ranger returned, so they could "compare notes," he said.

Gabe stepped to the bed of the pickup and lifted out the cooler that contained the sandwiches and three, gallon jugs of tea. Caroline had included plastic cups and a large bag of bite-size candy bars.

The law enforcement ranger reached for his buzzing cell phone. The ID showed a Rapid City number. "Mills," he answered. He'd returned to his office to check messages and eat a quick bite before heading back out. Volunteers had searched nearly a quadrant for the missing woman, which included yesterday afternoon's fruitless effort.

"This Bob Mills at Devils Tower?" the caller asked.

"Yes—what can I do for you?" He crumpled the plastic wrap with one hand and tossed it into the trash can beside the desk. The missing woman's neighbor had made dozens of ham and cheese sandwiches, delivered by her hired man, *Gabe* something. He'd seen him ride bulls in the local rodeo. Hard to forget a Black bull rider. He and the missing woman's boyfriend, whose name also escaped him, had come to help. Bob wished a better word existed for a grown man, hardly a boy, who was involved with a forty-seven-year-old woman. He was thirty-two, himself. The boyfriend had reported the neighbor lady's husband had just died, and here she'd made sandwiches. *Something to do,* he guessed, *but still. . .*

"This is Howard Solyst at Regional. Tom Robinson is under my care. Ah, he's coming to and keeps repeating something—sounds like *sane-ga,* then, some numbers. Mean anything to you? Could be delirium—he's had to be sedated, I'm afraid; he's risking a busted blood vessel."

"Yes, Dr. *Solyst,* is it?"

The caller confirmed and Bob resumed, "It's the name of a missing woman—and numbers, you said? Like what? You write them down?"

"We did—well, the nurse's assistant did, thinking it might be important. The man was agitated . . . okay—got a pen?"

"Yeah, thanks. Go ahead."

"44.5902 . . . and 104.7146. They're coordinates, right? Makes more sense now. Oh my," the doctor said, doubt creeping into his voice.

"Looks like it . . . yeah, and hey—thanks for the call, doc. Um, is Tom going to be all right?"

"Can't say yet. Do you want to be informed as to his condition? His chart shows no family. I only called because the park superintendent said you work with him."

"Well, *sort* of, but thanks, I appreciate it. And when he can talk, yes, give me a call, please—oh, and do *not* discharge him, doc, under any circumstances."

After the call ended, Bob sat a moment, then called the sheriff. The coordinates were close to those of the Tower itself.

Slightly different, so, nearby. He swore and entered the numbers in his computer. A map appeared with an arrow designating a point several yards off the lower trail. He printed the page, made copies and tore off the sticky note with the figures, putting it in his pocket.

"What the hell, Tom?" he said to the air and hurried out the door.

Milo Two Bears walked back to their campsite, to discuss the morning's search with his wife and to share a sandwich and candy bar with her. He interrupted her meditation and apologized.

"I have met Gabe," he said after. "He is in mourning; no, not for Senga, but for his friend—and boss—who died in the night. This . . . is a *difficult* time." He stepped to their box of food stuffs and chose a package of Fig Newtons. The strains of flute music ended and Moona'e pressed the button for the CD to start over.

"You don't think I'm playing this too loud, do you? I thought maybe Senga might hear it and know where to come," she said, while contemplating the player.

"As long as you don't run out of batteries," Milo half-smiled and drank from a thermos of coffee. "I better get back. Her friend's tuggin' on the reins," he said, meaning Sebastian.

"See you later," Moona'e said, "Find her," she added. "Time grows short."

When he walked into the midst of the search party, Milo felt a circulating buzz. Something had happened. He spotted Joe and walked to his side. "What is it?" asked Milo.

"The ranger has coordinates, he says. Here, I'll show you." Joe stepped over to one of the picnic tables where a stack of maps lay, weighted down by a stone. He took one. Milo had followed him and immediately recognized the spot marked with an arrow, but said nothing.

"Is this where we are looking?" he asked Joe.

"I—I'm not sure, but it seems likely. Why?"

"Joe, I want to take that boy, Joey—he's a good tracker—and his friend; I think her name is Lily. A student nurse. We'll go a ways from here—from *this* spot, I mean," he said, tapping the paper. "Now, please do not ask questions. I can hear you thinking, but I do not have any answers. And say nothing," he added.

CHAPTER 38
BEYOND HIS KEN

More park personnel were enlisted to join the search, now that an element of suspicious circumstances had surfaced in Tom Robinson's possible delusory admission. Having restored their bodies with food and drink, the larger assembly listened to Bob outline the afternoon strategy. He noticed among those gathered, the father-and-son campers who had witnessed Tom's accident—if "accident" described it. No one as yet had been detained regarding the hit-and-run.

The temperature had steadily climbed into the nineties, with promise of late afternoon rain. Bob had left his jacket in the office and thought he might have to return for it. His notes reminded everyone to wear sun block and a hat, if possible, and to drink water. Another ranger passed out bottles and handy water-bottle pocket clips available for sale at the Visitor Center Bookstore.

"All right, folks. Thanks for your help. So, with this new information, we might have a lead, but keep in mind that Miss Munro could be anywhere; in other words, keep your eyes peeled and don't overlook any possibility. Search under downed logs and check unusual impressions on the ground—that sort of thing, I'm afraid. I tried to round up a dog, but one isn't available until tomorrow—so there's that. The weather's a factor, of course, so it'd be great if this search could be concluded sooner than later." He surveyed the crowd for questions.

"Seems like a stupid question, Bob, but what do we do if we find her?" Lee Rogers asked. He'd brought the guest ranch staff and a van-load of kids to help; not something Bob would have done, and he privately told the Blue Wood owner to have an adult accompany every three or four guest ranchers, or Campers, as Rogers called them.

"No, not stupid," Bob replied. "Phone reception is spotty around the Tower, but try calling me." He recited the number and waited as several tapped it into their cell phones. "A shout works, too," he added. "Chances are she'll need medical attention." He was hedging his bets and could *hope* she'd require medical attention and not a coroner. There were murmurs, then silence. "And stay with her—she may be incapacitated; send someone back. Ranger Murphy will be here." He glanced quickly at the seasonal behind him.

"We'll fan out from the eastern park boundary first, then slowly—operative word, *slowly*—head for the coordinates on the map, eventually to merge in that vicinity. Everyone get that?" he asked and watched them nod. He'd already sent someone to the site, who'd reported back no sign.

They rose from the picnic table benches, pulling down hat brims or bills, to move en masse toward vehicles. Bob had remembered to instruct the entrance ranger to tell visitors to keep an eye out—if they planned to hike—to increase the odds of finding the woman. Tourists were always up for a little excitement, a fact that left a bad taste in his mouth.

Grabbing up his pack, the Cheyenne man had sidled over to where the boy, Joey, and the girl, Lily, were seated and, without speaking, he had quietly indicated they follow him.

They had slipped away unnoticed by all, save Sebastian, who kept his attention on Milo and the two young people. Using the pretext of a trip to the lavatory, located several yards from the shelter, Sebastian was able to slip behind the cement building and follow a line of shrubbery, all the while scanning ahead and behind against discovery. Milo had wished to steal away quietly. Sebastian did not wish to threaten the man's motive, believing it was likely critical. Gabe, Francesca and Joe might feel dismissed, perhaps insulted, but he would ignore this for the moment. Milo, it appeared, had an idea. He would catch up with the three soon enough.

Harboring no doubt that the Indian knew exactly how far behind he trailed, Sebastian nonetheless moved furtively through the forested area. They skirted the Tower at a wide radius and, once, they all ducked in unison, as a park vehicle passed along the road. Then, Sebastian noticed Milo, Joey and Lily cutting back diagonally toward the west face of the rock; in other words, heading in the opposite direction as the main search party. He wondered if he was making a mistake, if this Milo was leading him farther away for some reason.

When he judged it sufficiently safe to show himself, he hurried forward to catch up. "*Milo!*" he whispered, startling a doe from her grassy bed, surprising him in turn. He reared back and heard a low chuckle.

"They'll do it every time—'bout give you a heart attack, huh, man?" said Milo. The trio paused to wait for him. Beads of sweat shone on the faces of the youngsters, while Milo looked dry as bone, and Joey used the opportunity to swig some water, then handed the bottle to Lily. Sebastian read much in the gesture.

"Ah, thank you for waiting, and I won't ask why—yet. Let us not waste time. Shall we?" Sebastian started in the direction it appeared Milo was taking. The Cheyenne smiled cryptically at him and they resumed the trek through the woods, necessitating careful steps over crisscrossing downed timber; some of it blackened dead-fall from a burn. Sebastian recalled what the ranger had said about leaving no log unturned. He put this out of his mind for now and carried on. High grasses and low shrubs grew in the sunnier locales and, twice, they sighted turkey. The air felt fresher under the trees and smelled of warm vanilla and resin. Senga filled his being in a similar sense.

He noticed how quiet his companions were. They spoke little as Milo led them, and all scanned their surroundings methodically, as though eliminating information, which was precisely what they were doing, Sebastian decided. He adopted their tack.

After ninety minutes of systematically zigzagging along a wide swath of deep timber, they approached—*cautiously,* Sebastian remarked—an area marked by huge boulders and dangerous-looking pitfalls, if one were careless. The four stood above the tree line, what was named *the boulder field* in the park. Visitors were invited to clamber on the great stones, but to go further required a climbing permit. He noticed only two young boys and possibly their father moving in and out of sight. A hawk or falcon again screeched overhead. *The same?* he wondered. There may have been rock climbers clinging precariously to a column above as well, but Sebastian ignored all but the mission.

"Let's go sit in that shade for a moment. I have something to say." Milo pointed with his lips to an indention in the ground, on the north side of a rectangular stone—*hidden from view, save from above,* thought Sebastian. They stepped down into the wide impression, and Milo leaned against the cool stone with Joey beside him. Lily sat beside Sebastian, facing Joey, her legs stretched onto his lap. The young couple exchanged a look.

Milo drew from his jeans front pocket a small muslin bag, tied to keep the contents from spilling. He untied the knot and carefully extracted a pinch of what appeared to be cornmeal. No one asked; Milo did not volunteer, except to say, "I will not burn sage here; so, this other means. To promote harmony." He sprinkled the cornmeal beside them.

"Long ago, the *Tsitsistas,* or The People, were led to this place. . ." he began, gesturing gracefully with his arm. Then, he told them a story, abridged for time, with concern for a woman's safety, about a boy named Pup who grew up to be a chief and was the carrier of a *Thing.* "Capital T," Milo added, with a spark in his normally sober eyes.

"And you know where this portal is, ah—*was?*" Sebastian finally asked, after the listeners had sat tongue-tied for several moments when Milo finished.

"I have a rough idea," was all he said.

They remained seated for a moment longer, awaiting the old man's proposal. A chipmunk skittered above them and jumped from the stone to the ground and away. Milo slowly gathered together the strings on the cornmeal bag, tied them and returned it to his pocket, to pat it unconsciously. Then, he stood. Sebastian watched the man somehow calculate the distance between his head and the inward-leaning shelf above, marveling at how he didn't suffer a head injury upon rising.

"*Aho.* Let's find Missy." His pet name for Senga. "Joe-*ee,*" he addressed the boy, "This is a tricky problem. Not to be confused with 'old Indian trick,'" and he grinned, if sadly, at the boy, putting everyone at ease. "*You* will look for recent signs of movement through the trees, whether by a four-legged or a two-legged." Sebastian looked at Joey, who seemed to understand perfectly what his task was.

"Which way are we headed?" the boy asked.

"This does not matter, yet. I want to see if there was anyone at all in this area. *Go!*"

Joey went.

"Missy," he turned to Lily. All girls were Missies, Sebastian surmised. "You are a healer, this is so?"

Lily looked at Sebastian, then back to Milo in bewilderment. "I'm studying to be a nurse," she said slowly, and the Dane recognized the halting speech pattern of the young with the old. As though roles reversed at some indeterminate age.

"Good. That's what I said; a healer. You will come with me and *feel* where our Grandmother Earth is hurting. You know the pain that comes with your courses?"

Lily blinked and looked at Sebastian again, as though to ask for help. When none was offered, she turned back to Milo and stammered, "*My period?* Uh, yeah . . . *why?*"

"Because it's all the same, Missy. I believe I know what has happened to our girl, but you have a clearer sense of *where* it might have happened. Can you understand me?"

Sebastian grew impatient with Milo and his riddles. He was desperate to begin actively searching. The sun beat down on them and every passing minute could—

"You!" Milo spoke sharply and Sebastian turned to the voice. "You aren't *with* us again, my friend," the man scolded, meaning the time Milo sought an arrow shot by a "ghost" Indian beside Senga's cabin. On that day, Sebastian had taken his leave early. "Please—*this* time," said Milo, "it is more crucial than how an arrow came to be found beside a pond; your Missy is the arrow here."

The dark eyes of Milo penetrated Sebastian's already shaken defenses. The correction stung, as though delivered by one of his earliest teachers, to be followed by shame; but with the mitigating factors of age, understanding and humility, he was given to accept it and to apologize. "I am sorry, Milo. I am afraid—afraid for Senga—and I do not . . . I have *no ears* for what you say. But understand I *am* with you now. I promise."

The Indian stared at him for a moment longer, considering, then drew himself up to his full, former height, before age compressed his spine, and Sebastian allowed a mystery beyond his ken to manifest. The Cheyenne inhaled, turned and lithely ducked beneath the stone shelf, to emerge on the other side. Sebastian and Lily followed. Joey, moving parallel a few yards away, stepped along slowly, oblivious to all but his focus: the ground, shrubbery and young saplings.

Sebastian sorely wished his son-in-law were here. Peter was a trained investigator with Interpol; they might have stood a chance—his theory. These errant thoughts were interrupted by another stern look from Milo. *Gud! Does the man hear my thoughts?* He shook it off and desolation arrived in its place. His eyes stung with it and he stopped dead in his tracks.

"What is it, Sebastian?" asked Milo, not unkindly.

"What are we doing, Milo . . . if I may ask?"

The Cheyenne regarded him with compassion and chirped, like a squirrel, to Lily, who had moved ahead. She paused, turned and faced west; with chin raised and eyes closed, she sniffed like a bird dog on a scent. Frowning, she then pointed toward an outcrop.

"It's like what you said, Milo. I can smell it," she said quietly and glanced in Joey's direction, but he was just out of view.

"Smell what?" asked Sebastian.

"Come," said Milo, extending a weathered hand to the Dane's shoulder. The touch traveled to Sebastian's boots like a small electric shock. But try as he might, he could not sense whatever the girl thought she had detected. He only smelled the earthy heat rising from the forest floor and his own perspiration. Lifting the water bottle from the clip on his back pocket, he unscrewed the top, drank and held the container.

Two crows swooped through the trees ahead; the first *caw!* attracted the man's attention in time to watch the second bird, its wings fanning the air. There was no breeze but what these produced. He thought he could feel it, like a zephyr. A kiss of air.

They reached the outcrop and Milo told Lily to stay by him, while Sebastian was instructed to circle around. The girl made to object, but the Dane obeyed. After making his way up and over the rock-strewn hillside, he was stopped by the force of memory. The intriguing scene reminded him of a place from his youth; perfect for scampering and playing pirates with his brother.

Before him rose a large boulder and, behind, to its right in a cleft, a collection of smaller stones, almost certainly arranged—as though on purpose. An assortment of low-growing plants grew in and around these stones, all guarded by a twisted, old juniper. Taking it in, even from a distance, the impossible strangeness of the unnatural landscaping mystified him. He was contemplating it when he heard Joey.

"Milo," called the boy from several yards away. "The rain's erased most everything," Sebastian heard him say, ". . . but I found this—"

To see what the boy had discovered Sebastian quickly retraced his steps.

Using a twig, Joey held up a filthy, tattered blue-and-white bandana. Sebastian swallowed. Senga had one similar; but they were common, no?

"It's—it smells pretty gross," Joey said, trying to remain equal to the task.

"Bring it here," said Milo. "And Sebastian, go back—you could miss something if you leave now."

This was the astute remark he might well have earned from Peter, so, he turned back toward the rocks. The massive *Nakovehe,* or Bear Lodge, loomed beside its cleaved and fallen matter, an epic watchtower or, benign observer, perhaps, but always a presence. In *allowing* a fervent plea to the spirits of the place, Sebastian *dis*allowed a forced distinction between *to do* and *to be done by.* Not scrupling whether he was drawn by one pole, or repelled by another, the paradox overcame his skepticism.

At this precise moment, he noticed the odd shape on the ground in front of the peculiar array of juniper, stones and plants. He gingerly stepped over a downed limb and through a tangle of low shrubbery. Whereas earlier, the long shape might have been mistaken for a log—and perhaps a rotting one at that—*tree trunks,* he joyously apprehended, *do not grow white and honey-colored wisps of hair,* however soiled and caked with dried mud, as was the rest of the figure.

Like light, the information coursed through him: charcoal-smeared jaw and neck; eyes and cheeks hidden under dirty hair;

broken, blackened fingernails on hands, palms pressed together, outstretched; a tousled head resting languidly against a forearm. The soiled leather jacket—once the warm, dark-amber color of whiskey—now grungy; blue jeans, no longer blue, but streaked with dirt and gray dust. And between her thighs, where it had soaked through denim fabric, a bright, poppy-red stain shimmered in a shaft of sunlight. Another instant and the image resolved itself sufficiently—horrifyingly—to his mind and he ran to her.

She lay still as death.

"I found her—" he called from his knees, not loudly, but loud enough and, twisting to sit down upon the earth, he dragged the limp figure onto his lap in a tearful embrace. Tenderly brushing aside the hair, he beheld the face he most desperately needed to see. His tears further smudged the black streaks that marked her. *Like a child's war paint,* came the thought and his heart clenched in a vise grip.

His Senga—though barely recognizable.

Her pale cheeks were sunken, dirty and clammy. Her body light as air on his lap, and he thought he sensed, more than heard or saw, shallow breaths. Like a bird. Recalling the bottle he had laid aside, he reached for it, unscrewed the lid with his teeth and poured a few drops onto the fingers of the hand holding her head. Too much too soon was dangerous. He wet only her lips with it, and then, he waited.

Milo and Lily had approached with care. Joey turned away to use his phone, then joined them. The student nurse kneeled down and gently took the bottle away while shaking her head. She lifted a wrist to search for a pulse, then raised one of Senga's eyelids.

I watched Lily half-smile. Turning my head to the side, she explained, "So she doesn't choke," then, "She needs the blanket, Milo."

Sebastian choked back tears of relief. "She lives," he murmured.

Pulling the item from his pack, Milo covered my shoulders, torso and thighs as best he could. He knelt at my head and murmured something as Joey stood sentinel, respectfully silent.

Lily settled at my feet and raised them onto her lap. She worked to untie and remove the boots. *For the sake of circulation,* I dimly noted. The task required some effort, as they appeared to be held fast, and when at last the first came away, the girl grunted. She ran a hand along the sandy sole of my woolen-socked foot. She raised her eyebrows and fingers to Sebastian. He absently noted the gold flecks.

Above, a crow cawed five times, one for each human, to be answered by another bird in the near distance. The man, upon hearing it, looked up once again from the earth where he sat, to search the sky and beyond. In his arms, he held the woman as though she were treasure. The raucous crows met and, together, flew up beside the great stone, one that could be judged to be falling up, into air, where *Mysterious Movement* had once paused, the woman had once explained. And still it pauses. The man's gaze fell back to earth to search the woman's face, to find her eyes squeezed shut against the light. He heard the gift of a syllable.

"*Pooh.*"

CHAPTER 39
SWEET BURNS THE SAGE

*M*y Heart,
I write to you through our Francesca. I can write little in English; I am sorry. I have difficult things to say; forgive me. Both San Gabriele and the cards say you are in grave danger. To be alive is to court danger, this I know, but you are to avoid a certain man who will want you to go someplace dark with him. I am sorry I cannot be more specific. My sense of this is vague. I am sure your Sebastian likes you to go places with him! It is a thorny one.

I have discussed this with my friends, Sofia and Nadia, and we pored over the cards with great care in the event we missed something. Alas, we all come to the same conclusion. So, take care, my granddaughter.

Francesca's Nonno and I continue to find one another's company acceptable, and we often speak of you. We send you love.

Only love!
~Your Nonna in Italia
Write to tell me you are well and safe.

I lay three days in the intensive care unit, for a total of ten at the regional hospital, treated for shock, possible "cave disease" (histoplasmosis), as well as dehydration and its host of symptoms, mainly gut-ache; most days, hooked up intravenously to sodium chloride. Sebastian seldom left my side during the day. The question of my depressed immunity, however, required he wear a mask. At night he returned to his home named for Peace, and where he's brought me to continue my recovery from a too-eventful summer. We've returned to my cabin two times a week to water my garden and orchard. Once, we happened on Gabe and Caroline. I felt in a fog and wished no fanfare. Sebastian offers his entire self; what more could I desire?

Like a child, I think and speak in simple, declarative sentences and the odd, glib query.

I was told about Rufus before I left the ICU, but my heart knew; it's bleeding for Caroline. For us all.

Rufus, why did you have to go?

I'm here but for the sound of his voice urging me on, for the sight of his beautiful old face, and with thanks to the bats. . . One of them must have snatched my bandana as they careened by me in the tunnel, to drop it where Joey found it. Francesca discovered my hat on the other side of the Tower, snagged on a limb not far from the trail. She recognized it.

Healing is slow. Surprising *how* slow. To write is a slog through three feet of wet snow; the effort required to simply think—enormous. How for granted I've taken it. I completed the course of antibiotics and have returned to my herbs. Mainly, I am nourished by love, good food, teas, much water and a little daily exercise to help the bowels along.

After I was found (Sebastian tells me), I was rushed to the hospital. No surprise there. In cases of trauma, Western allopathic medicine proves more efficient than herbs, though several may serve alongside, such as St. John's Wort and verbena. My lover had carried me to the park road—not an easy task, given the forest floor. As Joey cleared the way for him, Lily held my feet up as best she could, to aid my heart. My sense of indebtedness cannot be overstated.

When the medical staff pronounced me stabilized, corresponding with the return of other senses (i.e., the cloying smell of sanitizer), I haltingly asked about the cave. All I saw were blank stares. This "delusion" was plainly attributed to my condition. The following day, when Sebastian had left to find something for lunch, Milo arrived with Joe and Moona'e. The piercing eyes of the old Cheyenne settled on me knowingly through the ICU window. He said nothing, save to ask if he could burn sage. "Only a little," he promised the charge nurse, who was Lakota. I wasn't surprised she'd agreed.

I watched Moona'e hand him his eagle feather to waft the thin tendril of smoke in my direction, never mind the glass. The nurse then indicated he extinguish the bundle, which he did, but somehow, I smelled it. In an instant I was back in the tunnel, following the sweet-sharp fragrance behind mysterious torchlight. This provoked some anxiety and I felt the familiar squirrel-cage-like dynamo of panic. Slow breathing, at another nurse's quick command, dispelled it. I hope the association will fade. The charge nurse threw Milo a look.

Through the window Joe stood by, resembling the *very* large, brown teddy bear he held up for me. Moona'e waved a king-size bar of dark chocolate, knowing my affinity. The three were returning to the reservation that afternoon. As a priest, Joe was permitted in the room to anoint me with Holy Chrism, the oil once reserved for the dying, now widely employed as a healing balm in the Church. My nominal catholicity did not object. Perhaps it was this word, *catholic,* meaning all-embracing, Joe honored and acknowledged in me. In any event, his soothing words flowed over me in a holy-water cataract of empathy and I felt lighter for them, cleansed of recent torment.

Star light, star bright, I recall thinking, still lightheaded. I'd lost a good deal of blood, apparently due to an irregular menstrual cycle brought on by hellish circumstances. (I'd quit my bleeding years ago.) This conjured the time Grannie had me squat on the Earth during my first period; I thought she was crazy. She was the opposite of crazy, whatever that is. Oh, yes; *sane, whole* and *holy*—from the same root. . .

At the conclusion of the rite, Joe took my hand, punctured by a needle; even with tube dangling, my very own *stigmata*. He kissed it through his mask and left the room. I asked to speak with Milo privately. The nurse hesitated, then allowed him in as family and I related the cave experience as coherently as I could. After, I asked him what had happened. Quiet for a long moment, he took a guess and made a cryptic remark about my being related to a certain arrow.

"We're all related, Missy," he added with a grin and palmed my forehead, magnifying the healing intent of Joe's oil. "It is passed down, that one of our holy men, Sweet Medicine, said this thing: 'There is a special magic and holiness about the girl and woman. They are the bringers of life to the people, and the teachers of the little children.'" He paused a moment, in seeming contemplation of his feet—possibly to give the words a proper steeping—withdrew his hand and lifted smiling eyes to me once more. Moving away, he said over his shoulder, "You feel better real soon, Missy," and pulled the heavy door closed behind him, following a terse order from the nurse in the hallway.

Sebastian missed my friends' visit, and before his return I pondered, and concluded (a laborious process still), that Milo had known where to look for me by ascertaining precisely where I'd been, confirmed by the GPS coordinates, and he'd purposefully allowed Sebastian to find me. Joe's canny adopted father will never admit this, in so many words, but I sensed it like fire in my head. A Truth.

Gabe waited to come after I was released from ICU, accompanied by Francesca and Caroline. Sebastian was present. My head felt much clearer by then, only to suffer the full impact of Caroline's and our loss. He explained gently how they'd accompanied the body of Rufus to the crematorium earlier in the day. I was slightly taken aback by this, assuming he'd be buried in a plain pine box—whole, entire and wearing his Dan Posts.

"Nah," said Caroline, when she guessed my thoughts. "We hadn't talked a lot about it all, but he'd told me he wanted this— when his time came."

"*It came too soon, too soon,*" I whispered. She didn't wait for me to ask the circumstances, but volunteered what the coroner thought. Rufus had, quite literally, worn out. He'd died of "congestive heart failure," the official phrase. She was being strong, incredibly so.

I watched my neighbor clutch my hat, newly cleaned and brushed, against her heart, like a life preserver. Sweet Francesca was solicitous, insisting Caroline sit in the room's only chair, at which she bristled and then sat. Gabe looked worse for wear, but in his eyes, not his person. He held his duty sacred toward his friend and boss and wouldn't let him down now in death. But he had some questions, if I felt up to it. I merely nodded and placed a hand on Sebastian's arm.

"When the ranger got word they'd found you, the search party mostly dispersed, but I could see that the matter of the coordinates rankled him. He had three others continue a search of the area, to find nothing."

He'd repeated Joe's *Halleluiah!* at my discovery and the Franciscan had quickly left them to go tell Moona'e. Gabe had noted the absence of Milo, Sebastian, Joey and Lily during their search, but he'd kept his own counsel. He now understood some of it, he said, but not all. Sebastian had offered no explanation earlier and Gabe hadn't pressed, believing the man deserved some peace. I knew Gabe wondered how Tom Robinson was involved, and why. So, I explained—the how, anyway, concluding with a weak reference to curiosity and dead cats, *never mind the nine lives,* which I quickly rephrased.

I related how Rufus helped me leave the cave by devising an eight-second bull ride. Gabe and Caroline exchanged a glance, for mention of Rufus, but also for the cave reference. *If not in a cave, then where had she been all that time?*—their mystery. If I was involved, they'd allow it. Gabe wanted to discuss it further, but Caroline insisted he wait until I felt better.

Jake had remained at the ranch for the day. "He's coming along, that kid. We're lucky that way," said Caroline.

Sebastian, who'd been quietly absorbing all from the edge of my bed, rose to locate another chair. He kissed my forehead and said he'd return in a moment. Francesca then handed me *Nonna's* letter, written on Florentine stationery, along with another sheet of paper, her translation. "It arrived only three days ago, *cara mia* . . . after Sebastian found you."

The letter, smelling faintly of jasmine (*of course*), spoke a warning. Unfortunately, too late. *Nonna's* window-angel, *Gabriele,* had prompted her to read her cards. During my visit last year in Italy, my grandmother had foreseen Sebastian's unexpected appearance at a concert she, Gabe, Francesca and I were attending. . . I opened the red, green and gold-lined envelope and pulled out the note. I could make out a few words. We used to write one another and she would try her "kitchen English," she called it, but that was a *long-ole* time ago. I turned to Francesca's account and shuddered as I lowered the page to my lap and closed my eyes.

"She knows you are safe, Senga. I called Carlo and he told her right away."

I thanked her, opened my eyes and slipped the note back into the envelope, folding hers into it as well and set it on the bedside table, after breathing in its scent once more. The others were naturally curious and I nodded for Francesca to explain. Caroline's eyes grew wide. Gabe took it in stride. I would show the letter to Sebastian later.

After a meditative moment, Francesca broke the silence. "Caroline—" She spoke the name sadly, "wants the *memoriale* for Rufus to be special—" pronouncing the word in Italian.

"When the dust settles," Caroline interrupted, adding, "It's for Rufus, and for you, too, Senga. I am just sick this happened to you . . . you look like warmed-over shit, hate to say." She gazed at me in such a way I felt the words reach in and massage my heart. She continued, "It'll be for Gabe and Francesca *and* all them Blue Wood folks; you know—a shindig. Sorta like the old days—well, *nah*. Not a dance. Don't much feel like dancin'. . . But I want it for Jake and Joey, and his girlfriend; yeah, I talked to Earl and Mae. Them, too, 'course. Hell, even Charlie Mays and that librarian friend of his."

"My boss—Muriel. So, half the county, in other words," I suggested. "Oh, Caroline—" Releasing my vigilance, I covered my face with both hands to suppress a wave of emotion.

"Don't now, Senga . . ." my neighbor urged.

At this Gabe grunted, as Caroline lightly punched his shoulder, and I clasped my hands under my chin. Sebastian, having just entered the room with a stool, questioned me with raised eyebrows. I rearranged my face to say, *Whatever Caroline wants. . .*

He set the stool beside sweet Francesca and bade her sit.

Everyone wanted to know what had happened to Tom Robinson. I told them I didn't know yet, but I was sure they'd know soon enough, given police scanners and gossip circles, at which Caroline piped up, "How else we gonna learn anything useful?" I was reminded of my Grannie and her penchant for usefulness. It seemed so long ago; another lifetime. *Was it? Had I renegotiated some boundary of time during my sojourn in the underworld?*

My friends patiently waited the return of my attention. I shook my head the once to the left, as was my wont, to dispel an errant notion, and I saw Sebastian exhale as though everything would again be fine. Remembering the calming properties of the cacao plant, I reached for Moona'e's bar of dark chocolate to pass around, after breaking off a square for myself.

I *craved* sweetness.

I told them I'd been interviewed, but only briefly, per doctor's orders. The sheriff had sat impassively taking notes as I related my ordeal—that I'd been held captive for however many days, until I found a way out. I'd gotten in this condition by some means and *clearly*, I'd emphasized, I hadn't done it to myself. It was exasperating, even for me.

"But no evidence of this place seems to exist, Ms. Munro," Sheriff Miller had declared, questioning my testimony. Perhaps my sanity. I asked about my herbal notebook—had it been found? I'd scrawled over drawings when blank pages ran out. The writing had eventually devolved to scribbling and some proved illegible, but much did not. The dates necessarily confused, I'd hazarded guesses in my notes, to maintain an approximate relationship with time. The phone battery had died within two days and, when told how long I'd been missing, I was incredulous. The sheriff dispatched a deputy to look for the notebook.

I did not want a full-scale search of possible cave entrances to be mounted at the Tower, so was in tricky territory. Claiming fatigue, I'd dismissed the sheriff with the weak assertion that sometimes things happen for which there can be no rational explanations. I remember closing my eyes and he'd left—just as I closed them later, bone-weary. All but Sebastian left after I fell asleep to my friends' murmurs. The last thing I heard was Gabe's Cajun sweet talk, "Now you get well, *chère*," and a light kiss, like an angel wing, brushed my forehead.

I craved sweetness. . .

Tom Robinson, I learned, was released from the hospital and placed under guard, due to files discovered on his work computer. What, I haven't been told. The driver of the car that hit him hasn't been found. The coordinates Tom muttered in the same breath as my name to a nurse's assistant have revealed nothing. *Strange* that.

Mysteries abound.

Sebastian repeated Milo's tale about the tunnel (or tunnels) having been sealed long ago. I described what happened to me, intermittently, tentatively, like literal waves on a gold-tinged beach, and this is what I believe: the night before I was found, Milo discovered the tamping bar and simply carried it off. He took a risk. *Why didn't he come for me?* Recognizing the location, the coordinates had simply confirmed his suspicions. His action might not preclude another steel bar reappearing one day, but I don't believe that the man who once saved me from myself in the Sara's Spring grocery store will return as a park employee. Did he think his action somehow made me his? I also learned he sustained some brain injury. The case is under review while the state hospital provides him bed and board.

If it were up to me. . . Alas, it isn't. "Not an element of the crime," says Charlie Mays, *where* I was held. Place doesn't matter, apparently. Kidnapping is a felony. False imprisonment, a lesser charge, also matters. However, my *personal* treaty and inconvenient vow (at least in the eyes of the justice system) remains to those who came long before: that I may neither show, nor tell anyone where I crawled into, or out of, Grandmother Earth. I gave my word to Milo and, earlier, to my captor, Tom Robinson.

Will my silence only serve to guarantee the man's release? Nonna, I'm not seeing something here.

"Oh, bother!"

Sebastian continued to sort his mail and grunted a question mark. We were in his study. I hadn't realized I'd spoken aloud. "I, um, said 'bother.' I guess. Sorry. I feel out of my body much of the time, pooh." Curled up in the burgundy leather chair opposite the desk, the comforting image could belie my claim.

His lips, tightly closed in concern, loosened with a sigh.

I studied him surreptitiously.

A beeswax candle burned brightly on the side table, placed there by my lover to warm my soul. He'd laid a soft, plum mohair throw behind me and I'd found myself drifting in and out of whatever consciousness is. I sat conscious of my surroundings, a warm cocoon. The quality of light streaming into his home shone markedly softer in late summer than when I'd first encountered it, in the aftermath of a destructive blizzard. His aunt and uncle's art collection, including brightly woven textiles, adorned the timbered walls.

Sebastian had left everything in his relatives' home as it was, in memorial, save certain pieces his brother had requested. Through the study door, I glimpsed the kitchen to the right and the guest room to the left. Overhead, I pictured the well-lighted, loft bedroom, dimly noting I hadn't considered it "our." This niggled.

"The Immigration Tunes" played on, dolefully, as random details about the cave *surfaced,* too fitting a verb for comfort. One—the image of a fully articulated skeleton of a huge animal, more plausibly a bear than my Middle Earth dragon. The bones had shone gray in the faint candlelight. Not bleached; their age beyond reckoning. As the image faded, existential despair took its place, more diffuse than acute. Bathed in my mental moonlight, a floating sense of Danica curled back from awareness, like a fish darting away, and I sealed my mind against all temptation for now.

Sipping good, strong coffee with tentative pleasure, I tried to savor the aroma and sweetness. I *longed* for sweetness. . . Despair be damned—*I'm here.*

Last night, after discussing Gabe and Francesca's postponed wedding plans, Sebastian proposed *we* marry. We were eating dinner—an impossibly good asparagus-brie quiche. Savoring my flaky bite, I waited too long to reply, or even react, for I could not *see* the prospect—not yet. After holding his blue eyes with mine and swallowing, I perceived the words that hung outside my body—waiting to be plucked up by a slow tongue. Like snowflakes already melted.

"The horizon of the future . . . *shimmers,*" I whispered, closing my eyes, "like the farthest sun-lit ridge on my grandparents' farm during an afternoon rain. . ."

I opened my eyes to a face clouded with puzzlement.

I'm treading water before the tide turns, I heard myself think. "Soon, I'll go home," I gently continued, "where I belong for the time being, to tend my books at the library; to tend my garden; to tend my soul." I held his eyes.

Taking a deep breath, his lips parted for a moment in resignation. Then, I leaned over, pulled his forehead to mine and held it a longer moment. Abandoning the dishes until morning, we climbed the spiral staircase to bed and made love with delicate, and exquisite, care for our bruised sensibilities.

During the summer, inexorable tides of desire and obsession had crashed against one another. When abiding in two persons, distinct and separated, these tides *may* ebb and flow. Inhabiting one person, they'll risk the rocky shore of belonging, to gamble all and to sometimes lose.

"And where is my mermaid this morning?" Sebastian interrupted softly. Leaning back in his chair, fingers linked behind his head, he regarded the ceiling curiously. *Or, was it sweetly?*

I rose and stepped round the table to where he sat, lowered myself into his lap and rooted for the sweet-smelling nook below his jaw, nudging my face into its perfect, rough contour.

"*Ahh,* here I am . . ."

CHAPTER 40
OF A LAMP AND A KISS
Two Weeks Later

"Gabe, it's me," Caroline called from outside his room. One of the horses nickered at the sound of her voice. Rufus' big bay.

He pushed the chair back from his desk, where he'd been immersed in his story, a welcome distraction from grief. "Coming," he said as he crossed to the door. Any thought of his old *patron* caused ache. He missed the man moment to moment, save when writing. The paradox of distraction. Opening the door, Gabe said, "Hey. Come in, come in."

She stepped up into the tack room, furnished with saddles, bridles, hackamores, blankets, trunks and cabinets of gear, including vet supplies. A heater in winter, a fan for summer; metal bed, small bedside refrigerator, desk, chair and lamp—all provided for his needs, along with the sink and curtained-off corner toilet. He showered in the house. A rubber storage bin held his clothing—against moths, packrats and mice, always a possibility—though he and Rufus had once taken pains to make it less so. Caroline studied the space thoughtfully.

"You're frowning, woman. What's wrong?"

She shook her head, "Oh, nothin', Gabe. Two things," she said more brightly, as she sat at the foot of the bed. "Not 'two things are wrong.' Ya might as well sit back down. You're workin', I suppose?"

"Yep." He returned to his chair, rotating it to face her.

"All right. This won't take long. Oh, what's Jake up to?" she interrupted herself.

"I have him shoring up that dam; we'd talked about it—Rufus and me—for about a year. Figured it was past time to get 'er done, as they say."

"Ah, well. Good. It's not too much for him?"

"Nah. I was going to check on him in a bit, anyway. What's up?"

"Okay, okay. You know how I took these lamps to Rapid a while back and the guy told me the one was a copy? Well, I showed them to another antique dealer yesterday when I went over—"

"I wondered what happened to it," he mindlessly broke in, glancing at the stained-glass lamp that had once lighted Jake's room, now on Gabe's desk.

"Well, this one here *is* the copy, but yours—I always thought of it as yours—anyway, it's the real McCoy. I never showed it to the other guy, afraid if one was phony, the other would be. Yeah—how 'bout that . . ." she said to his unbelieving eyes, showing less enthusiasm than the revelation merited, but then, they were all suffering.

"So, you sold it?"

"You bet. And here's the thing—parked outside is what I got with some of the money. I want you to think about it before making any kind of decision, though. Oh! Almost forgot. There's a box come for you in the mail—probably your books, right?"

She managed a wink, stood and smiled down into his face. "It's been one hell of a month, Gabe. Let's take the good where we can find it," and she leaned over to give him a quick peck on his cheek, to turn away after, seemingly embarrassed. He noticed her self-consciousness.

Oh, no, you don't, Miss Caroline. Drawing a deep breath, he said, "Yes, it has been that," sending her a sad smile of affection. He rose and walked toward the door, plucked his tired Stetson from a hook, pulled it on and stood waiting. "Well, you comin' or not?"

She stood by his desk. "This's a pretty lamp, too, dontcha think, Gabe? I mean, it's all right I sold the other?"

"It's a *beautiful* lamp, Caroline, and they're yours to sell. This one's a mite elegant for out here, but I appreciate it. I feel spoiled." They stepped out of the room and he pulled the door shut behind him.

She'd left the sliding barn door ajar to the sunshine and he wondered *what* was parked outside. They certainly didn't need a new pick-up or tractor, both vehicles being relatively "not old." And he'd heard no one drive up. His window was even open to allow a breeze. So, *what?*—and then he spotted it. Whoever had delivered it had left it on the other side of the car gate. Must've gotten a ride back, he figured.

Caroline, what have you done?

The RV was a mid-size model, not one of those behemoths that resembled a bus. It was—*intriguing;* all he could come up with, and he risked a quick glance in Caroline's direction. She'd been watching for his reaction.

"Well? Wanna look at your book first, or listen to my little idea?"

He could not imagine what she had in mind. Was she going to take a road trip, now that she had Jake and him to hold down the fort? What about the up-coming barn dinner she was planning (with his and Jake's help)? The combination potluck-memorial-new book gathering and reception for his and Francesca's wedding—the latter once again postponed. "And last, but certainly not *least,*" Caroline had emphasized, when listing the occasions, "a gathering for Senga and Sebastian—but *mostly* for Senga," she'd amended.

Gabe and Caroline had run into Sebastian the week before at Senga's cabin, when they met by chance to water the garden and trees. They discussed the barn dinner once more and told him he didn't have to bring anything.

Caroline later told Gabe that Rufus wouldn't mind sharing his *party,* she'd called it, with tears again springing to her eyes.

"Ah, so, what are you thinking?" he now asked Caroline, as he approached the recreational vehicle, more than a little curious. She followed on his heels.

"Here, I've got the keys." She tugged them from her pocket and handed them over as they passed through the people gate beside the grate. He inspected the vehicle closely for any evidence of roll-over or accident. Seeing none, he asked where she'd bought it.

"In town. You know the folks who bought the big house on the corner?"

He was familiar with the RV owners. They were newcomers, and retired. Another growing demographic in small-town, low-taxes Wyoming, he'd learned. "Are there Blue-Book prices for these things?" he finally asked.

"Oh, the deal went through the bank, so I suppose all that's figured in. I paid cash for it, though, so I've got the title and everything."

He glanced sideways at her, but only for a moment. "I would have checked it out for you, Caroline—I mean, the engine part of the deal," he said, with raised eyebrows.

"I had Jerry at the co-op do that, but thanks. I kinda wanted it to be a surprise. Well—is it?"

"Ah—yes, Caroline. It's a surprise, all right. Come on. Let's see what you got yourself," and he held out a palm for the keys, unlocked the storm/screen door and handed her up. She struggled with the first step and he caught her muttering about something or other, then he heard her cackle and, *law,* it made him happy, not having heard the sound in weeks. He stepped up and into the camper. She was already seated at the table.

"Sit down! Ain't it cute as a bug?" she asked.

It was and he smiled for her happiness. He sat down across from her. "So, why did you get it, Caro?" He said her name the way Rufus had, *Care-o,* and it wasn't lost on either of them. He hadn't realized he'd done it until she peered at him, but she let it pass.

"Okay. I just want you to think about this now. Don't say anything yet. You need to talk to Francesca, anyway. We—Rufus and me—we wondered about this for a while—I mean, what you and Francesca would do after you got married. We wanted you to stay on, even if Jake's here—the kid needs a *lot* more learnin'—so . . . how 'bout you two move in here, where you can have your own space—well, *sort* of—and, well, just think about it, will ya?" She gave him one of her exasperated looks.

He hadn't seen this coming and sat back, quietly digesting it, and not wishing to appear ungrateful, he took another deep breath, let it out with, "*Whooee* . . . now, you're something else, Miss Caroline—*Caro,*" he corrected, having decided he liked it. He made another sound, then slowly said, "First, I thank you for the gesture, and I won't, as per your wishes, answer yet. I'll speak with Francesca and get back to you."

She grinned, then related that after carefully inspecting the camper, she'd felt a little jealous (meaning envious, he mentally corrected) of the improvements over the years, remembering her and Rufus' early experience. While not exactly a hardship, they wouldn't have minded a *little* more comfort and room.

Caroline snorted with the memory and continued.

They could either park near the barn to access electricity, or, use a generator. She didn't particularly like them, she told him, but she'd happily put up with the noise to have him stay on. The only stickler would be in Francesca's having to drive to the Blue Wood to work. Caroline didn't even know if the woman would return to Italy, as she'd done the last few years to rustle up clients for the guest ranch and, more important, to visit her family. She asked.

He nodded, and kept nodding, trying to follow and absorb one unexpected thing after another. Caroline again smiled her catbird grin, then stood impatiently, wishing to show him every nook and cranny, of which there were many. The RV had been sold as "furnished," meaning dishes and various housekeeping supplies, curtains and the like. She told him she'd declined the bedding, having informed the sellers they could just keep that. She also thought a brand-new mattress might be necessary. He silently agreed.

Might work, he thought. He remembered several tales Rufus had related about his and Caroline's first months sharing a camper much smaller than this one. He was lost in one such story, when Caro tugged on his shirt. "Didja hear me?" she asked.

"Ah, no, sorry, I didn't. What's that, now?"

"I said, let's go look at your book, *Mister* Author."

He'd completely forgotten. "Oh, that's right!" and checked his watch. "But I need to go see how Jake's doing."

"Oh, he'll do. Come on. I wanna see your book!" and they stepped down, shut the door and crossed into the yard.

He turned once to re-inspect the RV. Caroline had reiterated that they could set it any number of places, depending on their need for electricity. His laptop and printer required it. And then, it occurred to him that he could still use the tack room as a study.

Jake would most likely stay in the house. Gabe wouldn't put this unexpected cart before the horse though, so shelved the notion and followed Caroline into the house to his short story collection, newly published.

His agent had been disappointed Gabe couldn't attend his own pub party, but understood. A reception was still being planned, however tardy. "No worries," the man had assured him. Early reviews had included accolades. He'd take the good where he could get it.

CHAPTER 41
YIN YANG

Jake helped his mother and Aunt Haley clear the table. The covered dishes and baked goods the neighbors and friends had dropped off at news of Rufus' death were nearly consumed at last, some having been frozen. Normally, at this time of year, the men would have stepped out to the porch, where Rufus would roll an after-dinner smoke. Now everyone stayed put, strung between kitchen and dining room. Caroline looked tired, Gabe thought, and he hoped she'd go to bed soon and let everyone fend for themselves. Tomorrow was the barn dinner and most details were sorted, giving him a measure of peace.

Francesca sidled up to him. "*Hey, meester, how about a little hanky panky?*" she whispered into his ear in a Brooklyn accent. Incongruous as it sounded, he almost spit out his beer, wiping his mouth with the back of his hand.

"Where did you learn that one?" he asked, recovering his poise.

"Mary. She likes *Jeemy* Cagney films. You know him?"

"Ah, yes. And I'm ready to go if you are. . ."

She nodded solemnly.

"Let me go tell Caroline. Wait for me?"

"Sure, *meester*," she said and smiled.

After goodnights and visiting the barn to give the cats their evening treat (holding the ginger back a moment to give the others a fair chance), and then making a general walk-through, he asked Francesca to hold up beside the camper, eyes closed.

"All right, you can open them now."

"Ahh, *Gehb!* It is so . . . so *bella!*" she cried as she scurried to the camper's door, festooned with twinkling lights.

Once inside, he lowered the shades, the windows opened to the air, and he tilted the fan to blow in the direction of the bed. Next, he poured a large glass of water. "Want some?" he asked.

"*Sì.* I am parched. Mary says this too."

"I figured." He poured a glass full and handing it to her, said, "I'll do my bathroom stuff, then you. That okay?"

"Okay, *meester,* but don't take all night."

His eyes widened at her growing acumen. Must come from her facility with languages, he thought as he finished drinking his water, set the glass in the dishpan-size sink and disappeared into the water closet, as he nick-named it. It was possible to take a shower in the tight space, but he'd chosen to continue using the one in the house. This one would do in a pinch, and Francesca didn't mind the small area. *Yet,* he thought.

He washed quickly, brushed his teeth and dabbed on scent Francesca had brought from Italy, of oranges and cedars. The narrow confines would take some getting used to, but a little organization goes a long way, and didn't they enjoy the prospect of countless acres beyond their threshold? They had discussed an outdoor seating area.

When he opened the bathroom door and stepped out, he smiled with anticipation. Francesca was sitting at the table, leafing through a magazine, wearing her robe and naked beneath, he knew. A candle burned beside her. After he undressed, she looked him up and down, made a sound of rolling r's, like a tigress purring, and slid out from behind the table. Their movements, of necessity, demanded choreography. She passed to his left and he to her right in a near square dance move, toward the built-in drawers. He heard the toilet door click shut, inhaled and let his breath out slowly.

The built-in bed was surrounded by windows. Normally, he wouldn't mind. He cranked one open on the north side of the camper, toward the grove, and closed the curtains, save one, to better allow a breeze. The sheets were cool, clean and smelled of sunshine. He slipped between and waited, allowing his thoughts free rein.

Leigh and Haley had returned, sans husbands, for their father's memorial. Haley's sons, Derrick and John, had come with her and he hoped the younger grandsons might visit more often. Billings was not far.

"Do you mind the wall, *caro mio?*" he heard after several minutes, welcoming the interruption.

"No. Come here, my sweet Francesca—" She climbed into the bed, after removing her robe and hanging it from its own special hook. There was a place for everything.

"I have missed you," he said, as he gathered her softly scented body, round in round places, firm in firm places, and toe-curling erotic in others. He held her a long while, then rose up on an elbow to draw the curtains apart, to permit more air, and to better see her in the dim light. The yin-yang of their bodies.

He breathed her in. "*Mmmm,* you smell like almond extract." With his fingertips, he lightly traced the contours of her body, from her heel, along her calf to her thigh, where she pushed his hand away.

"*It tickles . . . Gehb—stop!*" she whispered.

He grinned, made a noise and resumed stroking her stomach, then her breasts, with a heavier hand. He circled her hard nipples and, leaning over, kissed each softly, then hungrily before exploring her clavicle, neck and the side of her face. She moved to kiss his mouth with such urgency that her body followed in near-choking spasms of desire. She called out to him.

"*Now, Gehb—*"

"*Shhhh,*" he whispered, chuckling.

"And *you* are too quiet," she chided, "It is not *I* who am loud," she observed, in what he was learning was perhaps an Italian penchant for reordering opinion. She huffed and turned over, to face the galley. A breeze lifted the curtain hem into his face, bringing a clean scent of pine needles and humus. The bright candle flame on the table flickered, but wasn't extinguished. He lay back and admired her from behind. How could simply regarding the woman's *derrière* make his cock respond?

"Oh! I forget!" she said, looking over her shoulder, "I have a song for you; wait for me, *teedbeet!*"—her name for Chinese spring rolls and this bit of his anatomy, as if it were going anywhere without him. He crooked an arm behind his head after adjusting the pillows, and watched her consider her descent from the camper bed. After giving his cock a warm squeeze, to which he groaned, she slid to the floor and reached for her phone on the table. "I brought my speaker so you could hear it better . . . listen!"

There followed silken strains of a cello, followed by an oboe. He vaguely recollected the piece—*from a film?* It sounded Italian. From *The Mission.* Yes. *Amazing how music summons another dimension,* he thought; the concert in Lucca especially.

Francesca scrambled back in beside him as the melody enveloped them.

"It is called 'Gabriel's Oboe.' Do you know it? By Ennio Morricone—an Italian. I think of you when I listen to this."

He noted her use of "listen," and not merely *hear.* The active, versus passive participation. *Maybe they're two sides of the same coin, like yin yang.* "Yes, it's familiar. Thank you. It's beautiful, love."

The music fulfilled an accidental purpose beyond that of auditory pleasure—to cover her cries, and they fell asleep to the song's repeating play. In the night, he carefully climbed over her to turn it off, and then, for a long moment, he watched her quietly breathing.

He was filled with her.

CHAPTER 42
THE GINGER CAT
IS EXCEEDINGLY FAT

Hermione stands guard over the garden, wearing a bright blue cape, complete with hood, a happy find from the second hand store. The lining is sown in saffron-colored satin, of all things. The scarecrow makes quite a picture and belies her purpose, the second of which—and more important—to put me in mind of my Emily, who loved to dress the straw-stuffed creation. Not far away, four crows ignore the life-size witchy doll and caw from their platform. This morning, they paused to watch me cross from the cabin to the garden enclosure, their heads turning at the same time and angle. I must pretend I don't see them else they'll fly away.

After passing a quiet day alone, inspecting tiny bundles of mint, sage and lemon balm hanging in the garage to dry, and counting windfall apples for the deer, I considered a light supper of garden vegetables: tomatoes, corn, and cucumber and turnip greens with bacon. At dusk, the fairy lights on the juniper tree blinked on, and I sat down at my table to compose a letter to Joe, cup of linden and chamomile tea at hand and candle burning in the east window. A doe and her fawn eased by, pausing at the window.

> Dear Joe (I began) . . .
> Thank you, Milo and Moona'e, for all you did for me, and I am sorry for the trouble I put you through.
> September already. During my convalescence (such a fancy word), I learned that Einstein's quote—wait, let me find it. . . The distinction between the past, present and future is only a stubbornly

253

persistent illusion, *wasn't meant as a great scientific epiphany. He was simply trying to comfort a grieving friend. He died himself a month later. Time becomes less and less important as we age, I think. Less timely. Though certain things are certainly exigent, like picking apples after frost (not yet arrived).*

Three days ago, I returned from Sebastian's, and yesterday I went in to work for a couple of hours. My wandering mind returned fiction to reference (isn't it?). Muriel would have reminded me to drink more linden and chamomile teas. I taught her well.

Sebastian took good care of me after I was discharged from the hospital. We'd come here to water, etc., then return to Fred (have I said? Danish, for peace?). One night, he asked me to marry him. Yes!— but I couldn't say yes. Love is a form of madness. An overdose of dopamine, or is it oxytocin? Am I a coward? Am I mad?

Speak to me of madness. (Is that from some play?) What induces a man to ignore every warning and sign, to permit another woman's lunacy (mine is exempt) to infect him, as though it were a virus of sorts, like the common cold? Are there degrees of madness—as on a spectrum? Of course there are.

Remember Jason's Argonauts and the siren calls? This was like that. No mast apparently available to lash to—the crux. There's a discussion—the metaphor of the mast. But I digress. . . The fascinating thing about writing to you, dear Joe, is how I spot solutions embedded in my questions. Must review Rilke.

Back to sirens. (See how they are?) Sebastian and I have enjoyed a riddle game, featuring a certain mermaid (me) and a sailor (him), so here I include myself in the fishy race of seductresses. With no further distressing particulars, one of the last riddles I posed, or that was, more accurately, put to me from your end of the proverbial stick—the Universe—asked: What did the mermaid say to another who wanted to lure the salty sailor?

Nothing. I said nothing.

Either way, I dropped some cosmic ball and all hell broke loose, not to put too fine a point on it (which I am doing). If I were to respond now, what would I say? What could I say? The reply waits, if unspoken and moot, beside that of Sebastian's marriage proposal. I couldn't see it. See, as in envision. I expected a blazing neon sign, dear Joe. It's a matter of timing—my usual caveat. I'll allow both to steep longer. At least until I hear from you.

The question of madness, though—it's a temptation, isn't it? A mere excuse, but all the same . . . Let it be, I hear. Allow troubled waters to still. And they will. Breathe.

Speaking of water . . . Did you know there was precious metal on my feet when they found me? (Consider this admission under the seal of confession.) I'd forgotten about the gold-rimmed pond (yes!) until I was shown my ordinary pair of natural wool socks. Like Velcro, the fabric gripped the particles. Someone at the hospital had placed the socks in a plastic bag for me. You should have seen the nurse's perplexed expression. I'll squirrel them away with my other treasures. It was likely placer gold from alluvial deposits of sand and gravel; in this instance, an ancient stream bed. Sebastian's uncle was a geologist, did you know? He and his aunt used to pan gold for amusement.

Francesca translated a letter to me from my Nonna. She tried to warn me against following a man somewhere. Would I have heeded had I known earlier? I'll never know. Maybe. Yes, I believe I would have. Her Gabriele told her to read her cards. Chew on that little nugget for a while. Between Grannie and Nonna, I'm . . . blessed.

Enough for now. Give my love and gratitude to Milo, Moona'e and Sweet Sister Joan. I look forward to hearing from you, as always.

Peace be with you, friend,
Senga

I like to steep a letter overnight, to review in the morning, not trusting evening's mind. Clarity of morning equals constable of conscience. The next day found the words acceptable, and I gleaned some insight, as invariably happens when I write my Franciscan friend. I addressed the envelope and walked to my mailbox, then passed another day in the garden and orchard— bracing burdened limbs against the weight of apples and coming fall snows. At 4:00, I stopped and showered, in preparation for Caroline's barn dinner.

Joe's quote, on my bathroom mirror, called. A holy siren. By St. Bonaventure, it read: *Enter into yourself, therefore, and observe that your soul loves itself most fervently.*

What I was doing, yes? Entering into myself? Yet I was still overlooking, or willfully ignoring, a *Great Thing*—enormous and infinitesimal at once. Paradox *and* mystery, but only in the sense that I wasn't seeing it. It was as though I'd left a crucial puzzle piece of memory in the cave; an element I'd normally recognize in every cell of my body, but had forgotten.

I sighed and proceeded to dress.

Later at Caroline's, giddy Francesca and somber Gabe showed off the RV, decorated with twinkling lights. They discussed their postponed wedding; "But we are making a *pre*-wedding trip to New York," she explained as we sat in the camper's cramped galley. "*Gehb*—he calls the trip a 'backward honeymoon,'" she said, her brown doe eyes flashing widely in his direction. They'd accepted Caroline's offer to stay on in the camper, *whenever* they wanted. By the evidence strewn about, they'd claimed the place. (I also caught a light whiff of sex, my olfactory sense at this time remarkably keen.) Gabe reached for Francesca and pulled her close as I shrugged out of a shawl. It was warm in the camper, despite a whirring fan.

"Oh! Almost forgot," he said as he gestured to his fiancée, whose eyes had sparked with recognition at my unusual (for me) attire. Smiling, she reached to the bunk for something. By the wrapped, angular shape, I guessed a book. His book. I whooped a bit weakly, but they understood.

"I don't expect you feel like reading anything just yet," he stated in apology as I tore away the paper.

"Oh, what do you know—" I countered, inhaling as the words caught in my throat. I gazed at the splendid cover and exhaled. For the title, his editor had chosen *The Carnival Horse,* the very story Sebastian had read to me last fall. The dust jacket pictured a painted collage of carnival themes, the golden parade horse figurine peeking from the layers. It may have been a photograph. *Yes*—I thought, as I studied it. Reverently, I opened the book to find an inscription:

For Senga Munro, with Deep Gratitude for Your Friendship and Presence in my Life. Gabe Belizaire.

I brought the book to my chest, drew another breath and extended my bruised, but healing, I.V. pierced hand to his forearm. Squeezing it, I mouthed, "*Thank you.*"

"You are welcome, girl. Sebastian on his way?"

"*Mmmm,* we're—"

"Hello? You guys in there?" Joey. He'd enrolled at Black Hills State University and was taking a light freshman load to begin. Lee and Mary Rogers had paid his tuition. Lily was a full-time student and had promised to return to The Blue Wood in the spring, to Joey's frank delight.

Gabe sucked in his cheeks, still chewing on my reference. I waved my hand to forestall his curiosity. After a quick glance to Francesca, he called, "Hey! Yes—come on in, Joey. Lily with you?"

"Yep."

We heard light laughter, then, "We came to see the new bunkhouse. You mind?"

Gabe had stood and stepped to the screen door, to hold it open. "I suppose we can squeeze in two more," he said. "Come on in. Welcome to the hobbit home." Chuckling, he moved back, to lean against the counter. Lily stepped up first, followed by Joey, handsome in his favorite duds (minus spurs). The wide Montana hat brim barely squeaked through the doorway and he removed it, for ease of movement.

Lily, wearing a white prairie blouse and a long, cornflower-blue flounce skirt, appeared bemused as she took it all in. I caught her eye and nodded. She'd saved my life and I hadn't seen her since the day. I mouthed a thank you to her as well.

It was a week for expressing gratitude.

"Senga!" greeted Joey, seated beside me, the hat placed on the counter. I noted his knitted brow and wanted to smooth it. He looked healthy and happy; the wisdom would catch up. "Boy, the stories are a-flyin'," he said. "You going to set us straight?"

I gazed into his eager, young face. "Not today, Joey. And, thank you for looking for me. I-I don't think I could have gone another day . . . it's—" The word escaped me and the sentiment trailed away, like snuffed candle smoke.

The quiet that followed waited for something.

Another day. How long had I lain there, *on* the earth and not beneath? Just the one? Overnight? I didn't know. When Sebastian gathered me up, I happened to squint in the direction of the hole behind me, to see only an unfocused collection of boulders, brush and an old juniper tree.

"*Cara mia,*" Francesca spoke gently.

"Sorry, everybody," I apologized, then, "Let's go find libations! I'm ready—aren't y'all?" and I moved against Joey's hip to scoot him off the bench, Gabe's book still pressed to my chest. "I cannot wait," I said to him. "And I love your new, ah, hobbit hole," I added, grinning to each in turn. "Does Francesca—do you know about hobbits?" I addressed her.

"*Sì,* Senga! It is a very popular story. *Lo Hobbit.* You think we are *hobbits, cara mia?*"

I wryly laughed and we left the twinkling camper, now parked below the grove, tethered to the light pole by a long green electric cord. It stood in sight, if through the trees, of Rufus' chair on the front porch where Gus the Great was still sitting, or lying, vigil, nose on front paws. We joined the others milling at the barn.

Gabe wondered about Sebastian. *What happened?* He knew not to intrude, but *law,* it unsettled him. Nearly everyone Caro had invited was here. The Dane seemed to make a habit of not being where he was expected, and then turning up when he wasn't. So, maybe he'll come later, Gabe surmised.

He watched Caroline make her shambling way to the lighted barn entrance, where plywood on saw horses served as tables. Draped with an array of sheets, quilts and food. He and Jake had strung lights throughout the barn aisle, and outdoors between tree limbs. It reminded him of Italy. Rain wasn't expected, but clouds had gathered. Willie Nelson crooned from Jake's iPod and speaker on one of the tables.

Caro had wanted a simple barbecue with grilled hamburgers, corn on the cob, salads and desserts. Nothing fancy. And beverages—both kinds. He'd be putting her to bed at some incoherent point, he believed, and hoped it might be without her daughters' judgments raining down on the woman. When Leigh and her husband arrived after Rufus' death, he'd watched Jake negotiate the reunion with grace and maturity. The boy had grown in character by leaps and bounds, to use a cliché. He grunted; *but it's true.*

The girls appeared a mite uncomfortable on this second visit. If they'd come around more often, some of that would wear off, he thought. Jake was bunking in Gabe's room in the barn so Leigh could have his in the house—her former bedroom. Haley and her young boys chose to stay in Sara's Spring. Gabe was gratified to see Caroline's daughters show their mother respect and love. Both had pitched in like old hands with the dinner preparations. That they'd clearly loved their father was evident, despite the distance—physical and psychological. He knew all about that and resolved to call his father in the morning.

And so, he'd been busy, wanting to make the gathering as special for Caro as he could, given her stated parameters. He couldn't bring himself to call it a party, however, even if for Rufus. *Gathering* sounded more appropriate. Caro leaned on him daily to make decisions. He hoped it was a temporary thing, and that she'd get back on the horse soon, as it were. How to help her do that? he wondered.

"Gabe!"

He swung around to his name. It was Lee. He couldn't help but smile at the man's *bonhomie.* Never had he seen a more perfect pairing of the word with appearance. Save Santa Claus, whom Lee resembled more and more.

"Hey—how're you doing, man?" asked Gabe. "Hang on, will you?" and he finished jotting a thought, closed the notebook and returned it and pen to his shirt pocket. "Sorry."

Mary, brandishing two bottles of Stella Artois, caught up to her husband. "Here—want one of these?" she asked them both.

"I'll get another," and with no other word, she thrust the beers into their hands and scurried back toward the cooler. Gabe admired the ease with which she wore her "*cowboy chic,*" as she dubbed it. This evening, a brightly patterned *serape* and aquamarine boots figured. She'd removed the bottle caps, bless her.

He wanted to sit down and express his appreciation, or, admiration to Lee for helping Joey and gesturing toward a pair of chairs, he asked the man to join him. Interrupted by a thought, he itched to bring out his notebook again to record it. Instead, he stood transfixed, ignoring Lee's quiet "Gabe?" Then, taking a swig of his beer, he raised a tentative forefinger. He needed to witness the interchange between the women, which led to reflection:

Gabe considered his friends: one whose husband of sixty years had just died; the other having traversed purgatory since Ireland. *The riven face of Senga*—he had noted the new lines. Some ineffable quality had redefined her physical bearing; not so much through the loss of the long hair, but naturally. *And who wouldn't have aged?* It didn't matter, but still, it denoted *some*thing, and he struggled to identify the significance of that which is overlooked (including humanity as a whole). *Do we lose a certain facility or capacity for apprehending pain? Do we become inured to it? Or, do we normalize it, expect it; even anticipate it?*

He felt foolish debating her circumstances.

In the near distance, Caro and Leigh appeared to be discussing the mundane: the placement of dishes; the seating; the amount of ice in the cooler. *Ah, the practical beauty of food and feeding loved ones. . .* Caroline looked amazingly herself, he thought. Warm, if directive.

"I'm sitting down, Gabe," said Lee from behind. "Is she going to be all right, you think?"

Who? Gabe wondered. *Caro or Senga?* "Yes," he said, confirming for both, and turning, he said, "Sorry, man . . . it's just so . . ." and he backed to the chair, sat and took a long pull from the bottle, his thought incomplete. Lee made weather observations to which Gabe could feign attention.

His thoughts returned to Senga. Her hair had grown little in three months. Due to the ordeal, he supposed. The last time he'd seen her, she had shown him her dress, holding it up like a sixteen-year-old before a prom. *Made of silk,* she believed. Brownish-black. *Mahogany*; the threads shimmering in the angling sun rays like a beetle's back. It was a style called shirt-waist, like his mother used to wear before switching to pants. The gift package had arrived at the Blue Wood in care of Francesca; "For Senga, from her Nonna." It had included three such garments. From different periods in the old woman's life, doubtless. Wide borders of lace embellished the hems, "to make them longer," reported Francesca, owing to Senga's taller stature. She'd taken to wearing the old felt hat most of the time, a bobby pin clipping back the long white bangs. Less for style than expediency.

Upon leaving her, he had thought she would look *regal* in the dress, if that was the right word, and he sent her a quick prayer as he returned his attention to their friend, Lee.

"Is Sebastian coming?" Naturally, the man's opener would be.

"I don't know, man," said Gabe, finishing his beer in a long swallow.

They made small talk about the guest ranch and the success of the "Camp,"—in simplest terms—to refer to the three-week experiment. All but three of the young campers had indicated their wish to return the following summer and Lee was thrilled. Mary too, as the session had gone mostly well, thanks in large part to Lily and Jake who, being younger, were predisposed to connect with the campers, whom Lee called kids. Gabe sensed the man's pride in providing an opportunity for the city dwellers, some of whom had never been on a horse, much less away from home for an extended period. Lee would offer two scholarships for less privileged children next summer.

Gabe jumped up from the chair, snatching Lee's empty bottle, and told him he'd be back shortly with another.

"Sounds good, Gabe. Jim . . . he's still pining over that Russian gal," he added, effectively jerking back Gabe's attention. "They're emailing. I don't know what to think."

"Jim's solid, Lee. I wouldn't worry one way or another about it. Back in a bit," said Gabe, as he walked away.

Glancing back, he noticed Mary had taken his place and was handing Lee one of Lupita's mouth-watering stuffed mushrooms and another beer. Pete and the ranch cook had remained behind, perfectly satisfied to be alone at the Lodge, Lee had reported. Another group wasn't expected for a week, so Jim was catching up with some postponed chores.

Catching a glimpse of Mae and Earl just inside the barn, he made his way over, since Lee was set. Mae was perched on a chair Rufus had often used. A package balanced on her lap and one of the cats twined at her feet. The big ginger one, naturally, with a face the size of a chicken pot-pie.

"Want a cat, Mae? Good mousers," he called to her.

"Hey, you. I'll think about it. I like this one," she said, setting the box down and lugging the cat to her lap. It weighed more than it should have, due to bullying the others and eating more than its share.

"This is one of those deals where I pay you to take him. I call him Gordo. He's friendly, though. Tell you what—one of my books is included."

"Done!" said Earl. "Don't let us leave without it—and I guess the cat. How're you doin'? Haven't seen you in a while. . . We're so bummed about Rufus. Sorry, man. When we told Jane and Larry—in California—" he added, not knowing if Gabe remembered their names, "they couldn't believe it . . . just couldn't believe it. Said the man looked so alive—and happy. Jane said he *radiated* happiness. That's how she talks, you know."

Gabe understood. His *patron* had been shot through with life in the weeks before his death, as though infused with something extra. *Lagniappe.* And some secret ingredient. *What was that, Rufus? Can you please tell me?*

"*Hey, y'all.*" They turned to the Italian accent. It was Francesca, coming into the shaded aisle, holding plastic cups of some drink, likely prosecco, compliments of *l'Italiana.* She inhaled deeply, sighed and declared, "I love the smell of fresh pine."

In preparation for the dinner, Gabe and Jake had spread a truckload of shavings into the area, including the stalls. It had freshened and brightened the somber space. "Charlie and Muriel are here," someone muttered. Francesca furtively turned her head toward the entrance, "He's asking about the search." Charlie had not been free to help on that day.

Gabe saw Earl frown and glance at Mae, who looked down. They had heard an edited version.

"Just change the subject, you know—like Senga," said Gabe, referring to her facility with misdirection. For his part, he instead smiled at his fiancée, who wore his favorite blouse that accentuated his favorite breasts.

I grew self-conscious and withdrew toward the rear of the barn. "Where's Sadie? Out with the others?" I wondered aloud, peering into a stall.

"You can just ignore the man, chère, you know. He's just curious . . . I expect the sheriff shared some of what you told him; don't you think?"

Saying nothing, I gazed into my wine in the barn shadows, accented by horizontal slices of light shining between planks. I'd worn my lace-up boots with the silk dress and, by some magic, it worked. Ever practical. I'd known I was going to a barn yard.

Francesca threw Gabe a look, then wandered over. "Oh, Senga . . . do not worry, *cara mia*—we will—*come si dice? Ah, sì!* We circle the wagons around you—"

"—And Caroline," added Gabe. Mae and Earl chimed in, the ginger cat meowed and I turned to respond, shifting my gaze. We pivoted in unison to watch our hostess slowly moving toward us, followed by Jake, Joey and Lily.

Caroline lifted a cup of what I assumed to be whiskey. "I don't know any fancy toasts or anything," she said quietly, ". . . so, I'll just say I love you all, and Rufus surely did . . . We're gonna miss him, and we're all so thankful . . . I don't know how we're gonna get on with it, but we will, cause here—" she searched each face for a moment, ". . . here, we got us the best around. . ."

Turning to Gabe, she continued, "And *you,* you just go on calling me that, 'cause I feel more myself with how Rufus called me." Pausing, she quirked her mouth and looked into a distance we couldn't fathom, then, "And that made no damn sense, but I think you get my meaning. So, cheers, or whatever the hell you say at these things. . . Okay, enough. Let's eat. You grillin' or not?" Caroline addressed Gabe, her resolute anchor now holding her fast to the earth.

"Yes, Caro." He crossed to her, and placing an arm around her shoulder, said, "Let's go, kids. Come on, my sweet *eye*-talian girlfriend; Mae, Earl; oh—and Caro, we got us one less cat. How 'bout that!?"

"Which one? Not the ginger—I like the ginger."

"Now that's just too bad. . ." My friend would prevail in this one thing.

Mae stood and laid Gordo on the chair seat, where his gargantuan size spilled over the edges. The cat quickly tightened its curl and put its head between its paws, believing it was invisible.

"Oh! Wait, Caroline—" Mae called out, "Jane sent this to us to give to you. She said you'd *get* it."

"Huh? What's she done? Here, let me see."

We watched Caroline examine the brown paper-wrapped box, and Gabe held out his open pocket knife. She slit the end and pulled away the paper to reveal a CD player and a CD.

"That's a *real* nice brand, Caro," said Gabe about the Bose, as he closed his knife and slipped it back into his pocket. "What's the CD?"

She stared at the plastic case, turned it over and mewed like a kitten. "It's some music Jane played for us there," she said, handing it to Gabe, with tears in her eyes. "Go put it in the house, will ya? Thanks. I-I'll write to her tomorrow. Well, that was . . ."

Instead of handing over the player and CD, she turned away from us and headed toward the house, arms grasping the package to her breast, her shoulders heaving.

"I'll go," said Gabe, the CD still in hand. "Somebody, please start the grill."

CHAPTER 43
A TYPICAL, LATE SUMMER AFTERNOON

What do you want? is the customary question to a ghost, petty or otherwise. Why am I being hounded by a ghost? *Wrong question, Munro, I hear. Insufficient attention paid to the obvious* is a phrase also haunting me. I've been alone, not lonely. *But ghosts?*

Sebastian returned to Denmark, citing family and business concerns. A prestigious Dutch magazine published an article on the photographs. Odd; photos of the photos—mirrors infinitely reflecting themselves.

The venture continues to do well commercially, and he'll insist on splitting the profits with me. It seems I may consider possibilities beyond the subsistence farming of my upbringing and mere survival. I'm being glib; it was so much more—which is why I'm not too concerned with "possibilities." In truth, I may lack the knack for it. So, I'll decline the money and insist it was a labor of love. He'll laugh, ignore my wish, and a certified letter will arrive with a substantial check. I'll set it on the shelf, where it will remain until I see him again. When, I do not know—also, I'll trade cell phone technology for less invasive means: letters. The slow, more satisfying food of communication.

The large framed photograph stands where it has since Christmas Eve. I've searched the subject's face for understanding, for mercy, for forgiveness. . . They're all represented and offered for the taking, but the figure's pale, nude body looks spectral. Ghostly.

I am the ghost. *What do I want?*

I've wondered ever since my return from the cave. *Caves,* remembering Ireland. *Was I likewise a wavering arrangement of molecules to the two in the grotto? Ignored, dismissed and forgotten?*

Gabe. He came bearing leftovers from *The Gathering,* as he called it. I heard him mutter I'm too skinny; "gaunt," his word. Wants to fatten me up. The half pan of brownies should do it, I thought, as he set it on the flat porch railing, in order to open the door to the cabin. And then, we sat. After a moment, I wondered, maybe aloud, what *he* would have said to another who was luring away his lover. He sucked in his cheeks, mustache twitching this way and that, squinting as he thought, and he grunted.

"You're kidding me, right?" That's it? That's what she says to her?" Disbelieving, I reached unconsciously to touch my absent braid (as a charm of sorts). Realization dawned. I lowered my hand, blew out my breath and clasped my hands in my lap.

"Ahh, Senga . . ." I heard him say. "I mean—is your entire life at this moment hinging on the answer to a riddle? This ain't fairyland, sweetheart."

So, he'd heard me.

I thought about Sebastian's proposal, and what I'd written to Joe, about Jason being tied to the mast of the Argo, to hear the sirens' song and not be lured. Gabe sat back then grunted again. "The way I see it—and I don't know much—is that you are Sebastian's mast and he's yours. Gotta be that way, *chère;* at least I think so. So, maybe you're consorts, you know? Don't have to be *married*." And, with the pronouncement, my friend stood, took off his hat and, rubbing his head, declared, "I need a haircut," and pulled the hat back on.

He gazed, distractedly. Beyond the porch lay a typical, late summer afternoon in the Hills, noisy-hot with insects and frogs croaking in the nearby pond. I sat digesting his earlier remarks.

"Everybody left this morning," he murmured. "Francesca's working and Jake's in class." A long pause. "Listen, girl; Caro needs some woman time. I thought of you and your potions. Go see her . . . couldn't hurt." He smirked, and I caught my fist before slamming it into his eye-level thigh—for his skepticism.

"Thanks for the food, Gabe, and yes, of course I'll go see her. Soon. You're right." *As usual,* I added to myself. I hadn't properly attended to my own healing, much less pondered hers. We could help one another, I decided.

There is love, I remembered thinking earlier this spring, *and then there is what eventually blooms in the fullness of time: loving.*

"You know," he tossed over his shoulder as he ambled toward his pick-up, "I like fairytales as much as anybody. I never meant to dismiss your, ah, *metaphor* so lightly. I get it. More than you know, *chère . . .*"

Now what? I wondered.

"Remember when the Pied Piper disappeared with the town's children?" He turned to face the direction where hung the bit of red bandana.

"Yes. . . Why?"

"He lured them into a great mountain. Hard to say what happened after. This piece I'm working on, about small towns in Wyoming—the West in general . . . What's luring the kids away, girl? It relates to your riddle—if peripherally, I think," he added, ". . . and, I'd better get along. . ."

Yeah, well, I thought, dryly, *for cutting through the crap, you sure know how to pile more on, mon frère.*

I heard him chuckle and he waved with his back turned, adding, "It's *all* fertilizer, girl—and so are we, for that matter. Oh—" he paused and turned once more. "We spread Rufus' ashes along that new dam spillway. He wanted to plant willows there, so we will. Caro thought of it. Just so you know." He then touched his forefinger to his hat brim, smiled his sad smile, and resumed his leave-taking. As an afterthought, he stopped at the garage, entered and moments later exited with a scoop of peanuts for the crows' platform.

Pussy willows. *Salix discolor.* Simple to propagate, their inner bark, decocted, produces an anodyne related to pharmaceutical aspirin. Seemed fitting for Rufus; a pain reliever.

I thought I saw Gabe kiss his palm and wave it back to me as he reached the truck. He backed around and drove toward the highway, where he headed south for the ranch and Caroline.

I could smell the brownies. *Heaven on earth.* He'd also brought a plastic butter tub of macaroni and cheese, five hamburgers and two pieces of corn, all of which he'd placed in the refrigerator. Swathed in a tea towel stood a half bottle of Jim Beam, with note attached—*Rufus would have wanted you to finish this, medicinally of course. Caroline.*

A nip? I thought, and I wanted to sample a brownie.

They were the chewy variety, not cakey; food for the gods. The liquor *(spirits!)* put me in mind of Rufus immediately. Like magic. And, like magic (wasn't it?), I heard him. *Now, you think on me now and then, girl, but don't be thinking too much, like you do.*

That was the gist of it. Could have been my Papa's very words.

Feeling pleasantly at peace, I stood. At Emily's tree, I blew on one of the chimes for the sound, for the notion of conjuring a friendly spirit and to banish others. I thought about pouring some of the amber whiskey on the earth for Emily and Rufus, as Gabe's words returned to me, of masts and mountains and manure, and I laughed quietly. *Fertilizer all, indeed.* After reentering my cabin, I sank into my blue wing chair, leaving the door open to the air.

Dearie, there are no answers; only choices . . . and, *Sebastian and I chose one another.* Both sprung from memory, sailing through the open door as though slingshot from an ancient, dormant volcano. Alas, I surmised, the riddle game was just that—a facile diversion. But I'd chosen truth and not a false choice; then, I heard ringing in my ears.

Tracking the sound, I twisted in the chair and my gaze floated through the east window to across the ravine. Near the ponderosa where the scrap of red cloth hung, stood a woman, dressed in a creamy buckskin dress, fringed and beaded, her jet-black hair not how I'd imagine; it was cut—chopped, really, at chin level. I watched her slowly slump to her knees in profile to me. She stared to the south, and keened at a high pitch, her face a painful portrait of suffering. In her right hand, she wielded a knife and, in her left, a thick hank of hair. Then, she turned and looked straight at me, or, was it *through* me?

The landline phone continued to ring and, shaken, I glimpsed down to the caller I.D. *Sebastian Hansen,* it read. I watched my hand reach for the receiver.

When I looked back, the woman had vanished.

CHAPTER 44
THE SAVAGE BREAST
Copenhagen

R*egard any predicament, problem or matter that bothers you as the teacher,* his lover once cajoled, adding, "We are always whole, always, but being human, we tend to forget."

The normally placid face of Sebastian twisted as he struggled to recall the rest. . . . *Ah, yes. A difficulty (real or perceived) points to what we do not see or acknowledge. The cause is there; we just aren't aware—and we invariably miss crucial pieces of the whole. The completed puzzle?* she had added after sensing his bewilderment.

"But the whole truth, all at once, would overwhelm, my dear," he had countered.

Her expression had betrayed what she was thinking, and making a sound he had learned to translate, she then recited a line from Dickinson's poem, "Tell All the Truth, But Tell it Slant"—*The truth must dazzle gradually, or every man be blind.*

"By recognizing the hard parts, and not denying or diminishing their importance," she had underscored, "we come to value their significance and our own—beyond that of taking up space," she had quipped and he had laughed aloud. In a nutshell, it was her philosophy, passed down by her grandmother (she had noted), if in slightly different terms.

The conversation had taken place nearly three years before at *Fred,* his aunt and uncle's home in the Black Hills, when they had made the photographs.

He would work with her grandmother's idea, inasmuch as possible. Such concepts were largely personal and depended on the ability to factor in one's experiences. *But could it be universal?* he puzzled on a late summer afternoon in Copenhagen, as he sat, waiting, always waiting, on a bench at the harbor across from Hans Christian's Little Mermaid, also waiting on her rock.

Sebastian Hansen rarely drank to excess. In the past several months he had done so twice, once in Paris with a gallery manager and, more recently, alone, in his Vesterbro apartment. Both instances involved women—Danica Olsen and Senga Munro. The former had seduced him; the latter had loved him.

A third woman in his life, his daughter Erika, had tried to coax him from his apartment, without success, to attend his granddaughter's piano recital. Jytte was visibly disappointed, her brows knitted and her lips pressed tightly together, the image tossing another loadstone of guilt onto his already burdened back. The young girl had been upended by his appearance and he had heard her whisper to her mother, "*What's happened to Papa? He is not himself, Mama.*"

A quick glance in the hall mirror had confirmed this. Normally exuding a quiet confidence, if paired with slight melancholy (he *was* a Dane), Sebastian might have been called fastidious—if not strictly for himself, then in memory of his mother (by dint of training); she had taught him to take good care of his person, that it would better serve him when older. Erika had shot him a side-long scowl, a judgment he had recognized. After his wife died, two decades before, his daughter had moved out rather than live with morose depression, even if grief-driven. Her action had spurred his recovery.

"If you do not want to come with us, you could at least shave, Papa," she had muttered on her way out the door, ". . . unless your object is to grow a beard. If so, tidy it. . . Come, Jytte, or we'll be late."

The girl, bundled in her puffy winter coat against an unseasonable cold snap, had stepped over to her grandfather, whom she adored, her arms raised for a hug. "You smell sweet, Papa," she had whispered into his scruffy neck, adding, "It's all right," as she patted his back with mittened hand.

And then they were gone.

Having shared with his family the least information about the nightmare in Ireland, followed by Senga's silence, Erika and his son-in-law, Peter, had allowed him space. He felt their concern, but also their reserve, believing Senga was merely making herself scarce.

After Erika and Jytte left, he had sat frozen in indecision and humiliation, then he had stood abruptly to retrieve the bottle and glass from behind the large bag of muesli on the counter. The cereal essentially comprised his diet and he suspected Erika knew he was drinking.

Sebastian sighed, feeling stiff from having sat immobile too long in an alcohol-induced stupor. An ache in his left side caused him to jerk then shift in his chair. He welcomed the pain; a mere hair shirt would have only irritated.

In the dimly lit kitchen area, he rose clumsily from the table to switch on the stove light. *Too bright,* he complained, and turned it off. On the shelf, behind the wood stove in the living room, a single white taper, lighted new, had burned down to an inch. The wavering light provided his only company, apart from the spicy-green scent of caraway. (Another gift from Senga: the senses as guests.) Returning to his chair, Sebastian poured another half-glass of *Akvavit,* the aromatic source, and downed the liquor in one stinging swallow. It burned, igniting a spasm of coughing. The neighbor's dog set up a racket next door; its deep barks at last squelched by his master's muffled shout. After, all was quiet again.

He perused his surroundings blankly, until his eyes fell on the large photograph seen through his bedroom door, propped at an angle against the wall on a low stool. Of the thirty-plus portraits he had exhibited in Europe, Japan and North America, he had chosen only two for his home in Denmark. In dimension, each measured not quite life-sized, but dramatic enough to elicit a startled response at their intensity.

From the shadowy bedroom, awash in moonlight, the whites of Senga's eyes met his. The placement of the image in the bedroom, at first calculated, now mocked him. In the photograph, made in his Black Hills home and titled "Agency," Senga is sitting in his late aunt's armchair. Carved grape clusters and leaves peek from behind her imperious form as she focuses on the photographer. The black-and-white format contrasts her white, nude figure with the dark wood and shiny, taupe-colored upholstery.

The bright wall behind frames—within a frame—subject and object, or body and chair. With perfect posture, the subject's thighs and calves align with the seat and front chair legs, her forearms rest on the seat's arms, fingers splayed and slightly raised. A bird poised for flight, a mere suggestion. Her sex lies hidden in shadow, while her breasts appear sovereign, like those of the Sphinx, or France's Marianne, or any number of ship figureheads.

Unbound, center-parted and brushed to either side of her shoulders, long wavy hair falls like a curtain, to stop within inches of the floor.

"But no more," whispered Sebastian, his remorse palpable, like a small, dense beast squatting on his left shoulder. He had not been able to thwart the madwoman's quick purpose and swifter scissors. *And then she fell on them and died. . .* Her self-scarred breast pierced.

"A savage breast," he murmured, remembering.

His attention returned to the photograph.

Of serious mien and like bearing, Senga's power drew itself into a profound silence, the nudity revealing more truth than beauty. He longed to hear her particular music, which might have soothed his tortured soul. *White Clouds,* in translation. Then, dropping his gaze to his lover's bare feet, planted squarely on the dark, wooden floor, he spoke her name aloud, "*Senga—*"

Slowly, he raised his head and shuddered. Nausea bloomed in his chest. Through tightly closed eyelids, he watched a super-imposed image step from Senga's, maw agape in a silent scream, in mind to devour him. *Danica.* Thrown off-balance, Sebastian struggled to regain his seat, his muscles quivering with fright as he thrust out an arm in defense. He forced open his eyes. The hallucination ceased before reaching him, as if dreamed. The singular image of Senga sat by, again impassive, self-possessed and—unattainable. He rose and stumbled toward his bedroom to pull shut the door against the prior source of solace.

Anguish replaced the dying echo of her spoken name, and choking cries startled him, as though emanating from another source.

Elbows on the table, he wiped tears from his face and cupped his head in his hands. The ravaged cry welled up again, like a train engine rushing from a dark tunnel, pursued by a sobbing despair, and he wept until his chest heaved and burned with the exertion. Laying down his head on the table, he fell asleep at last.

He woke in darkness, save the velutinous glow of the Vesterbro night sky through the window. The candle had guttered in its holder on the shelf. Coals through the woodstove window burned feebly. His tongue felt thick and dry in his mouth and he thirsted for water. Desolation haunted him still, but less so. Weeping had exposed and invited a weary, shy peace, and he stumbled to the sink to drink a full glass of water and then another. After relieving himself, he splashed cold water on his bleary-eyed face, and then fumbled for two aspirins from his medicine cabinet against the incipient hangover.

His mobile phone lay on the table beside the tumbler and near empty bottle. Noting the information with chagrin, he heaved a sigh and checked the time. In Wyoming, it was eight hours earlier, or 4:13 p.m. Strange, he thought, the same hour he had rung months before; but Senga had requested a letter. *What else could possibly be said?*

He returned the bottle to its shelf, set the tumbler in the sink and, after wiping the tabletop with the dishcloth and drying it, he remembered the call. He had prepared to hang up after several rings, when someone had picked up.

"Senga! My dear. I thought I had missed you. I mean, I do miss you. Is this a good time to talk?"

The telephone had gone dead, as in a no-service area, but he had called her land line.

He had stood, trembling, the phone to his ear, as though it had all been an error, willing her to speak.

There *had* been an error, but much worse, the blunder.

Rather than brood, as he had done for the last few months, he would *do* something else. Consulting the mirror, he muttered a resigned oath in English and lifted his coat from the nearby closet. He checked for his gloves, mobile and wallet, pulled on a knit hat and scarf and stepped out the door. On the lighted steps of the building entrance, he paused a moment to inhale the salty, bracing air and to gaze into the night sky. It was past midnight.

From a distance came the whirring siren of an ambulance and the deep blast from a ship's horn. A harbor light streaked across the sky in a searching arc. Vesterbro, once part of the capital's red-light district, was not billed as a quiet neighborhood, and from somewhere came the measured rhythm of a bass drum, likely from a late-night club. This put him in mind of his coffee house, *The Four In Hand,* and, taking a chance it was still open, he turned in the direction of its genial atmosphere several blocks away. Nodding at a young couple who returned the greeting, he noted each carried a cloth sack of clinking glass.

"*Hej!*" the young man called after him. "Would you like to go to a party with us? The more the merrier, as they say!"

Sebastian halted, turned and, shaking his head, made to proceed in the opposite direction. The young woman begged, "Please! The occasion demands more revelers than are expected, kind sir! It's a celebration for an artist's first exhibit. He's brilliant! Come!"

He pivoted at this. The merrymakers resembled artists. *Free spirits.* Unlike him. Yes, he needed camaraderie; he needed . . . *mirth.*

"Thank you—yes, I think I will, but I should take something . . . a bottle at least. Will you wait for me, just a moment? I have something inside." The couple cheered and Sebastian rushed toward the apartment steps, to return moments later with a canvas bag.

So began a journey, to end near harvest time, of seeds sown in misbegotten corners, to reap a wasteland; of passing idle hours on a lonely harbor bench, lost in fallow dreams. . .

A sea gull screeched overhead. It was a Sunday in late September. Someone stepped between him and the view, and glancing up, Sebastian startled at his granddaughter's face. He sniffed, coughed and regarded the girl, whose frown and tear-filled eyes (once again) searched his own. Jytte moved to sit down beside him and, extending his right arm, he tucked her in against him and held her close.

"Oh, Papa," she said, "please, come back to us. We miss you so."

The sea bird cried and swooped to the wind-whipped breakwaters, where it calmly bobbed. Sebastian sighed long then shuddered, willing his mermaid to hear him. Tear-mottled pages from Gabe Belizaire made tiny flicking noises in his trembling left hand as it rested on the bench seat. Situated just so, the bench also caught the harbor breeze.

CHAPTER 45
SINGULARITY II

The sweet smell of earth in the tunnel filled my nostrils as breaths came more and more shallow. Having managed to cast my notebook through the closing portal with a fevered cry, I summoned remaining forces to coax one last push.

None were available.

I lay trapped, a beached mermaid, arms folded beneath my bowed head.

*Only enough space for spirit to pass—words and sketches—*I reckoned, with the little reasoning power (and *Sight*) remaining to me: Sebastian mistaking a fallen, long-rotten log near the portal . . . for me. I would also see (feel-taste-hear-drink-smell, *then* see) the devastation written on his face when he realized, and his calling to Milo, "I . . . I hoped. But—no."

The action of closing my eyes and resting a cheek on the earth had sparked images, a film rolling solely for my benefit, and I watched a story, a quantum possibility, unfold—of Sebastian discovering me with Milo, Joey and Lily attending. . . Then, a hospital scene, where Joe, Milo and Moona'e brought me chocolate, a teddy bear and sage—for smudging. . . Gabe, Francesca and Caroline, bringing news of Rufus. *Rufus?* Sebastian taking me to *Fred,* to recover, and asking me to marry him (but I couldn't *see* it, I told him); a fast-forward, to Caroline's gathering and my wearing the vintage silk dress Nonna had sent. *She predicted this. She knew I would follow some man somewhere.* Too late . . . *Too late* . . .

The bright cover of Gabe's book splashed across the screen behind my eyes, depicting a golden horse. *He finally won his prize.* And Francesca's spell for the protection of their friend: *Senga, we circle the wagons around you. . .* My friends as sturdy *Conestogas.* I liked that image. And finally, the visit with Gabe at the cabin, when he arrived laden with leftovers from Rufus' wake—*So she'll have something to eat when she gets back,* Caroline had told him.

Ah, yes. . .brownies.

I turned the other cheek to the cool earth to wait, and my sorrow sank into the earth with an exhalation.

For what seemed the proverbial year and a day, I haunted my environs. I would not leave my Emily. In the early evening of the last day, during the *gloaming,* I noticed the Indian woman beckoning me with cupped hand, fingers motioning me forward. Her other hand clutched a book of sorts. *My notebook,* I dimly noted. I noted too it was a wizened elder now standing beside the frayed scrap of red bandana on the hillside behind the cabin.

The tiny mirrors of Emily's decorated tree sparkled like sun-infused raindrops, sending flashes in all directions. A true Glory Robe. The air was still, and yet the chimes tinkled. Grannie's *It's all a one big one, dearie!* resounded, as my senses coalesced, and I smiled inwardly, loving my soul. Turning away at last, I made my light way up the hill toward the buckskinned woman. We fell in together and continued to the top of the ridge, to meet another sunrise just blooming over the horizon.

CHAPTER 46
THE SIMPLER

Three weeks before, relatively speaking, the Two Bears were making their way to St. Kateri's rectory, where Milo hoped to find Joe in. He had forgotten to call in his confusion. After a quick glance at the object in his wife's lap, he looked back to the highway and again to Moona'e. She widened her eyes and used her lips to gesture to the road ahead, just in time for him to hit a pot hole. He caught her wincing; her back was acting up.

"Sorry," he muttered. She remained silent.

At the church, Milo pulled into a parking place and shut off the engine. "Well, we're here," he said, unnecessarily.

"Yes. . . This is going to upset him, you know."

"I suppose. Let's go."

They left the truck and walked slowly to the door of the rectory, Moona'e clutching the bundle to her breast and walking gingerly.

Sister Joan answered the door. "Come in, come in. Good to see you. What have you got there, Moona'e?" she asked.

"Some*thing*—" The Cheyenne woman couldn't think of the word. She drew out the last syllable.

"Joe's upstairs. I'll call him," and she did just that. "Joe?! Two Bears are here."

Sister Joan chuckled and excused herself to prepare the customary coffee. Their last name tickled the holy woman, always had. Milo and Moona'e looked at one another, the bundle, and crossed the room to the sofa, where they sat down—the bundle on Moona'e's lap. She stuffed a throw pillow at her back, for support.

They heard Joe clomping down the stairs and he soon stood before them, wearing not his brown robe, but a knitted sweater and jeans. Unusual attire for him. The Birkenstocks and socks still in evidence, however, Milo noted. He stood to embrace his adopted son and friend. "Hey, Joe. Nice sweater. Somebody build that for you?"

"Why, yes. How did you know?"

Milo only smiled. The Eskimo-style pattern would have required the wool of two sheep to make, he figured. "Hey, we've got something here," he said. "You better sit down. Let's wait for Sister."

Joe leaned down and pecked the proffered cheek of Moona'e. "The back?" he asked, spying the pillow.

She nodded. "Good to see you, son."

The Franciscan sister returned, bearing a tray of steaming mugs of coffee, a sugar bowl and a pitcher of creamer. She set it on the coffee table and handed each a cup. Only Milo took sugar, to Moona'e's disapproval. He was pre-diabetic. *Like everyone,* he'd responded to his doctor.

"Looks like an old one," Joe remarked about the bundle.

"Yes. It is." said Milo. "Are you ready for a story? It's a mystery. Better brace yourselves."

Joe took a sip of his coffee to fortify himself. He glanced at Sister Joan whose frown threatened to freeze and tapped the space between his brows to call her attention. She relaxed.

"Please. Go on, Milo," urged the big Franciscan.

"*Aho.*" Milo took a deep breath and closed his eyes for a long moment. He asked for clarity, and then he began—

"Yesterday, Moona'e and I were called to Maynard and Erik Medicine Hill's place to help with an old bundle belonging to Maynard's great-great grandfather. Maynard's getting on and so, well. . . They asked me to perform the ceremony—to open this bundle and inspect the objects—as we sometimes do, you know." Here Milo paused to wait for permission to proceed. He resumed. "They live north of us, about ten miles."

Joe nodded; he was acquainted with the family, though they weren't parishioners.

"The fire was ready, and they'd built an altar for the bundle. You have participated, so I probably do not need to describe the ceremony."

Joe nodded again in agreement.

"The thong was about to disintegrate, so it was good we were doing this. I carefully untied the knot, but the rawhide broke anyway. The dust was thick. It had been stored for decades in a cave, south of Lame Deer. I did feel something waiting for me in this one though, so I unrolled it slowly and handed Moona'e the items, one by one, so she could smudge each in the sweetgrass smoke before warming them beside the fire. When I came to the last object, I was puzzled. It was a notebook. Spiral bound. About five-by-seven inches."

"An anachronism," offered Joe, his brows now furrowed.

Milo nodded. "I lifted it, and then nearly cried out, which would not have inspired confidence in old Maynard or Erik." His lips pursed, Milo turned to his wife, to gain confidence. "Printed neatly on the front was *Agnes Munro* and, beneath that, *Senga Munro.*"

Joe sucked in his breath and Milo kept his head lowered, hoping to avoid an interruption.

"My hand, it trembled as I showed it to Moona'e. She asked Maynard for permission to examine the notebook. He nodded, appearing as confused as we felt, and Moona'e—well. . . Do you want to tell it?" he asked his wife.

Moona'e took a breath and began, seeming to speak beyond her audience. "I recognized the notebook, only after seeing Senga's name. It bothered me, this *thing*. What did it mean? I asked. With my heart thumping like a war drum, I turned the pages carefully, in case of something loose in them—like we do, you know—a pressed flower, or a leaf. Toward the back, I saw where she had started to write—if you could call it that—more like a spider crawling over her drawings. She had run out of pages. . ."

She ran out of pages, thought Milo.

Here Moona'e shook and made a painful sound. Milo reached around her shoulders and held her a moment.

"I'll be all right. . ." she assured him, repositioning the pillow. "We asked Maynard if we could show you, Senga's friend, and tell you where we found it. He gave his permission. You see, my son, the bundle belonged to one who, long-long ago, helped seal the tunnels near the Bear Lodge." Moona'e spoke in a measured rush of words, as though something was chasing her through that tunnel, her husband thought, and he squeezed her hand.

After a moment, she untied a new rawhide string on the leather wrapper, withdrew the notebook with reverence and handed it to Joe with two hands. A sacred object. Their adopted son contemplated the object as though it might explode.

Moona'e nodded to Milo to continue as Joe rested Senga's words on his knees.

"I studied the notebook last night, my heart bursting. Our Missy had been tricked. She was held captive in the cave for all that time," he said. "I hold myself accountable for not unsealing an opening. Now, it is too late. I was under an oath, but I have made a terrible mistake, and one I'll live with."

Joe crossed himself and looked on his Cheyenne family with compassion. Sister Joan uttered a "Jesus, Mary and Joseph." Invocation; not blasphemy.

"Her notes end with her drinking some of the water from the pool," Milo continued, "and hoping for the best. The last entry describes a light across the way, *torchlight,* she writes, and her decision to investigate. She also mentions how tired she is."

Moona'e squeezed her husband's hand.

Joe turned the pages slowly, the first entries made when Senga, then called Agnes, was eleven years old.

"It's been over a year. My Lord, have mercy. . . Are there any dates?" asked Joe, still leafing through the pages.

"Mm-hmm. At first . . . then the last one, just the month and year, and that she had probably passed her birthday. Her forty-eighth. Also, some about this devil, Robinson."

"Gabe and Sebastian must be told. I'll. . ." Joe began, then, covering his face with his hands, he began to weep. Milo sat quietly and Moona'e stretched to place her hand on Joe's knee. Sister Joan seemed at a loss. Joe had witnessed much and had endured countless occasions for tears, yet had permitted so little expression of them. Sister Joan rose and left the room to give her friend space.

Milo rolled up and retied the wrapper. Laying his hand on it, he asked the Creator for peace—for the original owner, for Maynard and Erik, for Senga; for Joe and Moona'e; and last, for himself. Old Maynard had instructed him to do what he must with the white woman's book; that it was beyond his understanding. Milo was to return the leather wrapper when he could, and that he trusted him with it. The bundle's artifacts had remained behind.

Milo wondered if he trusted himself with the mystery.

Later, on their way home, it was Moona'e who gently reminded her grieving husband that Senga was only following her chosen path's direction, fearful as it may have proven, and to pray she had been given strength. Milo wanted to accept his wife's words, but he could not.

EPILOGUE

*D**ear Sebastian,*
I have your phone number, but cannot call with this. I hope you will get in touch, and let me know you received my letter. I am writing from Senga's cabin and watering the apple trees. I have taken on the responsibility, partly because I have a good hand in Jake and can leave for the time required.

What I am about to relate will likely confuse and upset you. I am sorry. More than you know. Please accept my inadequate expressions of compassion, and know that I—and many others—hold you in our hearts. It has been long since we have seen you, and I suspect you have been suffering in this limbo.

Enough preambles.

Two days ago, Joe Rafaela and Milo Two Bears arrived with a story I am still trying to sort. . .

He wrote it much the way Milo had told it. The Cheyenne elder was a born story-teller; a gift, however harrowing.

Arriving at Strickland's after lunch, Joe and Milo had passed the late summer afternoon on the porch with Gabe and Caroline. Francesca was working at The Blue Wood and Jake was in class. Gabe cleared his throat twice and squeezed Caro's hand once, to remind his employer (and friend) to refrain from interrupting. He could tell she was vibrating with nerves. When Milo indicated he was finished, Gabe asked Caroline if they could have coffee, and maybe some of the pound cake she had in the pantry. He knew the activity would settle her.

"We're making a visit to the Tower," said Joe. "To pray for Senga. Then, we'll head back home."

"Makes for a long day," said Gabe.

Caroline pushed open the screen door with the tray of coffee and cake before Gabe could jump up to hold the door open for her. She did not summon her usual acerbic remark.

Later, at the car, Joe pulled Gabe aside. "How are you, friend?"

Gabe gazed into kind eyes, shining from a face mostly covered with eyebrows, mustache and heavy graying beard. "I don't know, *Padre* . . . I truly don't, but thank you for coming all this way. I . . . *we* . . . miss her, and Rufus. It's a rough 'ole time."

The former professor graded his comments less than eloquent. They all embraced and Gabe watched the old sedan disappear down the gravel road.

He put down the pen and leaned back. The task of writing the letter to Sebastian proved ludicrous, even obscene, given the circumstances. And what did he know? What was missing, besides Senga, whose diary pointed to her being trapped underground, somewhere near the Tower? The extraordinary notebook lay open before him, its pages dusty, some smeared; like her arrowhead, a complete mystery, but one possibly containing the seeds of its own resolution.

Should he tell Sebastian he'd pressed Milo to show him and the authorities the location of the entrances? The old man, with tears in his eyes, would not bend. He said it only once: "It is too late, Gabe. Let her be, and please do not take this to the police. It is beyond their jurisdiction. But let her friend know."

Gabe resumed his task, relating Tom Robinson's role and the man's present condition. A judge had ordered him to the state hospital, under guard. Full recovery was "improbable," Bob Mills had reported. What had begun as innocent fantasy had devolved to dark obsession. This was as much as Mills could disclose, and he only passed the information to Gabe because he seemed to be as close to the woman as anyone—Sebastian having returned to Denmark. Gabe noted the ranger had said nothing about a tunnel, or a cave. *He must have wondered about the coordinates. . .*

The cabin door stood open to a late afternoon breeze, presaging a coming thunderstorm. He could smell it on the air, and taste metal. He liked to hear the creaking in the crowns of the old-growth ponderosas, and the *ssshhhh* of the wind. Like slow spring rain.

Oh, Senga, hon. A vise-grip squeezed his heart.

When he had revised the letter's first draft, he stood abruptly, stretched and crossed to the refrigerator where his two beers waited for him. Choosing one, he opened a drawer and laid a hand on an opener. After removing the cap, he drank down the contents then opened the second. The sharp taste of Stella Artois reminded him of the occasions he had shared a six-pack with his friend in her lair. . .

Gabe told Sebastian he didn't know what would become of the cabin and property. It was managed by a rental agency, due to the owner's failing health. *The agent,* he wrote, *told me the monthly payments had been maintained by you,* and what did Sebastian wish to do now? Not having heard from the agency, Gabe decided to postpone further action and was glad for it. Rob McGhee had been contacted and would come in the near future. For his daughter's ashes.

He called Senga's cousin, whose reaction bespoke affection. Colin would draw up her financial documents and send them; to whom? Gabe didn't know, but asked him to forward them and he would take care of it. He learned the Cheyenne people had been named beneficiary. Which rang true, he thought.

Gabe had never cared for the minutiae surrounding someone's leaving, but there was no body. He pictured carrion birds and wished he hadn't. He and Senga had once held a less-than-solemn discussion on the topic. Caroline was beside herself with what-if's and self-recrimination. Francesca as well. They had been dealt heavy blows. First Rufus, now Senga. *It's harder for those left behind,* Gabe's mother used to say.

Populated, pulsing rings of concentric circles—he considered Senga's tribe—counting her not-quite an orphan (citing her grandmother Maria Teresa, with whom Francesca had spoken). He continued to count: Joey and Lily; Jake (to a smaller degree, for his recent arrival, but he *was* mostly family). Lee and Mary Rogers. Their son Pete and, Lupita, his sweetheart. Jim, *The Compassionate One,* Senga had once called him, for his selfless effort to rescue the freezing Russian woman and her daughter. Chief Charlie Mays (her *sort-of* midwife) and Muriel, her employer at the library. Earl and Mae? Definitely. Rob McGhee—Emily's father—and finally, for always, Rufus. Even now. And, Senga's own family, a given, and, Sebastian.

Gabe wondered (on the page) if she ever truly apprehended how "liked" she was. He crossed this out as grossly inadequate and wrote *beloved.* She was, in his estimation, a rascal, but a loveable one. *Heyoka,* Moona'e had declared; Indian, for "sacred clown," she'd explained—*but so much more,* the Cheyenne had added. He had once read that people are liked for their qualities, but loved for their flaws. The platitude did not survive the letter's final edit.

They had cleaned out Senga's refrigerator some time ago. Francesca had helped give the small rooms a good "one-over," and both had found the task difficult. Emotionally. A sharp green smell had returned to the place, owing to an airing and Pine-Sol. *The ephemera a person chooses to cherish,* he'd remarked to his lovely Italiana, with no concluding sentiment or observation, save a pained expression.

He had only ever given Senga's bedroom a cursory glance upon leaving the bathroom.

While Francesca was emptying a cabinet of dry goods, he noticed the onion-skin stationary pages on the bedside table, illuminated in the window as in a Dutch painting. His curiosity too strong, he stepped over and read the contents of the letter. Setting it back down, he wished he hadn't snooped—his heart now doubly stricken. He sank down on the blue-and-white summer quilt, mindful of Sebastian having slept beneath it the night before the search and for days afterward. A haunted man, he had blamed Senga's presence, and absence, too much to bear, and had returned to Denmark.

The tragic knowledge in the bedside letter they now surely shared, thought Gabe. *I'm so very sorry, girl.* Francesca had asked him what was the matter, but he would not add to their misery. "This," he had answered, raising his palms to the cabin interior, "without Senga."

———

How quickly the hours had passed. The cabin's interior grew dim, and his stomach growled. He leaned over to switch on the lamp, bathing the room in amber, a virtue of its yellowed pine interior. It brought solace; the cockles of his heart needed warming, even if his body felt adequately comfortable in the early September air. Appeasing his hunger would have to wait.

Evening brought sheet-lightning in the south. Fingers of skeletal light stretched toward one another, from one end of the horizon to the other, what Senga might have called *inebriated fractals*. If it rained, and he hoped it would, the orchard would only benefit. Having left the door open to the air, he rose to shut it, first lifting the latch-string mechanism, then down, smartly into place. Now visible, against the wall, leaned the portrait. It gave him a start, as though his friend appeared behind the flirtatious eyes.

Once, he had admired the photograph for its beauty over truth. This night it only confounded him. He raised his cool bottle of beer to those eyes in homage, as his own welled with tears, "Well, here's to you, *chère*," and he took a swig, turned and sat back down, letting his eyes roam and fall wherever they would—the portrait, a scrupled exception. Of Senga, winding a clock. She and Sebastian had named the photograph "Behind Father Time." Tongue-in-cheek. In reference to her blurred *derrière*, and possibly Mother Nature's role.

The water well required electricity, and the orchard required water, so this breaker he would leave on, he decided, and switch off the remainder. After several minutes of *just sittin'*, he systematically went about unplugging lights and appliances, which were few (three lamps, a toaster, refrigerator and radio), then stepped outside to circle the cabin, just because. With sorrow, he noticed the darkened juniper and sent a prayer to mother and child. A hoot owl called in the near distance, followed by an angry clap of thunder and, still, no rain. Dry lightning posed a danger.

Indoors, he finished closing up the cabin as one would a seasonal retreat and, from the threshold, writing folder (including the notebook) tucked under his arm, he took a long look, in case he'd forgotten anything. Spying Rob's CD on the bookshelf, he grunted and crossed the short space to slip the case into his jacket pocket, saying, "Just borrowing it, hon." A song title had intrigued him: "Nothing's Lost, Nothing's Wasted; For Emily and Senga." A small bear, inscribed with symbols and fired to a shiny shade of obsidian (*Like you!* she'd joked), caught his eye. The Bear was a totem of healing. He had given it to her in 2006 for tending him after a rodeo injury. It fit neatly in the palm of his hand.

Please, take me, it called, and he did.

Before drawing the last of the curtains and drapes, he paused at the east window to watch the hillside be bombarded by continuous flashes of lightning, like a strobe, and he recalled his entreaty to Senga's mysterious hunter—

Find her, please—

Early the next morning, Gabe kissed Francesca softly on her forehead as she slept. He quietly left the camper and walked the short distance to Caroline's kitchen. A nearby nest of wrens had awakened, their *chirrs* insistent. The eastern sky, streaked with cloud layers, glowed from light mauve to indigo.

Jake joined them shortly and each noticed Caroline was tight-lipped. After he and Jake had sat down and swallowed a gulp or two of her good coffee, she told them (in a choked near-whisper) to take the four-wheeler, truck, shovels and picks up the canyon and beyond, to look for hot spots or smoke. She'd heard on the police scanner a fire had been reported during the night at Senga's place. The Volunteer Fire Department had responded, but the tiny cabin had already been destroyed—a tall pine beside it, the lightning rod.

"Most of the trees in her orchard were spared somehow . . . that's what they said. Hunh. *Her-money*—ain't that the name of her scarecrow?" added Caroline, still speaking softly.

Doesn't want the devil to hear her, thought Gabe, in case he was still out there causing mayhem.

That afternoon (having discovered no strikes or smoke on the ranch) Gabe drove to Emily's shrine, off the interstate. He stood a long moment before it. A thin wind whistled over the range, lifting a sharp fragrance of sage. Bending to a knee, he carefully positioned Senga's Spirit Bear, newly wrapped in a blanket of flannel, into the bowl. After blessing his friend, he turned for home.

ACKNOWLEDGMENTS

I write these notes in 2020, while our country undergoes great trials and tremors. Trips to see children and grandchildren are postponed. So many lives have been broken and lost to Covid-19. Masks and sanitizers join paraphernalia near our door. Practicing isolation, my husband and I continue along many of the same lines as our pre-virus existence, save for *sorely* missing the children. But sacrifice is needful, requiring our resolve, attention, and simple good sense. The Business of Writing during a pandemic is antithetical to promoting one's finished product, and I have missed the reading events and conversation.

Book One begins before Senga's birth. Her tragic circumstances balance precariously with another character's, Gabe Belizaire. After being mauled by a rodeo bull and taken in by Senga's ranching neighbors, the injured man is introduced to the wounded healer and a friendship develops. Each live as "other" in their chosen state; Senga, for her personal quirks and lifestyle, and Gabe, for simply, and unfortunately, the color of his skin. Far from their Southern roots, a sense of *Family* evolves naturally, even organically. The theme centers on loss, grit and restoration. The second in the series, *Starwallow,* explores desire, and the journeys necessary to bring one back to oneself. *The Simpler* delves into madness and obsession.

I have begun the fourth *Riven Country* book, but am concentrating on a non-fiction work for now, to be (possibly) released in 2021. Lacking Senga's *Sight,* I impart good wishes and prayer for the present and the future.

Realizing that some readers go straight to the Acknowledgments, I'll refrain from mentioning spoilers, but I do wish to acknowledge and salute the Second Civil Rights

Movement. Initiated by beautiful people of all shades, we beat the proverbial great drums: This Will Not Stand! resounds world-wide. May peace, love, justice and healing prevail.

My gratitude to The Demesne, *Ballyfin*, in Ireland, where I infused myself with its peaceful spirit of place. I passed two delicious mornings in its rooms in 2017, working on a passage that would surprise me when I understood where it was going. (No; we don't always know where we're being led—ask our Senga.) I thank the Gemini Birthday Picnickers for continued support and encouragement and, for one Irish trip for the ages: thanks, Gunda, Shirley, Candace, Barb and Joyce.

To early readers Laura Jones, AdriAnne Carrier, Linda Spears, and Kevin Sweeney, my everlasting *Namaste*. Encouragement personified, all. To my intrepid editor, Sarah Pridgeon, you're the best. To my husband Jeff, my love and gratitude always. To my son John and his family, all love.

Finally, I wish to express my appreciation and gratitude to the Wyoming Arts Council, The National Endowment for the Arts, and the Wyoming State Legislature for the developmental grants. We are fortunate to enjoy such a robust and dedicated agency in WAC.

I have dedicated this work to all who suffer. 2020 will be remembered for too many horrendous reasons, but also, for extraordinary courage and resolve. Stories may calm. I hope you receive some small comfort in these. Please leave a review, or contact me if you feel moved, and thank you for reading.

ABOUT THE AUTHOR

As a child, Renée lived in France and five Southern states, 'migrating' to Wyoming at eighteen to attend the university, where she earned a B.A in French. Having lived in rural Wyoming for over four decades, she remains its "student of place."

Renée and her husband, a retired school superintendent, tend an apple farm, a too-large garden, raise garlic and herbs—medicinal and culinary. Their children are grown and live out-of-state. In 2018, she was awarded the Frank Nelson Doubleday Memorial Award by the Wyoming Arts Council.

Renée sings and plays the odd musical performance, and practices family herbalism—which winds its way into her writing, "like possessed vines."

She is currently drafting a nonfiction narrative called CROFTER, *A Wyoming Homestead Manual and Radical Memoir, Rooted in Place*. A future installment in The Riven Country Series is in the wings.

To inquire about booking a speaking engagement, or to purchase inscribed books, please visit the following links:

reneecarrier.wordpress.com

reneecarrier11@gmail.com

Also by Renée Carrier

Nonfiction:
A Singular Notion, published by Pronghorn Press
Essays and Memoir

CROFTER, *A Wyoming Homestead Manual and Radical Memoir, Rooted in Place**

Fiction:
The Riven Country Series
Braeburn Croft Press

The Riven Country of Senga Munro, Book I
Starwallow, Book II
The Simpler, Book III

*Scheduled for release in 2021-2022

The Simpler